FORTITUDE

SCATTERED STARS: CONVICTION BOOK 4

FORTITUDE

SCATTERED STARS: CONVICTION BOOK 4

GLYNN STEWART

**FAOLAN'S PEN
PUBLISHING**

faolanspen.com

This edition published in 2021 by:

Faolan's Pen Publishing Inc.

22 King St. S, Suite 300

Waterloo, Ontario

N2J 1N8 Canada

ISBN-13: 978-1-989674-18-5 (print)

A record of this book is available from Library and Archives Canada.

Printed in the United States of America

1 2 3 4 5 6 7 8 9 10

First edition

First printing: August 2021

Illustration © 2021 Jeff Brown Graphics

Faolan's Pen Publishing logo is a trademark of Faolan's Pen Publishing Inc.

Read more books from Glynn Stewart at faolanspen.com

1

COMMODORE KIRA DEMIRCI had done many things in her life. She had raised sheep, flown starfighters, led fighter squadrons, dodged assassins, buried two mentors, performed covert operations, trained pilots and, most recently, commanded a mercenary fleet.

She had never in her life piloted a merchant starship—but even to *her*, the behavior of the ship on the tactical display was wrong. They were trying very hard to pretend they were normal now that Kira's ships were there, but they'd edged just a bit too close to the other ship in the nova stop for it to look right.

The blonde Commodore really had no place on *Pegasus*'s cramped bridge. The brand-new *Parakeet*-class fast attack destroyer, one of two Kira Demirci's Memorial Force mercenary fleet owned, was perfectly capable of handling this mission—and so was Caiden McCaig, *Pegasus*'s immense Captain.

Kira could come up with a dozen reasons why she *was* aboard *Pegasus*—it was the first time the two destroyers had been sent off on their own, McCaig was a former ground-troop commander, et cetera, et cetera—but if she was being honest, she was there because she was bored and the pirates harassing the New Ontario System were the biggest problem the Syntactic Cluster had right now.

"*Ancillary* is responding to hails and maneuvering as instructed," Gala Negri reported. The permanently tanned-looking woman was the destroyer's executive officer, a new recruit to Memorial Force.

Like so many. Kira had buried more friends than she liked to think about—and her mercenary fleet was expanding rapidly.

"And yet *Ancillary* is so very much in the wrong place," McCaig murmured. "I'm not wrong, am I, Gala?"

"No, sir," she confirmed. "I've done merchant shipping through this exact stop. We're two novas from New Ontario, and New Ontario has bugger and all for out-system security still. No one would be getting close to *anybody* else out here."

There was a tiny degree of surprise in Negri's voice. Kira wasn't sure most people would have caught it, but she was a bit surprised herself. She'd picked McCaig to command *Pegasus* because he had been a long-standing officer on the now-wrecked mercenary carrier *Conviction*—and she needed a destroyer Captain more than a ground-assault officer these days—but she'd worried how well he'd take to starship command.

The answer appeared to be *like a duck to water*.

Both of Kira's destroyer Captains were learning a new skillset. *Persephone* was commanded by Evgenia Michel, one of Kira's original Memorials who'd evacuated their homeworld of Apollo with her. Michel had lost both of her legs in a dead fighter in the battle that had turned the Syntactic Cluster around.

She was both unwilling to fly a nova fighter anymore and her mobility prostheses didn't really allow for it, either. So, Kira had given her a destroyer where the rest of those old hands commanded fighter squadrons.

"Captain Michel agrees," McCaig said aloud, probably communicating with Michel via a silent headware channel. "Do you have any *suggestions*, Commodore?"

From his sideways glance at the company's chief shareholder and unquestioned commanding officer, the destroyer Captain knew damn well Kira had no business on his bridge.

On the other hand, Kira signed his paychecks.

"Nothing so far, Captain," she told him. "Carry on."

"All right," he said grimly. "So, *Ancillary* is suspicious as all hell. How long does she have left on cooldown?"

"Jianhong radiation signature is unclear but present," Ionut Ayodele reported. A small Black man from Redward, Kira's main employer there, he was shorter than the Commodore and barely wider in the shoulders.

"I would guess at least an hour before she can nova," Ayodele concluded.

"And eighteen for us," McCaig murmured. A standard six-light-year nova required a twenty-hour cooldown for the class one nova drives used by large ships.

"Yes, sir," Negri confirmed.

"I don't think that leaves us many options, and Captain Michel agrees," the destroyer Captain said calmly. "Set an intercept course for *Ancillary*. Maximum speed. Stand by multiphasic jammers and the plasma cannon.

"Michel is confirming..." He paused. "Do we have that course?"

"Yes, sir!" the navigator confirmed crisply.

"Engage on my mark," McCaig ordered, clearly still silently communicating with Evgenia Michel aboard *Persephone*.

"Mark."

TWO DESTROYERS FLIPPING on their Harrington coils and blazing toward you at full speed wasn't something you generally missed. Within a minute of the change of course, *Ancillary*'s Captain's nervous-sounding response was being played on the bridge.

"Destroyers *Pegasus* and *Persephone*, my sensors have you on a high-speed approach vector," she said quickly. "Please advise your intentions."

The bridge was silent and Kira watched as McCaig ran a series of numbers on the screens attached to his command seat. Finally, clearly aware that every eye was on him, the massive two-plus-meter-tall Captain stretched his shoulders and bestowed a big grin on his team.

"Record for transmission," he ordered aloud, then leaned forward into the camera that would automatically point at his seat.

"*Ancillary*, this is Captain Caiden McCaig of the Memorial Force LLC mercenary company," he said, his tone calm and cheerful. "We are under contract with the Kingdom of Redward to enforce interstellar traffic and trade regulation under the Syntactic Cluster Free Trade Agreement, as agreed to by all systems within the Cluster."

That was even true now. The Bengalissimo System had been the last holdout, but the externally supported government there had collapsed and the newly formed Republic of Bengalissimo had signed on to the Free Trade Zone as one of its first acts.

"Per the terms of the SCFTA, all ships in the Syntactic Cluster are subject to close examination and potential search if duly authorized officers believe they have grounds for suspicion," McCaig continued.

"My officers have scanned your ship and course and are concerned your vessel's armament is sufficient to engage in piracy. Based on the recent incidents in other trade-route stops near the New Ontario System, we wish to carry out a closer examination of your vessel and an inspection of your ship's cargo and logs.

"Per the terms of the SCFTA, you will cease acceleration and permit our ships to match velocity and board."

He leaned back and glanced at Kira.

"Sounds about right?"

"We have the authority," she agreed. "Carry on, Captain. I'm not here to interfere."

Not unless things went really sideways, and Kira wasn't overly worried about that. The *Parakeet*-class ships were the Kingdom of Redward's newest and most advanced ships—which meant they were on par with the nearly obsolete heavy cruiser from her home sector Memorial Force used as a flagship.

But cubic meter for cubic meter, the thirty-two-thousand-cubic-meter destroyers outmatched anything in the Syntactic Cluster *except* Kira's *Deception*. A rogue thirty-kilocubic freighter with half a dozen light plasma turrets wasn't going to worry her.

There were real threats that freighter might conceal…but she wasn't expecting them there. And even if the ship *did* somehow conceal advanced nova fighters, she'd *still* trust McCaig and Michel to deal with them.

She really was only there because it was the only excitement going on.

"Incoming response from *Ancillary*," Negri reported. "Playing."

"My ship is no pirate, Captain," the woman's voice said harshly. "I will not tolerate this high-handed abuse of rights of passage that have been honored for decades!"

Kira heard several people around the bridge chuckle—and unless she was wrong, it was mostly the Syntactic Cluster natives who were finding the response amusing.

"I do not recognize your authority, 'Captain' McCaig. How do I know *you* are not pirates?"

"Well, then, she is being a pain, isn't she?" McCaig said loudly. "Negri—time to range?"

"Ten minutes, sir," the executive officer confirmed instantly. "Assuming she doesn't have jammers, we could handily disable her engines at that point."

"Oh, if she's a pirate, she has jammers," the big Captain said, before Kira could interject. "Not as good as ours, but that doesn't matter much for jammers."

The multiphasic jammer rendered functionally all communications and sensors except visual identification useless within a light-second of the emitter. Even visual analysis was degraded inside the jamming field.

"With jamming, we'll need to get within about a hundred thousand kilometers of her to guarantee a disabling shot," Negri reported. "Another minute or so."

"Understood."

The big Captain was silent, watching the range drop. "And their Jianhong signature?"

So long as the nova drive was emitting Jianhong radiation, it was still cooling down and couldn't be used. A military ship had baffles and shields to prevent that scan, but a civilian ship wouldn't take the expense.

"Hard to read," Ayodele noted. "I don't think they've got military-grade baffles or shielding, but there's definitely some attempt to conceal their signatures."

The bridge was silent. Kira didn't have much to contribute at the moment—she was a starfighter pilot, not a destroyer skipper. She had some ideas on how to operate a two-on-one intercept like this, but McCaig and Michel clearly had it in hand.

"Lay in plasma cannon one," McCaig ordered. "Target is fifty thousand kilometers ahead of *Ancillary*'s bow. Warning shot when you're ready, Commander Ayodele."

Memorial Force had expanded the rank structure from the three-rank version *Conviction* had used...but not by much. The department heads, squadron leaders, and executive officers all shared the vague title of *Commander*.

"Firing," Ayodele reported.

A flash of white light marked the tactical display, the near-light-speed burst of plasma blasting past *Ancillary* with tens of thousands of kilometers' clearance.

"*Ancillary*, this is Captain McCaig," McCaig intoned grimly. "I repeat my orders: you will cease acceleration and prepare to be boarded.

"Attempts to evade will be treated as an admission of piracy and I *will* fire into your ship. While I will *attempt* to disable her, I can make no promises.

"Heave to, *Ancillary*. This is not subject to discussion."

He turned to look at Kira again.

"I'm expecting them to pop their jammers in about five minutes," he noted conversationally. "It was either then or when we fired the warning shot."

"I was expecting them to jump at the warning shot," she admitted. "Do you have a plan for if they're actually innocent?"

"Close-range hull scan, search the cargo, inspect the logs," McCaig reeled off. "Exactly as I told them. If I'm *wrong*, the cargo will be properly certified and the logs will say they were well clear of the known incidents."

"Which we don't expect," she murmured.

"Indeed." He shook his head and tapped a command on his chair.

The bridge didn't show any differences, but Kira could feel the slight vibration of the battle-stations alarm. The active shift had been enough to get them this far—and, hell, might be enough to handle a single pirate. But why take the chance?

"Lost the target," Ayodele snapped a few seconds later. "Multiphasic jamming is active—looks like they jumped at the warning shot, sir. They were just slow about it."

"Probably have the jammers concealed," Kira suggested. She leaned back in her observer seat. "You seem to have everything in hand, Captain McCaig. Fight your ship."

The petite blonde Commodore didn't need to be there at all—and the only *real* question in her mind was whether her boyfriend or her business partner was going to lecture her about that first!

2

"WELL?"

Mercenary companies lacked most of the formalities for arriving and departing warships that Kira had grown used to in her time in the Apollo System Defense Force, but they were still *generally* more respectful than one-word questions.

Of course, the dark-haired and shadowy-featured woman *asking* the one-word question as Kira stepped off her shuttle was Captain Kavitha Zoric, *Deception*'s commanding officer—which made her Kira's Flag Captain, Memorial Force's second-largest shareholder, and Kira's main business partner.

Zoric didn't *need* to be respectful.

"Well, what?" Kira asked, stepping aside so as not to block the traffic out of the shuttle. She hadn't been the only reason *Pegasus*'s shuttle had shot over to *Deception*, after all. The big heavy cruiser—the single largest nova warship in the Syntactic Cluster for at least another year—was their flagship and central brain center.

"Well, did you get what you wanted out of attaching yourself to a destroyer patrol that you had no damn business being on?" the Flag Captain said sharply, gesturing for Kira to walk with her.

Kira snorted and obeyed her subordinate. *Deception*'s landing bay was currently *cramped*. Between her two fighter-carrying capital ships, Memorial Force was trying to cram eighty fighters into space meant for sixty—and her carrier was trash.

Literally—the common working name for freighter conversions like *Raccoon* was *junk carrier*, and after commanding the ship for nine months, Kira wasn't going to argue with the label.

"We caught a pirate," she finally told Zoric. "New Ontario was pleased and threw an added bonus onto the contract from King Larry. Helped confirm the whole concept of the shared-security side of the Free Trade Zone."

King Larry was Redward's ruling monarch and the central mind behind the Syntactic Cluster Free Trade Zone. His star system held Memorial Force's retainer, covering their ongoing costs in exchange for Kira making her four ships available to him at a moment's notice.

"From the report I skimmed, McCaig or Michel could have caught that pirate on their own," Zoric replied. She was leading the way through *Deception*'s corridors toward Kira's office, the Commodore realized, checking her headware's map of the ship.

That was a trap. It could only be a trap.

It was also a trap Kira deserved, so she swallowed her pride and followed meekly.

"Yes, they could have," she admitted. "But it was the first independent outing for either of them, so having me along as harmless supercargo was good for everyone's nerves."

"You mean it was good for *your* nerves to do something?" Zoric asked drily. "At least if you'd gone on patrol in *Raccoon*, you could argue that you're one of our best nova-fighter pilots and strapped on a Hoplite or a Dexter for your excitement.

"But we both know you're not actually qualified as a destroyer skipper and that any pirate we found on this trip wasn't going to justify needing a squadron commander, don't we?"

They were at Kira's office and she stopped, looking balefully at the door.

"We do," she conceded. "And you're not wrong," she admitted. "But Konrad is waiting for us in there, isn't he? Can I wait until *he* lectures me as well before I give my mea culpas?"

Zoric snorted and the door slid open at her mental command.

The man sitting on Kira's desk was *exactly* who she'd expected. Despite the obvious trap laid for her, Kira crossed her office and embraced Konrad Bueller before the copper-haired man could say a word.

"Good to see you," she told him.

"Good to see you too, despite your attempts to find *any* possible danger in the Cluster," the broad-shouldered engineer said with a chuckle. "How much of a lecture did you give her, Kavitha?"

"Pretty much all of it," Zoric conceded. "She's an idiot and she knows it. Care to explain *why* you decided to run off *without telling your senior staff?*"

That, Kira knew, was where she'd doubled down on the stupid.

This time, she audibly sighed and leaned against her own desk as the door slid shut, surveying the room. *Deception*'s flag officer's office wasn't large—nova ships were limited entirely by the cubage their drives could take into an FTL jump, not mass—but it had space for the three senior officers to hash out their problems outside of the eyes of their subordinates.

"That part was dumb," she finally conceded as she looked over the tiny amount of decoration she'd added to her office. There was a printed portrait of her family on their sheep farm on Apollo, a second portrait of her and Konrad Bueller trying not to grin like idiots, and a handcrafted model of an ASDF Hoplite-IV she'd commissioned one of the flight-deck techs to make for her.

There wasn't much else. She'd left Apollo with a single duffle bag of personal possessions, accompanying a set of not-quite-stolen nova fighters one step ahead of a team of Brisingr assassins.

"On the other hand, I'm bored out of my skull and needed to *do* something," she told them, agreeing with their assessment of her reasoning. "And I both made the decision in very short order *and* figured you'd try to talk me out of it."

"Which left me showing up to your office to find it empty without warning," Zoric said drily. "Your timed message was about twenty minutes too late for *my* nerves, Kira."

Kira winced.

"Sorry," she murmured. "It was supposed to be before your shift started."

"*I* just woke up to a timed message telling me you'd novaed out with McCaig and would be back in two weeks," her boyfriend told her. "You can't *do* shit like that, Kira. You have responsibilities."

"You two and Mwangi have *Deception* and *Raccoon* well in hand," she pointed out. "I knew I could leave Redward for a few weeks and things would be fine."

Kira *watched* Zoric roll her eyes in exasperation and wilted a bit.

"And if something had come up that required us to sortie the capital ships?" *Deception*'s Captain asked. "King Larry's people know I'm the second shareholder, but there's still a concern if they need me to commit to deploy *Deception* and *Raccoon*."

Kira wasn't entirely sure that *Raccoon* deserved the title of "capital ship"—the junk carrier was only five thousand cubic meters larger than the two thirty-two-kilocubic *Parakeet*-class destroyers—but Zoric had a point.

"I know," she conceded, then sighed. She'd been wrong. She *knew* it. She'd known it from the moment *Pegasus* had novaed out, if not before that.

"I know," she repeated. "I shouldn't have done it. But it's been six months since Bengalissimo got their shit sorted and sent 'Her Majesty' Rossella Gaspari to prison. The Institute seems to have written the Cluster off as a bad bet for now, and everything has been *very* quiet."

"Most people would regard that as a good thing," Bueller noted calmly.

"It *is* a good thing," Kira said. "But I went from the Apollo-Brisingr war to running from assassins to working for Estanza here and fighting the Institute basically nonstop for eighteen months.

"For things to be calm is *weird*. I don't know what to do with myself."

"We noticed," Zoric said, her tone now dry enough to sandpaper with. "But…please limit your search for excitement to, I don't know, contracts and Konrad's pants?"

To Kira's perpetual amusement, her lover was surprisingly easy to make blush. The Brisingr man—from the same nation she'd spent her first military career fighting—was older than she was, but still...*innocent* wasn't quite the right word, but it was close.

Embarrassable, she supposed.

"That's fair," she admitted. "But I'll point out that I was never in any actual danger—neither was anyone else. *Ancillary* didn't even *hit* our ships before they got close enough to disable her, jamming or no jamming.

"Redward's new destroyers are almost up to Apollo-Brisingr Sector standards now," she told them. "They can handle just about anything native to the Cluster—even some of the new cruisers!—until the next generation of Redward cruisers and carriers roll out."

"Fair enough," Bueller said. Zoric glared at him and he raised his hands. "I saw the *Parakeet* design before they even started cutting metal, Kavitha," he reminded her. "It's as good as the Cluster's got.

"Kira's not wrong that there isn't much out there that can handle the pair Redward sold us. They've done okay by us."

"Mostly," Kira muttered. *Deception*, at ninety-six thousand cubic meters, was the largest warship in the Cluster—but the Redward Royal Fleet had three one-hundred-twenty-kilocubic warships under construction.

Everyone, including Redward, agreed that Redward owed Memorial Force a carrier. *Conviction* had been the largest warship in the Cluster before *Deception* arrived, and John Estanza had taken his flagship to her death saving the Cluster from the Equilibrium Institute.

That left Memorial Force running around with a junk carrier they'd been given and waiting on a chance to *purchase* a new carrier from the Redward yards...but it wouldn't be the one currently under construction.

"They've done well by the Cluster," Zoric said grimly. "I mean, the FTZ now covers the whole Cluster again and they've got everything well in hand. They need more destroyers, but what interstellar power *doesn't*?"

"And the way they've set it up, Bengalissimo and Ypres carry at least half of the weight of that," Bueller noted. "Our ships... Well, I'm not sure they need us."

"They don't," Kira admitted. "Or at least, they won't once the new capital ships commission. Right now, no one wants to let *Deception* go, so they pay for everything else."

Her office was quiet for a few moments. She sighed and slid off the desk, taking her seat and triggering the artificial-stupid drinks machine. It rolled out of its concealed cabinet and started making coffee for the three of them—black for Kira and Zoric, heavily doctored for Konrad.

Because Kira *knew* Konrad's preferences, there were two blends of beans in the robot. Both were from Redward—coffee was a major export of the planet they were orbiting—but one was an export mix, serviceable but not excellent...and the other was the royal family's private blend.

"*We're* only really still here because a retainer that covers our day-to-day is actually pretty sweet," Kira told them. "But damn, it gets boring." She shrugged. "Eventually, I've been promised the chance to order a hundred-twenty kilocubic carrier at cost.

"I *trust* Larry and Sonia, which is a hell of a thing to say about Outer Rim monarchs, so here we are," she concluded. "And if the Institute sticks their nose back in the Cluster, we'll chop it off."

The Equilibrium Institute was an interstellar organization dedicated to *very specific* political ideals. Kira's understanding was that it was, at its core, a privately funded think tank out of the Heart. The resources of even a small private organization within two hundred light-years of Sol easily covered the expenses of waging private wars in the Rim twelve hundred light-years farther out.

But between her, the late John Estanza, and the rest of what was now Memorial Force, the Institute's intrusions into the Syntactic Cluster had failed both expensively and dramatically.

"So, we wait," she conceded with a sigh.

"And you, Commodore Demirci, *stop* running off without telling people," Zoric told her firmly. "If we need to send you on anti-piracy patrols to keep you sane, we can do that...but let's do it properly and with a plan, okay, boss?"

Kira snorted and nodded.

"All right, Kavitha, Konrad, you've made your point," she said. "I'll be good!"

3

EVEN WITH ZORIC handling most of the business of the four-ship mercenary fleet for the two weeks Kira had been gone, her headware happily informed her that she had a stack of messages waiting for her once her two senior subordinates left her be.

At the top of the list was a message flagged as priority from Stipan Dirix. The former Redward Army officer ran their semi-permanent dockside establishment in the Redward System and helped coordinate Kira's affairs with the locals.

There were, she realized, *several* messages from Dirix, of increasing urgency.

The most recent was just to call him, which Kira sighed and did.

"Stipan, what's going on?" she asked him. "Captain Zoric should have told you I was out-system."

"Oh, thank god," Dirix replied. "You're back in time. Zoric wasn't sure when you'd be returning, and we were running down to the wire on this."

"On what, Stipan?" Kira said. "I have six messages from you, and I'll freely admit I only read the most recent."

"Fair, fair," he conceded. "Queen Sonia *wanted* to have you at a grand reception *yesterday*, but since you weren't here, I gave her your regrets."

"Her Majesty knows I'm not in Redward full-time," she told her aide with a chuckle. "She'll forgive me this once, I'm sure."

"That would be my normal assumption, yeah," Dirix agreed. "But she seemed… Well, I wouldn't say Queen Sonia would show frustration to someone like me, but the fact that she *called me directly* says something, yes?"

Kira straightened in her chair. She'd been invited to a number of parties of various levels of privacy by Queen Sonia. Among other things, King Larry's wife was the true head of his intelligence services.

She also had a habit of trying to build up women across the star system, mostly by inviting them to parties so they could make connections with each other.

But *all* of the invitations Sonia had sent Kira had been recorded messages, often the digital equivalent of written invites, sent by the Queen's staff to Kira's staff.

If Sonia had directly called Stipan, something *important* was happening.

"I understand," Kira murmured. "Do you have any idea what's going on?"

"I know the grand reception last night was for some delegation of bankers from the Royal Crest," he told her. "They're here to discuss financing for a series of new infrastructure projects across the Cluster —people are here from the Yprian Federation, Bengalissimo…everywhere, honestly, to talk to them.

"My read is that the new stability in the Cluster is potentially going to see a *lot* of money flowing in—and Their Majesties want to make sure there's no offsetting flow of resources and power out."

That was always the risk with foreign investment, Kira knew. It was one of the ways a hegemon like the Royal Crest maintained their control.

On the other hand, the Royal Crest's banks provided the default interstellar currency across several hundred light-years of the Outer Rim, including the Syntactic Cluster. That gave them a *lot* of power, even before they started financing projects.

"So, I missed an important party, I take it?"

"Not as bad as it could be, I think," Dirix told her. "Because when she called me"—the mercenary administrator still sounded terrified by that—"she told me that I should get Zoric for today's event, regardless of whether you were back yet."

The big man raised his hands helplessly.

"We don't have many other senior officers she'd invite to something like that," he admitted. "Tamboli or Milani, I guess, but neither of them can speak for the company."

Kira had to hide a smile at the thought of the two nonbinary officers at one of Sonia's soirees. Dilshad Tamboli was self-admittedly a jumped-up shuttle mechanic turned nova-fighter flight-deck boss—and Milani, *Deception*'s chief ground trooper, never left their armor.

Ever.

"But Zoric could, even if I wasn't here," Kira noted. "On the other hand, I *am* here now. What kind of invitation am I looking at?"

"Private party at the Solitary Lodge," Dirix told her. "You're familiar with the place, right?"

"It was the first place Sonia ever invited me to one of these," Kira agreed. "That was where she recruited me for a suicidal covert op."

A covert operation that had ended up with her in control of an Institute-crewed ex-Brisingr warship—the ship that had become *Deception*. Almost as fortunately for Kira, in hindsight, had been meeting Konrad Bueller.

Of course, they wouldn't have ended up in control of *Deception* without Bueller, so that was a win all around.

"My impression is that this is a significantly larger event," her aide warned. "Invitation says outdoor barbecue party. Semi-formal, which in this case I think means *clothes you can clean ketchup off of.*"

Kira snorted.

"I hate burgers," she noted. That wasn't entirely true, but nothing she'd encountered in her adult life lived up to her father's mutton burgers. "So, I hope there are other options."

"It's the Queen's personal private retreat in the heart of a protected wilderness," Dirix reminded her. "Last I checked, they have a top-tier chef out there."

"And from what Sonia says, they're bored out of their minds," Kira murmured. "I sympathize. All right, Stipan. Make the arrangements. Captain Zoric and I will attend Her Majesty's barbecue.

"How long do I have?"

"Four hours. It's a midafternoon thing and it's already noon at the Lodge."

Just getting from orbit to the Lodge could easily take an hour, Kira knew. That didn't give her much time.

"Good thing I checked in with you first," she told him. "Anything else in my messages that will explode if I don't read it today?"

"Nothing from me, though that's not a perfect guarantee," he said. "I'll get in touch with the Queen's staff. Good luck, boss."

THE MOST CRITICAL component of Kira's emails was a note from Angel Waldroup—formerly the flight-deck boss of *Conviction*, now the flight-deck boss of *Raccoon*—that she'd rigged up some of the less-used cubage aboard *Raccoon* as a storage rack for class two nova-drive units.

The class two nova drives were a complex piece of technology. Unlike the class one drive, they required *very* specific gravitational and energy levels in the area where they were being produced. A class one nova drive had to be built on a planet.

Class two drives had to be built either on an asteroid or in an actively orbiting facility at a carefully calculated altitude. Once you had all of the pieces in place, though, they were actually mass-producible in the way the larger class one drives weren't.

Their *main* advantage, though, was having a far shorter minimum cooldown than a class one drive. A class two could cool down from a nova of a few light-minutes in a minute. A class one took a minimum of ten minutes to cool down, even from the shortest of novas.

That, combined with the class two drive's smaller size, had created the nova fighter. Kira's nova fighters could jump across a light-minute of space, engage a target, and then jump out after a minute.

Those hit-and-run attacks were devastating. On the other hand, the class two drive's *long-distance* nova cooldown was significantly longer than a class one's, which was why carriers existed.

Waldroup's storage solution was the answer to one of Kira's problems, though. Redward was the *only* system within a hundred light-years that could make class two nova drives, and they were willing to sell them to Memorial Force.

With the fabricators available to Waldroup, they could easily build nova fighters so long as they had the drives. Without the drives, their ability to build the rest of the plane was useless.

So, being able to store nova drives for later was *important*. It also might allow Memorial Force to dismantle some of their excess fighters, the ones that were currently crammed into every scrap of spare deck space aboard *Deception* and *Raccoon*.

Kira hesitated to do that, but given that they and their allies currently had a monopoly on nova fighters in the Syntactic Cluster, it might be an idea.

She sighed and put *that* thought aside for a later moment, firing off a thank-you to Waldroup.

They'd see what possibilities it opened later, but for now, her important messages were handled. That meant she needed to get ready for the party—and, thankfully, Queen Sonia wasn't so foolish as to expect Kira or Zoric to wear a *dress*.

4

THE SOLITARY LODGE was an intentionally rustic structure, a two-story building of raw wood and glass built on the edge of a lake at the heart of a planetary park. To Kira, the defensive screens shimmering in front of the large windows and the armor behind the wood were obvious, but the defenses were subtle.

Most civilian craft from the Outer Rim would never have picked up the anti-spacecraft missile batteries concealed in the woods around the Solitary Lodge, either. Kira's transport was a Brisingr-built combat shuttle, however, and the weapons in the forest stood out like sore thumbs.

The Lodge had been quieter the last time she'd visited. Her shuttle had been the only one parked on the concrete pads concealed beside the old-fashioned dock. Today, a dozen small spacecraft and aircraft were parked on the water—some of them directly, bobbing away on floating pontoons.

Given that the Lodge's two outer buildings were storage for water-craft and aircraft, that suggested there were more people there than the concealed haven was really designed to hold.

That said, there were several large open spaces carefully maintained around the house. As Kira and Zoric made their way up the dock toward land, Kira spotted that hand-carved wooden bridges had been laid over the brook that wrapped around the south side of the Lodge, connecting the two main green spaces to allow for a larger party.

There were at least three dozen people scattered across the Lodge's grounds, gathered in small clumps of conversation as half a dozen human servers made their way through with serving trays.

Kira noted Zoric examining the servers with a watchful eye and concealed a grin.

"It's one of Sonia's parties," she murmured to the other woman. "Every server is a commando."

She'd worked with several of Redward's elite army troops before. Their dedication to their missions was impressive—and one of their missions was the protection of their monarchs.

And unlike most of Redward's citizens, the commandos knew damn well how much Queen Sonia did.

Kira had barely finished the thought before they reached the end of the dock and the Queen of Redward herself appeared. The delicately tall woman was wearing a dark pink sundress that showed off her athletic frame perfectly, and gave the two mercenaries a genuine wide smile.

"I'm glad you were back in time to make this party, Kira," Sonia told her. "Welcome back to the Solitary Lodge. Welcome *to* the Solitary Lodge, Kavitha."

"Do you hold a lot of events out here?" Zoric asked after a modicum of a curtsy. Both of the mercenary officers wore a dark jewel-green jacket over the monochrome, temperature-regulating shipsuit of a spacer. For this situation, the shipsuits were a slightly iridescent black that rippled in the sunlight and offset the jackets perfectly—but they were still *entirely* functional.

"More during the local summer," the Queen replied. "It is a bit too far north here for winter activities other than hunting and skating, and neither Larry nor I are fond of either."

From what Kira understood, a significant number of King Larry's ancestors had been avid hunters and there was a network of lodges like this across the planet, part of the royal family's personal wealth.

Larry's distaste for hunting meant that many were barely used by the royals—a significant number were being rented out as hotels and tourist stops these days.

Of course, anyone who took the rotund monarch's dislike of hunting helpless animals for *weakness* had learned better by now, Kira hoped. Redward might be only one of sixteen signatories to the Syntactic Cluster Free Trade Zone and only one of the three recognized Major Powers of the FTZ, but there was no question in anyone's mind that the system was first among equals.

And while King Larry was a constitutional monarch, limited by law, tradition and personal morals alike, it was *his* hand behind that creation. Though the cheerfully charming woman in the comfortable dress in front of Kira had definitely had her part in it!

"Come. The staff will *complain* if I don't introduce you to their food before anything else!"

AN IMPRESSIVE DEFENSIVE array of tables had been assembled around a massive six-grill barbecue. The whole culinary fortification backed onto the brook, protecting the chef working away at the grills from excessive complaints or compliments.

Compliments, Kira suspected, were more likely. She wasn't entirely sure what the meat used in the burgers was, but it smelled heavenly enough to convince her to try one.

"Huh," she said after swallowing the first bite. "I'm impressed."

"You weren't expecting to be?" Sonia asked with a raised eyebrow.

"I grew up on handmade and hand-spiced mutton burgers my father made," Kira replied. "I don't trust *anyone's* burgers to come close enough to be acceptable. This is…acceptable."

The Queen laughed.

"I will attempt to phrase that more delicately to Em Caballo," she said. "She thinks she might have made the best burger in the known galaxy."

"Well, if it helps, *I* think she's right," Zoric said. "Damn, that's good."

"I will leave you to your food for the moment," Sonia told the mercenaries. "Almost no gathering at the Lodge is without ulterior motives, but today's are minor. Enjoy, ladies."

Kira concealed a smile at Zoric's momentarily pained expression as the Queen swept away. A pair of nonbinary local businesspeople swept in on the Queen like hovering vultures the moment Sonia was clear of the mercs, which earned a *different* pained expression from the mercenary Captain.

"I figured when it was out here," she murmured to Zoric. "Though the crowd is diverse. Most of the people here are... Well, they're the people I expect to want to talk to the Crest delegation in detail."

"You *know* these people?" Zoric gestured around.

"Most of the Redward people by sight and name," Kira admitted. "There aren't many I've had an actual conversation with, but I've met most of them.

"So have you," she reminded Zoric.

"I guess. I'll admit I've only paid attention to the military people at the parties you've brought me to," her business partner replied, shaking her head. "I mean, it makes *sense* that we're considered movers and shakers in the business world, but..."

"But we're still soldiers, even if we're soldiers for hire?" Kira finished. She took a moment to focus on her burger while Zoric considered that.

"I guess. Which makes me wonder what 'ulterior motives' Her Majesty has."

"Well." Kira looked around the crowd, considering the people she *did* know—and the ones she didn't know but could identify by the angular projections of Crest-style clothing.

"Most people here are civilian infrastructure," she concluded after a second. "Executives or major shareholders of companies that build large-scale ground, air or space facilities. Then, of course, we have the female and enby portion of the Bank of the Royal Crest delegation.

"Most of the ulterior motive I see here is giving the non-male members of that industry a slight edge in meeting their counterparts in the BRC group," Kira noted. "There's a *lot* of work on the table right now, across the Cluster but mostly focused in the Costar Clans Systems."

When Kira had first arrived in the Syntactic Cluster, the Costar Clans had been the major source of military actions in the area. The inhabitants of four marginal-to-doomed systems, they had survived by building the cheapest possible nova ships and stealing from *everyone*.

Redward had occupied those systems as part of finalizing the creation of the Free Trade Zone. They had the potential to help make the Kingdom of Redward an unimaginably rich five-star-system power —or to drag King Larry and Queen Sonia's nation into complete bankruptcy trying to keep their promises.

"So, Her Majesty wants to, what, handicap men in the bidding process?" Zoric asked.

"Not quite." Kira shrugged. "My own experience is that everybody, generally, listens to people of their own identifications more easily. Since Redward has a somewhat more male-dominated industrial and economic space than most, that can have a feedback loop effect that closes out everybody else.

"So, Queen Sonia uses the power of her position to enable women and enbies to talk to each other and form their own connections in an enabling space."

"Huh. Despite being here for years, I hadn't noticed that until you pointed it out," Zoric admitted. "I've seen worse sexism in the galaxy."

"I don't think it's even sexism so much as just like preferring to talk to like," Kira said. "Human nature. Like the fact that we're hanging out near the buffet table, talking to each other, rather than meeting the people around us."

Zoric chuckled.

"I'm not sure who here we *need* to meet," she admitted. "But from what you and the Queen said, I imagine there is at least one person we *should*."

"Almost certainly," Kira agreed. "So, I suggest we each grab one of those iced teas at the end of the table—the Lodge's staff makes *amazing* iced tea—and go see who we can find."

5

KIRA WASN'T REALLY surprised that the reality turned out to be someone finding *her*. She had one short conversation with a woman she knew—a continental vice-president for the company that made Astonishing Orange, her second-favorite Redward coffee varietal after the royal family's own private blend—and then spotted a pair of strangers specifically making their way toward her.

The Royal Crest's current fashion seemed to have escaped from the instructional images of a ten-year-old's geometry class. One of the two individuals approaching Kira wore what she *thought* was a dress that was formed into a perfect cylinder of the width of the wearer's shoulders and hips and descended down to just above their feet.

Their arms were still free to move, and she *presumed* they had some flexibility under the dress, but it was a quite distinctive outfit.

The dress-wearer was giving off strong "aide cum bodyguard" vibes, however, and Kira's attention slid to the person they were "definitely not" escorting. That worthy wore a similar distinctively angular-style blazer suit in dark gray, with shoulders that were clearly supported out past the wearer's body and then cutting inward to create a sharp triangle.

It was, as Kira understood it, an extremely masculine style by the

Crest's standards—but the gray blazer was buttoned just below the sternum, revealing one of the most delicately frilly pink blouses Kira had ever seen, carefully cut to expose more cleavage than Kira *had*.

Somehow, she was unsurprised when her headware pinged both individuals as nonbinary, using they/them pronouns. What *was* interesting was that her headware didn't give her much more information than pronouns and first names: the dress-wearing bodyguard was Voski and the gray-suited businessperson was Jade.

Kira was used to being aboard ship, where her headware could give her full lifetime files on her mercenaries or other military personnel. The blip of updating from silicon to organic memory was so familiar now that she barely registered that knowledge as not *hers* in any way.

The lack of that detail was interesting, and she bowed slightly as the two Cresters approached.

"Commodore Kira Demirci, yes?" Jade asked. They had darker skin, with a Korean-extraction tilt to their features, but with a sharp nose and heavy eyebrows.

"I am, yes," Kira agreed. "And you are?"

Both of them *knew* at least the basics from the implants in their heads, but humanity had hundreds of years of tradition behind pretending they *didn't* have computers in their heads.

"I am Jade," the stranger introduced themselves. "I am one of the directors of the Bank of the Royal Crest assigned to this expedition. This is Voski, my aide."

"A pleasure, Em Jade," Kira told them. "How are you finding Redward so far?"

Jade quirked their lips.

"May I be honest, Commodore?" they asked drily. "Between one Mid Rim soul and another?"

"I like Redward well enough," Kira replied, "but I won't hold your opinions against you, Em Jade."

"Please, Commodore Demirci, just Jade," Jade told her. They gestured around the party. "This is hardly formal enough to require Em this and Em that, don't you think?"

"As you wish, Jade," Kira said. She did *not* invite the banker to use her own first name. If Jade wanted to play identity games, that was fine, but Kira had paid for her rank in blood.

From the repeated quirk of the lips—not quite a smile but definitely amused—Jade picked up at least part of Kira's silent message.

"Redward is less backward than I expected," they finally said. "But it still pales against home. I have seen less well-amenitied cities on our direct client worlds, but I have seen far better, too."

Kira kept her face level. That was right. The Royal Crest maintained an explicit tributary empire—like the one Brisingr was busy setting up around her home system. Their "client worlds" were heavily restricted in their interstellar trade and provided resources and personnel to help maintain the Navy of the Royal Crest.

They were exactly the type of military-economic hegemon that the Equilibrium Institute had tried to force into existence in the Syntactic Cluster. The Institute believed that kind of hegemony was the only stable long-term interstellar political structure, after all—and the Royal Crest and their client worlds were one of the working examples of that in the Rim.

"It does grow on you if you live here," Kira murmured. She gestured around the Solitary Lodge. "Places like this are everywhere, I suppose, but I think they did a good job here."

"They did," Jade conceded. "And the Cluster's newfound stability is certainly appealing as an investment prospect." They shook their head. "Of course, while we *understand* King Larry's determination to keep control of Syntactic assets in the Cluster, it does limit the resources we're able to deploy.

"And there are, of course, those who question how long this stability will last. It was only a few months ago, after all, that the whole region was involved in a war."

"There aren't many threats in the Cluster to cause that again," Kira pointed out. "Bengalissimo and Ypres look to make more money as part of the Free Trade Zone than trying to break it. The Costar Clans are now under Redward control." She shook her head with a smile.

"With the Bengalissimo Republic, the Ypres Federation and the Kingdom of Redward all upgrading their fleets at a breakneck pace, I don't think anyone who tries to cause trouble here is going to enjoy it," she noted. "They're going to up to a Mid Rim standard soon enough."

"And your Memorial Force will be here to protect them until they are?" Jade asked.

"If needed," Kira agreed. "*Deception* will remain the most powerful warship in the Cluster for a while yet, though she's no longer as necessary as she once was. *Conviction*, in many ways, was more dramatic an influence on the Cluster than *Deception*."

"So I heard," Jade said softly. "Were you close to Captain Estanza?"

"He was a mentor and a friend," Kira murmured, swallowing the usual spike of grief. She had a lot of practice at hiding grief these days. She'd lost a lot of friends before she'd ever come to the Syntactic Cluster—and the fighting there had been no gentler.

"But he died doing what he swore to do," she continued. "He stopped the Equilibrium Institute and their patsies from wrecking the Syntactic Cluster."

Kira watched Jade and Voski exchange a glance. There were a *lot* of people who regarded the story about a third party interfering in the Cluster as a lie designed to permit the new Bengal and Ypres governments to wash their hands of the actions of their system's factions.

"I have heard the…theory about the Equilibrium Institute," Jade allowed. "I would be interested to hear your take on it, Commodore."

"For that, Jade, I will need to refresh my drink," Kira said carefully. She suddenly suspected that *this* was what the Crest bureaucrat was after—and that meant she wanted a few moments to think.

"Voski, can you grab the Commodore and myself new drinks?" Jade said instantly. "I see some free chairs over in that gazebo. Voski can grab us some food as well, if you wish. Shall we, Commodore?"

Kira smiled. She wasn't sure why the Bank of the Royal Crest delegation wanted her take on the Equilibrium Institute, but she now understood why Sonia had been so desperate to get *her* to this party.

KIRA WAITED for Voski to return with grill-roasted potato wedges and a full pitcher of iced tea before she said anything. The gazebo was surprisingly comfortable, a tucked-away seating area on the edge of the forest around the Solitary Lodge.

There was an energy screen between the gazebo and the woods, of course—but it was intriguing to Kira that both Jade and Voski both clearly made note of that shield as they took their seats. She expected the bodyguard to pick out the defenses, but the banker themselves? That was interesting.

"You seem quite determined to get my opinion on the Equilibrium Institute, Jade," Kira noted after trying the first wedge. Like everything else she'd ever been fed at the Lodge, it was amazing.

"I can think of a dozen reasons why the governments of the SCFTZ would make up a story to cover up the various conflicts of the last few years," Jade said bluntly. "While you are contracted with them, you have less reason to toe the party line than most.

"We are talking trillions of crests' worth of investment, Commodore Demirci. *Trillions.* While these are both sums that the Bank of the Royal Crest can lend and that we can reasonably expect the Free Trade Zone to be able to repay, it is my obligation to the people whose accounts and investments will be supporting and supported by those loans to make sure I fully understand the situation.

"There are already concerns in the halls of the BRC about the long-term stability of a free trade zone," they noted. "Any uncertainty around the likelihood of resumed conflict in the area changes our risk assessment—which will, at a minimum, drive up the rates we can offer the Free Trade Zone's members or even render those loans non-under-writable.

"Do you understand?" Jade asked.

"Mostly," Kira said. She wasn't an expert on loans or financing—Memorial Force was fortunate, in a lot of ways, that between their sources of hardware and the cash reserves assembled by both John Estanza and Kira's old CO who'd sent her out to Redward, they had *no* debt—but she understood the basics.

"What do you need to know, Jade?" she asked.

"You've only been here for two years, yes?" the banker asked. "And yet you now command a mercenary fleet that is arguably the third or fourth most powerful fleet in the sector? That seems to have been a...rapid rise, Commodore."

Kira snorted.

"I arrived in this system with a recommendation for a lawyer, instructions to talk to John Estanza, and six not-quite-stolen nova fighters," she told Jade. "I started flying for John Estanza off of *Conviction* and saw the first fight against the Costar Clans' 'Warlord Deceiver' first-hand.

"Until then, I didn't buy the whole Equilibrium Institute spiel that John had," Kira admitted. "But Davies—Warlord Deceiver—had multiple Mid Rim ships, nova fighters, even a class two nova-drive production line. Someone outside the Cluster had provided all of that.

"And we captured a man who confessed to *being* an Equilibrium Institute agent," she told Jade. "He tried to recruit me—and *re*-recruit Captain Estanza, who used to work for them."

There was a pregnant pause as Kira took a large swallow of her tea, then refilled it from the pitcher. She noted that Voski had retreated to lean against the entrance to the gazebo—still close enough to hear but far enough to secure their privacy.

If Kira had been worried at all, though, she also noted that one of the servers had positioned themselves to watch the gazebo and Voski. As she picked up the glass of tea again, she half-saluted the commando over it—and got a thumbs-up back.

She smiled. She *thought* she'd recognized the woman as one of the commandos who'd gone into Ypres with her.

"I'm surprised you'd admit that Estanza worked for the Institute, if they're all the Cluster says they are," Jade finally said into the silence.

"John Estanza, important as he was to me, is dead," Kira said quietly. "He died saving this Cluster from the Equilibrium Institute. I would fail at the task he set me if I protected his memory over telling the truth."

She did *not* note that there were still other former Equilibrium agents in Memorial Force. Konrad Bueller had been recruited by the Institute and sent out to the Syntactic Cluster with *K79-L*, the cruiser that had become *Deception*, and she had several no-longer-blackmailed agents among her pilots and crew.

"I see," Jade allowed.

"As for the rest of the last two years..." Kira shook her head. "*K79-L* was brought out here by an Equilibrium cover company. They used her to support the coup against the Ypres Hearth faction—and Institute agents murdered the president of Sanctuary to enable Hearth's conquest of the system."

She smiled thinly.

"Thanks to my mercenaries, and some Redward commandos, *K79-L* fell into friendly hands. *My* hands. Others dealt with the attempt to unify Ypres by force—and then Their Majesties helped birth the Ypres Federation as an alternative to conquest."

"Which almost brings us here, to a solidified Free Trade Zone and peace," Jade noted. "You believe the Institute story, then?"

"More than believe, Jade," Kira said. "I have been the one providing proof and weaving the pieces together for Redward. *Three times* we have encountered Institute agents in the Cluster—the first time, supporting Davies; the second time, aboard *K79-L*, trying to unify Ypres by force.

"The third time was when Queen Rossella Gaspari took control of Bengalissimo and waged war against the rest of the Cluster," she concluded. "Gaspari was an Equilibrium agent herself, but the key player in *that* mess was Cobra Squadron—and Cobra Squadron, Em Jade, was *always* an Equilibrium asset."

"You sound very sure of that," Jade noted drily.

"John Estanza was a friend and mentor...and a former member of Cobra Squadron," Kira pointed out. "Jay Moranis, on Apollo, was a friend and mentor and my commanding officer—and a former member of Cobra Squadron.

"And Lars Ivarsson, who died aboard the assault carrier *Equilibrium* when John Estanza rammed *Conviction* into her, was Platinum Cobra, the commanding officer of the rebuilt Cobra Squadron—and the last person to attempt to recruit myself, John Estanza and some others I *won't* name to the Institute."

The gazebo was quiet again. The sound of conversation from the rest of the party was more muffled than it should have been, suggesting that there was a lot more gear built into the unassuming structure than Kira had realized.

"You are very passionate about this, Commodore Demirci," Jade finally told her. "It is reassuring. It is easier to disbelieve the dry and measured words of politicians than the fury of a warrior who has lost friends."

"I'm glad," Kira said grimly. "I've paid enough for that certainty."

"You have, and I apologize for doubting you," the banker said. "I needed to be certain that the Institute was involved here. I thank you for your time, Commodore, though I have one more question, if you will indulge me with speculation."

Kira exhaled a long breath, intentionally forcing her shoulders to relax as she met the banker's gray eyes. Jade's expression was more sympathetic than she expected. The Crest enby was telling the truth, she realized, when she apologized.

"Very well," she told the banker.

"Do you think the Institute is going to come back?" Jade asked. "My napkin-math estimate says they spent somewhere in the region of eighty *trillion* crests on their various projects here, and I'm likely underestimating that."

"Sunk cost," Kira said bluntly. "I suspect the Institute has its fingers in a lot of different sectors across our region of the Rim. I *hope* that their influence isn't spread across the *entire* Rim, but I don't know."

Given that "the Rim" was every star system more than a thousand light-years and less than fifteen hundred light-years from Sol, Kira really did hope the Institute's influence was limited to only a portion of it.

"That said, my understanding is that the Institute is an entity of either the Heart or the Inner Meridian," Kira continued. "The funds they've spent to almost destroy this Cluster are a rounding error for a decently sized operating entity of those regions.

"But money they spend here isn't money they spend influencing other regions—and if their Seldonian calculations say that a free trade zone like ours is doomed, then why not simply wait for us to fail? Then they can give the strongest of whoever is left a hand up to become what they *think* the region needs."

Something in Jade's expression twisted at Kira's words.

"I see," they said, in a tone that sounded vaguely ill. "And what do you believe they think the region needs?"

"What they *told* me," Kira said pointedly, "was that their Seldonian psychohistorical calculations showed that free trade zones and similar egalitarian structures are doomed to failure within two to three decades.

"*They* believe that only strong central military-economic hegemons can maintain stability in a region. Anything else can only result in chaos and death on a massive scale, which clearly enables them to engage in the most immoral and vicious actions to avoid that."

Kira knew how much vitriol was dripping from her voice at the end—and Jade clearly picked up on *all* of it.

"There are some believers in similar projections in the Bank of the Royal Crest," they warned. "That is one of the impediments the SCFTZ is facing in their quest for financing arrangements."

"It becomes a self-fulfilling prophecy at that point, doesn't it?" Kira asked.

"Not if I have anything to say about it," Jade replied—and their tone told Kira there was more going on than the banker was telling her just yet.

6

THE POLITICALLY REQUIRED parties added a degree of glitz and glamor to the life of a mercenary fleet commander, but even those were merely more decorative meetings in Kira's mind. Her meeting aboard the battle station Green Ward the next day was more typical.

She'd traded the dark jewel-green jacket of her dress uniform for a plainer black jacket. Konrad and Zoric wore the same outfit—though only Zoric had insignia, wearing the stylized golden rocket that was the near-universal marker of a ship Captain.

The Redward Royal Fleet officers they were meeting were similarly dressed, though their uniforms had a profusion of insignia. In theory, at least, only two of the six officers didn't match or exceed Kira's rank.

On the other hand, no one in the room was going to pretend that Kira didn't stand on the same level as an RRF Vice Admiral these days, let alone the two Commodores or the Rear Admiral in the room.

Kira didn't know any of the RRF officers in the room well, though Vice Admiral Saga Idowu was known to her by reputation and role. The dark-skinned woman ran the Redward military shipyards— Konrad knew her significantly better than Kira did, as he'd been working through recurring contracts with the yards.

"Commodore, Captain, Commander," Idowu greeted them as an aide poured coffee for everyone.

A sniff confirmed that it wasn't Astonishing Orange, Kira's preferred purchasable Redward coffee brand, but it *also* wasn't Redward Premium Choice, the planet's main export brand.

While Premium Choice was drinkable to most people, Kira had been spoiled since arriving in Redward, and the export brand was mediocre at best by the system's standards. Whatever variety Idowu was serving was decent, though not fantastic.

"I wanted to touch base, first and foremost, and get your impression of the new *Parakeet*-class ships," Idowu told Kira after everyone had started their coffees. "You have a quarter of them and, from what I understand, they have now seen action under your command?"

"*Action* might be stretching it," Kira admitted with a chuckle. "Captains Michel and McCaig ran down a pirate near New Ontario, but they had her so outclassed, it barely qualified as a fight."

"That is a recommendation all on its own, I suppose." She paused thoughtfully. "The ships are maneuverable and their sensors and targeting systems are good. We didn't have to test their defenses, but their optical systems were enough to disable a freighter at a hundred thousand kilometers with a single shot.

"My comparison point is such that most Syntactic Cluster ships come up short, Admiral Idowu," she warned. "But the *Parakeet*s are much less so than most things I've seen out here. An Apollo ship has better miniaturization, which allows them to simply pack *more* into the same volume.

"Without the ability to include that extra Harrington coil or to put in that heavier plasma cannon, I'd say the *Parakeet*s are as good as you're getting out here."

At least one of the Commodores—Kira's headware said her name was Rachel Ermacora—looked positively mutinous at Kira's comments but remained silent at a sharp look from her superior.

"I appreciate your bluntness, Commodore," Idowu said with a chuckle of her own. "Part of the sale agreement, of course, was that your Captains would provide their impressions and sensor records."

She left that hanging and Kira swallowed a grouchy response.

"Of course," she finally said. "I will make certain that Captains Michel and McCaig pass on their reports to your people."

"That is all we ask," the Admiral said with a slight nod. "We've already begun construction on the second wave of *Parakeet*s, but we're still early enough that changes can be made."

Konrad coughed next to Kira and she managed not to twist in her seat to look questioningly at her partner. There was clearly *something* he was prodding the Admiral on.

"In terms of general background information for you to be aware of as part of your defensive contract, Commodore, we are expanding the yards underneath the Green Ward," Idowu told her.

The Green Ward was one of several massive asteroid fortresses that orbited Redward. Most inhabited systems had defensive stations of a similar ilk, vastly outmatching any nova ship that could be deployed by a comparable power.

Attacking an inhabited star system was a long way to commit suicide. Nova warships fought over trade-route stops, the mapped points that were safe to nova to, not star systems.

Most relevant to Kira, though, and likely the reason Konrad was poking the RRF Admiral, was that the Green Ward yards contained the three slips where the RRF was building their new capital ships. As part of the deal that had seen her keep *Deception*, Konrad Bueller had helped the RRF's engineers develop a 12X class one nova drive.

A class one nova drive couldn't be *smaller* than one thousand cubic meters—and the standard unit was a 10X unit, creating a ten-kilocubic ship. No one in the Rim, so far as Kira knew, had managed to build a class one that was larger than ten thousand cubic meters.

Redward hadn't even been up to that size when Konrad had got involved—but he'd changed all of that, allowing them to build a ten-thousand-cubic-meter 12X nova drive. And with that drive, a one-hundred-and-twenty-thousand-cubic-meter capital ship.

Three had been under construction for well over a year. They still had nearly a year left, but one of those slips was *supposed* to be used to build Kira a new carrier when it was ready.

"You're building new one-twenty yards?" she asked.

Redward already had smaller yards, currently building less-rushed versions of the *Baron*-class cruisers that had defeated the Bengalissimo and Equilibrium fleets. Without an active blockade, there was no reason to accept the outright dangerous pace that had built the first generation of those light cruisers.

"We are," Idowu confirmed. "Making sure that those yards remain protected will be a key strategic and operational objective if this system comes under attack, hence briefing you on them. While the Green Ward is capable of withstanding most threats, a surprise nova-fighter strike remains a concern."

All of which was true, Kira reflected, but didn't cover what she was thinking of. Konrad had almost certainly been involved in the process of laying out the new building slips and new ship designs—and *he* had clearly been thinking of accelerating Memorial Force's access to a new carrier.

Raccoon's limitations were very much holding the organization back at the moment, and all of Kira's officers were daydreaming of the day they would have a *real* carrier again.

So, she smiled at Admiral Idowu.

"Forgive my forwardness, Admiral, but the Redward yards are committed to providing Memorial Force with a one-hundred-and-twenty-kilocubic fleet carrier," she said. "Given this expansion of the yards, I expect that one of those slips will be put at our disposal for that project?"

There was a long silence as the RRF officers traded looks, then Idowu sighed and took a long swallow of her coffee.

"I am not aware of the exact details of the agreement between yourself and Their Majesties on that point," she noted. "The specification that *I* was advised of was that we would build you a carrier, at cost, once our own capital-ship needs are met.

"We currently have no one-twenty kilocubic ships in commission, so it is impossible to claim that our capital-ship needs have been met," Idowu concluded. "These new yards have already been flagged for the construction of two new battlecruisers and a fleet carrier for the Redward Royal Fleet.

"Once our first wave of construction is done and we have commissioned capital ships of our own, then—and *only* then—will we be able to spare heavy construction yards for the construction of capital ships for sale, even to valued and close friends such as Memorial Force."

There was a long pause, long enough to make it clear that Idowu had hoped to brush over that aspect of the situation.

"Which does bring us to the main point of this meeting, of course," she noted with what Kira suspected was false calm. "While most of our current construction is spoken for, we will have both seventy-five-kilocubic and thirty-kilocubic slips coming up available in the next six months, and you are on the *very* short list of organizations we are authorized to sell warships to…"

"THAT VOID-FROZEN LYING chunk of iced *waste*."

Kira had *felt* Konrad seethe the whole way back to the shuttle, but it wasn't until they were back on their own spacecraft that the engineer let loose.

"Bueller?" Zoric asked carefully.

"I helped them design the new yards, even make some refinements on the battlecruiser and carrier designs," Konrad told the two women. "I'm sure you both figured that. I've been doing contract work on the side for the yards whenever we're in-system.

"I kind of felt like I owed them that, after I drafted the plans that got so many workers killed."

Kira squeezed his arm. The rushed construction program that had put three *Baron*-class cruisers into commission for the war against Bengal had been hard on her lover. He'd worked with Redward's ship-building leaders and workers to assemble a plan that maximized effi-ciency…at a conscious sacrifice of worker safety.

No one had worked on those ships without knowing that was the deal, but Konrad had been the one making the final calls—and *hundreds* of workers had died to build those ships.

She wasn't sure he'd ever forgive himself for that.

"But…the big yards, I pushed back a bit," Konrad said. "I know we're a bit trapped here until we get that carrier, so I *thought* I'd got a commitment that we'd get a shot at one of those slips."

"And?" Kira asked.

"Idowu is *very* careful in her damn phrasing," the engineer snapped. "*When we've met our own needs.* Gods. That..."

"Breathe, Konrad," Kira said with a long sigh.

"After everything we've done for them, they pull that on us?" Zoric demanded. "'Just *for your information*, we have new yards that could get you what we promised but we're not making them available to you?'"

Both of Kira's main subordinates were apparently spitting nails. Kira didn't even *disagree* with them, but there was only so much they could do.

"Yeah, that was...frustrating of them," Kira admitted. She'd barely managed to keep her own focus on the meeting after that. "We did get them to commit to putting one of the seventy-five-kilocubic yards at our disposal."

"In six months," Zoric murmured. "So, what, we get a light carrier in eighteen months and a fleet carrier in three years?"

"It could be worse," Kira said. "Who else is going to sell a mercenary company anything they regard as a modern fleet carrier at all?"

"Hell, with three years to play with, we could go right to Sol and have the Federation build us something that's utterly obsolete trash by their standards—and still be back here before we get the ship Redward promised us!" Zoric snapped.

Kira raised an eyebrow at her Flag Captain.

"SolFed doesn't build armed ships for anybody," she pointed out.

The Solar Federation was the stars closest to humanity's home system, one of the few multi-system powers in existence and the unquestioned primarch of human space. Given that SolFed was fifteen hundred light-years away, Zoric was exaggerating how quickly they could get there.

"It would take us longer to find someone willing to sell us their surplus closer to the Core than it would take us to wait on Redward," she told her people quietly. "Let's not leap to suggestions that we know are almost impossible.

"Yes, that meeting was a bit of a knife in the back," she agreed. "But

Redward, overall, has treated us pretty well. They're still definitely selling us a modern—by their standards, anyway—fleet carrier. *At cost.*

"We can wait a couple of years for an at-cost carrier."

"You've been on our flight decks, boss," Zoric countered. "We have a contract that lets us purchase class two drives from Redward, but we have nowhere to put the *drives*, let alone the nova fighters.

"We're making it work, but we're pushing the limits."

"I know," Kira replied. "But the truth of the matter is that *no one* else is going to sell us a real carrier, people. And the Redward retainer is covering all of our ongoing operating costs, including all of our salaries."

She gestured at the three of them.

"*Raccoon* isn't a good carrier." That was just a statement of fact. "But we have four ships, and Redward is happy to pay for their crews and maintenance for now. The Syntactic Cluster is *probably* safe, but us being here helps *keep* it safe.

"Admiral Idowu might have been less than straightforward with us —and believe me, I'm going to make sure the right people hear about *that*!—but Larry and Sonia have played fair with us all along.

"So, we can wait for now."

Kira smiled thinly.

"Unless one of you knows someone with a better offer, anyway?"

7

FOR ALL OF the trials and travails of Kira's job—and her current rising undercurrent of sheer boredom—there was still something incredible about watching her squadron maintain formation and knowing that it was all hers.

Well, fifty-one percent hers. The rest of the ownership was split between Kavitha Zoric and the survivors of her original Apollo fighter pilots. Still, Kira Demirci held the majority share and was Commodore and CEO of the company.

Of course, *Deception* dwarfed the other three ships of Memorial Force. She was almost three times as large as the *Parakeet*s and well over twice the size of *Raccoon*. The junk carrier could still easily be mistaken for a freighter by someone who didn't know what a converted freighter-carrier looked like.

Her headware pinged an incoming call and she checked. She smiled when she realized it was Mel "Nightmare" Cartman —*Deception*'s Commander, Nova Group.

Cartman was one of the first people who'd made it out to Redward to join Kira and *also* one of her oldest friends. Her role as CNG for *Deception* was a bit of an odd fit, since Kira *also* flew off the cruiser and acted as CNG for the whole of Memorial Force.

"What's up, Nightmare?" Kira answered the com. *Deception*'s flag bridge was empty other than her, which gave her the privacy to be more casual than usual.

"Checking to make sure you haven't stolen a nova fighter and gone off on a one-woman crusade against tax fraud or something," her old friend said drily. "Still here, though?"

Kira snorted.

"I got bored and attached myself to *one* destroyer patrol," she argued. "From the way you all are acting, you'd think I'd been doing this every week for years."

"Because it was dumb and we want to make sure you *don't* do it again," Cartman told her. "Eventually, we'll feel you're sufficiently chastened." She paused. "Maybe."

"Wonderful," Kira said. "Well, I am still here. Sitting on *Deception*'s flag deck, watching a hologram of our ships orbiting Redward."

It was a notable sign of trust that her independently operated *warships* were permitted to orbit autonomously, without being required to dock with a station or being positioned under the guns of one of the asteroid fortresses.

Her four ships weren't much of a threat to a planet, but any warship could fabricate a Harrington-coil missile that would ruin a large city's century with pure kinetic energy. Only trusted warships were left to swan around in planetary orbit without escort.

Redward was basically home for Memorial Force at this point—but they *were* still independents.

"Well, since you're still here, it's Dinesha's birthday today," Cartman told her. "He's...well, I'm your other ship CNG, boss. I'm guessing you've noticed what he's doing, but I'm the one working with him."

Kira sighed. She *didn't* need Cartman to tell her what Dinesha Patel, the third-largest shareholder of Memorial Force and *Raccoon*'s Commander, Nova Group, had been doing. Patel had lost his long-standing boyfriend in the battle against Equilibrium and was...surviving.

"He's working too much and not coming up for air," Kira said aloud. "I'm familiar with the coping mechanism."

If for no other reason than that she tended to do the same thing.

"I checked in with Dr. Devin and *he* says that throwing Dinesha a birthday party with the old salts should be good for him," Cartman said. "I didn't go so far as to ask if Dinesha was getting counseling through Devin or someone else—I know the lines!"

Kira chuckled softly.

"A party would be fine, I agree," she said. "I'm guessing you've organized something and want me there? Does *Patel* know about this yet?"

"Yes and yes," Cartman replied. "I didn't think a *surprise* party was a good idea. We're all a bit squirrelly after Hoffman's death…and, well, it's not what he would have wanted."

Joseph "Longknife" Hoffman had been the most senior pilot to make it to Redward from the old Three-Oh-Three Nova Combat Group in the Apollo System Defense Force after Kira herself. He'd taken over as CNG aboard *Conviction* when Kira had moved to *Deception*, but she'd worked with him for over a decade and had known him well—if not as well as Dinesha Patel!

And Mel Cartman was right.

"My schedule is clear for the moment," Kira told her friend. "And if it wasn't, I'd make it so. Where do you need me and when?"

AS THE COMMODORE AND CEO, Kira knew she was going to have to leave the party early—that was even more true now than it had been when she was merely her friends' squadron commander. They *were* her friends, but they were also her subordinates, and her presence was always going to be at least a little suppressing.

Despite the space problems aboard both of their ships, Cartman had managed to take over a pilots' briefing room on *Raccoon* and clear it out for the party. There was a rack of torpedoes—*hopefully* with the hydrogen tanks for their cores and warheads emptied!—against one wall, but otherwise it looked almost normal.

There were only four of them there to start. Kira herself, Mel Cartman, Dinesha Patel, and Abdullah Colombera.

Patel looked tired. His beard had grown in enough to be visible on his darker skin, but he was keeping it enough under control to keep it from looking unruly. Still, his eyes were focused more on his beer than on his friends, and he was quiet despite Cartman attempting to engage him in conversation.

Colombera had been one of the troublemakers in the Three-Oh-Three. Now he commanded one of Cartman's squadrons on *Deception* and was usually completely professional.

That meant that *no one* was expecting the whoopie cushion when Patel took a seat next to the table of snacks. A loud, ear-shattering fart noise tore through the briefing room and shocked them all to complete silence.

Patel's bottle of beer hit the ground in the midst of that silence with a solid *thunk*, followed by a small burble as the liquid started to dribble out—and then *Raccoon*'s CNG burst out laughing.

Kira had to join in as the tension in the room, tension none of them had really acknowledged, snapped. After a second, they were all laughing.

A fifth voice joined them from the door and everyone turned to see Evgenia Michel make her way in. The bulky specialty prosthetics that had replaced her legs and pelvis weren't quiet, and they made their own clanking noise as Michel crossed to the snack table.

"A whoopie cushion, really, Scimitar?" she asked the squadron commander with a broad grin.

"Everybody here needs to stop feeling so damn sorry for themselves," the younger man told them all. "We lost Joseph. That fucking sucks. We lost Estanza. That's awful. We lost home. We lost the Three-Oh-Three.

"All we have is each other."

Colombera gestured around them.

"Except that's *bullshit*," he snapped. "Who's in this room, folks? A Commodore. A starship Captain. Two CNGs. And one squadron commander.

"We're not alone. All of Memorial Force is with us. That's our family now. A party with just the five of us isn't wrong, but it doesn't feel right, either, does it?"

Kira snorted.

"I bring Konrad and Kavitha to most things these days," she conceded. "You're all special to me, though. All of you."

She looked around, meeting each of their eyes. Patel and Michel were the worst; she had to admit that to herself. Patel had lost the man he loved—and Michel had learned the hard way that her nervous system rejected the regeneration tech available to Redward.

Out there, at least, they couldn't even get her to grow the nerves necessary to interact properly with prosthetics. The clunky, oversized units she wore were linked to her headware instead of properly interfacing with her regular nervous system.

Colombera picked up the dropped beer bottle and tossed it into the recycling chute.

"Whoopie cushions are old and crude, but no one looks for them," he said with an impish grin. "And this party needed the tension kicked. So." He looked around. "Are we going to have a party or a sob fest?"

"There's not enough room to invite anyone else, not with *these* legs," Michel said with a loud grin. "So, I suggest someone toss me a damn beer—and if no one *else* has the old dirty drinking songs memorized, they're in *my* headware!"

Kira laughed—and threw Evgenia Michel a bottle of beer.

Her old squadron still had some kick to it, it seemed—and she realized that Dinesha Patel wasn't the only one who'd needed the kick.

8

"WHAT DO we have on the plate this morning?" Kira asked.

The morning virtual conference was a standard of their last few months in Redward. All four ship Captains, both CNGs, Kira and Stipan Dirix all linked together from their assorted offices in a meeting that was supposed to keep everyone fully up to date.

"We forwarded those reports on to the locals on the *Parakeets'* performances," McCaig answered, the big man looking more amused than anything. "Interesting to know that we took them into action before the RRF did."

"Not much shooting going on in the Syntactic Cluster these days," Michel noted. "It's a fluke that *we* happened on *Ancillary*—they were going to get hit by someone, they were drawing too much attention, but the odds it was going to be us weren't good."

"That didn't work out so well for them," *Raccoon*'s Captain Mwangi noted. "And I saw the statements for our bonus on bringing them in. That was good work."

"That was easy," Michel admitted. "*Ancillary* was smaller than either destroyer. She was a thirty-kilocubic tramp that had had a handful of plasma guns welded on. She was never a threat to anyone except a merchant ship."

"And you handled her well," Kira pointed out. "So, let's not talk ourselves down too much, shall we? New Ontario was pleased to get the crew alive. My understanding is that they're hoping to track down whoever was buying their prizes—with the Costar Clans absorbed by Redward, the usual markets are no more."

"There's always *someone* willing to buy at a discount without asking questions," Stipan Dirix said grimly. "And stolen goods are never sold at a loss to the thief."

"This is true. We've benefited from that ourselves," Kira agreed.

That was part of why she'd managed to hang on to *Deception*, after all. It wasn't like Redward had paid for or built her themselves, and letting her keep someone *else's* ship was easy enough.

"*Raccoon* is about where we've been for the last bit," Mwangi told the others after a moment. "Waldroup is doing the best she can to keep things organized, but we've packed fifty-plus nova fighters into a deck designed to hold forty at a stretch.

"We're crowded and my launches are going to be short," he admitted. "That said, I can *get* those fifty fighters into space; it'll just take longer than it should."

"We'll need to optimize as best as we can," Kira said. "We know it's going to be a while before we get our hands on a real carrier again. We're going to be talking exact currency amounts with the locals, but we have a tentative plan for two more destroyers, a light carrier and a fleet carrier, but…"

"Nothing soon, I'm guessing?" Patel asked.

"Bingo," Kira agreed. "Eighteen months for the destroyers. Two years, minimum, for a seventy-five-kilocubic carrier. *Four* for the fleet carrier.

"So, we're going to be home-porting, if nothing else, in Redward for a few years," she told everyone. "Depending on what work we get over those years, we may buy a second round of ships after we get the destroyers and the CVL.

"We'll see. For now, I just have meetings with Pree and Yanis later to poke through bank accounts and see what we can afford."

That got her a chuckle. Pree—Priapus Simoneit—was Memorial Force's main lawyer in Redward, and Yanis Vaduva was the Force's purser. He'd held the same job for John Estanza on *Conviction*, and now he held it for the entire mercenary fleet from an office on *Deception*.

Kira was well aware of Vaduva's importance to the fleet. If he'd *wanted* to be in this meeting, he'd be in it. Despite his perpetually smiling cheerfulness when interacting with people, the purser vastly preferred accounts and text transcripts to meetings and conversations.

Part of his contract with Estanza had specified that he could not be asked to attend more than two hours of meetings per business week. Kira had duplicated the contract exactly when Vaduva had moved over to Memorial Force—and had never had a reason to regret it.

"Well, that's a good segue for me, I think," Dirix said after a moment. "We got a request for a meeting with the Commodore and Captain Zoric late last night. Potential contract."

Kira raised an eyebrow.

"Normally, we have a bit more information than that," she observed. "What have we got this time?"

"Very little," Dirix admitted. "Normally, I'd have rejected it and asked for more info, but in this case, I figured I'd leave that up to you two."

She exchanged a glance with Zoric.

"Okay, Stipan, stop beating around the bush," Kira ordered the ex-Redward Army officer. "What's going on?"

"The meeting request is vague as fuck," he told her. "No details on who you'll be meeting or what they want to talk about other than 'a contract.' But it was forwarded by Her Majesty's personal secretary, Em Hamasaki—and it *does* specify that it's from the Bank of the Royal Crest delegation."

Kira nodded slowly. That made...sense. As usual, Sonia was playing games. But she'd never lost out playing the Queen's games yet.

"I had a fascinating conversation with one of their directors at Queen Sonia's barbecue," she told the others. "If they were sounding me out for a potential contract, that would add another layer to that meeting."

Including a question around why Jade had asked so many questions about the Equilibrium Institute.

"Can we deploy to anywhere the Crest might want us to operate?" McCaig asked. "Our retainer limits how far we're supposed to be from Redward, doesn't it?"

"It does," Kira confirmed. "But there are allowances for us taking on other contracts, with enough notice to the Redward government— and if Sonia is forwarding the meeting request herself, I'm guessing they're willing to work with us.

"That said, it depends on how far away they want us to deploy," she continued. "There could be operations they need in or near the Syntactic Cluster, which should be fine. But if they want us to go all the way to the Crest *Sector*, that's a bigger deal.

"And raises the question of *why*. The Bank of the Royal Crest's largest shareholder is the King of the Royal Crest—there aren't many situations near home that they can't throw the *Navy* of the Royal Crest at."

The meeting was quiet.

"That said, Sonia's recommendation is a damn big deal," Kira noted. "Book the meeting, Dirix. Unless someone has some reason why we shouldn't even meet with them?"

"They're the biggest bank in four hundred light-years," Zoric said flatly. "I suggest we be prepared to go quite a bit out of our way to get in their good books."

"There are limits," Mwangi warned. "Let's not get too eager— banks aren't known for being *generous* employers, either."

"Captain Zoric and I will keep it in hand," Kira told them all. "We've both dealt with Mid Rim bankers before, after all."

While a good chunk of her people were now from the Syntactic Cluster, none of the people on the conference call were. Zoric wasn't even from the *Rim*—she was from a world only nine hundred light-years from Sol, which made her solidly from the Fringe.

"They're sharks, but they want something from us, and at the worst, we can always say no."

9

BLUEWARD STATION WAS the largest civilian orbital above Redward. It was attached to an orbital elevator that extended far past it, with the Azure Ward asteroid fortress at the far end acting as a counterweight.

Kira and Zoric were known by sight to most of the station's population now. With everything that had gone down over the last two years, the senior officers of Memorial Force were held up as heroes in a way that she suspected was *very* unusual for mercenaries.

"I'm not familiar with this restaurant," Kira murmured to Zoric as they followed the directions from their headware. "And I thought I knew everywhere of importance on Blueward."

"I know the name," Zoric said, eyeing the corridor ahead of them. "I've never been there, and I understand that Estanza only ever went there once." She shook her head. "It's not a restaurant as you're thinking of it, boss."

"What, it's someone's living room?" Kira asked drily. The name was simply Chef Concepta Pitt's.

"Not quite, but it's basically a kitchen and three attached dining rooms," Zoric admitted. "I thought reservations were booked a year in advance, so I'm a bit thrown that the Cresters have one."

Kira whistled silently. That was…different from what she thought of as a restaurant.

"Private and secure, I'm guessing," she said.

"Yeah. Like… *King Larry hosts ambassadors at this place* kind of secure."

"Well, it seems the Cresters think we deserve the best."

Their destination was a small door at the end of a row of high-end restaurants. If they hadn't had the directions, Kira would have thought they were looking at the entrance to the administrative offices of a restaurant.

But the name was right—CHEF CONCEPTA PITT'S was etched into the door.

Kira was about to knock, but the door swept open before she could touch it.

"Commodore Kira Demirci, Captain Kavitha Zoric," an elderly woman in a plain black tunic greeted them. "You are expected. Come in, come in."

Kira traded a glance with her subordinate and then obeyed.

This was going to be an interesting dinner—but she was suddenly confident that the *food* was going to be an experience all on its own.

INSIDE THE DOOR, the mercenaries were met by a pair of men that Kira instantly classified as "VIP Bodyguard, Standard Issue, Plain Clothes." Unlike the rest of the Cresters she'd met, they'd adopted Redward styles of clothing, but the way they carried themselves left no question in her mind.

The weapon scanner one of them produced also helped, she had to admit.

"I'm afraid I'm going to have to ask you to surrender your sidearms," the one with the scanner told them. "I didn't think those were allowed aboard Blueward, in any case."

"We have special licensing," Kira replied. The blaster pistol she wore concealed under her jacket wasn't powerful enough to damage the station's outer hull, but it could wreck an interior bulkhead at maximum power.

There was a reason they were restricted—and that she concealed the weapon. Now, however, she drew the weapon and offered it, grip-first, to the bodyguard.

Zoric followed suit a moment later, looking surprised at Kira's quick agreement.

Kira shook her head at her subordinate minutely. Whatever happened there today, no one was going to try to assassinate King Larry's favorite mercenaries on Blueward Station. They were safe enough there that she tended to forget there even *was* a death mark on her.

No one had tried to collect it since shortly after she'd arrived in the Syntactic Cluster.

"This way, please," the guard instructed after tucking both the sidearms into a secured case.

The elderly woman who'd let them into the restaurant took over the guiding duties again with a sharp look at the bodyguard. It was pretty clear the Cresters had taken over the space, and the staff weren't entirely enthused with that.

Kira gave a calm nod in greeting when their guide brought them around a corner, and they found Voski waiting for them outside a closed set of double doors. Presumably, that was the dining room they'd be eating in.

Her guess was that the narrow corridor they'd passed through was what took them behind the rest of the restaurants on the promenade they'd left. That would put Pitt's restaurant in the cheaper-to-rent space on a secondary corridor—but with a single access to the main promenade.

An interesting combination for an intentionally concealed restau-rant—and one that bodyguards like Voski had to adore. Today, Voski wore a Redward-style three-piece suit in black, with delicate purple blush and eyeshadow that blurred both their gender and their apparent sightlines.

"Captain Zoric, Commodore Demirci," they greeted the mercenar-ies. They glanced at the other bodyguards. "They are unarmed?"

The first guard presented Voski the case with Kira and Zoric's guns. "They surrendered their sidearms on request, ser."

"Your cooperation is appreciated," Voski told them. "Come with me, please?"

"That's why we're here, isn't it?" Kira asked with a chuckle.

JADE WAS ALONE in the room when their bodyguard let the mercenaries in. The Crester was standing in front of a fake fireplace, a mix of holograms, brick and heaters that gave the impression of a roaring fire at one end of the room.

The fireplace fit with the décor of the room in general. Kira guessed that most of the brick and stone was real, laid over the original metal walls to create the impression of an outdoor covered patio—supported by one wall that was showing an image from what she guessed to be one of Redward's many gorgeous parks.

Even the table, an intentionally rustic wooden affair, was designed to build into the illusion of being outside on a planetary surface while they were near the center of an orbital space station. It seemed to be working for Jade, at least, who was standing next to the "fire," warming their hands.

In almost complete opposition to how they'd been dressed when Kira had first met them, Jade wore an ankle-length ruffled skirt paired with a tightly fitted men's dress shirt. Given the curvature they'd displayed at Sonia's barbecue, Kira presumed the Crester was wearing a binder under the shirt—but the tailoring of both under- and over-garment was such that she couldn't tell.

"Commodore Demirci, Captain Zoric," Jade greeted them. "Please, have a seat. Chef Pitt will be with us shortly to discuss the menu and any adjustments required for allergies or dietary restrictions I was unaware of."

"Director," Kira greeted the Crester, gesturing for Zoric to take a seat while she leaned on the back of a chair herself. "I'm led to understand this place is normally reserved well in advance."

"It's amazing what you can buy if you ask nicely and put a large-enough sum on the table," Jade replied drily. "In this case, all three of tonight's reservees proved amenable to selling their reservations—and Chef Pitt also proved amenable to my making up her lost revenue."

"So, you took over the entirety of the most exclusive and expensive restaurant on the station to have this meeting?" Kira asked. "Doesn't that seem like overkill?"

"There is no such thing as overkill," the Crester replied. "Only success and insufficient effort. I can take no risks with this, Commodore. What we are to discuss must remain absolutely confidential, regardless of whether or not you accept my contract.

"Can you do that?"

"Negotiations are generally confidential, yes," Kira noted. "Unless you want me to move against Redward or the Free Trade Zone, in which case we will be having a *very* different discussion."

"Your honor does you credit, Commodore," Jade said. "I would have your name's word."

Kira glanced over at Zoric. There was a formal edge to Jade's phrasing, one that didn't mean much to Kira—Kira's word was her bond, but there wasn't any extra weight to her *name's word*.

From her subordinate's expression, however, the phrasing meant something specific to *Kavitha Zoric*. Kira was going to have to ask about that.

"Kavitha?" she said.

"You have it," *Deception*'s Captain said roughly. "Except as required to carry out the contract if we accept it, I will not betray this meeting. On my name."

"You have my word," Kira added. "This is all very cloak-and-dagger, Em Jade. Perhaps you would like to start explaining what's going on?"

"We will wait for Chef Pitt, I think," Jade replied. "She should be here any moment now. First, however, I think I should properly introduce myself."

They turned away from the fire and stepped over to the table with a quirky smile playing across their lips.

"I am Crown Zharang Jade Panosyan," they said quietly. "The heir to the Crown of the Royal Crest."

THE LAST OF the pieces fell into place for Kira as they discussed the menu with Chef Pitt. The white-uniformed woman listened carefully to each question and concern raised, and had an answer ready for each of them.

After five minutes, Pitt retreated from the room, telling them that the appetizers would be fifteen minutes, and Kira looked over at Jade Panosyan.

Zharang was an Armenian word, her headware told her. A legacy of the Panosyan dynasty's origins on Earth, it meant simply "heir" without any gender attachments. Jade Panosyan was their father's heir, which meant they were the heir to forty percent of the Bank of the Royal Crest and to the supreme command of the Navy of the Royal Crest.

The King of the Royal Crest had less direct control over the actual working government of the Royal Crest than many constitutional monarchs, but they were still the head of the military and the supreme justiciary.

It was an interesting balance, one Kira wasn't sure she trusted—but then, she wasn't a big fan of constitutional monarchies in general. King Larry had proven his worth to her, but the structure seemed inherently abusable to her.

Of course, *she* came from an explicit oligarchy where only people in the highest income tax bracket got to vote in planetary elections. She was aware of how limited her right to cast doubts on other planets' governments was.

"I had guessed that all of this cloak-and-dagger and secrecy meant you were not merely one of the directors running the delegation," Kira told Panosyan as they settled back down with glasses of water.

"I am also that," the enby told her. "There are three directors on this expedition. I am neither the senior nor the junior of them." They shrugged. "I will not pretend being my father's child didn't accelerate my path, but I was expected to earn my promotions. I have made the BRC a large amount of money, and I expect to do so again if the negotiations with the Syntactic Cluster pay off."

"I assume that seems likely?" Zoric asked carefully.

"At the moment, yes," Panosyan agreed. "There is no question that Ypres, Redward and Bengalissimo will be able to source whatever funds they need. The rest of the Cluster… Mmm. There is a suggestion that the main three powers act as guarantor to the others.

"If they all buy in to that, we can bundle the debt of the entire Cluster into a single subscription offering back home with an averaged risk. That will make it significantly easier for us to raise the funds and will work quite well."

They smiled thinly.

"My trailing commission on *that* deal will more than justify my being out this far."

Kira considered what Panosyan had said, then swallowed a grimace.

"But you want me to believe you came out here to talk to us?" she asked.

"Cobra Squadron were legends, Commodore Demirci," the Crester Zharang told her. "*Legends.* Someone inherits that weight—is it the people who destroyed them or the people trained by the first generation?

"How about the people who are *both*? Because that's Memorial Force, ladies. Each of you was the personal apprentice of a first-generation Cobra," Panosyan said grimly. "Moranis and Estanza—then both of you were at Estanza's right hand when he went to war with his old squadron.

"Cobra Squadron met Memorial Force…and Cobra Squadron is no more. If anyone is now a legend, it is you. So, yes, Commodore Demirci, Captain Zoric, I came here to meet you. To see what the leaders of John Estanza's legacy looked like."

"And?" Zoric asked bluntly.

"So far, I am reasonably impressed," Jade Panosyan told them. "Without *Conviction*, you are not the force that broke Cobra Squadron…and yet I see the heart and skill that did it still. So, I am here, and we have a contract to discuss."

"We only take payment in cash," Zoric told the banker. Kira swallowed her own amusement, wearing a level face as her Flag Captain continued. "We've had some problems with promises and payment in *trade* recently."

Kira wasn't going to challenge Zoric on that. She didn't think that a senior director of one of the largest banks in the Rim was planning on leaving them waiting for a promised carrier the way that Redward was doing.

"There are also limits on the missions we are prepared to take on," she noted herself. "Some of them are obvious: Memorial Force is far from capable of taking on planetary defenses. We do not operate in systems with hostile planetary forces. We do not take on suicide missions. We do not do commerce raiding."

She smiled thinly.

"We don't operate against the Syntactic Cluster and we don't do coups," Kira concluded.

The problem in Ypres had been *Crest* mercenaries that had signed on for a coup. Bengalissimo's coup had been carried out without mercenaries, but the same mercenaries had helped tip the balance in the Institute's favor.

Panosyan chuckled and took a sip of their own water.

"That's going to make this an interesting conversation, I think," they told the mercenaries. "But I ask your patience with me, as it *will* be worth your while.

"But." They raised a finger. "I *will* be asking you to operate in a star system with hostile planetary forces." They raised a second finger. "I *will* be asking you to participate in a coup." A third finger. "And I *will* be offering partial payment in trade."

Before Kira or Zoric could say a word, Panosyan laid a disk holographic projector on the table. A silent command activated it and a hologram appeared above the rustic wooden surface.

It took Kira half a second to pick up the scale, and then she swallowed her initial response to Panosyan's commentary as she studied the image of the starship. It was a squashed cylinder, two hundred meters long, twenty high and roughly fifty wide. There were clearly visible openings at the bow and stern, the accesses to a full-length flight deck. Even if the general shape hadn't been clear, the flight deck would have been the giveaway.

The ship was a fleet carrier—a hundred-and-fifty-thousand-cubic-meter *super*carrier, like even Kira's home system of Apollo couldn't build.

"That trade, in this case, would be the Navy of the Royal Crest fleet carrier *Fortitude*," Panosyan told them. "The *coup*, to be clear, would be against the Sanctuary and Prosperity Party that has taken over my father's government...and is, without question, a front operation for the Equilibrium Institute."

The image of the fleet carrier vanished as there was a knock on the door.

"Our food has arrived, but I hope I have at least earned the chance to make my pitch?"

Kira glanced at Zoric, several silent messages flying back and forth.

"You have our attention," she told the Crown Zharang. "But this is enough outside our comfort zone you're going to have to talk *very* quickly."

10

THE ARRIVAL of the soup and salad courses temporarily suspended the work discussion, leaving Kira to stew in her own mind as she ate the surprisingly bland food.

Her expectation of the food for the kind of specialty hole-in-the-wall restaurant they'd ended up at appeared to have been too high, but the food wasn't really the focus of her thoughts.

A hundred-and-fifty-kilocubic carrier was a massive investment, even excluding the hundred and fifty nova fighters she'd normally carry. What the *hell* did Panosyan want them to do that would justify that as only a *partial* payment?

Plus, Jade Panosyan's father—whose name Kira would freely admit she didn't know—was the ruler of the Royal Crest. He wasn't an absolute ruler, but he was still a powerful figure in the government of a powerful economic and military hegemon.

Unless Jade wanted a coup against their father, which sounded like all kinds of disasters, Kira couldn't see the point. They'd mentioned a political party, but…

Kira's mind was still swirling in circles when the soup course was cleared away and the server indicated it would be ten minutes to the entrée.

The door closed behind the server, and Kira leveled her flattest gaze on the banker and royal in the room with them.

"Talk," she ordered. "Because right now, I don't see what the hell you want, and *that* leaves me unlikely to take your contract."

That Queen Sonia had clearly set all of this up was buying Panosyan more time than Kira might have given the enby on her own, too. But there were limits to all things, even Kira's faith in the Queen of Redward.

Panosyan sighed and nodded. Glancing at the door, they shrugged.

"You are familiar with the Equilibrium Institute," they said. It wasn't a question. The whole point of their discussion with Kira at Sonia's barbecue had been to confirm that. "More familiar, in fact, than most people in the Rim.

"So, you know what their goal is in any given region, yes?"

"To create a military hegemon capable of enforcing peace," Zoric said grimly. "It's what they wanted to make Redward. It's what they *made* the Crest, isn't it?"

"Yes," Panosyan said bluntly. "The Bank of the Royal Crest and the Navy of the Royal Crest spent the best part of half a century under my grandmother, who was King before my father, creating our network of 'client worlds.'"

They grimaced.

"Our client worlds are blatant tributaries," they admitted. "Tied up in a net of loan obligations, treaties and defense contracts that leave them unable to carry out their own foreign policy or maintain significant nova-capable forces.

"They send money, resources—even *people*, through various placement and immigration programs—to the Royal Crest to support the Bank and the Navy."

Panosyan shook their head.

"My grandmother, King Kyung-Hee Panosyan, started out determined to protect the Crest from the threats around us," they said quietly. "That spilled into protecting the Crest's friends...and went rapidly downhill from there. I do not believe that the Institute became involved until nearly the end of her life.

"But by the time she passed and my-father-the-King"—the current

Panosyan heir reeled that off as almost a single word—"took the throne, the Sanctuary and Prosperity Party had been the Crown's favorite in Parliament for eleven years, rising from fifth-party status to junior partner in the ruling coalition over three elections."

The Crester spread their hands.

"My father was not…" They hesitated. "My father does not speak, even to me, of his decisions then. I believe that he feels he was weak. I *know* that he regrets his choices."

"Sung Panosyan has been King of the Royal Crest for twenty-six standard years," Zoric said quietly.

Kira figured that Zoric had looked up King Sung's name on her headware. She'd been considering it herself, but she suspected that the Cresters were running a scanner on the room to check for bugs.

That same scanner would detect her connecting to the station network for information.

"He has," the younger Panosyan agreed. "I was eight years old when he became King. And for twenty-six standard years, my father has supported and expanded the client network of the Royal Crest. He has maintained exactly the kind of economic and military hegemony the Equilibrium Institute desires—one with absolute control inside its own territory but also one lacking the strength to push outward.

"But that also means, my mercenary friends, that the majority of the worlds in our client network have been our clients for *more* than twenty-six years. To both my father and myself, that represents a responsibility.

"If a world pays us for protection, we are obliged to honor that task," they said calmly. "And as we bear that responsibility and honor that responsibility, it earns us the beginnings of goodwill.

"And goodwill represents *opportunity*."

Another knock at the door announced the arrival of the entrée— and Kira had more than merely food to digest as she ate now.

THE MEAL WAS GRILLED spiced chicken served over a bed of rice pilaf with vegetables. It certainly *looked* like gourmet food—but as Kira dug into it, she found it only reinforced her suspicion from the soup and salad courses.

Chef Concepta Pitt's kitchen was making its way on exclusivity and presentation *far* more than it was on making good food. That left Kira figuring either Chef Pitt had outsourced the actual cooking long before —or was just a marketing genius and a merely *okay* chef.

The other possibility, she supposed, was that Jade Panosyan's takeover of the restaurant for the evening had *seriously* pissed the chef off.

Still, the food at least dodged the usual bullet of high-end restaurants she'd encountered: the presentation had not come at the expense of quantity, and she was feeling pleasantly full by the time the servers cleared the plates away.

"And when would the guests like desserts?" the server asked.

"Bring coffee and brandy for now, then check in in thirty minutes," Panosyan instructed. "Thank you."

The servers had the drinks ready in a minute or so, then vanished to leave the three of them alone.

"You cannot expect that just keeping pirates suppressed is going to make your client network suddenly like you," Zoric said after a few moments of silence.

"No, I don't," Panosyan agreed. "But it's a starting point, one to build on if we make the right next steps. I believe that the relationships and political associations that we have built throughout our client network give us a chance few regions of the galaxy have.

"I believe, and my father is willing to lay the groundwork if nothing else, that we have an opportunity to convert the Royal Crest's client network into a true multi-stellar federal republic."

Whatever Jade Panosyan was, they certainly didn't think *small*. To Kira's knowledge, there were *very* few true multi-stellar states. That *Redward* was technically one now had drawn attention from significant distances.

"We're a long way from SolFed out here," Kira murmured.

"And I'm not trying to rebuild the Solar Federation," Panosyan replied. They poured small servings of brandy into three coffees and passed them across the table. "But we *already* have a lot of the structures of a multi-stellar nation in the client network; they're just all one-way.

"Converting that into an actual nation of partners will be difficult." They shook their head. "It will be my life's work, Commodore, but I need to clear one giant obstacle out of the way first."

"Hence us," Kira guessed.

"The Sanctuary and Prosperity Party is no longer the junior partner in a ruling coalition," the Crown Zharang told them. "The SPP has been the largest party in our Parliament for twenty years and held a non-coalition majority government for ten. Nothing...strange about that, I suppose. But they've now been in government, as either a partner or a sole party, for thirty years.

"And they have been using that status ruthlessly," Panosyan said grimly. "They have not gone so far as to create a single-party state, but they have taken *complete* control of much of the apparatus of the government of the Royal Crest.

"The Navy theoretically answers to my father, but Sanctuary and Prosperity members have been giving each other helping hands up for two decades. Loyalty to the Party now matters more, I fear, than skill—or loyalty to my-father-the-King."

Kira considered the situation as she took a sip of the coffee. At least Chef Pitt's had good coffee—she suspected there'd be a revolt if a high-end restaurant near Redward *didn't*.

"I'll admit, Em Panosyan, that I don't see how Memorial Force can help you," she said. "We have four warships and roughly eighty nova fighters. Against the might of the Navy of the Royal Crest, even ignoring the defenses of the Crest itself, we are completely outmatched and outgunned."

"We need to overthrow the Sanctuary and Prosperity Party," their host told them. "Right now, my father retains control of most of the planetary-level judiciary and law enforcement—and we have enough evidence to order warrants for the search of the houses and offices of the entire senior leadership of the SPP."

"Then why do you need us?" Kira asked.

"Because they control Parliament, the Guard and much of the Navy," Panosyan told them. "If we were to move against the SPP, my-father-the-King would be impeached within an hour—and the police officers trying to search SPP offices would be met by soldiers.

"Our best case would be civil war," they concluded, their voice soft. "The worst case…a swift replacement of myself and my father with a more cooperative member of the family. While no name comes to mind, I'm sure they could find someone obedient with some claim to the throne."

"You're afraid of a coup," Zoric said quietly.

"No. There would be no point to the SPP launching a coup at this point," the royal told them. "They control my world. While my goal is to restore my father to control of his government and hold new, free elections…what we are discussing is a coup against the functional government of my planet."

"A legitimately elected government, even if it is allied with the Equilibrium Institute," Kira noted. "They may be allied with my enemies, but I still hesitate to overthrow anyone's legitimate government.

"Not to mention that I still don't see any way this *isn't* a suicide mission."

She leaned back and took another sip of the brandy-laced coffee. She expected Jade Panosyan had an answer to both of those challenges, but she was curious what those answers were.

"Our best guess is that the SPP infiltrated and took control of our election monitors fifteen years ago," the Crester said. "Since then, it feels like entire blocs of our population have been disenfranchised— our official voter-turnout percentage hasn't changed, but the *number* of votes cast has declined dramatically.

"And this has gone hand-in-hand with the final rise of the SPP," they concluded. "I *do not*, Commodore Demirci, believe that the government of my planet is legitimately elected. *That*, in fact, is the main crime we believe we can prove. The wedge with which we believe, given the chance, we can bring down Prime Minister Maral Jeong and her entire organization.

"But I need you to give us that chance."

"You have a plan," Kira said. It wasn't a question—the situation as

Jade Panosyan had laid it out was insurmountable. So, if they *didn't* have a plan, there was no point to having the meeting.

"I do." They tapped the holoprojector disk again, restoring the image of *Fortitude*.

"*Fortitude* is the newest and most advanced carrier the Navy of the Royal Crest has ever built," they explained. "She is approximately three months from completion as we speak. Once that is done, she will undergo a series of trials of her onboard systems, including her nova drive.

"Her officers and crew have already been picked. They are SPP loyalists to a one. As part of her trials and to honor those officers, the Prime Minister and key members of the Cabinet are planning to make a secret trip aboard to inspect the ship and her crew."

"I'm assuming they are not so foolish as to make the inspection while the ship is away from the planet's defenses?" Kira asked.

"We are not certain of the schedule yet," their potential employer told her. "But we know that the nova-drive tests will be prior to the inspection. She will spend time in the outer system and at the nearby trade-route stops before the Prime Minister comes aboard.

"Where she will be vulnerable."

Kira drained her coffee and glanced over at Zoric.

"*What do you think?*" she silently messaged her Flag Captain.

"*I'm willing to take just about any swing at Equilibrium,*" Zoric admitted. "*But this is still risky.*"

"*On the other hand, we keep the carrier.*"

"How exactly do you see this working?" Kira asked aloud.

"You seize the ship, the Prime Minister and the Cabinet," Panosyan told them. "You nova to a nearby client system, where you pretend to be pirates and demand a ransom for Prime Minister Jeong.

"While she and her Cabinet are missing, we will take advantage of the confusion to execute warrants on the offices of the SPP. Hopefully, by the time we receive your ransom demand, we should have proof of Jeong's crimes."

The Crester shrugged.

"We pay you the ransom—the final portion of your cash payment—

and collect Jeong and the Cabinet to face trial. You leave with the carrier. Everyone wins."

"Except that the galaxy thinks we *stole Fortitude*," Kira pointed out. "That's not exactly a good thing for our reputation."

"I suspect most potential clients will work out the reality of the situation relatively quickly," Panosyan observed. "And others...well, that you stole a supercarrier from under the guns of a major power won't hurt your reputation.

"We will provide proper documentation after the fact to cover your ownership of her."

That didn't quite cover all of Kira's concerns, but she had to admit she was tempted by the carrier. Twice the size of *Conviction*—thirty kilocubics larger than anything Redward was building or her home system had.

"And the cash payment, Crown Zharang?" Zoric asked.

"*Thank you*," Kira messaged the other woman. That was important as well.

"The majority of the payment will be *Fortitude*, of course," Panosyan pointed out. "She cost just over one hundred *billion* crests to construct, after all."

"The construction cost of the carrier won't cover the operational expenses of our fleet," Kira said. "To take on this mission, we will need to negotiate at least a temporary release from our retainer with Redward.

"That leaves us absorbing approximately four million Redward kroner a standard month in costs," she continued. "That's roughly two and a half million crests. The value of the carrier is enough to potentially convince me to take this mission, but you will still need to cover at least a standard fee in cash."

"Twenty million," Jade Panosyan said instantly. "Five million on signing the contract. Five million on reaching the region of space around the Crest. Ten million as the 'ransom' for Prime Minister Jeong."

That wasn't much more than their standard *retainer* for six months. On the other hand, while the mission was going to entail a *lot* of risk— and Kira was hesitant around including the carrier as part of the value of the package—even only including *one percent* of the carrier's value would make it one of their most lucrative contracts ever.

"That covers us," Zoric said in her head.

"The risk is insane," Kira pointed out. *"I want to stick a knife in Equilibrium and this is a huge opportunity, but it could go very, very wrong."*

"So, we plan for everything we can and get ready to cut loose if we have to," Zoric replied. *"I think we can do it—and that carrier is a hell of a carrot to lure us with."*

"I want her," Kira admitted. *"Is that impacting our judgment?"*

"That's why Panosyan has her on the board. But…how else are we going to get a carrier *this year, let alone a supercarrier? I'm in. But you're the fifty-one percent."*

Kira inhaled and nodded.

"Commodore?" Jade Panosyan asked.

"We're in," Kira told them. "We'll need to sort out some details here in Redward, but we're in."

11

"YOU WANT US TO *WHAT*?"

Commander Milani was, as always, clad in full body armor from head to toe. Today, their armor was a dull black color—except for the inevitable red dragon writhing around in a fit of what was either rage or passion. Kira wasn't sure.

The command meeting was larger than she really liked, but Memorial Force was far larger than even Conviction and Memorial Squadron combined. *Raccoon* was enough smaller than *Conviction* had been that the cubage difference wasn't as large as it could be, but it was still four ships instead of two.

Which meant Kira's meeting aboard *Deception* had four Captains, four executive officers, two Commanders, Nova Group, herself and the ground-force commander.

The meeting room was large enough for them with room to spare—but *Deception* had been designed as a secondary flagship when she'd originally been laid down. She'd been intended to lead groups of destroyers away from the carriers.

"The plan calls for the ground forces to board *Fortitude* in deep space and seize control from her crew," Kira told Milani, glancing around her officers. "She will have a minimal crew, likely with only limited security forces aboard, as she's undergoing her trials.

"I *presume*, though we have no data yet, that *Fortitude* will be escorted by other NRC ships that we will have to destroy," she continued bluntly. "Identifying the appropriate moment to make the strike will be key to carrying this out successfully."

"The Navy of the Royal Crest," McCaig repeated, his voice stunned. "They could surround her with *battlecruisers*, sirs. We're a bit out of our weight class here."

"And that's why we're going to play this *very* carefully," Kira agreed. "We have received an advance payment that will cover our operating costs for the journey to Crest, so we are committed to at least making the attempt.

"That said, one of the things I *do* have is a complete listing of the current strength of the Navy of the Royal Crest, and they'd have a great deal of trouble filling space with battlecruisers," she noted. "Their pre-*Fortitude* ships are comparable to the best of Brisingr or Apollo's fleets, Twelve-to-Thirteen-X ten-kilocubic nova drives, pushing one hundred and twenty to one hundred and thirty kilocubics.

"Inside those parameters, they have six fleet carriers and six battle-cruisers," she told them. "They have another six older carriers in the ninety-to-one-hundred-and-ten-kilocubic range, along with ten cruisers in that range.

"All told, they possess twenty-eight capital ships supported by eighty-five lighter warships, including four fifty-kilocubic CVLs."

There was a long silence in the briefing room and Kira smiled.

"So, yes, they have sixteen carriers to our one—and their *baby* flat-tops are bigger and better than our one," she agreed. "They have sixteen cruisers in play, all bigger than ours, plus another eighty-one destroyers and corvettes.

"The Navy of the Royal Crest is a first-class military by Rim standards. Which makes them, what, eighth-rate by the standards of the whole galaxy?"

That was where Apollo and Brisingr tended to get classified, and the Crest was in roughly the same league as Kira's home system and their enemy. Redward was still clawing their way into *ninth*-rate standards, though Konrad Bueller had given them some handy kickstarts.

That worthy leaned forward thoughtfully, looking at the hologram of the Crest System that Kira had hanging over the conference-room table.

"If they follow usual practices for first-round trials after completion, they'll only have about twenty-five percent of the crew aboard *Fortitude*," Bueller noted softly. "Security contingent will be yard security, not real marines or commandos. They *might* have some fighters aboard to test the systems, but in the main, she'll be mostly empty for the first nova trials. Just in case."

"All evidence suggests that the inspection will take place while her nova drive is cooling down somewhere in the outer system," Kira said. "If we can take control of her *before* she novas to the ship with the Cabinet, we should be able to minimize the evidence of combat."

"Sir, we have eighty mercenary ground troopers across four ships," Milani pointed out grimly. "I have faith in my people—Captain McCaig will back me there—but to take control of a hundred-and-fifty-kilocubic carrier? That's a big ask."

"What would you need to make it less of an ask, Commander?" Kira asked them.

The dragon snapped across Milani's chest and hissed.

"Full schematics of the ship would be a start, but I'm guessing we have those?" Milani asked.

"We do," Kira confirmed.

"I'll need to go over my people's gear list," the mercenary ground trooper admitted. "I have a few thoughts around breaching-and-intrusion gear that I don't think we have. Our armor is as good as Redward can get us, so there's no real upgrades there..."

They shook their head.

"We've accepted a signing payment from our employer," Kira told them. Everyone in the room knew who that employer was—and no one else, even in Memorial Force, was going to find out from them. She trusted her people.

"If there is anything we can acquire in Redward that will make this mission easier, get me and Dirix a list in the next twenty-four hours," she continued. "That goes for everyone, though most of that weight is on Milani."

"I have some thoughts too," McCaig rumbled. "If you want them, Milani?"

"Against this mission? I'll take 'em, Captain," Milani told their old boss.

"The other thing to remember, folks, is that the NRC is supporting a client network of twenty star systems," Kira reminded them. "Even if everything goes to shit, we are not fighting an entire eighth-rate navy with a ninth-rate mercenary squadron."

"Somehow, that isn't as reassuring as you think it is," her boyfriend, *Deception*'s XO and engineer, told her as he studied the map of the star system. "They only need to get *one* carrier-cruiser group on top of us, after all. Even one of the older ones can match *Deception* and *Raccoon*."

"We will plan this to the *n*th degree," Kira promised. "And if I don't think we can pull it off, we *will* bail. But if we can do this, we might just change the fate of twenty star systems...and give the Equilibrium Institute an even bigger fuck-you than *anything* we did out here in the Syntactic Cluster!"

AS THE STAFF planning session dispersed, with most of Kira's people heading to the shuttles that would return them to their ships, the room eventually condensed down to just her and Konrad Bueller.

"This mission is ridiculous; you know that, right?" he asked softly. "A single mercenary squadron against the Crest. Relying on intelligence that could damn us all if it's even slightly wrong—and heading into space where we have *no* locals aboard.

"I checked," he noted. "We have people from sixty-eight different home planets in Memorial Force, but none of them are the Crest. We're in unknown territory there."

"I know," Kira told him. "And, from what I can tell, we're in *Equilibrium* territory—a system where a group of their active agents have taken near-complete control.

"But we're not fighting *any* of that, Konrad," she said. "We're hitting a weak spot and creating an opportunity. Leverage, my dear. If we hit the right spot with the right amount of force, everything turns the way it should."

"Or your source of force bounces and is ruined because you miscalculated," he replied. "This is risky. If we get it wrong…"

"We bail before it gets that far," Kira promised. She wasn't sure how easy that would be—if nothing else, paying the Panosyans back would be a pain—but she'd do it before she'd lose the squadron.

"I want to stick a knife in the Institute's eye as much as anything," Konrad admitted. "So, I'm in, all the way." He chuckled. "I'm just throwing an anchor out to windward, Kira. We are risking *everything* here."

"I know. But Jade Panosyan definitely found the carrot to bring me in," she told him. "There's some risk around stealing a carrier in trials. Think you'll be able to get her fully operational?"

He snorted.

"Almost certainly," he said. "Depends on what I have access to, obviously. I'm assuming not Crest yards, but if we bring her back here? Yeah. Anything they broke building her, I can fix."

"I'm planning on coming back here," Kira agreed, but a thought struck her and she grimaced. "I'll take a copy of that list of folks by homeworlds, by the by," she told him.

"I suspect more than a few of our Redward and Cluster natives will want the chance to step aside before they get dragged halfway across the Rim," she said. "Replacing them will be a minor headache, but I'd rather deal with that than have people in Crest who don't want to be there."

"Makes sense to me," Bueller agreed. "Maybe ask the King and Queen if we can recruit from some of the RRF?"

"Maybe even temporary swaps," Kira said. "I know we have a few people with family and kids here. Long-term, I'm still planning on home-basing out of Redward, but this will be a four-month journey."

"Four months we're not getting our retainer, too," her lover pointed out.

"Don't remind me," she sighed. "I have an appointment with

Admiral Remington in a few hours to have *that* discussion. *Hopefully,* *we can negotiate a temporary pause on the contract and resume it* *when we return.*

"But that might not be politic for her."

Admiral Vilma Remington was the commanding officer of the Redward Royal Fleet and the person officially responsible for negotiating contracts with Memorial Force. King Larry was definitely known for putting his substantial literal and metaphorical weight on the process, but the signature on the paperwork was Admiral Remington's.

"Good luck," Konrad said with a chuckle. "We seem to have quite a bit of work to do."

"And I've got another wrench for you, Konrad," she told him.

"Oh?"

"We haven't operated outside the reach of the RRF's logistics network since we acquired the destroyers," she pointed out. "We need a support ship. I need you to find me a freighter that can haul torpedoes, parts, food, fuel…Memorial Force needs a logistics ship."

Her boyfriend grimaced but nodded.

"Am I trying to rent one with a crew or buy one?" he asked.

"Buy one," she told him. "We're not going to need *less* logistics in the future."

"All right. But I'm telling you right now: I am *not* commanding her!"

Kira laughed.

"What, the power core isn't complicated enough for you?" she asked.

"Unlike you, my love the nova-fighter pilot," he said drily, "*I* like being on the right side of a whole lot of armor."

12

KIRA NOTICED the increased security in the flag officers' section of First Ward, the central command station of Redward's fixed defenses, before she reached Remington's office. It wasn't an entirely obvious thing—three troopers where there was normally one. Commandos scattered through security posts that were normally RRF military police.

The four clearly soldier-boosted men in suits outside Remington's office answered the question before she could ask it, though. Soldier boosts—a generic term for any of several mixes of biological, genetic and cybernetic modifications to make someone faster and stronger— didn't do anything that couldn't be matched by armor, though they *were* lower-profile.

While someone like Kira could pick out the noticeably faster reflexes and slight twitchiness of soldier-boosted guards, they still served a purpose in covert missions and as low-profile bodyguards.

In *this* case, she recognized them as Redward Secret Service, which meant that King Larry had once again inserted himself into the negotiations around his key mercenary force. With a concealed sigh, Kira gave the guards a familiar nod and stepped into Remington's office.

"Admiral Remington," she greeted the older woman sitting

perfectly upright behind the desk. The silver-haired woman was eyeing her already-present companion with an exasperated air.

"Your Majesty," Kira continued, bowing slightly to the notably overweight King of Redward. Lawrence Bartholomew Stewart, First Magistrate and Honored King of the Kingdom of Redward, waved a coffee cup at her as he delicately kicked a chair over to her.

"Take a seat, Commodore," King Larry ordered. "Vilma, grab Demirci a coffee, please."

Only the King would ask his top Admiral to grab someone a coffee, but Remington didn't even seem *bothered*. Of course, as she rose to grab the coffee, Kira felt the distinctive sensation of a communication containment field sealing around the office.

Her headware no longer had access to the station network. Given that they were inside an asteroid fortress ten kilometers across with fifty thousand Redward fleet personnel and soldiers aboard, that meant they probably couldn't be *more* secure.

She recognized the smell of the coffee as Remington handed it to her.

"I see His Majesty brought his own coffee," she observed.

"It usually gets sent ahead of him," the Admiral said with a chuckle. "Though I am sufficiently in favor to have a stock of Royal Reserve of my own."

"So does Demirci," Larry noted. "My wife spoils you both—she has *excellent* taste in friends and allies, in my opinion."

"I feel like I may have been anticipated," Kira murmured as she looked at the two people in the office. "I was not expecting His Majesty to be here."

"Did you miss that my wife set up the entire situation with you and the Crown Zharang?" Larry asked drily. He airily waved a hand. "We know...just about everything," he concluded. "More, I suspect, than Em Panosyan thinks we do. But that's our stock-in-trade.

"Despite everything we have accomplished together over the last few years, Redward is still a very small fish in the real pond," he noted. "The Free Trade Zone *combined* is still a small fish in the real pond.

"So, we must be well informed if we are to avoid catastrophe. Well informed—and well equipped with powerful friends."

"Jade Panosyan qualifies, I assume," Kira said.

"Exactly." Larry took a swallow of his coffee. "Of course, learning about the Sanctuary and Prosperity Party's links to the Equilibrium Institute does impact my willingness to do business with the Bank of the Royal Crest."

"But you need their money."

"Or the entire Free Trade Zone project may fail," he admitted flatly. "More specifically, without an external source of financing to acquire resources from outside the Cluster, the reconstruction project for the Costar Clans Systems is a fragile edifice at best. We have a fifty-fifty chance of the whole thing collapsing."

"And if the reconstruction project collapses, not only will it bring back the Cluster's largest homegrown threat, but it will almost certainly bankrupt Redward along the way," Remington finished.

"We have the structures and resources to paper over the cracks for a while," Larry said. "Possibly long enough for the Clans to start contributing back to the Kingdom's coffers—but right now, I am King of five star systems and four of them are giant black holes I need to fill with money.

"The Bank of the Royal Crest is the largest player for that kind of financing in this sector of the Rim, but currently it sounds like that deal will be pouring money into the hands of people who have tried to screw over the entire Cluster."

He sighed.

"Not to mention that the degree to which the BRC's contracts are trying to eat into the sovereignty of everyone in the Free Trade Zone makes my skin itch," he noted. "I think I'm going to win that fight, but that doesn't change the part about us funding the Equilibrium Institute."

"So, you *really* want me to complete this contract," Kira said drily. "That does make the discussion I'm here for easier on me, doesn't it?"

"Remember that there are also some real questions being raised in the Hóngsè Chéngbao about us keeping Memorial Force, given how calm things have become," Remington replied, her tone equally dry.

"No one is saying we shouldn't hire you if a crisis arises, but the retainer itself is being challenged on several points."

Kira shrugged.

"To be fair, that's a *you* problem," she said with a chuckle. "I want a temporary pause on the retainer: minimum four months, extendable to six."

"Bluntly, Demirci, we can't give it to you," Larry told her. "If you're *here*, working, doing patrols and catching pirates, I can lean on people and point to your actions. But once you're gone and we're getting by without you?

"It'll be a lot harder to sell people on paying you."

"That's not a selling point on me taking this contract," Kira pointed out. "Though, I suppose, I could take the contract and not come *back*."

She watched them both wince.

"We would strongly prefer if Memorial Force were to return to Redward after you complete this new contract," Larry told her. "While I can't maintain the retainer, I *can* help in other ways."

"I'm listening," Kira said. "I mean, accelerating when we get our carrier from *you* will help."

"I did *not* know that Admiral Idowu was telling Commander Bueller that his help would lead to you getting a carrier from the new yards," the King said grimly. "That promise should never have been made—which means we probably should have paid Commander Bueller significantly more for that contract."

Kira shrugged. She couldn't get *too* worked up about that—they were talking maybe a fifty-thousand-kroner difference in a meeting where she was negotiating over losing a retainer of *four million* kroner. A month.

"I can't accelerate your access to our yards, and we're already offering cost-only construction contracts to you," Larry noted. "What I *can* do is put a ten-million-kroner bonus in escrow, to be paid out to Memorial Force upon your return to Redward, and cover the costs of your shore office for the time period you're gone."

Ten million kroner—a bit over six and a quarter million crests— would mostly cover their expenses for the months Kira expected to be gone. It wasn't like Memorial Force's operating expenses were *actually* four million kroner a month. They hovered around three, depending on what Kira's people did in a given thirty days.

The shoreside office on Blueward Station, on the other hand, only consumed about a hundred thousand kroner a month. Larry could cover those expenses out of his pocket change, and everyone in the room knew it.

"You really do want us to take this contract, don't you?" Kira murmured in amusement.

"Knowing what I know now about the Royal Crest, I'm uncomfortable getting as far into bed with them as it looks like I'm going to have to," Larry admitted. "It's looking more and more like Redward, Bengalissimo and Ypres are going to have to countersign for *all* of the Cluster's loans.

"That helps protect the sovereignty of our smaller partners, but it also puts a heavy economic risk on our largest three powers," he continued. "While everything I have suggests that none of the loans and projects we are taking on represent a major risk, so long as we're careful, it will give the Crest a lot of leverage in the Cluster.

"I am...uncomfortable with that leverage resting in an entity under the control of the Equilibrium Institute." He spread his hands. "The process has moved far enough along that backing out now would be a political nightmare.

"So, *I* need the Crest...fixed."

"In several senses," Kira murmured. "Regime change is not going to leave them in a position to lean on that leverage for a while, is it?"

"The thought had crossed our minds," Remington said—and butter wouldn't have melted in the Admiral's mouth from her expression.

"All right. Here's what I *need*," Kira told them, raising a hand. "That ten-million bonus is enough for us to come back—assuming we *survive* this—but I have a few immediate problems you can help with."

"I'm listening," Larry said.

"I'm going to have somewhere between twenty and a hundred people who aren't going to want to leave the Cluster," she said. Her minimum count was based on people with young children in Redward, so she was *extremely* confident in it.

Kira Demirci had the motherly instinct of the average fish, she knew, and even *she* wouldn't want to leave a toddler behind for six months.

"I need to replace them, ASAP, with people I can trust. That means RRF secondments," she told them. "We'll bring them over at equivalent ranks, but I'm going to need techs, petties and probably at least half a dozen pilots."

She wasn't overly worried about officers or senior noncoms, but her techs and junior petty officer equivalents were going to take the lion's share of the sabbaticals—and she needed every one of them she had.

"Done," Larry agreed, without even a glance at Remington. "And we'll take any of your hands that want it into the RRF, at least temporarily. If we're keeping you around, it'll be good practice for everyone."

"Thank you," Kira said quietly. "I can't really justify paying them to sit around here."

"But we can pay them to do basically the same jobs they did for you," the King said. "What else?"

"I need people who've pulled this damn stupid stunt with me before," Kira said. "I don't know if you can spare Brigadier Temitope, but I need commandos—at least a platoon, and preferably as many of the people who went aboard *Deception* with me as you can find."

Remington laughed aloud and Kira raised an eyebrow.

"Hope is more briefed on this than most," the Admiral told her. "And now I owe her fifty kroner."

Brigadier Hope Temitope was one of the most senior officers the Redward Army Commandos had—but as *Colonel* Temitope, she'd led the Redward component of the operation that had taken *Deception* away from the Equilibrium Institute.

"We can't spare the Brigadier," Larry admitted. "But I will ask her to recommend a commando platoon to send with you. She likes you. You'll get her best."

"Then that should do it, Your Majesty," Kira said. "I won't pretend I like losing the retainer…but I'll be damned if I'll let the chance to poke the Institute in the eye pass by, either."

13

"GATHER ROUND, gather round and listen up well," Kira barked as she stepped into the pilots' lounge on *Deception*.

While both *Deception* and *Raccoon* had their own Commanders, Nova Group, everyone understood that Kira would fly a nova fighter in action and command the combined group. She was both the Commodore and *Memorial Force*'s nova-group commander.

Still, she wasn't in the pilot's lounge much. Traditionally in the ASDF, even squadron commanders stepped lightly in the lounge—and the CNG only entered when something absolutely critical was going on. This was the space for the pilots, not their commanders.

The only reason she'd spent much time in *Deception*'s lounge was that it was where the cruiser's Brisingr designers had put the simulator pods. There was only so much space to spare on a ninety-six-thousand-cubic-meter cruiser for the fighter wing and its supports, after all.

Like most pilots' lounges she'd been in, this one was messy but not dirty. No one in space would allow a ship compartment to actually get *dirty*. There were still empty dishes that hadn't made it to a dishwasher yet, jackets strewn randomly about, and a collection of cushions and pillows that were never in the same place twice.

Right now, the space also held twenty-five pilots. Mel Cartman had made sure the word was leaked that the Commodore was coming to speak to the pilots, so they were *all* there—and the lounge wasn't designed to have twenty-five people in it.

"Not much gathering around, I suppose," she said with a chuckle as she took in the crowd. "So, I guess I'll settle for listening up. Anyone missing?"

"Everyone's here," a lithe raven-haired woman said from the back of the room. "Hark to the Commodore's words, people!"

Kira laughed at Neha "Backstab" Bradley. The pilot's callsign had been born out of the fact that she'd been an Equilibrium plant in the fighter-pilot training program Kira and John Estanza had run for Redward—but she'd been blackmailed, and her intel had *broken* the Institute's network in the Redward System.

Still, the RRF had refused to take her and she had come to work for Kira. She was a perfect representative of what this meeting was about, though—she had a toddler living on Redward.

"I don't need to ask if you've been paying attention to what's going on," Kira finally said. "Every one of you knows we're prepping for an op. A big one—and the *smarter* folks in this room know that there's not much going on in the Syntactic Cluster that calls for a big op, is there?"

She let that sink in.

"I'm not here to brief you all on the mission before us," she continued. "There'll be a time for that when we're well away and preparing for battle. What I'm here to tell you, because I owe you this, is that we're going outside the Syntactic Cluster and we're going to be gone for months.

"Best guess is four to five. Might be six, even seven," she said. "Memorial Force, despite what we do, is not a military. I don't have you all locked into contracts that say you can't leave. I know you all knew this was a possibility, but I don't want anyone feeling trapped.

"So." Kira looked around. Backstab was definitely looking concerned, but she wasn't the only one.

"There are terms in your contracts around notice and buyout and all of that shit," she told them. "I'll assume you're all familiar with them and not reiterate. That said, I'm not a monster—most of the time —and I've made some arrangements.

"Anyone who isn't comfortable spending six months outside of the Cluster and away from Redward, talk to the CNG in private after this," she instructed. "We've made arrangements to swap a small number of pilots with the RRF, at least temporarily. We send you to their orbital squadrons and they play musical chairs to send me people up to your weight to replace you."

That got her a few chuckles, but there were worried and concerned looks as well.

"Look." She pulled a seat over to herself and sat down. "I'd rather go into action with all of you, but I owe you this chance. We'll call it a sabbatical for the folks who take it, and we'll talk about what that looks like when we come back.

"I won't hold staying in Redward against anyone and I will *not* stand for any of *you* holding it against anyone," she told them. "We'll be home-basing out of Redward for a while yet, but I suspect that a lot of our future operations are going to look like this—extended deployments to other sectors.

"We've helped bring peace to the Syntactic Cluster. That means we've got to go further to find work—but find work we shall."

BRADLEY WAS at Kira's office door less than five minutes after Kira sat down. Unsurprised, Kira had the young woman's preferred coffee mix waiting when she allowed Backstab in.

"Have a seat, Neha," Kira told the younger pilot. "I was expecting you."

"Despite telling us to go to Nightmare?" Bradley asked—but she took the seat and the coffee.

"Nobody ever admits that the bosses have favorites, but everyone in the nova group can point them out all the same," Kira admitted. "After everything you went through to get here, Neha, I feel more responsible for you than most of the pilots we recruited here."

The young woman nodded steadily, but her hands trembled slightly as she drank from the coffee cup.

"I…was wondering…well, if the transfer deal applied to me," she told Kira. "The rest of the pilots from the training program *chose* to be Memorials. I...was discharged from service with the RRF."

"You were," Kira agreed levelly. "Bringing down the Institute's spies here got you out from under treason and espionage charges, but even Queen Sonia couldn't keep that from tainting any chance of you flying for the Redward Fleet."

Bradley looked much less steady now.

"I see, sir," she admitted. "But I... But Jessica..."

"Jessica is with your mother these days, right?" Kira asked gently. Jessica was Bradley's daughter—the not-quite-two-year-old daughter the Equilibrium Institute had kidnapped to force her cooperation with their plan to infiltrate the training program.

"Yes, sir. The Queen encouraged me to reach out after...everything," Bradley said quietly.

"Your situation is the most complicated," Kira admitted. "But you're also among the pilots and crew with the most powerful reason to *want* to stay in Redward. So..."

She shrugged.

"You were discharged without prejudice from the RRF and returned to the training program as an explicitly Memorial recruit," Kira noted. "The sabbatical exchange that has been discussed is *not* a commission in the RRF. Those taking it will remain officers of Memorial Force under detached subcontract with the Redward Royal Fleet.

"Which means, Pilot Bradley, that your previous interactions with the RRF are completely irrelevant."

Kira could *hear* the raggedness in Bradley's exhalation, despite the younger woman's efforts to control her emotions.

"Are you sure, sir?"

"I checked, Neha," Kira said quietly. And Queen Sonia had leaned on the people setting up the program on the RRF's side, though she wasn't telling Bradley that. "If you want to take the sabbatical and remain here, there will be no issues."

"I... I have to, sir," Bradley told her. "I can't be away from Jessica for six months, not right now."

"I agree," Kira replied. She'd been preparing a backup plan where

Neha Bradley was transferred to their shore office for the six months, before Sonia had involved herself.

"So, I'll make sure you're on the list for that subcontract," she told Bradley. "It'll all be taken care of, I promise."

First, though, she had to get over to *Raccoon*, where she'd give a similar briefing and have, she estimated, three only *somewhat*-less-complicated conversations with pilots there.

Some days, she missed just running from assassins.

14

"That's better than I was expecting," Kira admitted after Bueller listed the number. "My guess was we'd lose ten of the pilots and at least forty of the crew."

"Our people mostly like their jobs, their colleagues and their superiors," Zoric said, glancing around the half-virtual senior officer meeting.

Kira, Zoric and Bueller were the only ones currently aboard *Deception*. The other three Captains were on the call, but it was still a small meeting of the core leadership. Kira would have preferred to pull Patel and Cartman into even these meetings—especially as Patel was the company's third-largest shareholder!—but the two nova-group commanders were currently at the RRF's Pilot Academy.

Giving a commencement address, of all things. Kira was busy enough that *she'd* been able to get out of it, but given that her people had been at the heart of the training program that had become the Pilot Academy, *someone* from Memorial Force had needed to give the address.

"I'll admit it's a warm, fuzzy feeling to have people stick with us as we go into the deep beyond," Kira said. "The *headache* will be when we get back and need to swap our RRF loans for our originals.

"Some of them will end up joining the RRF permanently, I suspect."

"We'll have to deal with that then," Michel noted. The mechanical-legged woman grimaced. "I'm hoping we're getting *good* people from the RRF, though?"

"I trust Remington that far, at least," Kira replied. She'd trust the RRF a bit further than that, in fact, which meant she wasn't overly worried. "I'm starting to focus more on what's in front of us.

"Konrad, how'd the freighter shopping go?"

"Well, that depends," he admitted. "Last I checked, we're only getting twenty million crests in cash for this whole affair."

"Given that we're promised a hundred-billion-crest carrier, I'm not side-eyeing the cash payment too hard," Zoric said. "But that sounds like a problem?"

"I found a perfect ship for us," Bueller told them. "Same class as *Raccoon* pre-conversion, so forty-five kilocubics. Secondhand, which puts a bit of a handle on the price, but in good shape.

"Even secondhand, though, well…she's thirty-five million kroner."

Kira nodded calmly, though she heard both McCaig and Michel inhale sharply in surprise.

"That's more than we're getting cash for this whole mission," McCaig pointed out.

"And that's why I wanted to check in with the senior officers before I closed the deal," Bueller replied. "I've got lines on a few cheaper ships, but this one really matches our needs—plus the extra cover of helping hide *Raccoon*."

"Secondhand merchant nova ships don't generally go for much less than half a million per kilocubic," Zoric pointed out. "And that's *crests*, not kroner. She's exactly what I'd expect for a ship like that."

"We're going to need logistics support for this mission—and for most missions after this," Kira said. "While I intend to continue home-basing out of Redward until we get our carrier from them, we're not likely to see a lot of operations in the Syntactic Cluster.

"That means we need a decent support base, a ship that can haul fuel and munitions and all of the other matériel of making war." She looked at her subordinates. "I think we buy the ship Konrad has found, but I'm open to counterarguments."

Everyone in the meeting except Bueller had at least *some* shares in Memorial Force, but Kira held fifty-one percent—to Zoric's twenty and Patel's eight. Michel and the other old Apollo hands had four apiece. The last nine were scattered through old *Conviction* hands like Mwangi.

"I agree," *Raccoon*'s Captain said calmly. "The price is quite reasonable, honestly, and we need the support. I wouldn't mind having somewhere to stuff spare torpedoes and class two drives, even though I'll be *damned* if I'll give any of them up!"

McCaig sighed, a surprisingly gentle sound from the massive man, and nodded.

"I'm not going to argue with Demirci, Zoric *and* Mwangi," he told them. "I'm just a grunt with a share in the company who's learning how to skipper a destroyer."

He was doing far better at that than Kira had dared hope, too. It was probably going to matter.

"I know my vote is irrelevant at this point, but I agree," Michel said with a chuckle. "I haven't been aboard *Raccoon* since I got grounded. With the amount of space I take up these days, I almost felt bad for visiting!"

"You're always more than welcome, Captain Michel," Mwangi told her. "But yes, my ship is feeling a tad cramped these days."

"All right," Kira said. "Konrad, close the deal as soon as you can. We're going to be picking up a platoon of Redward commandos along with our pilots and crew, and the freighter will probably be a handy place to store them."

"That'll make Milani happy," McCaig said. "The task you've set them isn't impossible, but it's certainly not easy."

"And if it wasn't Milani, I might be concerned," Kira replied. "But I know them. They'll get it done."

"Your faith in my former subordinate is touching," McCaig said. "Are we going to learn more about what we're getting into before we send them on a near-suicide mission?"

"That's next up," Kira told them all. "We need eyes on the ground in the Crest. While there is intelligence that we can *only* get from the Crown Zharang and their allies, I don't want to be entirely reliant on them.

"I want to take a forward party to the Crest ahead of the fleet and scout the yards and everything else I can find."

"And by *take* you mean going yourself?" Zoric asked.

"If I'm going to commit this entire mercenary fleet to a potential suicide mission, I want to put *my* eyes on the target," Kira replied. "Only problem I see is the timeline. I've started mapping out civilian transport to the Crest, and it's looking like eight weeks, minimum.

"Versus five to six for the rest of you. If I take a scouting party ahead now, working subtly, the rest of Memorial Force might just beat us there!"

"We have three months until the trials, correct?" Mwangi said. "We'll want to wait here and double-check everything before we move out, anyway."

"But you can also ask our employer for assistance in travel," Zoric suggested. "They may have people moving back and forth with messages. I don't know how much authority even three directors and the Crown Zharang of the Royal Crest have to sign off on hundred-tril-lion-crest loans on their own!"

"From what Jade said, you might be surprised," Kira noted. "But you're right. They may be able to get us a ride that won't take two months."

"You'll want to keep the team small," McCaig told her. "In a perfect world, I'd say take Milani, but...that won't work. They're needed to coordinate the integration of the commandos."

"The fact they don't take their armor off wouldn't be a problem?" Mwangi asked.

"They have a medical-prosthetic version that they wear in places they cannot go armed," Milani's former boss told the carrier Captain. "And a doctor's note, for that matter. Even *I* don't know what Milani looks like under the dragon armor."

Milani, Kira reflected, had managed something truly unusual in their time: a physical and gender presentation that people found strange. And *that*, she knew, just amused the hell out of the mercenary commando.

"Take Bueller," Zoric said after the amused chuckle faded. "My suggestion, in fact, would be just the two of you and a handful of commandos to protect you."

"I was figuring that Bueller was needed here," Kira admitted, glancing over at her lover. They hadn't talked about it in advance, though she hadn't been planning on leaving for a week or so yet. "With bringing in new crew and everything…"

"Not having him will suck, yes," Zoric agreed cheerfully. "On the other hand, do you know what will suck more?"

She glanced around the virtual meeting.

"If we steal that carrier and something *fails* because the Crest shipyards screwed up something basic. Bueller is the best engineer we've got and the most familiar with the tech level we're looking at for *Fortitude*.

"If anyone can identify a problem before the ship launches, it's him. If the trials are going to fail before the inspection ever happens, we need to know that chance exists."

"The more time I have to look at the ship instead of the schematics, the better I can judge her," Kira's boyfriend admitted. "But there's only so much I can do from the outside, and I don't get the impression we're going to be able to get aboard her in advance."

Kira chuckled.

"Not a chance in hell," she said. "From what Panosyan has said, the SPP is treating that ship as their own private baby. She might be Navy of the Royal Crest, but every officer and spacer aboard her is going to be a Sanctuary and Prosperity Party loyalist."

"Damn. That's fucked-up," Mwangi said grimly. "They're playing political games of that level with their fleet?"

"System defenses are probably more reasonable," Kira pointed out. "The nova fleet can afford to be a bit weaker if it's loyal. It's not a trade *I'd* make, but I'm not surprised to see politicians making it.

"Especially politicians who are fudging elections and working with the Institute." She smiled. "I'm more willing to assume malice on their part than incompetence, but I will be happy to find failures of theirs along the way."

"We can hope," Zoric said grimly. "Even if this all goes according to plan, we're up against a lot of firepower."

"I know," Kira allowed. "Hence wanting to get an *exact* figure on what we're dealing with. I'll see if I can borrow a courier from the Bank of the Royal Crest.

"Worst-case scenario, I start booking passenger tickets while you all prepare for war!"

15

"WINE, KIRA?"

"Please."

Kira accepted the glass Voski offered her, smiling to herself as the bodyguard retreated to the door of the borrowed office. Today, Voski wore a similar dress to the one they'd worn at the barbecue—and from her headware's complaints, she figured it was stuffed full of electronic-warfare gear.

"The office is swept for bugs four times a day," Jade Panosyan told her. The Crest Royal was leaning back in their chair with a wine glass of their own, wearing an old-fashioned pantsuit. "Voski re-swept just before you arrived and is running a few...toys, let's say.

"This space is secure."

"You'd know better than I if the Institute has agents out here," Kira pointed out. "We broke their network less than a year ago, but I assume they're rebuilding it."

"Potentially not. They do seem to have written the Cluster off as a bad investment for now," Panosyan observed. "Of course, they believe the Free Trade Zone will inevitably fail in a decade or two, so they will prepare for that and wait."

"Bastards," Kira murmured. Her anger with the Institute's very existence had lost much of its heat with time and exposure, but that made it no less intense. That was why she was even *doing* this contract.

"I can't argue that point," Panosyan agreed. "I saw that this was officially a social call. I'm assuming you don't want to talk to the BRC about a loan at the moment, so what do you need?"

"I might talk to you about a loan when your planet isn't run by my mortal enemies," Kira said drily. "Until then, we're working toward a better future."

"Always," the Zharang agreed.

"I need transport to Crest that won't draw attention," Kira told them. "I want to take a scouting party in ahead, to see what intelligence we can pick up on our own. It's not that I don't trust you, but…"

"I'm a banker, Commodore," Jade Panosyan reminded her with a chuckle. "*Trust but verify* is a golden standard for us. I'd expect no less from you."

They took a sip of their wine as they considered thoughtfully.

"There are several options," they finally said. "First, as I've assumed you've already investigated, there is standard commercial travel. You'd need to stage through a few different locations, and it would take some time."

"My research suggested eight weeks," Kira replied. "I was hoping you'd have a better option."

"We could charter a ship specifically to carry you to, hrm, Guadaloop, I think," the banker told her. "From there you could take commercial transport for the last hop, which would only be a couple of days.

"The charter shouldn't draw too much attention, because you aren't heading directly to the Crest, though Guadaloop is one of the more important client worlds with a semi-permanent NRC station," Panosyan continued.

"It might end up drawing more attention, then," Kira pointed out. "Since you and your delegation are here, a charter from here to a system *near* the Crest might catch NRC attention more than one directly home."

Panosyan nodded slowly and took another sip.

"This is true," they agreed. "A charter directly to the Crest, however, would also draw attention. Especially if no members of the delegation were aboard and there were no critical messages carried. Anyone debarking from that vessel would likely draw Institute attention."

The office was silent, but Kira saw the grin creep onto Jade Panosyan's face.

"Which means, of course, that someone from the delegation must return to the Crest to cover your arrival. I've done more than enough work here to earn my commission. Normally, I would prefer to see the negotiations through to the conclusion, but it is entirely believable for me to return to the Crest to start the back-end process of preparing the syndication of the loan.

"It's both justifiable and makes me look like I'm avoiding real work to those who don't understand banking, which fits with some of our enemies' prejudices toward me," they noted. "I can offer you transport on my yacht, and that will allow us to avoid some of the suspicion."

"Wouldn't we still draw attention as strangers on your ship?" Kira asked.

"If you came all the way to the Crest with me, yes," Panosyan said. "But…" They tapped the wine bottle with their glass before finishing their drink. "This wine is one of my favorites—I'm somewhat known for it, in fact—and it comes from Guadaloop.

"Several of my and my father's favorite wines are from that world, so it would be entirely expected—if I'm already evading the full weight of my duty—for my ship to stop at Guadaloop and pick up a supply for home.

"I have friends and contacts in the system, and we should be able to smuggle you off the ship there without drawing attention," they continued. "It will likely be easier, in fact, to do so in the Guadaloop System than in the Crest.

"From there, you can hire commercial passage and arrive in the Crest almost completely unnoticed. We will arrange drop-box communication and coordination, and I will make certain that a sublight ship is placed at your disposal.

"Getting you back to your squadron will take a bit more effort but should be doable."

They raised a hand in caution.

"I cannot guarantee your safe arrival in the Crest," they warned. "The Sanctuary and Prosperity Party has loyalists everywhere, who may find you suspicious. While I *believe* that only a core group in the Party is sufficiently aware of the Equilibrium connections to see you as a threat..."

"Just the fact that there are mercenaries in the Crest may draw unwelcome attention," Kira said grimly. "The thought has crossed my mind, but we can't get away from it."

"I presumed you understood, but I wanted to be certain," Panosyan told her. "I will make the arrangements for our sojourn. It will have some positive aspects as well."

The Crown Zharang of the Royal Crest grinned like an impish child.

"My ship is comfortable but not large, my dear Commodore. In five weeks, we will have plenty of time to get to know each other!"

16

THE NOVA YACHT *Yerazner* fit Jade Panosyan's description to a tee. Kira couldn't help herself from mentally measuring and guesstimating dimensions and statistics as their shuttle approached the ship.

Yerazner—Armenian for *Dreams*—was an egg shape sixty meters long and twenty meters wide at her widest. A significant portion of her upper half was given over to a transparent dome twenty meters across that contained a garden and a pool.

Given her length and lines, Kira estimated the yacht at about sixteen thousand cubic meters—probably based around a fifteen-hundred-cubic Eleven-X nova drive. Despite the garden dome on her upper half, the yacht looked to have powerful engines and, Kira suspected, at least some concealed guns.

Still, at sixteen thousand cubic meters, she wasn't a big ship. The dome took up two thousand cubic meters of her volume—*not* a small sacrifice. The presence of the transparent open garden was the single clearest sign of the ship owner's wealth.

Kira suspected they could have *gold-plated* the ship for less than it had cost to add the two thousand cubic meters used for the dome. Still, for a long trip, she could see the value.

"Approaching shuttle, this is *Yerazner* Flight Control," a professionally calm voice said in her headware. "I have you on my files, but please submit your manifest and passenger list to confirm."

"Transmitting, *Yerazner* Flight," Kira replied. The runabout she was flying was barely big enough for four passengers and their luggage—well, at least when the luggage included two full sets of combat armor.

Her two escorts—Jerzy Bertoli and Aleifr O'Mooney, two of Milani's most experienced troopers—weren't taking any chances with the Commodore's safety. They might be planning on spending the entire mission in plain clothes with concealed blasters, but they'd brought *everything* they might need.

"We have the manifest and passenger list," the Crester on the channel told Kira. "Just to confirm, the, ah, *special equipment* is staying on the shuttle, yes?"

"That's the plan, *Yerazner*," Kira confirmed. "It's there for if we need it, not for us to create a need for it."

The Crester laughed.

"Fair enough. You're clear all the way, Basketball," they told Kira, using her fighter callsign. "The skipper will be waiting in the bay; boss is in the gardens.

"Welcome aboard."

IF KIRA HAD SOMEHOW MISSED who, exactly, Crown Zharang Jade Panosyan was prior to that point, the people waiting for her on the shuttle bay deck would have been the most blatant clue yet. There weren't many organizations in the galaxy whose reputations spread beyond their own star systems—and the vast majority of them were space fleets and fighter squadrons.

The Dinastik Pahak *had* nova fighters. There were, in fact, two of them parked in the shuttle bay Kira had landed her shuttle in. Hussar-Six heavy fighters, they had a small but potentially significant technology edge over anything else in the Redward System—though the yacht only had space for two of them.

But the Dinastik Pahak were not *just* nova fighters. Their reputation hadn't spread as far as, say, Cobra Squadron, but Kira recognized the gold-on-black uniforms of the half-dozen armed guards waiting for her.

The uniforms still retained much of the angularity of Crest fashion, but except for the gold shoulders and the star on each Pahak's left breast, they were midnight black. The base was a shipsuit, like most uniforms Kira was familiar with, though the cut and armor were different.

The Dinastik Pahak were bodyguards and guardians, the most junior of them twenty-year veterans of the Navy and Army of the Royal Crest. Chosen for skill and loyalty, they guarded the royal family of the Crest.

Somehow, Kira was expecting Voski to be one of the people meeting her in that uniform. A second, older Pahak officer stood next to them, wearing the standard golden rocket of a starship Captain on her breast as she gave Kira a crisp salute.

"Welcome aboard *Yerazner*," Voski told Kira. "Captain Sung-Min Jung, please be known to Commodore Kira Demirci and Commander Konrad Bueller of the Memorial Force Mercenary Company."

"Captain," Kira returned the dark-eyed Pahak officer's salute. "I appreciate the Zharang's invitation to travel with them. I'll admit, I wasn't necessarily expecting the Dinastik Pahak. I thought you only escorted their father, the King."

"King Sung is our primary charge, yes, but a secondary detachment of the Dinastik Pahak exists to guard the Crown Zharang," Captain Jung told her. "Their Excellency prefers we not be obvious when they are working, but all of their security is from the Dinastik Pahak.

"Of course, their wife also has a Pahak detail, but Em Loretta almost never leaves the Crest."

Kira smothered her curiosity. She was a contractor *working* for Jade Panosyan. There was no reason for the Crown Zharang to have mentioned their wife to her, even if the lack seemed unusual.

"I don't believe either of you have met Konrad Bueller before," she said after a moment, gesturing her boyfriend forward. They'd known who was coming, but while Voski had introduced Konrad, they hadn't met him.

"He's Memorial Force's senior engineer," she noted. She swallowed any particular embarrassment in favor of necessity and smiled in amusement at herself. "He and I will be sharing quarters, which I hope makes your life easier."

"Zharang Panosyan had informed us as such," Jung told her. "We have rooms set aside for all four of you, as instructed. The Zharang has requested that Em Voski escort you and Commander Bueller to the garden once you've been shown to your rooms."

She made a small, amused sound.

"While I suspect you could find the garden on your own, we'll show you around first."

THE SUITE of rooms that *Yerazner*'s crew gave Kira and her people was clearly designed for *exactly* the purpose it was being used for. The whole suite, combined, was maybe two hundred and fifty cubic meters, but it was set up to put Kira and Konrad's room at one end and the guards' rooms next to the access from the rest of the ship.

It was surprisingly securable, and Kira left Bertoli and O'Mooney to that task while she and Konrad went up to the dome.

There was a tinge to the air in the entire ship that she wasn't used to, but it wasn't until the doors slid open into the garden dome that she finally realized what it was. The scent of flowers and fresh leaves, diffused by the purification and recycling systems, was rippling out from the massive garden dome and filling the entire vessel.

In the dome itself, the scent of unknown flowers was clear, and Kira found herself walking a stone-lined path through purple-flowered bushes in Voski's wake. Only a few meters from the entrance, the path gave way to a hedge-enclosed pool that rippled in an artificial breeze.

"The water is part of the ship's systems as well," Jade Panosyan's voice said from Kira's left, and she turned to find the Crown Zharang watching her. "Everything in here is linked into the ship's environmental systems. We're using the plants to purify both the air and the water, though the pool is entirely as extravagant as it looks."

They were sprawled in a sun lounger, grinning up at Kira, and gestured toward an empty pair of folding "beach chairs."

"While I appreciate the garden and abuse the hell out of it," they continued, "this was my grandmother-the-King's thirtieth wedding anniversary present to herself and her husband. She was far more inclined to spoil herself than I or my father, but... Well, we already owned *Yerazner,* and it seemed wasteful not to keep her at that point."

Kira chuckled and took a seat on the chair. A quick glance at the arm of the chair revealed it had roughly twenty-six different possible shapes, including the extended lounger form Panosyan was using.

For the moment, Kira remained seated upright—though Konrad sank about fifty degrees after he sat down and then made a contented sound as he discovered the massage features.

A drinks robot rolled out a few seconds later in answer to a silent command from Panosyan, and the Crown Zharang chuckled.

"Like I said, Kira, my ship is comfortable," they observed. "Crew of twenty, plus, what, another twenty bodyguards, Voski?"

The bodyguard was still standing, though they were now leaning on a decorative stone wall. There were more than enough chairs for them to sit, and Kira didn't have the impression that Panosyan would mind.

She did have the impression that Voski sitting at the pool was a long-standing discussion between the two of them.

"Forty-two all told," Voski agreed. "All of us have individual rooms with more-than-sufficient amenities. Your grandmother was always determined to reward service, and your father agreed with that sentiment."

"Well, where my father and grandmother agree, who am I to argue?" Panosyan asked. They shook their head and accepted a drink from the robot themselves after it had provided Kira a virgin margarita.

The Crester's drink was definitely *not* virgin, Kira saw.

"My grandmother always knew where her loyalties lay," the Crown Zharang continued calmly. "In another era, they might have hung 'the Great' on her—and that is never a title that isn't drenched in fucking blood."

Voski didn't even conceal their wince.

"Perhaps you should lay off the tequila slightly, Jade?" they asked.

"Please, Voski, if anyone in this damn galaxy needs to know just what the Royal Crest has been up to for the last eighty years or so, it's Demirci," the Zharang said. "My grandmother built our network of client worlds. Her only loyalty was to the Crest, her only goal, our prosperity."

"Other worlds would benefit only where it served the Crest."

Panosyan shook their head.

"I won't say our client worlds aren't better off than they were before they were pulled into our network," they conceded. "But I suspect most of them would have been better off still if left alone.

"We can't change the past," they said sharply, taking a swallow of the margarita. "But we can change the future, and that's what I hired you for."

"We're leaving shortly?" Kira asked.

"We already did," Konrad pointed out.

Kira glanced "up," to the transparent ceiling of the dome, and saw that he was correct. The stations and world they'd been orbiting were now rapidly falling behind them.

"*Yerazner* has the smoothest Harrington coils we could source," their host told her. "Two hours to the first nova. Twenty-six days to Guadaloop. Barring trouble, the biggest concern between now and then is going to be when we run out of Redward Royal Reserve coffee."

"I'm more worried about our stock of tequila from home at the moment," Voski said drily. "We might be down to a mere fifty or so bottles."

"Damn. If we run out, we might have to break open that pallet of rum from Ypres," Panosyan replied. "I sincerely doubt we're going to have any *real* shortages, Voski. You wouldn't let me drink that much."

"I am always concerned about the potential threats on our route," the bodyguard reminded them all. "This ship draws attention to itself. That helps with your plan, in many ways, but it also draws dangerous eyes."

"We'll deal with that if it happens," the Crown Zharang replied. "It didn't happen heading out; I'm not really expecting it heading back." Their smile thinned. "And this ship is far from defenseless."

17

AFTER ALMOST FOUR WEEKS, even the luxurious accommodations and extensive entertainment libraries aboard *Yerazner* were growing old. Kira had learned the names of every plant in the garden dome and had even helped transplant a wisteria bush—from Earth itself!—that had outgrown its pot.

It managed to be even more boring than sitting aboard *Deception*, doing paperwork and playing guard dog for the Redward System. The last day found her in the room she shared with Konrad, watching the last few episodes of an Apollo media series she'd missed the end of.

Somehow, when she'd been fleeing her home system one step ahead of the Brisingr Shadows and their covert ops assassins, making sure she had a way to get the last season of *Rising Guardians* hadn't crossed her mind, after all.

She was realizing that she'd been better off missing it, and considering pinging Konrad to see if he wanted to have sex again when the familiar faint sensation of nova aboard a starship rippled through the room.

"We've arrived," Konrad's mental voice said in her head. *"Welcome to Guadaloop, Kira. Ready to get to work?"*

"You have no fucking idea," she silently replied—and *heard* his chuckle from the sitting area at the center of their suite.

"I think we *all* have some idea," her boyfriend said loudly through the cracked-open door. "I think we're all going nuts. It's a comfortable ship, but..."

"But I'm not equipped to sit very well," Kira agreed, stepping into the sitting area and looking around at her team. "Are we ready for the actual job, people?"

"Sneaking off this ship without getting seen, renting transport for the runabout to the Crest, and entering an arguably hostile system under the eyes and guns of hostile nova warships?" Bertoli asked calmly.

"That's the mission, for now at least," Kira said.

"We're as ready as we're going to be. I don't know what *Yerazner's* crew is planning for cover. We'll start loading on the shuttle straight away."

"I'll check in with Jung and Panosyan," Kira agreed. "Need me for packing?"

"Hardly, Commodore," Bertoli said with a chuckle.

"That's the last time you call me that for a while," she told the merc. "It's Em Riker now, until we're back aboard *Deception*. Kira Demirci is known to the Institute. Let's hope they're not watching for us."

"We can run silent and we can run deep," Konrad told her softly. "They won't see us coming, even if they are looking for us. We'll make sure of it."

"I hope so."

"ARE YOU AND YOUR PEOPLE READY?" Panosyan asked before Kira could say a word. The Crown Zharang was on *Yerazner's* bridge, a baroquely decorated but small control space designed for only four people.

"The boys are packing as I speak," Kira agreed. "Everything we need is on the runabout. We've got ideas for getting from here"—she gestured out the window at Guadaloop's star—"to the Crest.

"But getting off of this ship without being associated with you is going to be the hard part, I suspect."

"Please, Commodore, I have a plan," the Crown Zharang said with a smile.

"I assumed. Except you didn't tell me it," Kira pointed out.

"I had six, actually," Panosyan replied, their voice suddenly deadly serious as they looked at the main display. "It depended on who I could get in touch with once I was here. My first and second plans fell through, but I think this one will work better anyway."

"That's reassuring," Kira said. "What's the plan?"

"Jung, flag our friend."

An icon on the screen flashed bright green. It took Kira less than five seconds to note that it was on a converging course with *Yerazner*.

"Local mining-ship captain," Panosyan said. "Name is Evelina Razc. Longer ago than I care to think about, she missed one too many payments, and her ship was up to be seized by the BRC. I was system manager at the time, one of my first senior roles. She ran one of my subordinates a hell of a sob story and got herself kicked up to my office.

"Since the sob story was *true* and her mother *had* just died of cancer, I made an exception on humanitarian grounds and re-amortized her loan." The banker shrugged. "It was the right thing to do—and we were going to make more money if she kept paying us than if we seized and auctioned the ship.

"She proved me right, but she always said she owed me. Figured this was as good a time to call that in as any."

And now Kira understood why Jade Panosyan had been so insistent on using Guadaloop as the relay point. If they'd been system manager for the Bank of the Royal Crest there for any extended period of time, they were probably owed a list of favors as long as Kira's arm.

"It's a pretty small favor, all told," the banker noted. "Razc adjusted her course just a little bit to make her run to the refinery cross our course. She'll be 'in front' of us with regard to the orbital scanner networks and the NRC's Battle Group *Final Usury* for just over two minutes.

"During that window, we'll drop your runabout and you'll vector your course to sweep in to the refinery with Razc's ship," they finished. "Arrangements have been made for you to have an officially filed course from the refinery to Guadaloop itself."

"Everything will appear normal to anyone who isn't aboard *Yerazner*," Jung said. "*Final Usury* and her battle group have no reason to suspect anything. They may still have sensor drones deployed around the system, however, and that's why you'll want to stick close to Razc's *Moonshine*."

"I've already agreed to have dinner with Admiral Avagyan," the Crown Zharang added. "Dafina is a cousin-in-law. I don't *think* she's an SPP supporter, which means I should be able to call in a favor and bury any oddities even if we screw this up.

"Not that I expect us to screw this up."

Kira chuckled grimly.

"*I'm* flying the runabout, people," she reminded them. "I'm pretty sure I can outfly *Final Usury*'s sensor drones if we can pick them out."

She considered for a moment, then shook her head.

"I have to ask, though. Your planet is known for banking, and you seriously named a fleet carrier *Final Usury*?"

"I've mentioned my grandmother was a stone-cold bitch, yes?" Panosyan asked.

18

TO KIRA'S hopefully concealed surprise, everything proceeded exactly according to plan. She was still watching the red icons on her display of the half-dozen sensor drones they'd picked up from the Navy of the Royal Crest carrier group in-system, but everything she could see said they'd made it to the Shaqvilla Refining Center without being detected.

"Flight SRC-Seven-Seven-Nine, your course is registered," a bored flight controller told her—as if her shuttle had just launched from the big station ahead of them. "We have you on standard vector to Guadaloop Actual; please confirm."

Kira checked half a dozen bits of data in her headware before answering—not least making sure she knew what the standard vector to Guadaloop *was*.

"Shaqvilla Control, this is SRC-Seven-Seven-Nine," she replied once she was certain. "Three passengers, on standard vector to Guadaloop Actual. I confirm."

"Safe flight, SRC-Seven-Seven-Nine," the controller said. "Everything is green on our end. Carry on."

Kira smiled to herself as the channel dropped.

"What?" Konrad asked.

"Either someone slotted in false data of us launching from the station—or more likely, the bored-sounding traffic controller I just spoke to was decently bribed," she told her lover. "We're now on an officially registered course and I've coded the autopilot."

She rose from the controls and stretched. The runabout shuttle was tiny, designed to be stored on ships that were only ten thousand cubic meters in total. It was basically a three-meter-diameter cylinder seven meters long—and it had Harrington coils and antigravity systems stuffed into it.

Every space aboard the runabout was cramped. There wasn't enough space for any kind of internal separation, which meant that she could hear Bertoli snoring on the fold-down bunk.

"Four more hours," Kira warned her companions. "Guadaloop Actual is the main orbital, an elevator center point like Blueward Station at Redward. To get there, we're passing through the battle station perimeter."

"That shouldn't be a problem, should it?" O'Mooney asked. The red-haired young mercenary looked nervous but ready. Kira knew that Milani and Bertoli had handpicked her for this mission, though, which meant she almost certainly *was* ready.

"We have a properly registered local course now," Kira told the ground trooper. "So, the Guadaloop Orbital Defense Command will almost certainly ignore us."

"GODCom," Konrad muttered. "Somehow, I doubt that was accidental."

"Probably not," she agreed. "But, truthfully, GODCom isn't our problem. Even if they've seen this entire maneuver, we're not a threat to them. They'll just track us back to *Yerazner*."

"At which point they'll ask the Crown Zharang about us or decide not to interfere in the Crest's affairs," Konrad concluded. "This is what my people are doing to our home sector, isn't it?"

"Yes," Kira said bluntly. "In my more-honest moments, I'll admit that being a *friend* of Apollo had its downsides too, but we were a long way short of this level of military threat."

O'Mooney was looking at the data on Kira's screens over the Commodore's shoulders.

"That looks like a lot of firepower to be threatened by anyone," she said.

"Roughly equivalent to Redward's defenses," Kira agreed. "Eight heavy orbital battle stations, a fleet of eighty monitors. But GODCom is the *only* military Guadaloop is allowed. I think their treaty with the Crest allows them four nova ships totaling no more than one hundred kilocubics."

That wasn't even four destroyers, not without being generous with the term. That was four *corvettes*—though, from what Jade Panosyan had said, Guadaloop maintained a light cruiser, a corvette, and two gunships in that cubage.

"And if they break that treaty, the Navy of the Royal Crest seizes any shipping that leaves the system," Konrad said grimly. "Even most of the Syntactic Cluster's systems are functionally immune to invasion and conquest, but you can only do so much if you can't *leave* your star system."

Kira grimaced.

"Like the Apollo-Brisingr Agreement on Nova Lane Security?" she asked him.

"I already said that this was what Brisingr was doing back home," Konrad pointed out. At O'Mooney's confused look, he sighed.

"Kira's homeworld and mine wrapped up an ugly war about three years ago with that beigely named treaty," he told the bodyguard. "In exchange for Brisingr not fucking with Apollo themselves, Apollo turned over security of the sector's trade routes to Brisingr.

"Which means the Kaiserreich's navy has been imposing the *exact* kind of blockages that Guadaloop is afraid of and extorting pretty similar treaties with the systems around our homeworld," he concluded. "To give Apollo's leaders some credit, they snuck a require-ment for a minimum allowance of half a million cubic meters for the system fleets into the Agreement."

Kira arched an eyebrow at him.

"I didn't know that," she admitted.

"It came up in my briefings before I left the Navy for Ghost Explo-rations and, well, the Equilibrium Institute," Konrad said quietly. "*We* knew that it was part of the deal, but it was buried in the appendices, and I think a lot of people only paid attention to the main treaty provisions with regards to Apollo and Brisingr themselves."

"Where did they bury assassinating Apollo's pilots?" Kira asked, letting bitterness tinge her tone.

"I suspect the Shadows kept `that` piece out of the formal documents," he said. "The longer I'm away from home, the less I like what Kaiser Reinhardt has made of my people."

Kira exhaled a long sigh and waved away the edge in the room. After a year, she and Konrad had had most of the fights they could really have over the state of affairs between their homeworlds.

She wasn't sure there was much to choose from between a constitutional oligarchy and a constitutional monarchy, in any case. Being a "Friend of Apollo" prior to the war hadn't been *cheap*, and she wouldn't pretend—now, at least—that her home system hadn't been running their own disguised tributary empire.

The only point in Apollo's favor she could see was that most of the "Friends of Apollo" she'd worked with during the war really had regarded Apollo as an ally, a first among equals, not an external conqueror.

"Like I said, we have a few hours left to get to Guadaloop Actual," she reminded them. "We should be able to find transport for the whole runabout to the Crest from there.

"I won't claim smooth sailing—there's a six-nova-ship Crester carrier group in Guadaloop orbit, after all—but we're on our way and there's not much we can do until we're in the Crest itself."

"Do you need someone to spot you on the controls so you can grab a nap?" Konrad offered.

"No, but we're going straight to a hotel for a nap when we get to the orbital!"

THERE WAS a certain relief to falling asleep in a normal spacer's hotel on a normal orbital. Kira would never—*could* never—complain about the ridiculously comfortable auto-adjusting beds aboard *Yerazner*, but they were almost *too* nice.

The more-standard comfort of a decent spacer hotel was fine and, after a month on Panosyan's beds, a novelty.

Kira's "nap" managed to turn into a full night's sleep, which surprised no one. Not even her.

She woke up to find the wall of the hotel room covered in holographic projections as Konrad Bueller worked through the shipping and ticket listings.

"Finding anything useful?" she asked, sitting up in bed and intentionally letting the blanket fall off her. They weren't in much of a rush, after all.

Her lover was focused on his work, however, and paid more attention to her question than her uncovered flesh.

"If we're willing to give up the runabout, we're not going to have any problem at all," he told her. "There's at least one passenger ship heading to the Crest every day. Most of them aren't big—we're talking stuff about the size of *Yerazner* but rigged up for regular passengers— but there's a regular back-and-forth."

"But the runabout?" Kira said, folding her arms over her chest as she focused on work as well.

"Hauling sixty cubic meters of spaceship is a bit more of an ask," Konrad admitted. "We'd be paying for quite a bit of cargo on one of the liners if we tried to bring all of the troopers' gear, so it could easily end up a wash.

"Or, I guess, it would if we didn't need cabin space either way."

He leaned on his fist, studying the charts.

"It would take less than a day to ship all of us but *not* the shuttle," he said thoughtfully. "Three or four to find a shipping slot large enough for the shuttle—but most of the ships with that kind of space don't take *passengers*."

"So, what are you thinking?" Kira asked. She had her own thoughts, but she was curious what his solution was. *She'd* hauled six nova fighters across a hundred and fifty light-years by taking a maintenance job on the freighter carrying them.

That wouldn't work for four people making a one-system hop.

"It looks like there are a few mixed cargo-passenger ships, for people who want to send supercargo along with the goods," her lover said. "Most of them are running longer distances than to the Crest. We might be able to stick ourselves on one of them that's making a stop in Crest, but that will take more research and we'll need to negotiate something in person."

"The other option is just straight-up hiring a ship," Kira suggested. "There's got to be a few ten-kilocubic tramps that make the regular back-and-forth run, right? They can carry the runabout easily enough and would have space for passengers.

"They wouldn't be on all the fancy boards, though," she continued, gesturing to his set of displays. "We'll find them by wandering the docks and asking bartenders more than anything else."

Konrad snorted.

"That was the obstacle I saw to that option, yeah," he agreed. "So, my dear boss, shall we wake up your bodyguards and go wander the docks and buy some drinks?"

"Sounds like a plan," Kira agreed, though her grin widened as he *finally* turned to look at her and took in her nakedness. "In a few minutes," she purred.

19

GUADALOOP ACTUAL WAS BUILT in the oldest traditions of mid-orbital-elevator stations. Positioned at the geostationary midpoint of the massive cable that stretched from the surface of the planet to an asteroid fortress counterweight, it was a massive ring around an elevator transfer station.

The ring didn't rotate for gravity—modern gravity systems meant that was unnecessary—but the structure allowed the orbital elevator to pass through on its way up to its counterweight. A docking station in the center of the ring handled the cars as they stopped and off-loaded their cargo and passengers.

Only a small portion of the cars that crawled up and down the sixty-thousand-kilometer cable continued on toward the counter-weight—most were civilian traffic that didn't need to go anywhere near the battle station.

The entire outer edge of the ring could theoretically act as a dock for spaceships, but tradition put the docks on the upper side, away from the planet. The biggest ships still had to dock at the outside edge, but the entire upper surface was used as docking stations.

And the half-dozen decks beneath that surface were officially the "docks." A large orbital like Guadaloop Actual would have several million cubic meters of storage in those decks alone, surrounded by spacer hotels and bars and everything else that serviced the transient spacer.

Kira and her people had booked rooms just beneath the main docks area, intentionally putting themselves outside the chaos of those working spaces. Now, however, they headed back into them.

"Ninety-five percent of shipping and ninety-nine percent of passengers are run through the digital exchanges," Konrad reminded the others. "Most of what's left is gray at best, with some of it being completely illegal and concealed on ships that are carrying cargos set up through the exchanges."

"There's basically two places to look if we're looking for something nonstandard in a short time frame," Kira added. "The first is the actual physical exchange office, which is usually right in the middle of the busiest section of the docks. The second is the midrange spacer bars. Cheap bars are where the crews will hang out, but we're looking for a low-end owner-operator.

"They won't be in a cheap bar, but they probably won't be in the *nice* bars, either."

All four of them were in civilian clothing—plain shipsuits with jackets, mostly. In Kira's case, the jacket was real sheepskin leather from her home village over a layer of blaster-resistant webbing. The jacket had *stopped* blaster fire for her once.

Given that it was a gift from her not-quite-estranged brother, it hadn't needed to do that to be special to her. She still appreciated that aspect of it—and owed her life to her brother's paranoia.

"Do we even know what the different bars are going to be?" O'Mooney asked.

"Oh, believe me, they're easy to tell apart," Bertoli told his subordinate with a chuckle. He pointed out a sign that they were walking past. "See that?"

"Yeah."

"So. Small, discreet, sign. Visible from the main thoroughfare, but nothing to draw attention to it, right?"

"Right..."

"So, that's a top-end bar, probably requires membership in a travelers' club or something like that," Bertoli explained. "The top-end owner-operators are in there, as are the captains and senior officers of the big lines. The lines basically subsidize the travelers' clubs."

"Oh." O'Mooney studied the sign for a moment.

"Then if you look over *there*"—Bertoli gestured, and Kira swallowed a snort of amusement when she saw the faux-neon sign that he was gesturing at—"*that* is a strip club, probably with an attached brothel. We're going to call that a *culturally* cheap bar, even though it's going to have the same prices as a higher-end drinking establishment."

The younger commando chuckled.

"So, we're looking for a place with a clearly visible sign that isn't neon and has minimal implied boobs and dicks?" she asked.

"Bingo," Bertoli said. The mercenary scanned the hallway they were in—a triple-wide, double-high corridor that likely encircled the entire station on this level—and then pointed down the hall. "Some of them are also restaurants, like that one." He paused. "What the *hell* is 'Tex-Mex'?"

"Classical Earth cuisine," Konrad said. "So, that's food and midrange bar. Probably a good place to start. Think they do breakfast?"

"They're in the docks," Kira pointed out. "That means you can get any meal you want at any time of day by station clocks. And I haven't met too many people who can screw up toast and eggs over the years.

"Let's go grab food and eavesdrop."

KIRA'S preferred breakfast was buried in a smaller, near-hidden section of the menu that was easy to miss next to the glittering pictures of something called "huevos rancheros."

It wasn't that the restaurant's specialties didn't look *good*; it was that she was generally quite specific in what she'd risk at an unknown eatery. Eggs on toast were hard to screw up—and this restaurant didn't.

The specialties that came out to their table a few minutes after they ordered looked good, she had to admit, but her meal looked exactly as she was expecting—and for the first meal of the day, that was *important*.

Their server was a middle-aged man with a mustache only a few millimeters short of requiring a hair net—probably saved from that ignominious fate by what appeared to be the application of industrial levels of wax.

Kira wasn't sure if she'd spent too long looking at the mustache or what, but she realized the man was returning her regard levelly.

"Thank you," she told him before turning her attention to her food.

The restaurant was decently sized, with eighteen tables of various sizes. There were some empty tables, but most of the place was full and there was a quiet burble of conversation for Kira to try and eavesdrop on.

She had to check to be certain that it was actually breakfast time by station clocks—though that didn't necessarily mean anything for the individual clocks of assorted ships.

"The food is good," Konrad murmured, keeping his voice quiet enough not to interfere with everyone stretching their headware's audio processors to listen in on other conversations. "Coffee is...not."

Kira took one sniff of the cup and chuckled.

"We've been spoiled," she admitted—but she went for the glass of hydroponic orange juice as well. Like the eggs and toast, it was standard the galaxy over. If there was a civilian orbital station in the galaxy that didn't have a hydroponics farm somewhere, with wheat and oranges in layered tanks, and chickens wandering around the floor to make maximum use of space, she'd never been aboard it.

None of the conversations she was overhearing were helpful. Everyone she could hear was a mid-ranking officer on a line freighter, reporting up a corporate hierarchy and flying on a schedule.

And mostly complaining about said hierarchy and schedule.

"I think this place is a bust, but at least the food is good," she told her companions, echoing Konrad's words. "Let's finish up and see what else we can find."

"Head toward the exchange office and buy half a dozen coffees on the way?" Bertoli suggested. "We'll *slosh* by the time we get there, but it'll give us a few chances to listen in."

"Agreed," Kira said. "I'll settle up the bill while you all finish."

The restaurant *could* have used the station network to handle payments, but that often required a subscription fee. A stand-alone payment terminal, like the one they were using, was a fixed non-variable connection to the network and hence cheaper.

But it required Kira to walk up to the host station and give the terminal mental instructions. Their heavily mustached server was leaning against the host lectern and nodded calmly to her.

"Your bill is loaded up," he told her, his voice notably higher-pitched than she'd expected. "Good to go."

That reduced the amount of work *she* had to do to a single back-and-forth mental confirmation with the terminal. It only took a few seconds, and she gave the server a nod.

"Thank you," she said again. "Tell your cook they do a good job. We're not from around here, and we were impressed."

"Lots of visitors come through here," the server told her. "I'll let Cookie know. You're Apollon, Em?"

"Syntactic Cluster, these days," Kira said. "Galaxy moves on, you know."

"That I do," he agreed heavily. "That I do."

20

THE NEXT TWO bars turned out to have espresso machines, at least, which allowed Kira to follow Konrad's example of burying bad coffee under sugar and milk. She'd once been able to drink any coffee black, but Redward truly had spoiled her.

The complex flavored lattes also kept them waiting in the bars for long enough to eavesdrop around. They hadn't heard anything suggesting there were tramp owner-operators on Guadaloop Actual at all—which suggested that either they'd misjudged which bars the tramp crews would hang out in...

Or that Guadaloop Actual *itself* was too expensive for tramp freighters. There were other orbitals for cargo transfer, after all. Guadaloop Actual was just the one attached to the orbital elevator, which made it the most efficient...and hence the most expensive to dock at.

Still, her worst-case scenario was that the exchange office's staff would be able to tell her where to look to find captains looking for a quick charter. Most likely, the office would be able to help them set up exactly the type of booking they needed.

It was just almost certainly going to take longer than Kira liked.

"Another bar up ahead," Bertoli said. "We're still a good ten minutes' walk from the exchange office, unless we want to find the transit system?"

"Walking is good for us," Kira replied. "I don't even want to *think* about how many calories are in those damn lattes."

She wasn't one to count calories or watch her diet or weight—she spent enough time exercising one way or another to not have to worry about it—but multiple flavored lattes sounded worrisome even to her.

"Let's check out that ba—"

A freight truck hit her in the middle of her back, smashing her forward and sending her sprawling onto the ground. The entire dispersal net buried underneath the leather of her jacket flashed to hot, the heat almost scalding even through her shipsuit.

"Down, *down!*" Bertoli snapped.

Kira was still blinking blearily when O'Mooney grabbed her and started pulling her across the metal floor. A second blaster bolt hammered into the floor where she'd been lying—and she heard the distinct sharp buzzing of a military-grade stunner as Bertoli returned fire.

"I'm fine," she finally managed to gasp to O'Mooney. "Help me up."

The grip shifted, helping lever Kira to her feet—and into the doorway of the bar they'd been headed toward. O'Mooney had her own stunner out. It was an ugly-looking heavy pistol shape, with a two-part folding stock that locked onto the wielder's forearm to control recoil.

"I'm fine," Kira repeated. "*Go.*"

More blaster fire echoed in the hallway, and Kira hoped that at least *some* of it was from Guadaloop security forces. Her people were a long way from Redward, and she hadn't spent the time and money to pick up new weapons licenses for Guadaloop Actual.

Their stunners were pushing the limit of what was authorized for civilian use aboard the station, but they weren't carrying blasters at all. From the growing bruise and likely heat rash on Kira's back, someone else *was*.

"Em?" a nervous looking young woman hailed her. It took her a moment to realize the local was the bartender slash barista serving the bar. "You okay?"

"I've been shot," Kira said drily. More blaster fire echoed outside. "But I'm fine."

"I called station security, but the response time is six minutes," the bartender said grimly. "I'm...guessing none of those blasters are yours?"

A scream outside cut off with distinct finality, and Kira drew her own stunner.

"None of them," she said calmly, locking the weapon onto her wrist. "Keep your head down, Em. Sorry to have brought this to your bar."

"Ahem," someone coughed, and Kira looked over to see a scrawny-looking man with a ragged white beard watching her. Like her, he wore a jacket over a shipsuit. Unlike hers, the jacket was a relatively standard plastic faux-denim material—and had clearly seen a lot of heavy wear over the years.

"I *like* this bar," the bearded man noted, producing the blaster version of her arm-locking stunner and snapping it into place. "Ramirez, Martinez, on me."

Two more people emerged from the booth behind the stranger: a man and woman, both clearly in their late thirties. All three of the strangers were dark-skinned, with similar angular features that suggested some familial relationship.

And all three were clearly armed with personal blasters.

"My name is Tomas Zamorano," the ragged beard told her. "Would you like some help, Em?"

"My people have stunners," Kira said. "I'd *love* any help you can give."

"Thought so," Zamorano replied. "*Baile Fantasma*—let's go!"

With a hopeful smile, Kira followed the three spacers out the bar door.

THE THOROUGHFARE HAD EMPTIED in the moments Kira had been in the bar. There were blast marks scattered across the walls, and a mobile repair pod had ground to a halt in the middle of the corridor. The pod's driver was on the ground, very clearly dead, and both Konrad and Bertoli were hiding behind the vehicle.

O'Mooney was tucked into the doorway of a convenience store a few meters from the bar. She was slumped to the floor, curled around a wound of some kind but still holding her stunner level and firing the occasional blast along the corridor.

The *hiss-crack* of multiple blasters told Kira their attackers hadn't gone anywhere—and drew her attention to them. There was no way in *hell* the black-cloaked figures with the blaster carbines had gone unnoticed prior to opening fire—but she recognized them.

The outfits were a hologram, an unidentifiable but standard image created to conceal the identity of the Kaiser's assassins. What the hell were Brisingr Shadows doing in Guadaloop?!

She opened fire, her stunner jerking back against her hand with recoil as she shot at the lead figure. Her emergence took them just enough by surprise that she managed to land the charge. The Shadow stumbled backward, whatever defensive equipment they had insufficient to negate the full impact.

The other two Shadows were readjusting their fire already—but Zamorano and his crew had also been identifying the threat. Blaster fire cut through the Shadows like a sword of deadly plasma. One of them went down instantly—and more stunner fire from Kira's companions caught the same Shadow she'd shot.

She could hear running footsteps in the distance—hopefully station security—as she slid in behind the wrecked pod with her boyfriend and bodyguard.

There was another crackle of blaster fire from Zamorano's people, and then silence fell in the corridor.

"Clear," a voice declared.

"Clear," Zamorano replied. "Check on the wounded woman, Martinez."

"On it," the young woman agreed.

Kira gestured for Konrad and Bertoli to follow her as *she* headed for

O'Mooney. The redheaded mercenary looked up at the four people converging on her with a pained smile.

"I'm not fine," she whispered. "I think I'll live, but…"

"We'll get you a doctor," Kira promised. "Let me see."

"I have a medkit," Martinez told them, the spacer woman producing the case from inside her coat. "Should be able to patch you up until medical gets here."

O'Mooney nodded, winced and lifted her arm from where she was covering the blast wound. It looked bad—a direct hit had burned through her concealed dispersal vest and shipsuit alike. Her skin was just *gone* across a six-centimeter chunk of her stomach.

"This will hurt," Martinez warned—and had a plasti-skin spray going before O'Mooney could say a word. "Just covering muscle," she continued after the mercenary had finished swearing. "Guts weren't burned through; your armor did its job. Not as well as we'd *like*, of course, but it did its job.

"Station security will get you to a doc. You'll be fine."

"Thank you," Kira told the woman. "And your…boss?"

"Boss," Martinez confirmed. "Third cousin twice removed, something like that? Really just my boss."

"Thank you, Ercilia," Zamorano said, materializing out of nowhere. "Josue is talking to the security; I wanted to let you deal with your woman. She okay?"

"She needs a doctor," Kira replied. "Which means I need to talk to security anyway."

"That's how it goes," he agreed calmly. "Lieutenant Sanna is decent folk; she'll take statements while you rush the Em to medical. I'm going to be the one in real trouble, anyway."

"They came after me," Kira argued.

"Yes, but I killed two people and you didn't," Tomas Zamorano said calmly. "You're going to make that up to me, aren't you, Em…"

"Riker," Kira told him, carefully using the fake name she'd used in the past. "Kira Riker. And yes, I owe you, Em Zamorano."

"It's *Captain* Zamorano," he told her with a chuckle. "And good. I like people who recognize their debts."

21

LIEUTENANT SANNA WAS AN OLDER Black woman with strange patterns of paler skin visible across her face and hands. Dressed in pale blue armor to stand out in crowds, she was giving direction to the rest of the Guadaloop Actual security people when Kira stepped up to her.

"You have a wounded woman, I understand?" Sanna asked sharply.

"I do," Kira said. "We need medical attention."

"A rescue pod is on the way; they'll be here in two minutes," the Lieutenant replied. "Will she be okay that long?"

"Someone got a medkit to her; I think so."

"All right. Your name?"

"Kira Riker," Kira replied.

"All right," Sanna repeated. "Walk with me, Em Riker."

The blue-armored vitiligoed woman led the way over to where the Shadows had fallen. Their holograms were down now, revealing an ordinary-looking pair of spacers in gray shipsuits.

"Any idea who these people were?" Sanna asked.

"I saw the holograms they were wearing," Kira said grimly. "I'm from Apollo, Lieutenant. I know Shadows when I see them."

There was a long pause.

"Assume I *don't*, Em Riker," the security officer finally told her. "Because I don't have a damn clue what you're talking about."

"Brisingr Shadows," Konrad interrupted, the big engineer stepping up to Kira's right hand. "The elite assassins of the Kaiser's covert operations departments." He shrugged. "Supposedly, anyway. In practice, my understanding is that they're *any* Brisingr espionage agent given a kill order."

"They use the holograms for anonymity."

"I see," Sanna said slowly. "We'll get real IDs on these two, then," she concluded with a gesture. "The blasters are unregistered and unlicensed, which would be enough to put them behind bars for a bit if they were still breathing.

"As it is, well." She sighed. "Captain Zamorano is claiming that both kill shots were him and in self-defense. I'll be reviewing the footage, but I understand his logic. What *happened*, Em Riker?"

"They shot me in the back," Kira said quietly. "My jacket has dispersal matrix and armor layers, so I lived. Then they...kept shooting."

"Probably saw the thermal bloom from the dispersal net on optics and realized you were still alive," Sanna noted. "GAS does not approve of assassination attempts, Em Riker, though I'd love to know *why* they'd have taken a shot at you."

Kira could guess. If she'd been IDed, there was still a *significant* bounty for turning her body—or even a recording of her death—in to a Brisingr embassy. That was almost certainly accompanied by an active kill order in Brisingr covert ops.

And it made sense there'd be Brisingr spy cells operating near the Crest. She hadn't anticipated that.

"I don't know, Lieutenant," she lied to Sanna as the white-painted emergency pod hurtled to a stop near them. Two white-uniformed medics were checking on O'Mooney within seconds, and Kira sighed in relief.

"I'm going to *hope* that whatever you're not telling me means that I won't be seeing further incidents on my station," Sanna said coldly. "I do not like other people's trouble coming to my station, Em Riker."

"I don't like being in trouble anywhere, Lieutenant," Kira replied.

"Not sure if they're after me or Konrad over there." She gestured to her lover, currently *also* going by Riker. "He's *from* Brisingr."

If they did have any grudge against Konrad, she was glad the Shadows had shot her. She knew he was wearing an armor vest, but it was more in line with what O'Mooney was wearing—and O'Mooney was being loaded into an ambulance.

"I'll take a formal statement while we walk to the clinic," Sanna told her, producing an official-looking recorder. "From all three of you," she noted, gesturing at Konrad and Bertoli.

"What about Zamorano?" Kira asked, looking around for the Captain.

"I know where to find Zamorano," Sanna said calmly. "*Baile Fantasma* is under lockdown until I'm satisfied that we don't need to lay charges. He's not going anywhere without his ship."

TREATMENT IN A CLINIC on the primary orbital station of a planet well over a hundred light-years from your current residence and health insurance was neither free nor cheap. Kira had yet to meet any clinic that *wouldn't* treat most injuries first and sort out payment afterward—but she also recognized the blatant relief from the human administrator when she asked how to pay.

That worthy was leaving, looking reassured—not least by the material amount of crests Kira had transferred to the clinic at his request—when Sanna stepped back into the waiting room.

"Well, we've IDed the pair of bodies cooling in my morgue," she told Kira. "I believe your spiel about Brisingr Shadows, sadly, but they're not Brisingr. They're local—born on Actual, in fact. No criminal record, nothing.

"My guess is that they were local assets recruited by Brisingr to watch our shipping," the security officer continued. "But that will take a lot more investigation. Not least since the one your people stunned never arrived at our lockup."

"What happened?" Kira asked.

"Paperwork mix-up; they were transferred to the surface," Sanna said crisply. "Where they appear to have disappeared."

"Ah." Somehow, Kira wasn't surprised that whatever cell of Brisingr's far-flung intelligence operations she'd run into had a way to get their people free. "That's unfortunate."

"Yes. It does support your theory, though," the Lieutenant noted. "I have nothing on your people, Em Riker, if you're worried. You were attacked, responded with an entirely rational level of force and, thankfully, escaped mostly unharmed."

"I have words for Captain Zamorano and his hero complex," she said, "but even there, I expect the footage to be open-and-shut. I need to go through the process because there *are* two bodies in my morgue, but everything I've seen suggests they deserve to be there."

"I'm sorry for the headache we're giving you," Kira murmured. She'd taken off her jacket and was surveying the damage to the back. "Does your station have any leatherworkers?"

"Not subtle, Em Riker," Sanna replied. "I'm not certain about the leatherworkers—probably not any who can work with plasma-dispersal nets and particulate armor. I get the impression that's a specialized combination."

"Fair," Kira said with a chuckle. She'd managed to get the jacket fixed after the first time she'd been shot wearing it, but this time, she wasn't sure she had the resources. "I'll see what I can find."

A white-uniformed nurse stepped into the room.

"Are you the folks waiting on Em O'Mooney?" he asked.

"They are," Sanna told the nurse, gesturing to Kira and her companions. "I'm done here, I think. Good luck, Em Riker—but I hope you forgive me when I say I hope you find your way off my station sooner rather than later!"

Kira turned her attention to the nurse.

"Yeah, we're waiting on Aleifr O'Mooney," she confirmed. "How is she?"

"She's out of reconstruction and in recovery," the nurse told them. "Doctor says she'll be fine. Between the armor she was wearing and the near-immediate plasti-skin application, there was no serious damage to her intestines.

"We had to rebuild the abdominal muscle wall and she won't be able to engage in heavy activity for at least six weeks, but she'll be fine," the nurse concluded. "She's asleep now; doctor wants to keep her unconscious for at least eight hours and then in the clinic overnight for observation."

"I'm not arguing with medical professionals," Kira said. "Thank you."

22

LEAVING the hotel the next morning, Kira found Bertoli attached to her by a far shorter metaphorical leash than normal. Even *Konrad* was hovering, and her boyfriend generally knew better.

"Clinic, then Captain Zamorano's ship," she told them. "We probably *don't* need to be a six-legged creature for the trip."

"Someone *shot you* yesterday, Com—Riker," Bertoli told her, cutting off his use of her rank before he really shoved his foot in it. "My job is to keep that from happening."

"And your jacket is a write-off," Kira's lover added, glancing around the thoroughfare corridor as he spoke. "Get me the tools and I can fix the armor layers, but even if I get the tools and materials, I have no idea how to patch leather."

"I'm still wearing armor," she pointed out to the two of them. "And I'm not exactly comfortable using either of you as a layer of ablative *meat*. So, some space, please."

Konrad was already moving back a step, but Bertoli leveled his most mulish gaze on her as they continued.

"I'm *also* armored," he reminded her. "And, bluntly, *ablative meat* is part of my job description. I'm supposed to keep you safe—if I come back and you don't, Milani *will* kill me."

Kira's ground-troop commander did not glory in the title of "the terrifying fucker in the dragon armor" without reason, she knew. On the other hand, she was *reasonably* sure they wouldn't shoot a subordinate for failure.

Reasonably.

"Bodyguarding is fine," Kira told Bertoli. "Being more intimate with me than my clothes or my lover, that's a bit much!"

Konrad didn't even bother to conceal his chuckle at that. They were currently claiming to be *married*, both using the false surname Riker, though she suspected they were a long way from making that a reality.

Neither of them had ever been married, and at their age, it didn't seem like something to rush into.

That was apparently the right tack to take, and Konrad's chuckle probably helped. Bertoli nodded, his face still set in a stubborn cast, and stepped back a single pace. He was still closer than he'd been the previous day, but she couldn't argue with that.

He was, after all, correct. She had been shot...and she was more than a bit surprised by how little that bothered her. The first time she'd been shot, she'd followed it up by the entire chaotic mess of evacuating every surviving member of her former nova combat group from Apollo.

She'd assumed her blaséness about the shooting had been pure adrenaline. This time, though, she had no such excuse for brushing off that someone had nearly killed her. She was used to that in space combat, but she could count on her fingers the number of times she'd been shot at without a nova fighter around her.

"Come on," she told her companions. "Let's go collect O'Mooney and then see about getting on with the job."

O'MOONEY WAS UP, dressed and walking around her room in the clinic when they arrived. A young Black man in scrubs was asking her questions and getting her to go through careful motions, looking up as Kira and her companions reached the door.

"Good morning," he greeted them. "I'm Dr. Tygan. I took over Em O'Mooney's care this morning."

"How are you feeling, Aleifr?" Kira asked. "Not every day you get shot in the gut."

"Stiff and I don't want to do push-ups," O'Mooney replied. "Otherwise decent. They do good work here."

"We try," Tygan said cheerfully. "The wrap we've put over your stomach should stay in place for at least the next forty-eight hours. After that, you can take it off to shower, but we recommend putting it back afterward for at least another week."

He looked the group over, clearly taking in the shipsuits all of them wore.

"I'm guessing I can't get you to come back for a checkup in nine days?" he asked.

"We're shipping out as fast as we can find transport, Doctor," Kira told him. "I'll make sure we find a doctor for Em O'Mooney wherever we are in nine days, though," she promised.

"And you'll *go* to the doctor we find, right, Aleifr?" Bertoli said firmly to his subordinate.

"I got shot," O'Mooney said brightly. "Believe me, I'm going to be good about the doctors!"

"That's a good plan," Tygan told her. "Be careful with abdominal movements of any kind until you've had that check-in. We'll download all of your treatment details to your headware."

"Thanks, Doctor."

The Guadaloop doctor studied O'Mooney's posture for a moment, then gestured for her to sit on the bed as he turned to look at Kira.

"She's had a full regen pass over her abdominal muscles," he told them. "Dr. Lionel also did some regen work on the intestine and stomach, just to be sure, but there was minimal burning there.

"Currently, though, all of that is being held in with plasti-skin. Between that and the wrap, her skin will naturally regrow properly and quickly, but we're still talking days, not hours," he warned. "The lighter she can take it for at least the next two weeks, the better."

"We can manage light duty for Em O'Mooney for at least that,"

Kira said with a glance at Bertoli. Most of what they were doing right now was *light duty*, after all. No heavy lifting or anything like that.

"Good." Tygan sighed. "She's as fine as anyone who took a blaster bolt to the guts yesterday can be. Her armor clearly served its purpose, though; as you can imagine, we didn't exactly salvage it intact."

"That's expected," Bertoli rumbled. "I have a spare vest for her, though I'd *hoped* we wouldn't need it."

"That's the thing with armor," Kira noted. "You rarely even expect to use it—and you always *hope* not to."

"I wouldn't know," Dr. Tygan replied. "She's clear to be discharged. There'll be a long list of things she's to do and avoid doing, but she'll have that in her headware. I recommend against walking for more than ten minutes," he reminded O'Mooney over his shoulder.

"For the next forty-eight hours, at least."

"We can make sure of that," Kira promised. "Though that means I'll need to sort out whatever this station has for taxis."

"Talk to the artificial stupid at reception," Tygan told her. "It can summon a pod for you."

THE REASON KIRA hadn't noticed the transit pods, it turned out, was because they were almost completely silent—and ran on the *ceilings* of the triple-high main thoroughfares. Using antigravity coils, the pod dropped to the ground to pick them up outside the clinic.

"Destination?" a chirpy artificial stupid asked. This one didn't have a holographic representation, since its designers had probably assumed the pod itself was enough of a "body" for the AS.

"*Baile Fantasma*, please," Kira instructed it.

There was a momentary pause—probably as much for effect as anything else, the AS should have been able to identify the dock Zamorano's ship was at instantly—and then the cylindrical pod smoothly rose back to the ceiling and shot away.

"Which one's that?" O'Mooney asked.

"The three strangers who helped us out yesterday have a ship," Kira told the trooper. "I believe Zamorano is the owner-operator, and security had them at least temporarily locked down. I'm hoping they're the right kind of hauler for our needs."

She figured it was fifty-fifty, but she owed Zamorano for helping them and was happy to repay that by overpaying for the transport she needed.

"*Baile Fantasma* is a small mid-distance freighter," Konrad noted, his tone absent in the manner of someone mostly in their headware. "Sixteen thousand cubics… Wait, the fuck?"

"Konrad?" Kira asked.

"Tau Ceti–built," her lover told her. "That ship is fourteen hundred light-years from the yard that built her. Don't get me wrong, she's *old*, but I don't expect to see even *old* SolFed ships out this far."

"Well, isn't that fascinating?" Kira murmured. "Now I'm more curious about Captain Zamorano than I already was. On the other hand…" She shrugged. "We have our own secrets, people. Unless Zamorano turns out to be an Institute operative, I don't think we need to know his."

Further conversation was interrupted by their arrival at the dock. The ceiling-mounted taxi pods were *fast*—though Kira noted that they had not yet descended to the floor and had a moment of concern.

"Payment, please," the AS chirped, and she realized *why* they were still stuck on the ceiling. That was one way to make sure no one tried to stiff the computerized taxi—with the doors locked and a seven-meter drop to the gravity plates, refusing to pay was *not* an option.

JOSUE RAMIREZ WAS STANDING NEXT to the airlock door leading to the ship, his casual slump masking his rapidly tracking eyes and the slight tension to his muscles.

Kira hadn't really had the time to study their helpers yesterday, but the concealed readiness of the dark-skinned man guarding the ship added to her impression of something hidden. *Baile Fantasma* was more than she appeared to be at first glance.

She just didn't think their secrets were going to matter to her.

"Ah, Em Riker," Ramirez greeted her, unfolding from his slump.

"I'll ping the Captain and let 'im know you're here." He looked over Kira's companions. "I hope the doctors took good care of you, Em," he told O'Mooney, giving the younger mercenary the slightest of bows.

O'Mooney wasn't Kira's type, but she recognized that the trooper was attractive as her own gender went. So, it seemed, did Josue Ramirez.

"They do good work here," O'Mooney replied with a nod that was just a touch too lingering.

Kira kept her chuckle silent. Neither of the pair were the *kids* she wanted to label them—O'Mooney was thirty-two and Kira would eyeball Ramirez around the same age—and Kira figured they knew *exactly* what they were doing.

"Captain says he's pleased to hear from you and asks if you'd like to join him aboard for coffee," Ramirez said after a moment of calm silence.

"We'd be delighted," Kira said. "I want to talk to him about that debt I owe him…and maybe some work."

23

LIKE EVERY FREIGHTER Kira had served on, *Baile Fantasma* was cramped in her living quarters. The mess, at least, was a decent size—but the corridors that Ramirez led them through to get there were barely two meters high.

Kira, who was petite by any standard, had no problem with the corridors. Konrad and Bertoli both seemed a bit perturbed by the low ceilings, but everyone was used to starships. It would be fine.

The mess was set up more like a large family kitchen than the traditional cafeteria style. One wall held two stoves and assorted other preparation spaces, and three decently sized tables with chairs took up the rest of the space.

While there were only a dozen chairs in the space, Kira could see it easily being increased to eighteen without much difficulty. Adding another table could get them to twenty-four, though it would be a bit cramped at that point.

She couldn't see a sixteen-kilocubic freighter needing twenty-four crew—and neither, it seemed, could Captain Zamorano.

"I promised coffee," that worthy said with a chuckle, laying out small cups on the counter by the kitchen. "Spanish-style espresso. If you haven't had it, it'll be a treat."

"I'm always willing to try new things when it comes to coffee," Kira said. The cups were definitely sized for just espresso with no fixings—and after the previous day, she wasn't sure she wanted to see a latte again for a while.

Each of her companions accepted a tiny cup, as did Ramirez.

Ramirez shot back the contents of the cup in one swallow, passing the empty back to Zamorano.

"I need to get back to watching the lock," he said. "Have a good meeting, folks."

Kira took a careful sip of the espresso, then followed Ramirez's example. There just wasn't enough of the rich liquid for sipping.

"That's different," Konrad said. "I like it."

"Old family tradition," Zamorano told them. "Slight differences in pressure and temperature from most espresso machines; creates a richer brew."

"Thank you for sharing," Kira said. "I appreciate it."

"Always. You are on my ship; I am your host. Can I get you anything more?"

"More espresso?" Konrad asked hopefully, and Zamorano chuckled.

"I'll start another round," he agreed. "It will take a few moments."

There turned out to be a specialty machine with six spouts tucked into a cupboard in the kitchen. It folded out and Zamorano filled it with water, carefully turning off one of the spouts, and then set it to brewing with several spoonfuls of coffee.

"So, Em Riker, what do you want with the humble captain of a humble ship?" he asked.

"You saved my people's lives, Captain," she told him. "I'd like to repay that, if I can. I'm also here looking for transport and wondering if you can help."

"Hence trawling your way through the bars and coffee shops of the dock district," the captain observed. He saluted her with the espresso cup he was about to fill. "I did some poking after we met, Em Riker. You're walking a careful line between avoiding attention and finding what you're looking for.

"And we've already seen at least part of the reason demonstrated."

"So we have," Kira agreed. "Lieutenant Sanna said you'd be released from lockdown quickly enough?"

"It's a formality and both she and I know it," Zamorano told her. He brought a tray of espresso cups over to one of the tables, gesturing for everyone to sit. "I give it another day at most. It was pretty open-and-shut. You were there."

"I was, and I appreciate your intervention," she replied. His casualness about having killed two people, though, didn't fit his intended image of a "humble captain of a humble ship." "We all do. So…I know how you can help *me*, Captain, but I'm wondering how I can help you?"

"I can think of a few ways," *Baile Fantasma*'s Captain said. "But my helping you may well incur additional favors, so why don't you tell me what *you* want and I'll assess if I should be upping my favor?"

Kira swallowed the second espresso, putting the tiny cup down and leaning back in the simple wooden chair, studying the man across the table from her. Like the two subordinates she had met, Zamorano was dark-skinned and sharp-featured. He had a ragged mostly-white beard and short-cropped, likely dyed, pure black hair, and his brown eyes danced with amusement at her.

He was utterly relaxed, as if the result of this conversation was utterly meaningless to him—which was either a fantastic negotiating trick or a sign that he was *not* a merchant captain.

Or both.

"I need transport for the four of us and a sixty-cubic-meter runabout shuttle," she told him. "To the Crest, with all paperwork registered, clean, unquestionable. We want to avoid any kind of attention, official or otherwise."

"And you want to do so quickly; otherwise, you'd have talked to the transport broker," Zamorano observed. "They could book that for you, but you'd be looking at two, maybe three weeks. There aren't a lot of slots for someone hauling both a shuttle and passengers."

"Exactly."

He smiled.

"I can do that," he told them. "Let's say…standard cubage and passenger rates per nova, plus fifty percent. It's an awkward trip, hitting the Crest from here, and I might not be able to fill the rest of the cargo.

"We need to make it look good if you want to avoid those questions."

That was pricey...but not unreasonable for the speed and oddity of her request. In hindsight, Kira should have just planned to dump the runabout—but she *couldn't* do that with the shuttle full of armor and guns.

"That's fine," she told him.

"But that's not my favor," Zamorano said with a smile. "I'll do that and I'll fill the hold as best as I can. I'll make a profit on that and I will be easily able to find work to get me *out* of the Crest.

"But even that is a favor to you, not me," he continued. "So."

"So." Kira held his gaze levelly. Her companions were silent around her, though she drew support from Konrad's presence—not least out of the certainty that if he *did* disagree with what she was doing, he'd have pinged her with a headware message by now.

"What do you want, Captain Zamorano?" she asked.

"Three things," he told her. "The same thing, really, but to three people. I need letters of introduction."

That was...dangerous. Kira *Riker* didn't know anybody she could write useful letters to.

"*He knows.*" Konrad's warning was unnecessary, but Kira appreciated it anyway and squeezed her lover's thigh under the table.

"To whom?" she asked softly.

"Sonia Stewart. Jade Panosyan. Henry Killinger."

The three names hung in the air like the Sword of Damocles. Konrad was right.

The Queen of Redward.

The Crown Zharang of the Royal Crest.

And...a dead Apollo nova combat group Commander?

"Henry Killinger is *dead*," Kira pointed out rather than engaging with the fact that the person she was pretending to be wouldn't know the other two.

"Henry Killinger would be very pleased to know you think that, Kira Demirci," Zamorano said quietly. "He's currently buried up to his neck in about eleven kinds of treason and isn't talking to strangers.

"I *really* need him to talk to me. I also would very much like to have a conversation with Jade Panosyan." He waved a hand in the air. "Sonia Stewart is more of an opportunity than anything else. I don't think I'm going to have many encounters with people close to her inner circle this far away."

"How long did it take you to work out who I am?" Kira asked softly.

"I haven't trusted the name someone gave me in over forty years," Zamorano said bluntly. "You should have done more to adjust your face, Em Demirci. My headware flagged you the moment you ducked into the bar. That death mark drew our attention."

The mess was silent.

"You're no merchant captain," Konrad finally said as Kira was still thinking. "And this ship...What the *fuck* is SolFed Intelligence doing out here?"

"Oh, *well* done."

The silence continued for a few more seconds, then Zamorano chuckled loudly.

"I am not fully up to date with events in the Syntactic Cluster," he noted. "I was aware that *K79-L* had fallen into your hands, Em Demirci. I was not aware that Em Bueller had fallen into your hands with her. A good choice, it seems.

"I was aware of John Estanza's death. You have my sympathies." He shook his head.

"And yes, Em Bueller is correct. I, this ship and every member of her crew are operatives of the Solar Federation's Interstellar Intelligence Service. The records on *Baile Fantasma* are correct, if you're wondering. She is two hundred and eighty-six years old."

The spy snorted.

"I'm a bit younger than she is, but I've come just about as far," he told them. "I'm Earthborn, which makes being out here an...experience, let me tell you. But..."

He shrugged.

"SolFed tries to keep an eye on everything everywhere," he noted.

"With a three-thousand-light-year sphere of generally accepted *civilized* space and an unknown number of colonies beyond that sphere, believe me when I tell you the effort is futile.

"This ship represents a significant percentage of IIS's assets in this region."

"And you don't mean the Crest Sector," Kira murmured.

"No," he agreed. "This IIS operation region is four degrees of the Rim. A little over one percent of a region of millions of cubic light-years. Apollo and Brisingr fall into the region. As does the Syntactic Cluster. We have... Let's just go with 'far too few' assets to even maintain intelligence updates across the Rim."

"Why are you telling us this?" Konrad challenged.

"Because you guessed," Zamorano said with a chuckle. "And because you, Kira Demirci, *can* give me documents that will get me connections to those three people. I don't think anyone else in the galaxy could get me all three—and I've been trying to find a way to connect to Killinger for a while."

"But he's *dead*," Kira reiterated.

"He faked his death," Zamorano told her. "Easy enough when a hostile intelligence service is doing their damnedest to kill every Apollo ace who isn't directly related to a member of the Council of Principals. After faking his death, he went underground.

"I have reason to believe he is gathering a private fleet of warships as the various systems concede to Brisingr's demands and officially decommission their nova fleets.

"But since he's officially dead, he is being utterly paranoid about who he makes contact with. You don't find Henry Killinger. His people find *you*."

"And you think he'll listen to a letter from me?" Kira asked. She'd flown with Colonel Henry Killinger. He'd been a close friend of Colonel Jay Moranis, *her* nova group's commander and mentor.

"I think he owes you his life at least twice over," Zamorano noted. "I think that might buy us a conversation he and I need to have." He shrugged. "With both Stewart and Panosyan, I *know* a letter from you will open a door, but with Killinger, it's only a chance—and at that, it's still worth getting you into the Crest to me.

"So. I know who you are and can guess why you need to be in the Crest without anyone knowing. You now know who I am and what I want. We put money on it, so no one else asks questions, but it's really down to whether you're willing to write those letters or not."

"You already saved my life," Kira pointed out. "And if I can't trust SolFed Intelligence to get me into a system without drawing attention, a whole bunch of urban legends and case studies I've read are wrong.

"So, let's do it."

24

BAILE FANTASMA WAS SADLY LACKING in gold-plated butler robots or any other outright magical tricks that legend might have expected from a ship built in the Solar Federation.

Of course, the general rule was that for every ten light-years a world was from Earth, tech was a year and a half behind on average. Economic development often lagged even further, but the general rule said that a ship built today in Guadaloop was the equivalent of a ship built two hundred–plus years ago in Tau Ceti.

And *Fantasma* was almost *three* hundred years old. The ship had probably been heavily updated in hidden sections, but Kira and her people were genteelly restricted to the passenger sections and the cargo compartment she was parking their shuttle in.

"You down and locked, Basketball?" Martinez's voice asked in her head the *exact* moment she'd shut down the engines.

"I am," Kira confirmed. "Is there a safe path out?"

"Highlighted on the deck in lights," the freighter officer told her. "Keep to the path, Basketball. I've got a couple standard TMUs floating into that cargo compartment."

"Got it, *Baile Fantasma*," she said. "Watching the lights."

A Ten Meter Unit—or Ten Meter Equivalent Unit sometimes—was

the heir to the standardized cargo containers of old Earth. Five meters high, five meters wide, and ten meters long, every cargo ship in the universe was built to handle them.

Baile Fantasma had four cargo holds, cavernous spaces attached to the "bottom" of the ship, that were ten meters high, ten meters wide, and twenty long—officially, though any hold always had a few extra centimeters for maneuvering. Hold One now had Kira's runabout parked at the far end, but that still left enough space for Martinez to slide multiple stacks of cargo containers into the hold.

There was nothing so luxurious as air or even *gravity* in the container hold, but Kira's shipsuit was capable of handling the lack of both of those. The designated path was lit up in bright yellow on the floor, leading from her shuttle's exit ramp to an airlock that presumably provided access to the habitable portion of the ship.

Still, Kira paused on the path to watch the containers come in. Each had its own small set of Harrington coils, controlled by remote from the cargo handler's office, and they came in one at a time.

The first TMU was visible in the light from the planet behind it at the open entrance to the hold. Kira watched as it slowly rotated in place to align with the opening and then slid forward. There were literally *centimeters* to spare on three sides of the container as it slid broadside toward Kira.

It rapidly came to a complete halt, five meters from the back wall and barely a meter from Kira's shuttle, and then silently locked down into its slot. The bottom half of Kira's view of the hold was now blocked by it, but she could see another container aligning itself with the entrance.

Her shuttle was taking the space of two of the containers—more for safety than anything else—but Hold One would still take six two-hundred-and-fifty-cubic-meter cargo containers, stacked in three rows, each two TMUs deep. The other three holds would take eight, presuming Zamorano had acquired enough cargo to fill them.

The ship would have a fifth hold somewhere that was designed for less-standardized cargo. That one would be pressurized and gravitized by default and would often be used as a gymnasium if it was only half-full.

Still, Kira's math said that *Baile Fantasma* only had nine to ten kilo-cubics of cargo space in an eighteen-kilocubic hull. Most freighter designers aimed for a seventy-five percent ratio of cargo space to overall hull space, which suggested the IIS ship had probably been designed around four-to-five kilocubics of machinery and living space.

Which left *another* four kilocubics, give or take, of volume that she couldn't account for. Zamorano almost certainly had schematics saying they were taken up by absolutely innocuous things.

Kira, on the other hand, knew damn well who she was flying with.

"SO, anything about this ship screaming 'love me, love me' to the engineer?" Kira asked Konrad as she dropped onto the bed in their guest quarters.

"The fact it's still flying after two hundred and eighty-six years, without a single system even suggesting that it's overdue for maintenance or otherwise rusty?" her boyfriend asked. "Also, the mattress is already scanning your back and calculating the optimal level of elasticity for you."

Kira glanced down at the normal-looking bed.

"You're kidding, right?" she asked. Self-adjusting beds were common enough, but they usually took a few minutes after you lay down to find the right balance.

"Nope." Konrad pointed to a small dot above the bed. "Scanner is right there. It's scanning us both whenever we're on the bed, sitting or lying down, and constantly adjusting."

"That's not three hundred years old," Kira said.

"Forty or so, I'd guess, at most," he agreed. "Probably self-maintaining to a large degree, like most of the ship. There's a reason there's only three people aboard—and space for us."

She paused thoughtfully.

"I...honestly thought we just hadn't met the rest of the crew," she admitted. "Zamorano has been sufficiently closed with us, in some ways I could buy him hiding us away."

"*Maybe*," Konrad said. "But I'd also buy this ship being mostly self-maintaining. There's a lot of small stuff that has artificial stupids in it that you wouldn't expect. I suspect there's a fleet of self-repair drones that *are* being kept out of our line of sight, because no tramp merchant ship out here would have them.

"But let's be honest: *most* sub-twenty-kilocubic ships can be *flown* by three. Or one. It's the maintenance that becomes a problem, if you don't have repair drones or something similar."

"You think the ship is smarter than we expect?" Kira asked.

"I think this ship is more *anything* than you expect," he replied. "I'm not going to go poking and see if I can chat with the computers; let's put it that way. I'm not sure I'd like what I found."

The implications of that were...scary. Rumor had it that SolFed had small-scale true AI, but that rumor had been present for a long time and Kira had never heard of anyone having *proof*. Complex artificial stupids that could fake sapience for extended time periods? There were even a few of those in the Rim.

Not many, though. Not least because faking sapience beyond what was needed for customer service wasn't actually *useful* in most contexts. True AI would, in theory, be enough more flexible to add value on its own—but the few experiments she'd heard of in the Fringe had been closer to asteroid-fortress-sized than ship-computer-sized.

"Step carefully, my love," Konrad said after a moment. "Today, Captain Zamorano is a useful ally, but his *sole* job is information-gathering for the Solar Federation. I imagine he has strict limits on what he is allowed to do—and those limits could easily end up with us getting cut adrift at a very awkward moment."

25

"WOULD you like to join me on the bridge, Em Demirci?"

Captain Zamorano's question interrupted Kira's breakfast on the second—and last—day of their short trip. She looked up at him in surprise and arched an eyebrow.

"And here I thought you were keeping us out of all of the scary parts of the ship," she observed. "Are we there yet?"

"We'll be novaing in about ten minutes," the IIS agent told her. "I figured you'd be more concerned about getting a look at the Crest than you were at seeing a pair of trade-route stops."

"I would certainly like to get a look at the system," she agreed. She glanced over at Konrad, who gave her a tiny go-ahead gesture.

"May I bring my coffee?" she asked after a second, gesturing at the Americano on her table—a diluted espresso that had turned out to be *Baile Fantasma*'s crew's caffeinated drink of choice.

"Of course. Why would we ever look at Mr. Radar without having first visited Mr. Coffee?"

Kira assumed that there was something behind the phrase that made Zamorano sound less insane to himself, but she simply nodded and smiled as she grabbed her coffee.

"Lead the way, Captain."

He bowed slightly and led the way through a door that had never opened for Kira and her people. The corridor on the other side of the bulkhead didn't look any different from the parts of the ship she'd been allowed in, but there was still a momentary spike of excitement.

Just what did the IIS hide on their intelligence ships?

The answer, at least for this part of the ship, was "nothing unusual." Kira wasn't surprised, but she was a bit disappointed.

"Apparently, my Em Ramirez and your Em O'Mooney were quite disgruntled to realize that her doctor's orders precluded horizontal exercise," the SolFed Captain murmured as he led her down the hall, past a series of unmarked doors.

"We've all been there, I suspect," Kira replied. She'd had more than one fling that had been specifically time-limited by a journey on a shared ship. "Though most of us haven't had the desire prevented by being gut-shot."

"Hell of a first impression your enemies make, Em Demirci," Zamorano told her. "And that's not even delving into the darker waters you swim in."

That, she suspected, was as close as the man was going to come to admitting anything about the Equilibrium Institute. There was no way the Solar Federation's intelligence service *didn't* know about the Institute, but that they hadn't *done* anything about it, well.

That suggested a lot of things to Kira—the ugliest and most likely being that the Institute was carefully operating in a place where SolFed truly could not be bothered to care.

"Here."

There was no door leading to the bridge. An entire bulkhead *dissolved* into the roof, turning a wall into a double-wide door in a moment of dramatic active nanotech. Zamorano grinned at Kira's shock.

"Carbon-nanotube-reinforced active nanomaterials," he told her with an impish grin. "Key systems in the ship are surrounded by a bubble of them. For *most* people, I program them to fake a door...but it's kind of fun to show off sometimes."

Kira shook her head reprovingly at the spy.

"Isn't it dangerous to expose so many of your secrets to me?" she asked, following him onto the bridge. The space looked normal enough—a quarter of the space was taken up by a holotank and four stations were positioned in a shared working space—despite its odd defenses.

Only Ercilia Martinez was in the room, holding down the navigation station, which reinforced Konrad's suggestion that *Baile Fantasma* might only *have* three crew members.

"Are you ever going to be able to admit that you were in the Crest at this point in time, Em Demirci?" Zamorano asked drily. "You're traveling under an assumed name, dozens of light-years from your mercenary fleet, and hiding from everyone.

"You're here doing prep work for a covert contract, one you haven't told me about." He raised his hands as he dropped into his seat. "One I'm not going to *ask* about," he noted. "But to betray *my* secrets would require revealing some of your own.

"Dangerous ones of your own."

He smiled.

"Plus, you now command a powerful mercenary force rapidly building a legend of its own. It will be useful for me, I suspect, for you to know who I am in the future."

"Maybe," Kira said calmly. "It's still a risk for you, isn't it?"

"Everything I do is a risk," Zamorano pointed out. "On the other hand, if I never take risks, it's difficult to build a network of trustworthy contacts. For example, now that you know what I do, would you be prepared to act as an informant for us?"

She blinked, taking a moment to glance around the bridge. The screens and holograms were all using standard iconography. They were at one of the trade-route stops—the heavily mapped chunks of space that were safe to nova to—that serviced the Crest.

There were two dozen other ships of assorted sizes visible on the scanners, including a pair of Navy of the Royal Crest destroyers. *Those* made Kira a bit nervous, but that was the reality of her current situation. She was going to be under the guns of the people hunting her for a while.

"I'm a tad twitchy about conspiracies and shadows, Captain Zamorano," she told him.

"I understand," he said. "To be clear, I'm not asking you to do anything active—not even betray confidences or nondisclosure agreements or…anything.

"Currently, IIS has *no* assets, whatsoever, in the Syntactic Cluster," he continued. "We are reliant on news reporting that reaches places like the Crest Sector and our assets in place here. You can imagine, I suspect, how accurate or complete that data is."

"You didn't even know Konrad worked for me," Kira noted.

"Exactly. What I need, Em Demirci, is not a spy. What I need is someone who can aggregate news and public reporting from across the Cluster, apply some level of sense and local knowledge to flag the egregious falsehoods, and forward it to a drop point by standard interstellar post."

That was a multiply redundant system of "pay the ship going that way to carry a few terabytes of data" in the Rim. Even in the Crest Sector, there weren't dedicated mail couriers. A standard post packet would make its way from Redward to the Crest in anywhere from sixty to ninety days, but it *would* get there.

"If you're *willing* to put Memorial Force's analysis teams to work for me and actually prepare intel briefings to go with that—based on unrestricted information, of course—I can arrange for a formal contract to cover those expenses.

"On the other hand," he chuckled. "While I would insist on paying you for your information if you simply do the news aggregation, we both know you're wealthy enough, it wouldn't make a noticeable difference."

It was relatively easy for Kira to forget that she was technically fabulously wealthy by most standards. The vast majority of that "wealth" was tied up in the value of Memorial Force's ships, investments and contracts. There was an investment portfolio run in her name, left to her by Jay Moranis and John Estanza and regularly expanded with her salary and bonuses, but that was *comfortable* wealth, not *buy nova carrier* wealth.

"My concern, Captain Zamorano, is far more about what SolFed is likely to do with that information than anything else," she finally said.

"Do you want the truth or the fancy appeal to honor and justice?" Zamorano said with a sigh.

"The truth, if you please," she told him.

"Nothing," he said flatly. "That information, even with the intel briefings and everything else, will go to an analytics office in the Inner Rim section of their operational zone. It will be aggregated with the data from another few hundred star systems into a report that gets sent to SolFed.

"Most likely, even that report won't be read by the time it reaches the Federation. It will be several years old at that point," he said quietly. "But it will be used to provide background information on the state of the galaxy for the Federation. It's my job to make sure that we *have* that data, Em Demirci, but I have no illusions about the level of activity that SolFed is prepared to engage in out here."

"I see," Kira said slowly. That turned it into a probably harmless source of extra revenue, but still...

"Think about it," Zamorano told her. "We have some time still. Martinez?"

"Standing by to nova; sixty-second countdown," the other officer replied. "Was about to interrupt."

"Well, Em Demirci, are you ready to see the system it has taken you so much effort to get to?"

KIRA HAD ALREADY NOTICED that novas aboard *Baile Fantasma* were ever so slightly—but noticeably—smoother than aboard most ships she'd served on. Any full-size nova ship with a class one nova drive was a far gentler experience than a nova fighter, but *Baile Fantasma*'s nova was almost ignorable.

Standing on the bridge, watching through the sensors as the ship displaced itself in the space-time continuum, it was obvious. One moment, they were hanging in deep space, with only a few dozen other ships visible.

The next, after a barely perceptible twist of reality, they were in a star system. A brilliantly white F_0 star of almost twenty solar masses, the Herald had burned its six closest worlds to uninhabitable crisps. Six gas giants swung around in the outer portion of the system, their various types and fluids providing the fuel for a massive modern industry.

And hung between the two sets of six was a single perfect world. Minimal axial tilt. Eighty percent water and several large continents. Two large moons for easy access to resources without damaging the ecology of the habitable planet. Everything humans could desire.

"The Damned," Martinez introduced with a grandiose tone to her voice, highlighting the six inner worlds. "The Grand." She highlighted the six outer worlds. "And the Crest." The habitable planet lit up.

"Welcome to the Crest System, Em Demirci," Zamorano told her. "Five point two billion human beings, one of the most heavily inhabited systems in the outer hundred and fifty light-years of the Rim.

"The Damned and the Grand also have individual names, of course, but the only *important* one is Rampant, here." One of the moons of the innermost gas giant lit up. "Rampant is, thanks to the interface of the Herald and the Grand Duchess, the gas giant it orbits, habitable.

"Less amenable in many ways than the Crest itself, it is technically a military reservation with the rest of the Grand Duchess, home to a hundred million support workers and military family members. The Navy of the Royal Crest runs their main shipyard above the Grand Duchess."

Which made the Grand Duchess Kira's main target, and she focused her attention on it. There wasn't much data at this range, unfortunately, but she could see the energy levels that spoke to Zamorano's explanation.

"Ninety percent of the system population lives on or above the Crest itself, of course," he continued. "That's where we're headed. No civilian shipping contract from out-system would ever let a ship approach the Grand Duchess—we'd get one warning."

"And then we'd be vaporized?" she guessed.

"That depends on whether the nova fighters they sent out decided we were a threat or not," Zamorano told her. "If they decided we were harmless but stupid, a nova destroyer would be sent to board us."

"Pleasant," Kira murmured. "Though Apollo had a similar area around Hephaestus."

Redward, now that she thought about it, didn't. They kept their military secured zones quite small and centered around the asteroid fortresses guarding Redward itself. Part of that had to be concentrating resources, though. Both Apollo and the Crest could afford to build a second set of monitors and asteroid forts to defend a gas giant and the infrastructure there.

Baile Fantasma was already heading toward the Crest. The planet was even more heavily defended and industrialized than Guadaloop—the client system hadn't been a significant step up from Redward.

The Crest, on the other hand, had *six* orbital elevators positioned at equal distances around its equator. Each had an orbital battle station acting as a counterweight, with a civilian station at geostationary orbit three-quarters of the way up.

Each orbital elevator acted as the anchor for constellations of civilian and military platforms, with refinery and factory platforms concentrated under the defensive shell—and leaving the majority of the planet's space free for satellites and spaceships.

Rich as the Crest was, though, Kira wasn't there for the habitable planet. She was going to need to get closer to the Grand Duchess—hopefully, once she'd reestablished contact with Jade Panosyan, the Crown Zharang's assets would suffice to get her runabout to the military reservation.

On the other hand...even *Deception*'s sensors would have been getting more data from the military reservation than the screens and holograms around her were showing.

Kira sighed.

"How badly *are* you degrading your sensor data to conceal your full abilities from me?" she asked Zamorano and Martinez.

Fantasma's Captain laughed aloud.

"I can't answer that," he told her. "I really can't, Em Demirci."

"All right," Kira conceded. She looked at the data for the Grand Duchess and considered her options. "Let me ask a different question, then: how much better data can you get me on the Grand Duchess and the military reservation if I agree to be your agent in the Syntactic Cluster?"

The bridge was silent for a few seconds.

"Quite a bit," he said, his voice suddenly perfectly serious. "If you agree to those intel briefings, for the Syntactic Cluster or wherever else Memorial Force ends up, I'll give you our full passive scan of *part* of the Grand Duchess. We'll need some time to clean up the data, but I can have it ready for you when we land."

As he'd noted when they'd talked about it, Kira didn't need his money personally. Even the contract for Memorial Force wasn't likely to make a huge difference to the bottom line of the mercenary company.

It was favor-for-favor...and while she wasn't entirely certain she could trust Zamorano completely, she suspected that the SolFed Captain would trade fairly with her.

"Done. I want everything you can get me on the capital ship yards," she told him. "And as detailed a scan as you can get of any carriers under construction."

Zamorano nodded slowly.

"Done," he echoed. "I'll have Ramirez start on the scan and data prep immediately. I'll have a contract and delivery details for you to pass to your people by the time he's done.

"As I said, Em Demirci, I see value in you knowing who I am. I think we will both benefit from today—and I look forward to working with you again in the future."

"I'd look more forward, Captain Zamorano, if I actually expected your employers to *do* anything out here," Kira admitted.

He sighed and nodded.

"I know," he admitted. "But we all have our duties, Em Demirci. Even your loyalty, as a mercenary commander, isn't only to money."

26

THE RUNABOUT LEFT *Baile Fantasma*'s hold as cleanly as it had entered it. The cargo containers were all gone now, well on their way to whatever destination they'd had, leaving the hold more than clear enough for Kira's small craft.

Everyone was back aboard the shuttle now, going over their tools and their data as Kira checked with the flight control for Crest Charming Station.

"Confirmed, Control, all identity documents and manifests are uploaded," she told the person on the other end. That person probably had half a dozen artificial stupids helping them, but the Crest seemed to agree that a human should have the com channel.

"So...you and your husband, Em Riker, plus your business partners?" the flight controller asked. "The manifest is all personal supplies that aren't intended to land?"

"Exactly," Kira confirmed. "We're in-system to play tourist and have a meeting with the Bank of the Royal Crest with regard to financing a major business expansion. Having our own spacecraft always has its value, though it makes booking flights a pain."

Ramirez had gone through their false IDs with a toolset of his own while they'd been aboard the spy ship, a freebie thrown in with their data on the carrier construction. Kira had been confident in the identification that Panosyan's people had set up for them—but she doubted that SolFed Intelligence had made the profiles *less* solid.

"That's all cleared," the controller told her. "If you are bringing anything onto Crest Charming or anywhere else in the system, beyond clothes and personal effects, you'll need to clear it with security and customs in your location.

"Whatever remains on the shuttle is fine, but your visa does not authorize you to engage in the sale or trade of goods. Understood, Em Riker?"

"Of course," she agreed. Putting everything on the manifest as "personal supplies" had helped cover up the fact that she had armor and significant weaponry aboard. She didn't expect to *need* that gear—but if they were landing power armor and blaster rifles, they weren't going to be playing nice with *customs*.

"You're cleared to shuttle port one-five-niner," the controller said. "Course is downloading to you now. I require a headware validation stamp on the paperwork."

"Of course." Kira reviewed the file the local had sent back, and then returned it with her validation.

"Let me be the first to welcome you and yours to Crest Charming Station, Em Riker," the local said. "I hope you enjoy your stay in our system."

The channel closed and Kira checked the course they'd given her. It wasn't far—but it also wasn't fast. If there had been no other shipping around, she probably could have put the shuttle at the port in under five minutes.

Given that her contact screen was practically *covered* in other ships, shuttles and space stations, she figured she needed to stay on the course they'd provided.

"We on our way?" Konrad asked, dropping into the copilot's seat.

"We are. Everything is clear. Between our friends on *Fantasma* and our friends who live here, we're clean and legally registered."

"And so, it's time to start looking around," he said. "I can tell you one thing?"

"Oh?" she asked.

"I'm not going to need as close a look at *Fortitude* as I expected," her boyfriend told her. "*Fantasma*'s data is better than we were ever going to get with the runabout's scanners at any reasonable distance.

"It's going to take me a bit to go over everything Zamorano gave us, but I think I have enough to make my assessment of *Fortitude*." He chuckled. "And the two battlecruisers and the other carrier they're building in the same yards."

"I didn't want to get *that* specific in what I asked the Captain for," she said. "How badly bugged is the data? I'm assuming it's going to call home to Zamorano."

"Me too," Konrad admitted. "But I can't find it. Which, unfortunately, does not mean it isn't there. My best guess is that the hardware and software this ship has is at least twenty or thirty years out of date by SolFed standards, but..."

"That still puts it way ahead of anything we have," Kira murmured. "So, we can assume that Zamorano knows that we're focusing in on *Fortitude*." She sighed. "Oh, well. Price of the data, I suppose."

"With this data, I'm not sure how much scouting we really need to do," her boyfriend told her. "I think I have everything I need on the ship."

"We still need final confirmation on the planned course for the trials, and then I want to check out the nova stops they're planning," she said. "Anything *in* the Crest is probably too risky, but I doubt they're jumping to a standard trade-route stop for the tests of their new carrier."

"You think they're going to hop around the system and use a dark stop for the long-range test?"

A "dark stop" was a trade-route-stop equivalent that wasn't added to the civilian maps. They were just as thoroughly mapped, but that mapping was done entirely by the local military, and the stop was used solely for their purposes. While a dark stop's mapping wasn't as regularly updated as a standard trade-route stop, it was still sufficient for a safe nova.

And a dark stop would be a spot the Navy of the Royal Crest would assume to be completely safe.

"You're thinking of jumping them at the dark stop?" Konrad asked, continuing the thought without waiting for her to answer his first question.

"It depends on their sequence," Kira told him. "The twenty-hour cooldown of a full-length nova will definitely help us get any evidence of our takeover secured before we meet with anyone else—but if the inspection is *prior* to the full nova test, then that's useless to us."

She shook her head, keeping an eye on the contacts around their shuttle. There was a *reason* this part of the flight wasn't left to autopi-lot, even though the artificial stupids were doing most of the flying.

Something could always go wrong.

"So, thanks to Zamorano, we're skipping our first problem of getting a good look at *Fortitude*," she concluded. "We're still going to need details on the trial plan and a nova ship to run around the local area in.

"Both of those I'm hoping to get from Panosyan." She grinned. "And if the Crown Zharang is feeling particularly helpful, they may even help us get *out* of this system to rendezvous with the fleet."

They had three weeks until they were scheduled to meet the fleet, at a randomly selected trade-route stop four novas from the Crest. Depending on just what was going on with their target, that should give them at least three *more* weeks to actually plan their strike.

"Once we've docked, I'm going to leave it to Bertoli to see if he can source us a hotel that's secure enough for our needs," Kira continued. "If we can't—and I only give it fifty-fifty odds at best—a lot of our planning sessions are going to be taking place in here."

She gestured around the runabout.

"What about you and me?" Konrad asked.

"*You* are going to stay on the runabout and go through that data," she told him. "Unless you think there's something else you should do?"

He laughed.

"No. We've got a lot of information and a lot of detail. More than I expected to have at this point, so that's what I was *hoping* you'd let me do."

"'Let,' the man says," Kira snarked. "Like I could *stop* you digging into a massive pile of fascinating technical scans."

"There are definitely ways you could," he murmured with an artfully arched eyebrow.

She grinned at him and he promptly flushed.

"You're getting better at that," she noted. Her adorably embarassable boyfriend would need a lot of practice before he could really handle dirty jokes at his own expense. He could handle them in general—he *was* a warship engineer—but his defenses cracked when his own sex life was in play.

"It amuses you, so it's worth learning," he told her. "What are you going to be doing?" he asked, looking at the massive expanse of steel that was the nearest side of Crest Charming.

"I'm taking O'Mooney and hitting three random dead drops from a list of seven possibilities on Charming," Kira said. "We need to make contact with the Panosyans."

"It is Jade we'll be working with, right?" Konrad asked, raising a thought that hadn't even occurred to Kira. "I mean, King Sung is behind all of this. He might want to be involved himself—or have other agents."

"I *think* part of the cover of this, if it goes wrong, is that Jade is operating on their own authority and at least half-intending to overthrow their father, the King," Kira said slowly. "I don't think they'll want to shift our contact person at this stage in the game—not when the Crown Zharang is *here* to keep up that role."

"Though they are the Crown Zharang," her lover said. "And they've been gone for a few months. They might be swamped."

"We'll know in about twenty-four hours, I suspect," Kira admitted. "That's how long they said it would take to get back to us from the dead drops."

"You know, I hate all of this cloak-and-dagger," he said calmly. "And I hate a lot of what I did for Equilibrium. But I'm glad to be here with you. If it wasn't for..." He trailed off, then sighed.

"I can't change it, and *nothing* would be worth what happened." His voice was sad now. While *Deception*—then *K-79L*—had been under

Institute control, her Captain had ordered the extermination of all of the witnesses to an attack on a Redward warship.

Of the former Equilibrium crew members with Kira now, Konrad had been the most senior then—and he hadn't been in a position to stop the ship destroying dozens of asteroid colonies and killing tens of thousands of people.

"I know," she told him gently.

"You're as close to worth it as anything could be," he finished, his tone awkward. "But...damn the Institute to hell."

"That, my love, is quite literally what we are in the Crest to arrange."

27

"I'VE CHECKED the apartment three times, and O'Mooney has gone over it as well," Bertoli told Kira. "It's clean. I'm...honestly surprised, though the place was on the list Panosyan gave us."

"I'm guessing they're not even listed on the directories, then," Kira said. They were in one of a bloc of eight rental apartments tucked onto the end of one of Charming's higher-end residential zones.

"I don't think so," O'Mooney agreed. The youngest mercenary was slumped in a chair against the wall, looking gray enough to make Kira feel guilty for dragging her all over the station.

Walking slowly was "light duty," sure, but six hours of it had clearly been more than O'Mooney's healing could tolerate. Thankfully, they weren't going to be doing anything tomorrow—and Kira was going to make sure the younger woman spent the day resting in the apartment.

"So, what have we got?" she asked Bertoli.

"Four rooms, a sitting area, a kitchen, laundry...it's basically a high-end apartment they keep ready for guests," the trooper told her. "Well secured, too. There's copper and lead netting in the walls to interrupt anyone trying to eavesdrop from outside."

He shrugged.

"And if my sweep came up that empty, and this place is used by the people I think it is, the staff sweeps them regularly when they're not in use," he concluded.

"So, we've basically stumbled on to the people who rent to senior executives from Crest," Kira observed. That fit sufficiently with their cover, so she wasn't *too* worried about it—though she was also relying on the discretion of their temporary lessor.

"Only one thing stinks," Bertoli told her, glancing around the room. The space was comfortably decorated with a collection of individual chairs. The chairs all looked one step short of providing a massage when you sat down, but there was also a distinct lack of multiple-person seating.

Very clearly a business unit.

"And what's that?" Kira asked.

"They were expecting me," the trooper said grimly. "I *hope* that's because our employer put the word out, but it still makes me worry."

"I suspect they wouldn't have talked to you if they hadn't been expecting you," Kira admitted. "We're relying on their discretion either way, Jerzy. Keep an eye on everything, but so long as the bug sweep is clean…"

"We're definitely not being listened to, not unless we're dealing with someone with *much* better tech than I've ever encountered," the merc confirmed.

"All right. Go get Konrad," Kira ordered. "O'Mooney and I will hold down the fort here, watching for our host's people to show up."

"You think they're going to come right here?" O'Mooney asked.

"Unless I miss my guess, there's a Dinastik Pahak security team in one of the other units that is busy setting up security perimeters and distractions as we speak," Kira said with a smile. "They need us in an environment they control…but I believe we may have just rented an apartment in exactly that.

"So, yes, I expect them or their people to come here. And I want Konrad to tell me how deep a hole that carrier is going to be before I talk to them."

ONE LOOK at her lover told Kira there was another priority before the briefing. He clearly hadn't quite noticed it *himself* yet, but the color had faded from his face. It was half-concealed under his excitement, but Konrad Bueller clearly hadn't *eaten* while the rest of them had been sorting things out on the station.

"Stop," she told him as he opened his mouth to ask a question. "You, Konrad, are going to eat a sandwich before we have this briefing. Bertoli?"

"I surveyed the kitchen, and the staff stocked it while I was sorting out payment," the trooper said. "Sandwich duty it is."

Konrad nodded slowly—and then collapsed into one of the chairs, equally slowly, as his incipient blood-sugar crash caught up with him.

"Okay, that's probably a good plan," he admitted. "But…I've got a lot to tell you."

"And the five minutes to eat this won't hurt," Bertoli replied, sliding a plate with a sandwich into Konrad's lap—and then following suit with plates for Kira and O'Mooney. "*All* of us should stop and eat, yes? Please?"

"Old soldiers know their priorities," Kira agreed with a laugh. "Thank you, Bertoli."

Calling Bertoli 'old' was exaggerating, but the point stood—and the quickly produced sandwiches were good, too.

"All right, Konrad. Brief us," Kira ordered once they'd all eaten. "So far as we can tell, this place is secure."

"She's a hell of a ship," the engineer said. "I knew what Panosyan said about her, but it's different to actually go through a full high-resolution scan of the lady."

Konrad laid a holoprojector puck down on the coffee table and gestured a hologram of the carrier to life. It looked almost identical to the one that Jade Panosyan had used to get Kira and Zoric on side with the mission, though…that had been a schematic.

This was a visual of the actual ship.

With a few gestures, a wireframe version of the schematic appeared over the ship, highlighting various sections.

"Her outer hull is entirely complete, including her defensive turrets," Konrad told them. Six large protrusions blinked, along with twenty-four smaller ones. "That's six dual heavy guns, each as powerful as the system *Deception* mounts, plus twenty-four lighter, single-cannon, antifighter turrets."

That put the carrier at twelve turreted plasma cannon, only two guns short of *Deception*'s own arsenal. That made *sense*—the carrier was half again the cruiser's size—but it was still intimidating.

"Currently, the only exterior work still in need of completion is her sensor installations," the engineer continued. "Those are usually installed as a single bloc and *should* be in by this point in her construction. They've probably had a production delay elsewhere, but so long as the installations arrive before she's due to deploy, it won't hold them up.

"It's harder to assess her internals," Konrad continued after a moment. "Even with the scans we have, armor and dispersal networks get in the way. That said, I can confirm that her nova drive is installed, all of her fusion cores are installed, and I'd say she's *likely* got her entire Harrington complement installed."

"So, she's basically done, is what I'm hearing?" Kira asked.

"Yes," her engineer told her. "*Fortitude* could probably fly out of there today. My guess is that, outside of the sensor installations I mentioned, she's in final finishing mode. They're installing *beds*, people, not guns."

"And fighters?" Kira said.

"None aboard, but we got a good glance into the deck at the equipment," Konrad said. "It's all there. She's fully capable of acting as a carrier right now. Most of the next six weeks is going to be final touches, system tests and boarding the initial trial crew."

"So, what's holding them to the original schedule?" Bertoli asked. "I'm just a grunt, Commander. Sounds like if they needed that carrier, they could rush her out."

"Easily, but it would be a risk," Konrad answered. "That's basically what we did with the *Baron* class. Those cruisers deployed with yard techs on board still running tests and never had anything except the most abbreviated trials. We, however, were running a construction operation while Redward was under siege.

"The Navy of the Royal Crest, on the other hand, is effectively at peace. They have no serious enemies that they're worried about, and their existing fleet is more than capable of maintaining their client network.

"While *Fortitude* and the sister ship they have under construction will represent a major upgrade in the NRC's strength, there's no rush for them."

"But they are ahead of schedule, aren't they?" Kira asked softly.

The apartment was silent for a few seconds, then Konrad nodded.

"About two weeks," he told her. "So, they may have shifted the schedule from the last data we had. I can't see them having shifted it enough to threaten our original timetable, but the danger is there."

"We'll make that nova when we get to it, I guess," Kira said. "There's nothing we can do to accelerate Memorial Force. At this point, they've already left the Syntactic Cluster, let alone Redward."

"What are our next steps?" Bertoli asked.

"First, we make O'Mooney sit down for a day and heal," Kira told her people with a smile. "We're waiting for contact at the moment. You and I, Bertoli, will go for a walk about the station in the morning to get a feel of the lay of the land, pick up some physical newsletters to go with the network downloads.

"We came to the Crest for a lot of reasons. One of them is to find out whether or not this Sanctuary and Prosperity Party is as much trouble as we were sold."

"You think they might not be an Equilibrium front?" her boyfriend asked. "That Panosyan sold us a false bill of goods?"

"I think *they* believe that the SPP are an existential threat to the Crest as they want it to be," Kira said carefully. "My own assessment is that if the SPP aren't an Equilibrium front, they're still doing exactly what the Institute wants.

"But I want to confirm that with my own eyes and ears listening to the people of this system. Not trust the person who hired us to carry out a coup. Make sense to everyone?"

"Oh, god, yes," Bertoli muttered. "You're the boss, boss. I'll over-throw anyone you tell me to—but I *am* assuming *you've* done the research."

She smiled thinly.

"And tomorrow, Bertoli, that is exactly what we're going to do."

28

"MARAL JEONG IS the best thing to happen to Crest," the shopkeeper cheerfully exclaimed at Kira's gentle prompting. "I mean, things were starting to go downhill *fast* when she took over as PM. People were talking about dissolving the *client network*, like we were some kind of conquerors!"

Kira took the neatly tissue-wrapped jacket thoughtfully.

"Really? I didn't know that had ever been a conversation around here," she said.

"The client network is a mutual-aid setup, but there's a lot of bleeding hearts on the Crest that think we're taking too much for what we give," the woman told Kira. "But I serve the merchants who haul around this sector and go elsewhere, too.

"It's safer where the NRC guards than it is anywhere else around here. Everyone tells me it's *more* than worth helping support the fleet!"

Kira smiled and nodded cheerfully—while wondering if the giant Sanctuary and Prosperity Party poster behind the shopkeeper's head was part of why everyone was careful to talk up the Crest's empire to her.

"Thank you," she said, transferring the price of the jacket and picking it up. "My husband will love this!"

Today, she was playing tourist, with Bertoli trailing around in the mode of a bored personal assistant. Most people who knew soldiers would register him as one of some kind—but a *lot* of executive personal assistants were ex-noncommissioned-officers, all over the galaxy.

A lot of the same skills, plus a PA who could act as a bodyguard usually only cost a bit more than a bodyguard—and less than having both a personal assistant *and* a bodyguard.

"Well, she was obvious before she opened her mouth," Bertoli muttered, falling in beside her and sliding the jacket into his collection of bags. "But she's not the only one."

It wasn't an obvious thing. No one had plastered propaganda posters all over the main thoroughfares, but Kira and her bodyguard were in Crest Charming's largest shopping promenade. The posters weren't in the shared public spaces—but they were in a *lot* of the private places, people proclaiming a clear allegiance to the Crest's ruling party.

She'd never seen this much active flag-waving before.

"How many of them do you think mean it versus have the posters up to protect themselves?" Kira asked.

"Most, from the conversations we've had," the trooper told her. "Hmm. I see an opportunity, boss."

"What kind?" Kira asked. She followed Bertoli's gaze and spotted the group. "*Oh.*"

A pair of Navy of the Royal Crest Commanders, clearly a couple—but with shoulder flashes showing the two men were from different ships—were finishing up their own shopping trip and walking in the direction of one of the promenade restaurants.

The *opportunity*, however, was the trio of petty officers attached to the pair of lovebirds. *They* were in clear beleaguered-minder mode, clearly having been coopted as much to carry baggage as provide security.

"Think the officers are smart enough to buy their escorts lunch?" Kira murmured as she studied them.

"They borrowed three petties to carry their bags," Bertoli said. "So, either they're popular enough that the crew will do that for them, in which case they're the type to buy lunch...or they *don't care*, in which case it's seventy-thirty they won't."

"Either way, we can eavesdrop on a pair of O-Fives and see what they think," she said. "Best case, I'll listen in on them...and you go commiserate with the petties. If the *officers* don't buy them dinner..." She left the sentence unfinished.

"Can I expense lunch for four?" Bertoli asked drily.

"Of course!"

THE TWO OFFICERS lived up to Kira's middling expectations, talking to the hosts to arrange to check the bags and then putting the petty officers up at a different table—and making it clear that they were paying for the petties' meal.

Of course, *that* meant that they casually ignored the growing line of other customers behind them. Civilians, even merchants and tourists, clearly didn't register on the same priority as their crew.

Once the NRC group had headed in to their tables, Kira stepped up the hosts and palmed a fifty-crest physical credit chip onto their podium. That was as much as the meal was likely to cost, which made it more than the hosts were going to see in tips.

"Can you sit me within hearing range of that pair of fancy uniforms?" she asked.

"Of course, Em!" one of the hosts replied cheerfully as the chip disappeared. "Right this way."

If the other host *didn't* trust her compatriot to give her part of the bribe, they didn't have time to argue before Bertoli stepped up to the podium behind Kira—and repeated the same trick.

It wasn't as subtle as Kira would like, but there weren't many options for making sure they were within eavesdropping distance of their marks. The only people they were really drawing attention from was from the restaurant staff they were bribing—who almost certainly did *not* care.

As the second host moved away with Bertoli in tow, a holographic artificial stupid appeared behind the podium and greeted the next guests. This was a higher-end restaurant—hence having human staff at *all*—but they could only afford so many human hosts.

Kira's guide led her to a table just on the other side of a three-quarter wall from the two officers. As she took her seat, she realized there was a privacy field along the wall. She'd have difficulty hearing through it, but this was as good as she was going to get.

Then the privacy field dropped—*just* between her table and the one with the two NRC officers. Her host gave her a wink.

"I hope the table is to your satisfaction," he said. "The table interface will have the menu and can take your order. There's a call command if you have any questions; it will bring a stupid who can summon one of us if it can't answer."

"Thank you," Kira told him.

He vanished and Kira brought up the menu—but her focus was on the other side of the wall.

"It's a mess," one of the two men was saying. "Jorge is saying that his promotion board was *grilling* him on his volunteering for the Liberals. He thinks he's stuck at Commander forever."

"He's actively spending his free time working for the opposition, Egemen," his companion pointed out. "With all the rumors flying these days, they have to make sure no one is thinking about backing a coup."

"Still, aren't we supposed to keep our politics to ourselves?" Egemen asked. "I mean, I voted SPP, not saying otherwise—Jeong's fantastic—but it doesn't feel like I should have to tell the promotion board that, you know?"

That was...bad. Even *Kira* knew that was bad. She took a moment to glance through the menu, ordering a vat-protein burger and fries. Her focus today was *not* on what she was eating.

"The whole thing with Captain Simonsson is still rippling through the Navy," the unnamed officer said. "Mutiny doesn't sit well with the higher-ups, no matter what claims she makes of illegal orders. Step *carefully*, Egemen. Your board is what, in a week?"

"Yeah. Six days," the man replied. "I even know which cruiser I'm probably getting, *if* I pass the board."

"You're Crest to the bone, Egemen. You believe in the same things as the folks they want in charge. The Sanctuary and Prosperity Party is moving in the right direction; we both know that. Tell the board that when they ask, and you'll be fine."

"I know, I know," Egemen. "But, Zahid, doesn't it feel wrong that our politics matter at all?"

"Lorelei Simonsson was as apolitical as you can be and be a battle-cruiser Captain," Zahid replied. "And *she* defied orders and tried to arrest a BRC system director! Command is worried about the rot that's setting in.

"It's not that they're looking for folks to blindly follow SPP into hell or some bullshit like that, love. They're just using it as one more metric to make sure you're aligned with the Navy and the Crest.

"Now, come on. We're supposed to be *celebrating* the fact that you're up for Captain, Egemen, not trying to navel-gaze the whole damn fleet. Pick a wine, damn it!"

The conversation turned to calmer topics and Kira swallowed a curse. That had been a *fascinating* piece of trivia to catch. The SPP had clearly managed to take control of the promotion boards, enough that they were using loyalty to the Party as a metric for advancement.

Jade Panosyan had *not* suggested that things were that bad. They'd implied that there was a definite cadre of SPP-loyal officers in the NRC, but this was far beyond that. Control of the promotion boards would rapidly become control of the fleet, one way or another.

Right now, Kira could assume that a good chunk of the Captains and flag officers were still more loyal to the Crest than to the SPP...but it was starting to sound like she needed to assume anyone she was dealing with in the Navy of the Royal Crest was loyal to the people she was trying to remove.

If the ground forces and orbital defenses were equally contaminated, the Panosyans had a *problem*.

KIRA AND BERTOLI had returned to the apartment before either of them could really brief the other. Outside of the suite of rooms they were regularly sweeping, they had to assume they were being recorded and listened to at all times.

Careful sleight of hand could let them bribe people, but conversation in quiet corners *was* going to get run against an AS algorithm.

"O'Mooney's asleep," Konrad told them when they came in. "So, let's keep it down a bit? The kid is more beat than she's letting on."

"'The kid,' Konrad, is a thirty-two-year-old mercenary ground trooper veteran who boarded *Deception* with us," Kira pointed out. "Just because you have a decade of life experience on her…"

"Fair, fair," he allowed. "She also just got gut-shot and is trying to pretend she's fully functional. So, if we can manage not to wake her?"

"I wasn't objecting to that part," Kira admitted. She stepped over to the apartment living room "window," a screen showing an image of a garden that might have even been on the station somewhere. It had a collection of small trees and shrubs gathered around a sand garden that someone had raked an infinity pattern of red stones into.

"Bertoli?" she asked.

"SPP has this place locked down tight," the commando told her. "It's not an overt thing—there aren't people marching down the thoroughfares with purple armbands or anything like that—but enough people are fully on board with everything they're doing, at least on the orbitals, that people aren't really going to talk about supporting anyone else."

"That was my read as well," Kira said. "To give the Cresters *some* credit, these orbitals live and die by the intersystem traffic. They have to be afraid that would go away without the client network. These are some of the people who are most aligned with the Sanctuary and Prosperity line."

"Almost as much as the Navy," Bertoli said grimly. "I listened in on that trio of noncoms you sent me to, boss. Their ship's XO, Egemen Baris, is up for promotion to Captain. His crew adores him, from what they said, and will probably follow him into hell."

"But?" Konrad prompted.

"They think he's an SPP bootlicker, too," the bodyguard told him. "They don't *care*, from what they were saying, but they definitely knew he's following the party line there."

"I was eavesdropping on Commander Baris and his partner," Kira said to Konrad. "According to them, NRC promotion boards are asking questions about political loyalties and volunteering. Baris isn't comfortable with that...but he's definitely SPP. His partner was telling him that was to his advantage."

"Those three petty officers figure he's a shoo-in because of it," Bertoli noted. "They might have volunteered as his 'security detail' normally—he's known for tipping the crew who help him out off-ship, even though that's technically against regs—but right now, they are sucking up *hard*.

"They think he's getting a brand-new cruiser and they want to be keel-plate owners on it."

"He apparently thinks the same, so long as he clears the promotion board," Kira said. "Which means he expects he's going to clear the board; he's just having normal nervousness."

The apartment was silent for a few moments as Kira traced the red stones in the Zen garden with her gaze.

"If the SPP owns the promotion boards, they own the NRC," Konrad said into the silence. "If they own the NRC, they own Crest Orbital Command and they own the Army of the Royal Crest. If they have *that* much dominance in the military..."

"Then the fact that King Sung Panosyan is the official commander of the military forces is irrelevant," Kira replied. "I don't know what the Panosyans' plan for that is, but the judicial coup that I was told about? They're going to run into a very real, very *armed* counter-coup."

"So, what do we do?" Bertoli asked quietly.

"What we're paid for," Kira said with a long sigh. "And we trust that the Panosyans know what the *hell* they're doing with their own planet."

29

IT WAS no surprise when Jade Panosyan arrived in the apartment the mercenaries were renting. What *was* a surprise was that they came in through the window screen, the garden suddenly fading away to reveal a utility access door.

Three blasters—illegal on Charming Station, but after the mess in Guadaloop, Kira had agreed to let Bertoli smuggle them in—focused on the door as it opened to reveal the gold-and-black uniform of a Dinastik Pahak bodyguard.

"Good afternoon, everyone," Jade Panosyan murmured as they stepped through the door behind their bodyguard with Voski in tow. "If we could manage to *not* shoot each other today?"

The Crown Zharang wore an insignia-less uniform in a monochrome gray that didn't match any of the Crest's service branches. There was presumably a binder under the shipsuit, but the combination brought Jade Panosyan to an androgynous anonymity that would pass unnoticed in most places.

"I wasn't planning on shooting anyone," Kira told their employer. "On the other hand, the apartment rental company didn't tell us there was a door there."

She glanced at Bertoli.

"It eluded our scans?" she asked.

"Scans were for bugs, not doors," the commando said, glaring at Voski as his Pahak counterpart emerged behind Panosyan. "Though I would have expected to find them anyway."

"It's just a utility corridor for the staff to have easy access to all of the apartments," Panosyan told them, settling into one of the chairs like they owned the place.

Which, Kira was reasonably sure, they did.

"Now that you've given us our daily shot of adrenaline, welcome to our temporary abode," Kira said. "I'd offer a seat, but you already claimed one."

The door closed and the garden image reappeared as Voski took their minion over to the other door and checked it.

"Em O'Mooney is recovering well, I hope?" Panosyan asked.

"She is," Kira confirmed. "We got lucky."

In more ways than one, but she wasn't going to bring IIS into *this* conversation. She'd given Zamorano his letters. He'd make contact with the Crown Zharang on his own terms, and Kira didn't have enough loyalty to *either* of them to get further involved.

"I presume you've had a chance to engage in some investigations since your arrival?" the royal asked. "I hope that you haven't found anything to change your mind about the contract?"

"Not that isn't buried under the ten million crests you already paid me," Kira said drily. "Though I worry you understated just how deep the Sanctuary and Prosperity Party's grip runs."

"It is worse than I like to admit," Panosyan conceded. "But that doesn't change your part of this mission."

"No. Which means I need assets, access and data from you," Kira told the Zharang. "I hope you have a plan."

"Access is…difficult but doable," their employer told them. "I can get *one* of you into the shipyard. I can't get them aboard *Fortitude*, but I can arrange for you to get into the building slip itself with a royal inspection team."

"Konrad?" Kira asked, glancing over at her lover. She wasn't sure if that was still necessary with the data Zamorano had given them—but, on the other hand, she wasn't entirely sure she wanted to give away that they had that data. Even to Panosyan.

"If I can get that close, even if I can't get aboard the ship, I can learn a lot," he said. "Especially if your people can help me drop a few glorified bugs in the area."

"Maybe," Panosyan said. "I can't be certain. I'm not yet sure how fully I'll be able to bring the inspector into the loop. I *know* I can get him to agree to bring someone along as a civilian advisor, but I don't think we'll be able to bring in the rest of the team—which would make bugs hard."

"That's fair," Konrad conceded. "Even just walking the slip and studying the carrier from there has value."

"As for data, I'm working on it," Panosyan said, turning to Kira. "There's a lot of moving parts. It looks like the whole event has been moved up by a week, and there's definitely a whole new level of paranoia running through the NRC and the SPP right now."

They shook their head.

"I am the Crown Zharang," they noted flatly. "I *will* be able to get the full schedule of the trials and the inspection—I've already confirmed both are still happening, just eight days ahead of the schedule I had while we were in Redward."

"It's five days from our rendezvous to Crest," Kira pointed out. "Eight days means that when we return to the fleet, we only have a week to get into position. Instead of almost three."

It was actually less than four days from the rendezvous point to Crest, but underselling and overdelivering was a good habit to be in as a mercenary.

"That's not something I can change, Demirci," Panosyan told her. "I think it's going to take me at least a few more days to get my hands on the finalized schedule. Hell, it might be a few more days before they even *have* a finalized schedule."

"Which brings me to assets," Kira said. "We need a nova ship to investigate the route. One that won't draw attention if people see it— and preferably one we can run back to Memorial Fleet, too."

She was starting to think she should have just bought a ship in Redward and sailed it all the way here on their own. Except there was no way she could have done that without drawing attention. Getting the runabout in had been hard enough—but worth it to give them a fallback point with armor and guns aboard.

"I could get you that tonight," their employer said calmly. "I'm not *going* to get you the ship until I have the full route and schedule, but I've made arrangements to put an NRC high-security courier at your disposal.

"Every officer and spacer has been fully cleared by the Dinastik Pahak, and the Captain was a schoolmate of mine," Panosyan concluded. "They are, without a doubt, loyal to the Crown of the Royal Crest."

"And that won't draw attention on its own?" Bertoli asked. "That sounds…attention-drawing."

"It's not that the ship won't draw attention; it's that a high-security courier has an excuse to be *anywhere* and no one is going to question her captain," the Zharang told them. "Everyone aboard has the highest security clearances.

"So far, the divisions in our fleet haven't caused officers to start mistrusting couriers that they think are working for 'the other side,' so to speak."

"But that division is starting to be a thing, isn't it?" Kira asked softly.

"Yes," Panosyan conceded. "It's worse than it was when I left. There is a clear and active group of SPP officers in the Navy of the Royal Crest, and they are comfortable enough with their power base to make moves I didn't expect to see for a while yet."

The apartment was silent, then Kira sighed.

"Who is Captain Lorelei Simonsson?" she asked.

"Until two months ago, she was the commanding officer of the battlecruiser *Penalty Fee*," Panosyan told her. "Currently, she is in prison, awaiting court-martial for mutiny."

"Most systems don't take that long to try someone for mutiny," Konrad pointed out.

"Most systems don't have a political party trying to make sure that the military judge is one of theirs in a system where both the military and judicial organizations are *supposed* to report to my-father-the-King," the Zharang said grimly.

"Simonsson and *Penalty Fee* were posted to the Zabata System," they told the mercenaries. "One of the outer client worlds. The system director of the Bank of the Royal Crest there is a long-standing donor and backer of the Sanctuary and Prosperity Party, assigned to a client world that's never been…entirely content with their status."

"What happened?" Kira asked.

"The director decided to *remind* the Zabatans of their position and make an example of a larger owner-operator that was delinquent in their payments."

Panosyan shook their head.

"It wasn't even *good business*," they complained. "The captain could have easily been offered an extension that would have made the bank *more money*, with all historical evidence suggesting they'd have managed it.

"Instead, Director Traver ordered the ship interned. Except his timing was *very* specific, such that the ship could easily escape. Which, sensibly, they tried to do—so Director Traver ordered Captain Simonsson to seize or destroy the ship."

"And she refused," Kira murmured.

"Oh, she didn't just refuse," Panosyan said with a chuckle. "*Penalty Fee* is a hundred-twenty-kilocubic battlecruiser, and she was the largest nova ship in the system, bigger than the entire fleet Zabata is allowed combined.

"Simonsson broadcast on the shared military frequencies that if anyone *else* tried to obey Traver's orders, she would shoot them the fuck down."

"I like her already," Bertoli said. "Is she single?"

Their employer chuckled, then shook their head sadly.

"Of course, there are actually structures that allowed Traver to give that order, though they're intended for far more serious crises," they told the mercenaries. "The SPP is now using those systems to say that

Simonsson is a traitor, basically. Simonsson is saying the order was illegal and unethical."

"Which I assume it was?" Kira asked.

"Yes."

Jade Panosyan shook their head.

"The Crest has been a *mostly* benevolent hegemon for my father-the-King's entire reign," they noted. "Some of that is the rose-colored glasses of being the one in charge, I'm sure, but we have not been as bad as we *could* have been.

"And the reason I can say that is because we're starting to get a lot *fucking* worse," they concluded. "And neither I nor my-father-the-King are going to stand for it. That's what all of this is about, Em Demirci."

The room was quiet.

"I was already in," Kira reminded the Zharang. "And we were *always* in for more than the carrier. Though the carrier helps, a lot."

"I'd hope so," Panosyan muttered. They shook themselves and surveyed the mercenaries with a calm expression. "I assume it will be Commander Bueller who will be accompanying the inspection team?"

"He's the only one qualified to judge a ship like that," Kira confirmed.

"You'll need to be at shuttleport sixty-four at eight hundred hours station time, day after tomorrow. Formal work clothes and shipsuit," they instructed Konrad. "I'm not certain yet if you'll be meeting the team or picking them up on the way, but that's where and when the shuttle will be waiting for you."

"Understood."

Panosyan met Kira's gaze.

"I'll have the trial plan and the inspection schedule for you as soon as I can," they told her. "Once I have that, I'll let you know how to get in contact with Commander Eireen Hamilton, your courier CO.

"I'd trust Eireen with my daughter, let alone my life," Panosyan concluded. "She'll keep you safe, find you what you need and get you back to your fleet. How long do you have?"

"Twenty days, but we need five for travel time," Kira replied. "Two weeks until we need to be moving to the trade lanes."

"Understood," the Crester said. "We'll make it happen, Commodore. Everything depends on it."

They shook their head.

"I was only gone for six months and everything has visibly gone downhill," they said quietly. "We *have* to succeed."

30

AFTER A WEEK OF "BEING A TOURIST," including sending her boyfriend off into the belly of the beast for two full days, and *weeks* of acting like a civilian, even aboard Panosyan's vessel, it was a relief for Kira to step off the runabout in an insignia-less black military shipsuit.

Her companions were a step behind her as she crisply saluted the Chief Petty Officer waiting for her in the NRC's dark gold uniform shipsuit.

"Welcome aboard *TVM-Six*," the Chief told Kira. She was a tall redheaded woman with her hair pulled back into a tight bun. "I'll be finding a space to put your shuttle," she continued, glancing around the small boat bay.

There was only one other shuttle in that bay, not much larger than Kira's runabout, and Kira saw the Chief's point. *She* wasn't sure where to put the runabout other than where she'd landed it!

"My apologies to the bay team," she murmured.

"I *am* the bay team," the Chief replied. "Chief Petty Officer Daniella Lewinsky. I'm the deck officer, shuttle pilot, shuttle maintenance crew, and backup navigator for *TVM-Six*.

"The skipper is on the bridge, but she asked me to get you landed and settled. Unfortunately, we don't have much space for anybody. I hope bunk beds aren't a problem?"

Kira laughed.

"How many people does this ship carry?" she asked.

"Crew of sixteen, Commodore Demirci," Chief Lewinsky told her. "We each have our own quarters, but there's no real allowance for passengers. Why put aside two rooms for passengers when you can squeeze in another Harrington coil, after all?"

Kira was familiar with the type of ship. The courier had two defenses: a full set of multiphasic jammers and a power-to-weight ratio comparable to a nova interceptor. It had the same class one nova drive as any other starship, but its sublight maneuverability made it hard to catch and harder to hit.

"Bunk beds are fine," she told the Chief, gesturing her companions forward. "I once served on a cruiser converted to carry a single squadron of nova fighters. One room for six pilots—and it was three months before it even *had* bunk beds."

Hammocks had been the order of the day, and she wasn't sure her back had forgiven her yet.

"Well, we at least have the beds," Lewinsky told her. She glanced over the other three mercenaries. "I was only given one name," she noted softly. "My understanding is that was the plan, to try to keep some level of confidentiality."

"Everyone aboard *TVM-Six* knows your mission and who you're working for, Commodore. We serve the Crown of the Royal Crest. You're safe here."

"I trusted our employer's judgment on that," Kira said. "Bunk beds, huh? I'll need to coordinate with Commander Hamilton shortly, so I guess we should get started."

AT TWELVE THOUSAND CUBIC METERS, *TVM-6* was far from tiny. The courier was a slightly squashed cylinder eighty meters long, half a meter wider than she was tall. She had no guns, limited cargo space, and only the one small boat bay they'd landed in.

The cramped nature of her interior had been a design choice, squeezing out as much space as possible to allow the ship to fit three fusion cores into a ship size that would normally carry two, and to install enough Harrington coils to need all three of the fusion plants.

Some spaces, though, had not been sacrificed on the altar of speed. In Kira's experience, the engineering spaces around those coils and power cores would be spacious—and the bridge was large and comfortable.

With the bridge's handful of workstations, it could also serve as a secure conference or briefing room—an intended feature of the design, one that left Kira and Konrad alone on the bridge with Commander Eireen Hamilton.

Hamilton was a short woman with night-black skin and an absolutely piercing gaze. Kira had the distinct feeling that the NRC Commander had identified that she and Konrad were a couple within ten seconds of their walking onto the bridge.

The question for the moment, though, was whether the woman could identify the key parts of their target's schedule.

"We now know everything we're going to know about *Fortitude* herself," Konrad noted. "Our employer has provided the full builders' schematics, and we have close-in scans and visual data. I have a few thoughts on what to do with all of that, but that's not really your problem, Commander Hamilton."

"No, it's not," she agreed. "And I'm probably happier that way." She shook her head, looking at the map of the system hanging in the middle of her bridge. *TVM-6* was on her way outward from the Crest itself, heading toward "the Grand," the system's gas giants.

"I'm not the largest fan of this whole operation," Hamilton continued. "I don't know all of the details, but I can put together the pieces I have. I'm scouting the route of *Fortitude*'s launch trials with a quartet of mercenaries on board.

"Given that among the schedules I've been given is the *Prime Minister*'s schedule, I suspect I have a damn good idea what I'm helping with. I trust Jade. Beyond all reason, apparently, but this still goes against the grain."

"Do you expect me to convince you to go along with this?" Kira asked bluntly. "Because that's not what I'm here for. I've been hired to help the Crown Zharang deal with a *problem*, Commander. I was told you were in and fully briefed."

That was a slight exaggeration, but from the sounds of it, Hamilton was close enough to fully briefed that Panosyan *should* have just fully briefed her.

Hamilton snorted and shook her head, running her hand over her shaved scalp.

"No," she conceded. "Jade told me enough. I'm in. But the Sanctuary and Prosperity Party is a symptom…not the disease. I'm not sure removing them by force is going to solve any problems."

Kira sighed.

"We're not assassins, Commander," she told the other woman. "At the end of the day, part of what I'm going to get paid for is delivering the Prime Minister to Crester police. The Crown Zharang has a plan.

"I'm not privy to it all either," she admitted. "But I know they want Maral Jeong to stand trial."

"And here you say you're *not* supposed to be convincing me," Hamilton murmured. "That actually helps. Though…" She ran her hand over her scalp again in a clear nervous gesture. "I won't pretend I wouldn't be doing this even if I thought you *were* just planning on killing Jeong.

"I really do trust Jade Panosyan that much. I just would like it a lot less."

"I appreciate the honesty," Kira told Hamilton. "To return it in like: if this was a targeted assassination, I would not have taken the contract. We'll keep our own peace on details of our part, but I can assure you of that much."

"Fair. To work, then?"

"To work."

"Finally," Konrad muttered—but he was grinning widely enough that Kira figured even Hamilton wouldn't take it the wrong way.

"I assume they're following a standard trial pattern?" he asked.

"Yes. We do the core tests over twelve days, but the part that we've been talking about is the actual *flight* trials," Hamilton told them, waving a series of lines and spheres onto the three-dimensional map of the star system.

"The first technical flight trial will happen in twenty-four days, two days before the rest of the flight trials," the NRC officer continued, highlighting the first line and sphere. "That will move *Fortitude* to the gunnery range on the far side of Grand Duchess from Rampant, where she will test her weapons and, according to the schedule, her fighter-handling equipment."

"She's taking on fighters there?" Kira asked. "For the rest of the tour?"

That was a complication.

"Looks like three squadrons out of the Blue Scarlet Combat Group," Hamilton confirmed. "They're an elite formation that usually operates off of *Valiant*, the current flagship. But *Valiant* carries a hundred and twenty fighters and bombers. They can spare eighteen heavy fighters."

"Do we have a solid listing of what they're getting in terms of pilots and birds?" Kira said. "That could be complicated."

"Nothing is *solid*, but my understanding is that the selection will be warped by the chance to meet the Prime Minister," the NRC officer told her. "So, almost certainly Blue-One, Blue-Two, and Blue-Three. The most senior and elite squadrons, equipped with brand-new Hussar-Seven heavy fighters."

Kira nodded slowly. A brand-new heavy fighter from the Crest almost certainly outmatched her Weltraumpanzer-Fünf planes—but probably not by much. The Weltraumpanzer-Fünfs *were* the current main heavy fighter of the Brisingr Kaiserreich Navy.

Her interceptors and fighter-bombers were about on par with the Fünfs. Her interceptors were Hoplite-IVs from Apollo, and while her PNC-115 fighter-bombers were an older design than the Hoplites or Weltraumpanzers, they were also from the *Fringe*, not the Rim.

Between *Deception* and *Raccoon*, she was definitely bringing in enough fighters to take on even eighteen new heavy fighters with elite pilots. The problem was that if even *one* of those fighters novaed to report, they were going to be in real trouble.

"We'll work with it," she said aloud. "How long will they be doing gunnery and landing trials?"

"Two days," Hamilton told her. "Actual flight trials will start in twenty-six days, eight days before the original schedule Jade said they gave you."

Kira nodded. She only had seven days before she needed *TVM-6* to be heading for Memorial Force, but that was already part of the plan. They shouldn't need *that* long.

"There will be twenty-four hours of real-space flight trials on her Harringtons in the region of Grand Duchess," Hamilton said. "That will be followed by a series of novas of increasing length over another twenty-four hours.

"Then they will make a full-length nova to security point six." A new icon flashed up on the side of the map, marking a light-hour-wide zone six light-years from the Crest. "They will be there for twenty hours while the novas cool, and then they will nova to *here*, above Grand Prince, where *officially* they will be engaging in a maneuvering test with the cruiser *Terminal Loss*."

"And in reality, they're meeting the Prime Minister and a good chunk of her Cabinet?" Konrad asked.

"Exactly. *Terminal Loss* is scheduled to pick up the PM and five Cabinet Ministers seventy minutes before *Fortitude* novas to Grand Prince. She'll nova there ahead, with her own escort consisting of a battlecruiser and an assault carrier.

"The Prime Minister's classified schedule says that the two ships will rendezvous and the PM and Cabinet will spend six hours aboard, inspecting the Crest's first hundred-and-fifty-kilocubic warship and glad-handing with the SPP loyalist crew."

"I'm guessing the schedule doesn't phrase it that way," Kira said.

"No," Hamilton admitted. She inhaled deeply. "Looking at this, I have to admit…"

She trailed off.

"Commander?" Kira prodded.

"The Prime Minister. The Deputy Prime Minister. The Minister for the Navy. The Minister for the Client Network. The Minister for Internal Security. The Minister of Communications."

The list didn't mean much to Kira initially, but as she thought about it, a sense of impending doom swept over her.

"If I was planning a coup to remove the King and impose a one-party government on the Crest, those are the Ministers I'd want in a private, absolutely secure, meeting, aren't they?" she asked.

"That's what I was thinking as well," the NRC officer said. "We might not be the only people thinking about a coup, Commodore. The Crown Zharang may just be moving *first*."

"I hope we're moving first," Konrad said. "Now. Kira...we can take *Fortitude*, but I'm wondering if she's going to actually be alone. Light-speed delays give us some chances, I suppose."

"We need to be careful relying on that," Kira warned. "If someone sees us jump the carrier, even if it's twenty or thirty minutes later, they can still warn the PM and short-stop the entire damn mission right there.

"Whenever we hit them, we need to either *not* be seen—or if there's a chance of us being seen, it has to be *after* the rendezvous with *Terminal Loss*."

She considered the Grand Prince rendezvous point. "Do we know what ships *Terminal Loss*'s escort will be?"

"There are at least two battlecruisers and two assault carriers that could get pulled in," Hamilton replied. "Those are just the ships with Captains I know to be SPP loyalists. They may even swap out a fleet carrier, depending on availability and what they think they can swing without drawing attention."

Kira nodded slowly.

"We can't reliably jump and secure *Fortitude* while fighting off two cruisers and a second, fully functional carrier," she noted. "I think that negates *any* plan of hitting them while the PM is aboard.

"That limits our options. A lot."

She looked at the map and sighed.

"She's not being officially escorted at any point, right?" she asked.

"No, but they'll have set the trials to coincide with when other ships are around," Hamilton said.

"Do we have those schedules?" Kira asked.

"If I don't already have them downloaded, I have the authority to get them," the courier captain said. "Give me a minute."

OVERLAYING the patrol patterns on *Fortitude*'s trials made it very clear that the Navy of the Royal Crest were far from incompetent. The new fleet carrier might not be officially escorted during her nova and sublight flight trials, but that was because she didn't *need* to be.

The sections of the outer parts of the Crest System the nova tests would take her to were under near-constant patrol by either nova fighters or lighter ships. Several of her early novas would take her to the projected positions of outer-system monitors, ships even larger than *Fortitude* herself but incapable of nova travel.

"There is no way in hell we can take on the monitors," Kira observed, looking at a rough set of statistics for the Crest's defensive ships. The sublight warships were a good chunk of why a civilized star system was regarded as uninvadable, after all.

"So, that rules out most of her test stops in the Crest," Konrad agreed. "What about the security point?"

"That's probably your most likely opportunity," Hamilton agreed. "I've also got a point here, between her two longest in-system novas. Someone miscounted *Fortitude*'s cooldown, she'll be able to nova fifteen minutes before the schedule calls for."

Kira chuckled.

"Which means she *will* nova fifteen minutes before the schedule calls for, most likely," she agreed. "What kind of gap does that open?"

"She's jumping almost three light-days out-system, so there is nothing else out there," Hamilton replied. "The *plan* is sending her out to a standard surveillance point where they regularly deploy ships to scan for troublemakers."

"But if she jumps early, she'll be alone out there for..." The NRC Commander ran the numbers, then shook her head.

"Seventeen minutes," she noted. "That's...nothing. And the next ship to show up is *Penalty Fee*. Her crew is basically on a punishment tour—but her new Captain is an SPP diehard."

"If we play the right games with timing and jammers, it's...

doable," Kira said. "But that is *not* a window I want to work with. Who's at the security point when they're there? Those are usually quiet."

"Usually," Hamilton agreed. Security point six appeared next to the display of the Crest System, lighting up with its own patrol routes. "Except…" She exhaled.

"Mapping mission," Konrad said, looking at the data. "Looks like a trio of destroyers. We… We could take them, Kira?"

"We could make no mistakes," she said softly. "With eighteen nova fighters in play, we'd need to send our bombers against the destroyers unsupported—and if we miss *one* shot, we lose everything.

"A single nova ship, whether it's a fighter or a destroyer or *Fortitude* herself, getting away wrecks the whole plan. We need to arrive at Grand Prince with *nothing* to make us appear suspicious.

"When are those destroyers supposed to report in?" Kira asked.

"They're on a cycle; one checks in every twenty-four hours," Hamilton told her. "There's a check-in right before *Fortitude* arrives, which means…"

"One will be expected to check in four hours or so after she leaves." Kira studied the map.

"Those are our two biggest weak points," she admitted. "Here, in the seventeen minutes before the battlecruiser arrives, and here, where she'll only have three destroyers in company and will be six light-years from the Crest."

The three of them looked at the hologram.

"I need to see both places," she concluded aloud. "Yes, I know they're both basically empty void, but…there may be something I can't see from a map."

"And then?" Hamilton asked.

"Then us mercenaries need to get to the rendezvous point and you need to get back to your normal job," Kira said. "If you leave us floating in deep space for a day or two, that will help cover your tracks a bit as well."

"My tracks are pretty covered already," Hamilton said. "But fair enough. Let's go check out this empty void and see if inspiration strikes."

31

THERE WASN'T much to choose between one patch of void and another. Even the security point was empty, the destroyers not scheduled to start their mapping sweep for several weeks still.

Looking at empty space didn't give Kira any inspiration. She found herself spending hours just sitting on her bunk, cycling through data in a virtual display only she could see.

Raccoon carried six Fastball bombers—a refined evolution of the Screwball improvised bombers they'd used against Equilibrium— which she could support with six heavy fighters and twenty-four fighter-bombers.

But if she sent all of her heavier nova fighters against the three destroyers, she'd only have thirty-one interceptors—including her own bird—to go up against eighteen advanced heavy fighters in the hands of elite pilots.

Sixty-seven nova fighters against a ship that was supposed to carry a hundred and fifty was definitely an…interesting challenge. So far as she could tell, though, *Fortitude*'s guns would be safed after their firing trials.

They wouldn't be quickly unsafed. The risk was someone escaping and bringing the rest of the NRC in before Kira could move against the Prime Minister.

"Still ruminating?" Konrad asked, settling down onto the bunk beside her. The single cramped room they had aboard *TVM-6* didn't lend itself to much privacy, but their companions weren't going to object to them leaning on each other.

"Trying to balance the options," she admitted. "Every so often, I wonder if just hitting *Fortitude* while the Prime Minister is aboard is even that bad an idea. It takes a lot of the timing issues out, after all."

"Except that the Prime Minister is going aboard while the nova drive is in cooldown," her lover pointed out. "Full cooldown, thanks to the nova from security point six. That's *twenty hours* the carrier has to be sublight, and she isn't *that* fast.

"So, you'd have to punch out two capital ships, board a third and do all of this while hoping not one of seventy-odd nova fighters makes a jump for help. I'm no tactical genius—I leave that side of things to you, Kira—but that seems...unlikely."

"Trying to take out eighteen fighters and three destroyers at the same time is also a pain," Kira admitted. "And we have the same problem at the security point of cooldown. If we take her after she completes a six-light-year hop, she's got a twenty-hour cooldown, which means we need to make sure no one within twenty light-hours sees us."

"Grand Prince isn't even that far out, is it?" Konrad asked.

"No," Kira admitted. "Which is a problem for the main plan. We *might* be able to ambush the Cabinet's escort with *Fortitude*'s guns at close range with no jammers up, punch them out and avoid anyone escaping if we control the ship, but...Grand Prince is only three light-hours from the *Crest*, let alone anything else."

"So, we need to, what, capture the PM and hold them incommunicado for twenty hours without anyone noticing?"

"That is what it looks like, isn't it?" Kira asked.

She spread her three options in the air in front of her and tossed the visual to him with a thought and a hand gesture.

He linked into the display and brought up something else. The schematics and details on...*Fortitude*'s fighter-launch systems?

"Sixty-five seconds," he said quietly. "That's the minimum scramble time for *Fortitude*'s fighters, assuming they have pilots in the cockpits ready to go. That seems like…a factor."

"Standard nova-fighter combat sweep is sixty seconds; that's why the carrier has defensive guns and would have a combat space patrol up," Kira noted. "Her guns are *supposed* to be offline, but those heavy fighters will be up."

"Not all of them, though, right?" he asked.

"No," she murmured. "Maybe two-thirds when they realize they're alone in the outer system."

Sixty-five seconds. And while she generally focused on the *cooldown* time of a nova drive, there was also a warm-up time of about a minute.

"We need to take out the fighters within a minute and start the commando landing almost immediately after, no matter what," she said aloud. "It doesn't matter whether we have seventeen minutes or twenty hours; we have to move *fast*."

"That's what I was wondering about," Konrad told her. "Whether we were thinking too much about the timing."

"I think we were thinking about the *wrong part*," Kira replied. "If we grab *Fortitude* at the security point, she *has* to be at Grand Prince for twenty hours. There's no way around it; that's just what the physics says."

"And?" her boyfriend prodded, clearly content to have provided his contribution and to now serve as someone to lay out the plan to.

"But they haven't officially scheduled *any* of their escorts except for the 'maneuvers' with *Terminal Loss*," she said. "So, those destroyers aren't *expecting Fortitude*. Which means…if she doesn't show up, no one is going to notice.

"If we take her before she's supposed to jump out…that point is already several light-days out. The *risk* is that if *Penalty Fee* doesn't report in, that'll raise questions. But if we manage to fool *Penalty Fee*, no one is going to see the actual attack for days.

"And then we nova out on schedule…and only go a few more light-days. Tighten up our control, link up with the rest of Memorial Force to solidify the plan, and then nova to Grand Prince on schedule.

"With *minutes* of cooldown on the drive instead of *hours*."

"Might work," Konrad said. "Only thing I'll point out is that they may be able to tell. Even with warship shielding, if they're looking, they'll see the wrong levels of Jianhong radiation."

"Maybe," she agreed, then looked away from her virtual maps to face her chief engineer. The man who, in addition to being her boyfriend, was one of the best engineers and gearheads she'd *ever* met.

"Can you fake it?" she asked bluntly.

"My dear, I never fake *anything*," he said with mock indignation. That faded into a grin. "But I can *definitely* produce some *extra* Jianhong radiation by exposing a couple of spare class two cores when we make the nova.

"I'm pretty sure we can cover it."

"It has to be perfect," Kira said grimly. "*If* we take *Fortitude* without being caught, we then meet the Prime Minister and her escorts with *just* the carrier.

"And the ten million credits we're supposed to be paid for finishing this mess says that Maral Jeong has a nova pinnace for her personal craft. If we screw up, she is going to nova the hell out and leave her escorts to deal with us.

"We won't get a second chance."

"Then we'd better not make any mistakes," Konrad told her. "No pressure, right?"

"Right."

32

WAVES of brilliant blue light flickered across the runabout's displays, a mix of Cherenkov radiation, Jianhong radiation and regular light that blazed across the empty space of the trade-route stop.

An alert woke Kira from her nap in the pilot's seat as the nova pulses flashed across her scanners and identity beacons began to trickle in.

"They're on time," Bertoli noted from the copilot's seat. "I can't say I loved two whole days in the runabout, cycling between two bunks and two chairs that fold back, but our friends are on time."

Kira chose to ignore the complaint, focusing in to validate the identification. It was easy enough—even there, in the Crest Sector, few nova ships approached a hundred thousand cubic meters.

She still thought *Deception*'s lines were ugly, the warship cut in the blocky and angular shape preferred by the Brisingr shipyards for ease of construction, but the ship had definitely grown on her. Compared to the rough cylinder of *Raccoon* and the logistics freighter, she was *definitely* a more modern and powerful ship.

The distinction was less obvious versus the two *Parakeet*-class destroyers. She could see Konrad's influence in the fact that the *Para-

*keet*s looked more like Brisingr ships than the older Redward destroyers she'd seen, but their systems showed his influence as well.

"That's everyone," she said aloud. "Are O'Mooney and Konrad awake?"

"I'm awake," Konrad said, her lover stepping up into the cockpit. "O'Mooney probably had an alarm set for this, too, but she's not bothering to get up."

"I'm awake," the youngest mercenary called from the back of the shuttle. "But there is *not* enough space for four in that cockpit."

"I am not going to miss this runabout," Kira noted, entering the commands to bring up her Harrington coils. *Deception* was almost two full light-minutes away, so it was going to be a while yet before they were aboard.

But they could *see* home—and two new nova flashes appeared next to them as a pair of Weltraumpanzers dropped into escort formation around the runabout.

"Basketball, this is Purlwise," *Deception*-Charlie's commander, Akira "Purlwise" Yamauchi greeted her. "Confirm ID, please?"

"Sending, Purlwise," she replied, pinging him with her Memorial Force codes. "It's damn good to see you all. Safe flight?"

"Safe, yes. Boring, mostly," the pilot replied. "Though when we get back to Redward, a few of us are going to find the gentleperson who sold Commander Bueller *Lady Tramp* in a back alley."

That had to be the logistics freighter…and didn't sound good.

"I'll have Zoric brief me, I suppose," Kira allowed. "You're our escort in?"

"All the way, Commodore. It's good to have you back."

"EVERYTHING WAS fine until we hit the third static-discharge stop," Zoric told Kira and Konrad a few hours later, gathered in Kira's office breakout room.

They hadn't managed to sleep yet. Kira hadn't even *seen* her quarters—and they had an all-senior-officers briefing in less than an hour.

The rush was probably unnecessary, but the longer everyone had to plan for what was coming, the better.

"So...eighteen novas from Redward and already outside the Cluster," Kira observed. Nova ships built up a mix of electrical and tachyon static on the hulls and on the nova-drive cores themselves with each jump.

It was easily discharged in a significant gravity well, but that required a nova into a star system, which added a delay to travel. A number of systems had received significant economic benefits from being spaced roughly thirty light-years apart along the common trade lanes—including both Redward, at the center of the Syntactic Cluster, and Ypres, at the "entrance" to the Cluster from the rest of the Rim.

"Yeah. That's when *Lady Tramp*'s Harrington coils started to fail," Zoric said. "Fortunately, Captain Woodcock is an old RRF engineering hand and realized what was happening before we'd lost more than half."

"*Half?*" Konrad exclaimed. "I *checked* her coils."

"From what Laure said, you did," Zoric agreed.

Kira wasn't familiar with Laure Woodcock, but her headware confirmed that Zoric had hired the woman away from the RRF to command their logistics ship. Her file said she'd been an engineer turned logistics-support officer, but Redward didn't deploy outside the Cluster and didn't need logistics or repair ships.

That limited the opportunities for a woman like Woodcock to command her own ship—which was probably why she'd jumped at the chance to move to Memorial Force.

"Then how?" Konrad asked.

"Woodcock's people checked every coil after that," *Deception*'s Captain told them. "They didn't *say* anything, but the systems automatically record replacement dates."

Kira could guess what that meant—and from the way Konrad started gritting his teeth, she wasn't wrong.

"They swapped them all?" he demanded.

"All of them," Zoric confirmed. "Woodcock figures they either had the old coils in the shop already or traded them. The ones they pulled had almost seventy-five percent operating lifetime, on average.

"The ones they installed were all on their last thousand hours," she said grimly. "Worth maybe a *quarter* of what the ones they pulled were worth. Woodcock says that even if they bought the ones they installed and just sold the original ones, they probably cleared half a million kroner on the switch."

"Dark alley. Right," Konrad gritted out.

"More *send everything to Pree*," Kira corrected. "You or Milani might break the asshole's legs—Pree will *end* his entire business."

Why send thugs when she could send lawyers, after all?

"We had replacement coils for the fleet on *Lady Tramp*, of course, so Woodcock was able to get everything running again without us losing too much time," Zoric noted. "I'm a fan of both thugs *and* lawyers in this case, boss.

"Those coils could have failed at a far worse time than us heading into orbit for static discharge—and Woodcock's people are still going over the rest of the ship."

Kira winced.

"How bad?" she asked.

"Worst was the nova-drive discharge capacitors," the Captain said grimly. "They only swapped half of those, at least, but one of their swap-ins already had a hairline fracture. She'd have made it to the Crest, most likely."

"And not made it back to Redward," Konrad replied. "Dark alleys and lawyers, yes."

Kira snorted.

"It's fixed, though?" she asked.

"Woodcock thinks so," Zoric confirmed. "Everything else is fine. We picked up new crew, new pilots—you know some of them."

"Oh?" Kira asked.

"I figured I'd make life easier and reorg so all of our RRF pilots were in one squadron flying RRF planes," her second-in-command told her. "I'm glad I did that, because I'm not sure I could have justified asking *Colonel Sagairt* to do less than command a squadron."

"*Helmet* is aboard?" Kira demanded. Teige "Helmet" Sagairt had commanded the original single squadron of battered ex-Crest nova fighters Redward had owned when she'd arrived.

He'd remained one of the key officers and pilots of the RRF's expanding pilot corps ever since. Last she'd heard, he was slated to skip several grades straight to Admiral and become the official CO of the nova-fighter corps.

Now she had to wonder if anyone had told *Sagairt* that.

"Yes, sir," Zoric confirmed. "On *Deception,* leading Delta Squadron. I had six Sinisters, as opposed to PNC-One-Fifteen clones, so that made sense as a place to put the RRF loaners."

"I'll have to touch base with him and see just what he is thinking," Kira said.

The Redward Royal Fleet's Sinister nova fighter-bomber was *heavily* based on the PNC-115 fighter-bombers that *Conviction* had once carried and *Raccoon* still did. It was not, despite its heritage, a perfect clone.

While Kira's pilot/copilot teams from the PNCs could easily handle the Sinisters, the RRF crews were more experienced with that specific variation, so Zoric's change made sense.

"Fair enough," Zoric agreed. "Our various Redward loaners have settled well. I suspect that someone—either Remington or Sagairt himself or *both*—was very careful about the people we got. They haven't lorded being regular military over our people, nor have they insisted on, well, any more spit and polish than you do."

Kira smiled. That had been a shock for some of *Conviction*'s people when she'd first come aboard. She'd let a lot of the rules and regs of military service go, but there were also rules and policies that made *sense,* and she'd enforced those on *Conviction*'s fighter group.

Now that mix of mercenary minimalism and military discipline ruled across her entire mercenary fleet.

"So, we're doing okay?" she asked.

"We're ready for war, Kira," Zoric said grimly. "But while our people are *willing,* I'm pretty sure we can't fight the Crest. Do we have a plan?"

"The beginnings of one, that we'll hash out with the rest of the senior officers when we have the full conference. A lot of data to run through as well," Kira told Zoric. "The Crest is in worse shape than I thought, politically. The SPP basically has complete control and is pretty obviously moving to change *de facto* to *de jure* by removing King Sung.

"The question isn't whether Jade and Sung are right to move against the SPP," she noted. "The question is if it's already too late. Either way, though…"

She sighed and shook her head.

"Worst-case scenario I see is that we pull this off and then have to dump the PM and her Cabinet somewhere because no one is going to pay for them," she admitted. "So long as we manage the *mission*, we still walk out of this with a carrier."

"We've got command-and-override codes to take control of her, *if* we can take physical possession of her," Konrad added. "Which, I guess, is where that all-officers briefing comes in?"

"That part of the plan is on Milani and McCaig," Kira agreed. "But I want everyone in the room to talk about it as we go through the pieces.

"There's going to be very little slack to work with."

Zoric nodded slowly.

"How little?" she asked.

"Seventeen minutes."

33

KIRA FINISHED LAYING out everything they knew about the situation on the Crest and the planned timelines of the trial and paused, studying her audience.

Even for a mercenary fleet of five ships, counting *Lady Tramp*, it was a lot of people. Two fighter-group commanders—Cartman and Patel—four ship Captains, four XOs and the ground-force commander. And her.

She didn't know the executive officers well, other than Konrad obviously, but the warship Captains were all old friends and colleagues. There was no one in the mixed virtual/physical conference that she didn't trust.

"Any questions?" she asked.

Milani leaned forward, the dragon on their armor flickering around their helmet as they did.

"I've been reviewing the schematics of the carrier," they noted. "Are there any significant changes that will impact the boarding plan?"

"Konrad? You got a better look at *Fortitude* than anyone else," Kira asked.

"So far as we can tell, the schematics our employer provided are still fundamentally accurate," he told Milani. "I have a comparison drawn up between the final builder schematics and the mid-cycle drawings. I'll pass it on after the meeting, but there's nothing that should impact the boarding. Flight deck, Engineering and the bridge are all in the same places."

"Good." The armored mercenary leaned back again and shook their head. "Right now, the plan is to load a platoon onto each destroyer and make a close-nova approach. Shuttles should be in space for under thirty seconds and land simultaneously.

"So long as the flight deck is clear, we should be able to get four shuttles down in one go and deploy all sixty ground troops in one wave.

"Do we know what kind of security is anticipated?"

"There are not supposed to be any internal defenses other than standard security surveillance," Kira replied. "We've confirmed that she will not have her standard Army of the Royal Crest security detachment aboard, but I would assume we're looking at at least a security platoon for the ship herself, likely backed by a platoon of executive security personnel for the Prime Minister.

"*They*, after all, know she's doing the inspection."

"So, equal numbers, but we have surprise and heavy weapons," Milani concluded. "All right. We hit them fast and hard, take Engineering and then sweep the rest of the ship to clear up survivors as the prize crew comes aboard."

"'Fast and hard' is good," Kira told the ground commander. "Because our timing is going to be ugly."

She tapped a command, zooming in on the part of *Fortitude*'s schedule that was relevant.

"They've set up the trials to use their existing patrol pattern to remove the need for escorts," she noted. "Since the ship needs to swan around most of a star system and its environs *anyway*, it makes sense and is surprisingly efficient.

"But *if* the nova drive performs as expected, *Fortitude* will arrive at her final in-system nova point fifteen minutes early," she continued. "Her expected company there won't arrive for seventeen minutes.

"That is the *only* break in the schedule," she told them. "All other options require us to engage other defenders. If we deploy in this window, we have to deal with her combat space patrol and make sure no future fighters launch."

"And remove any debris from the initial dogfight," Michel pointed out, the former pilot looking grim. "Collect or vaporize; we can't have evidence if there's a ship coming—unless we're planning on taking down that ship as well, anyway. This is pretty far out."

"It is, and that's what makes this possible," Kira agreed. "But the ship that's showing up is one of their more-modern battlecruisers. We *cannot* fight her, which means that by T plus seventeen, every sign that we were there needs to be either aboard *Fortitude* or gone."

Everyone was silent again, looking at the timing.

"We can deploy localized jammers once we're aboard," Milani said after almost a minute of silence. "That will enable us to complete the boarding op if we haven't fully secured the ship by that time.

"But you'll need to have the prize crew aboard at T plus ten, maybe T plus twelve at most. We will not have fully secured the ship by then."

"It's a risk," Kira agreed. "The bad news is that *Fortitude* will be expected to communicate with *Penalty Fee* as well, so that won't buy as much time as we'd like. The *good* news is that *Penalty Fee*'s crew is currently in the doghouse, so they won't be surprised if *Fortitude*'s prize crew ignores them for a bit."

"So, we'll have twenty, maybe twenty-five minutes to storm and sweep an entire hundred-and-fifty-kilocubic carrier," Milani said quietly. "Because if we miss *anyone*, their headware will be enough for them to com a battlecruiser a few light-seconds away when we drop the jamming."

"And we'll need just seventy-five minutes to cool down the carrier's drive," Konrad observed. "After that, *we* control how far she novas, which gives us some interesting options for dealing with the Prime Minister, but...we're stuck on that hour in *Penalty Fee*'s company."

"We can make that work," Kira replied. "But we need to take the carrier first. We have the...strategy and operations, I suppose," she said with a smile. "We know what we're doing, why, where and when.

"So, now, people, we need to work out how. One carrier. Eighteen advanced heavy fighters with elite pilots. Seventeen minutes."

All of the data on the display slid aside into a three-dimensional "scratch pad" everyone could access. Kira dropped *Fortitude* into the workspace and added six fighters.

"We can assume two squadrons are aboard the carrier," she noted. "That's our starting point...and then we'll make contingency plans for if they're *all* deployed."

PUTTING TOGETHER the first cut of the plan took three exhausting hours. When it was finally over, Kira wasn't even sure it was good.

She *was* sure that there was no point in grinding the twelve most expensive minds in her fleet against it. The holograms winked out and she was left alone with *Deception*'s senior officers—and realized Zoric, Cartman and Milani were all regarding her and Konrad like hungry owls staring at a field mouse.

"When did either of you last sleep?" Milani asked, the ground-force commander, as usual, faster off the draw than everyone else.

"On the runabout," Konrad replied. "I think Kira was sleeping in the pilot seat when you all arrived."

"On a shuttle," the mercenary commando echoed. "In the *pilot seat*...and then you decided to run an hour-long briefing and three-hour planning session."

They turned to Kavitha Zoric.

"Captain, permission to call the company CEO an idiot and have commandos drag her to her quarters to make sure she sleeps?"

Zoric chuckled, but her gaze was very focused on Kira.

"Both the CEO and my XO need to go fall over," she noted. "We nova in ten hours. If I see *either* of you before then, I *will* give Milani that permission.

"Am I clear?"

"Who pays who here, again?" Kira asked with false plaintiveness.

"I own twenty percent of the company and I'm pretty sure I can get forty-nine percent of the shares to vote that you need to go lie down,"

Zoric told her. "So. Boss. You're no longer on covert ops duty, which means you need to be awake enough to *think*."

"She's not wrong, Kira," Konrad told her.

"My *plan* was to go to bed next," Kira replied, her plaintiveness slightly less false now as her senior subordinates—her *friends*—ganged up to mother her.

"Then shoo," Zoric said. "Go."

34

DECEPTION HAD A FULLY functional flag deck, designed to act as the home base of a senior Commodore or junior Admiral leading a cruiser group. The *K70*-class cruisers had originally been designed as independent capital ships operating with destroyer support, after all.

Even when they'd grown too obsolete to risk being deployed where heavier Apollon ships could find them, they'd kept the facilities—and now Kira was making full use of them again.

Which meant that right now she was watching sixty nova fighters make an enthusiastic attack pass on empty space. The target, of course, was simulated in their systems. So were their guns and even their multiphasic jammers.

While Memorial Force was currently alone at the trade-route stop, they didn't want to hash up real space for other people. While multiphasic jamming was only fully effective within a light-second of the emitter, the chaos traveled outward at lightspeed and could ruin someone's day if it hit at the wrong time.

"Your people are good," she told the man standing next to her. "I'm impressed."

"I handpicked the best from the volunteers," Colonel Teige "Helmet" Sagairt told her. The brilliantly copper-haired man grinned.

"You've made quite an impression, you know. I had *complaints* from people who didn't make the list of pilots we were lending you."

"To be sent into a fight you knew nothing about beyond that it was outside the Syntactic Cluster and I was getting paid for it," Kira murmured. "I'm actually touched."

"You came from nowhere and saved our planet and our Cluster at least twice, Commodore," Sagairt said. "I know you were paid for it and paid well, but money doesn't clear some debts. The Redward Royal Fleet's nova-fighter wings exist because of you, and we know it.

"Plus, I think everybody figured you weren't going that far unless you were sticking a finger in Equilibrium's eyes—and the RRF has its own accounts to settle with those assholes."

"That's true enough," Kira agreed. "I'll admit, I was surprised to get *you*."

He chuckled.

"You've heard the rumors, then," he said.

"That you're supposed to be getting stars and put in charge of a semi-independent fighter corps?" she asked drily.

"Those ones, yep," he agreed. "That's *why* I'm here."

Kira looked away from him to watch *Raccoon*'s Fastball bombers carry out a perfectly sequenced strike on a virtual cruiser with virtual torpedoes. For a group of pilots that had never seen a bomber a year earlier, her bomber crews were smooth as silk.

"Are you trying to *avoid* that promotion?" she said.

He laughed at that, then winced as he looked at the screen behind her.

"What?"

"Well, your *Raccoon*-Alpha and -Bravo squadrons just *pincered* my poor *Deception*-Deltas," he told her. "I'm checking the metrics...yeah, that dogfight was a bloody massacre." He shook his head. "My people are not up to speed with yours yet."

"My people are also learning, most of them," Kira admitted. "I'm worried about these Blue Scarlets. We've got the numbers edge, but everything I'm seeing says the new Hussars can match the PNCs and Sinisters for gunpower and the Hoplites for maneuverability."

She shook her head.

"A heavy fighter that can dance with my interceptors and shoot with my fighter-bombers is not what I want on the other side," she admitted. "Though, to be fair, they have to leave their torpedo behind to match the Hoplite-IV's maneuverability."

Her Hoplites only barely had enough plasma-cannon firepower to really threaten a real warship. The PNC-115s, on the other hand, were a decent threat even *without* their torpedoes, as were the Weltraumpanzers.

The new Hussars carried a single torpedo, like her Hoplites, and, also like her Hoplites, suffered for maneuverability when they did so. Even with the torps, the Hussars weren't a threat to *Deception*...but the threat for *this* operation was their nova drives, not their weapons.

"And who knows if they're carrying them," Sagairt agreed. He shook his head. "As for the promotion they're talking about, when I say it's why I'm 'here,' I mean 'here on this flag deck with you,'" he clarified.

"I'm here to learn how to command a nova-fighter group from the best example I have available," he told her. "Do I think you're perfect? No. Do I think you're damn good at this job? Yes.

"Plus, you're around and you were willing to let me join you to observe the exercise," he continued. "Availability makes up for a lot of shortcomings, Commodore."

"I'm both flattered and vaguely insulted, Colonel," she told him, but she laughed. "Seriously, you're, what, *apprenticing* yourself to me for this mission?"

"Between you and Cartman, I'm getting a good feel for a completely different way of running an organization of nova fighters," he pointed out. "And I'm watching you manage the nova fighters from the half-step back I'm going to need to use once they hang those stars on me.

"It's a learning experience for me, and one that will serve both me and Redward well."

He smiled sharply.

"And if the last time I strap on a nova fighter is to ram a torpedo through an Institute plan, I will regard it as time well spent."

Kira snorted, keeping her eyes on the exercise.

"Well, if you want apprenticing, it's a good call to mention it," she observed. "Because half of what you need to know goes on in my head —assuming my methods are even worth observing. Apollo runs an entire three-month intensive training course for officers moving to starship or full nova-group command, but I never took it."

She'd been supposed to, but then Jay Moranis had warned her that the death of one of their other squadron commanders was fishy as all hell—and told her to retire and get out of Apollo.

Gods, did she miss the man. John Estanza, too, the old troublemaker. The pair of them—comrades in Cobra Squadron and Equilibrium alike before they'd learned better—had put her where she was. They'd set her up to be successful, wealthy and the commander of a mercenary battle fleet that would have few equals when she was done.

And she'd trade it all for having both of them back.

"You've spent more time in the cockpit of a nova fighter than I have," Sagairt said quietly. "You've commanded a nova-fighter squadron in more actions than I've *flown* in. You're the best option I have to learn from, and I don't give two flying rats whether you got the formal training or not.

"I'm sure as hell not getting any formal training before I take command of an entire planetary nova-fighter force!" He grinned. "So, feel free to start narrating your thought process if you think it'll help, boss.

"Because I am ready to learn...and I need to."

"All right." Kira swallowed and looked back at the map. "First thing to note, then, is that we're watching by squadron right now," she told him. "We'll analyze by individual pilot afterward, but that will just be a quick run-through to make sure the squadron commanders don't miss anything.

"So, we're comparing performances of squadrons—their maneuverability, their formation-keeping—and if you look *here,* you can see that Purlwise and *Deception*-Charlie squadron are still occasionally flying like they're in fighter-bombers, not heavy fighters."

Sagairt nodded slowly as she continued, pointing out the places where the pilots and squadrons on the map were failing that could be fixed—and the places they were doing exceptionally that needed to be praised.

If he was to lead Redward's nova-fighter corps, he would need to be able to identify *both*.

"ALL RIGHT, PEOPLE," Kira said into a virtual debrief when everyone was back aboard their respective motherships.

Dozens of pilots and copilots looked up at her in various stages of exhaustion, and she smiled. It was a well-practiced smile, one she'd learned when she'd taken on her first squadron command eons ago.

Her smile projected sympathy for their exhaustion, understanding of their failures...and a warning that she was about to lay some of those failures out for everyone to see.

"For a first run at the series of simulated scenarios, that was decent," she told them. "Normally, I might even say good. You understood the scenario parameters, were keeping your simulated and test novas to the right cycles, and flew like you knew what you were doing."

That was a higher bar than it sounded. Even the best pilots could lose track of the cycle time and spent sixty-five, seventy, even eighty seconds in the battlespace. The class two nova drive had a minimum cooldown of sixty seconds, and it was almost *never* a good idea to spend more than that around the enemy.

"Against any opposition in the Syntactic Cluster, you'd be looking good," she told them. "Against most pilots in the Rim, even, this would be a promising start.

"Except everything we have says that the Blue Scarlet Combat Group is an *elite* formation, handpicked for this mission because they are guarding both the most powerful warship the Crest has built *and* their Prime Minister *and* the leadership of the political party that is well on its way to securing total control of the Crest.

"We can safely assume, pilots, that we are looking at opponents just as capable, just as skilled, just as *dangerous* as the Cobra Squadron pilots who came after us for Equilibrium."

Those veterans had easily taken two of the Cluster's newly commissioned pilots with each of them when they'd gone down. Kira and her allies had *smashed* Cobra Squadron in the end, but the price—even excluding the loss of *Conviction* with John Estanza and Lakshmi Labelle—had been high.

"So, today was…acceptable," Kira warned them. "That said…"

She looked around, meeting gaze after gaze in the physical briefing room aboard *Deception* and through the virtual link to *Raccoon*.

"Performance today *was* acceptable," she noted. "And that is against a metric of us needing to go up against an elite combat formation in less than two weeks.

"Which means, pilots, we have work to do. But this is not a lost cause and we *can* take Blue Scarlet—and do it, I think, without losing a single damn one of you.

"Because in my perfect future, people, I bring everybody home from this mess *and* I get a fleet carrier *and* we help the Crest short-stop a move to a one-party government *and* we stick a knife in Equilibrium's back."

She could feel the energy in the room improve as she continued and her carefully practiced smile turned into a near-feral grin.

"We are going to go over every single place today that you fell short of my hopes," she told them, but that energy buoyed them. "Not because anyone is to blame but because those are where we need to practice on the next round.

"Because very, *very* soon now, we are going to go up against the elite of the Navy of the Royal Crest and *you*, Memorial Force's nova-fighter pilots, are going to make *them* look like amateurs.

"Who's with me?"

35

THE FINAL DEBRIEF was a *lot* smoother than the first one. Kira even let Sagairt lead the briefing as practice, which her people were taking in good humor as he walked through the multiple sequences of their training program.

When the RRF officer finally sat down, Kira stepped up and gestured for everyone to pay attention to her. The crowd was expanded over the usual, and they were actually on *Deception*'s flight deck, to allow for space for the officers from the other ships and for at least all of the squadron commanders to be physically present aboard the flagship.

"Colonel Sagairt has been suffering from the unfortunate fate of having volunteered to be apprenticed to me for this operation," she told them, an explanation she hadn't given any of the pilots prior to this.

"I hope the process hasn't been as awful for him as I fear," she continued to a chorus of chuckles. "But here we are, everyone. For the *terminally unobservant*, we are currently sitting three light-weeks from the Crest System, with the navigation departments already working on the novas to drop the fighters and ships of the strike into the correct positions at the correct time.

"It is…" she paused, letting the timer in her headware tick down, then continued dramatically. "T minus thirty-six hours *exactly.*

"This was our final training run. You will spend the next thirty-six hours resting and preparing for heavy combat," she continued. "I'm not going to stop you doing dogfighting exercises or anything like that, but there will be no more scheduled training between now and T zero."

She gave them a moment, smiling.

"Unfortunately, those of you paying attention may *also* remember that Memorial Force brought along a particular regulation from the Apollo System Defense Force," she told them. "And that is that no one is permitted alcohol in the thirty hours before a planned combat operation."

Kira waved around the flight deck.

"That includes me, the spacers, all the officers, but is mostly meant for you lot," she told the pilots. "But since that deadline doesn't kick in for six hours, most of you have encountered the Apollo pre-mission tradition of the strike party."

Stewards were rolling tables into the room behind her people, quickly forming a near-solid line across the eight-meter-wide fighter deck.

"*Deception*'s stewards have outdone themselves with a spectacular spread for you," she told them. "Most of the crew will be getting the same spread in their messes, but this is the big party. It's the one with the Commodore!"

That got her more laughs, but most of her people were eyeing the food and drink behind them now.

"I'm not going to keep speechifying," she promised. "You've done good, people. We're as ready as we are going to be. So go, eat, drink, be merry."

She didn't finish the thought aloud, but she knew most of the older pilots would do it automatically.

Eat, drink and be merry—for tomorrow we die.

KIRA KNEW that the Commodore could only stay at the party for so long. Her presence would inevitably suppress the *enthusiasm* of the event—though there were aspects of that she was planning for as she carefully positioned herself near the punch table.

She was just in time, in fact, and caught Evgenia Michel's hand as the destroyer Captain was about to add something to one of the bowls.

"Ev," she said warningly. "Just what is that?"

"A mild thirty-second hallucinogen," Michel said cheerfully. "Well, it is when mixed with alcohol, anyway. It's completely neutralized by the cannabinoids in *those* punches." She waved the small pouch at several of the mixed drinks.

"Hallucinogens are fine when people are *consenting* to them," Kira pointed out. "They make for a terrible prank."

"That's why it's mild and short-duration, and Scimitar and I hang around to keep an eye on people," Michel insisted.

"How many times have we had this argument?" Kira asked.

The destroyer Captain paused thoughtfully, her heavy metal legs adjusting with clearly intentional drama.

"Twenty-three," she answered. "Which is why Abdullah is coming this way with a sign."

"A sign?" Kira asked, not quite following—until the dark-eyed form of Abdullah "Scimitar" Colombera, *Deception*-Bravo's squadron commander and Michel's age-old partner in crime, appeared and placed a small tripod with a hand-lettered sign next to the punch bowl Kira and Michel were arguing over.

MOON JUICE. CONTAINS HALLUCINOGENS.

"*Now* can I add the powder?" Michel asked with a laugh.

"You're still supervising the damn bowl, kids," Kira told the two officers, chuckling herself. *Consent* was the critical part. Slipping drugs into the drinks was a prank she couldn't allow—at least *two-thirds* of the prank at this point was the knowledge on Michel and Colombera's parts that Kira or Zoric would catch them—but a labeled hallucinogenic drink was…fine.

"Of course," Colombera agreed cheerfully. "But if you call us kids, do we have to start calling you the Old Lady?"

"If you call the Commodore the Old Lady anywhere that *I* can hear you, you might start finding the systems in your quarters surprisingly glitchy," Konrad told the two Apollon officers as he materialized. "I won't do anything to damage the ship, but I understand that unexpected cold showers are *fantastic* for increasing efficiency!"

Michel shivered dramatically.

"Be good, Scimitar," she told her partner in crime. "I don't trust my engineer not to do *exactly* what Bueller tells her."

"That's because Em Hoang knows what's good for her," Konrad replied. "Something I'm not entirely sure either of *you* has ever worked out."

"Please, Konrad, neither of them is past thirty-two," Kira said. "Their brains haven't fully developed yet."

"Yet you gave one of them a destroyer," he pointed out.

"I didn't say *my* brain had fully developed." She scooped up two chilled bottles of beer and passed one to her boyfriend.

"Now, are you two done seeing if you can make me jump?" she asked her pranksters.

"That's the last thing involving spiking the punch, yes," Michel said virtuously.

"If it wasn't so unethical I twitch to think about it, I'd have Konrad shut down your legs to protect everyone else," Kira told the younger woman firmly. "Nothing injurious. Am I clear?"

"Yes, sir," Michel said crisply. "We *did* learn a sense of proportion along the way, didn't we, Scimitar?"

"No, Ev," Colombera corrected. "*I* learned a sense of proportion. *You* learned to listen to me."

KIRA SOON FOUND herself holding up a wall, with Konrad, Zoric and McCaig gathered around her. It was hard for the senior officers to get involved in the party—Michel was managing it right now, but Kira suspected that it would become harder for the young woman as time went on.

"Are we ready?" Zoric asked softly.

"Fighters are," Kira told her. "Maybe more training would help, but there's a point where you just have to accept that you're as good as you're going to get in the time you have. If we make them train up to the final moment of the strike, they'll be exhausted when they *start*.

"So, we rest them for a day and then we go in."

"I'm not liking being the delivery vehicle for the commandos rather than leading them," McCaig rumbled. "Milani was always my best, and they know the job as well as I do, but…it's hard to let go."

"I can't argue," Kira admitted. "*I'm* flying a nova fighter in the strike."

"Which we'd say you had no business doing if you weren't one of the two or three best pilots in Memorial Force," Konrad said.

She truly appreciated that her lover hadn't even *tried* arguing with her on that. Konrad Bueller had pushed back on her taking a nova fighter out before—and when he'd done so, he'd been right. And part of how she knew that was how often he *didn't* push back on it.

"Are the commandos ready?" Kira asked McCaig.

"Our people are good. Redward's are…better," he conceded. "Once everyone's in armor, soldier boosts don't matter *much*, but the fact that the RA commandos are boosted to eleven certainly doesn't hurt them.

"Milani knows what they're doing, and they've been running virtual training ops the whole time. The timing is everything, but once the destroyers are in the battlespace, the shuttles will be in place in under ninety seconds."

"And then you'll be gone," Kira noted with a sigh. "This whole thing is risky as hell and swings on what Panosyan does on the Crest itself."

"No updates from them?" Zoric asked.

"No, and we weren't expecting any," Kira told them. "The plan is what it is, people. We *also* need to relax, even if none of us are good at it."

"What are you implying, sir? That Memorial Force's senior officers may be workaholics?" McCaig asked. "I, for one, am offended by the suggestion that I am less than brilliant at *anything* I put my mind to."

Kira had to laugh at the big man and then kept smiling as Mel Cartman materialized out of the crowd.

The Apollon Commander, Nova Group, was carrying an entire *case* of chilled beers that she started passing out.

"I figured none of you were going to be in the middle of the crowd, and I *knew* Kira would be finishing her first beer about now," Cartman told them.

Kira traded her now-empty bottle for one of the full bottles in the case. Once all of the bottles in the case were swapped for empty, a small light on the case told them to put it on the floor—an artificial-stupid steward support drone was coming to collect it.

"Cartman and I have been doing these parties for a *long* time," Kira observed. "She has the timelines down to an art."

"And this one is better for everyone than just the old Three-Oh-Three hands getting sloshed together," Cartman said. "That just depresses Dinesha. He keeps looking around and expecting to see Joseph."

Kira nodded.

"Where *is* Patel?" she asked. *Raccoon*'s Commander, Nova Group, was there somewhere.

"Getting plied with drinks by Tamboli," Cartman said. "I do believe my flight-deck boss is testing to see if he's sufficiently recovered to be seduced."

Dilshad Tamboli was the intentionally androgynous former shuttle maintenance shop boss who ran *Deception*'s fighter deck. To Kira's knowledge, Dinesha Patel was bisexual but monogamous, so any interest on Tamboli's part would have been unrequited while Joseph Hoffman had lived.

It might still be now. Grief was a funny thing—but Kira didn't begrudge Tamboli trying, so long as they didn't push hard enough to upset or hurt Patel.

"Is someone keeping an eye on that?" she murmured.

"Yeah," Cartman agreed. "Milani."

"That seems helpful," Kira said. "Good."

Milani was the only person at the party in full body armor, which made them an extremely handy chaperone and watcher. They were capable of both subtlety and a *lack* thereof as they saw fit—and Kira trusted their judgment.

"Everything seems to be safely in order," Konrad observed. "Should we be considering retiring and letting the party carry on?"

Zoric chuckled knowingly.

"*I'm* going to keep an eye on things for a bit still," she noted. "If, say, my CEO and XO want to go bang like bunnies, I'm sure I'll be able to handle the situation without them."

Konrad almost managed to not blush that time. It was a faint coloring, one that Kira and the others likely only saw because they were expecting it.

"I don't know if that's your executive officer's plan," Kira told Zoric, winking at her boyfriend, "but it's definitely *mine*."

36

THERE WAS a moment in the wait where everything shrank down to
the timer. It was on the screens in the nova fighter around Kira. It was
in her headware. Everything else was secondary to the countdown to T
zero.

Five minutes.

Kira forced herself to exhale, running her hands over the familiar
lines and controls of the Hoplite-IV nova fighter. Most of the interceptors in Memorial Force were clones now. They had the fabricators for
manufacturing Hoplite-IV parts and had used those, combined with
Redward-built class two nova drives and Harrington coils, to build
exact duplicates.

Her fighter wasn't. It was one of the original six nova fighters she'd
smuggled out of Apollo with her. She'd arrived in Redward with a
duffle bag full of cash, a lawyer's address and six nova fighters.

So many things had changed, but her Hoplite-IV hadn't.

She smiled as she remembered that wasn't *exactly* true. Just past
where her right hand normally sat was a small statuette. Formed by
hand out of bits of scrap metal from *Conviction*, the model was hardly a
thing of great artistic beauty. It was a crude facsimile of a Hoplite inter-

ceptor flying over a mountain, only really identifiable as such if you knew the intent.

But Konrad Bueller had made it for her with his own hands as a favor and a good-luck charm. The fighter flew over the mountain, after all, and that was supposed to represent that she'd always rise above any obstacles.

It was silly and ugly and dumb and beautiful and thoughtful and romantic—and she loved it more than words could say.

Three minutes.

Kira carefully breathed in, then out again, and opened a channel.

"All squadron commanders, check in," she ordered. "Confirm fuel and ammunition status for your squadrons."

There shouldn't be any surprises there, but they had the time. Every fighter was in space around her, almost seventy nova fighters and bombers waiting for the order.

"*Deception*-Alpha reports hundred percent fuel, hundred percent ammunition. No torpedoes," Cartman reported almost instantly.

Ammunition for a nova fighter was the plasma capacitors that fed their close-range cannon. They could be refilled from the microfusion plant that powered the starfighter—but not at nearly the pace they emptied. Usually, a fighter would use up half of their capacitors in a sixty-second pass and recharge about two-thirds of what they'd lost in the sixty-second pause before the next strike.

"*Raccoon*-Alpha reports hundred percent fuel and capacitors. No torpedoes," Patel's voice said crisply.

That covered both of her CNGs and their direct squadrons. Both were interceptor squadrons of Hoplite clones. Carrying their torpedoes would have sacrificed the maneuverability they were going to need—and they weren't planning on destroying *Fortitude*.

"*Deception*-Bravo," Colombera's voice checked in. "Full fuel and ammo. No torps."

"*Deception*-Charlie," "Purlwise" Yamauchi reported. "Full fuel and ammo. One torp per plane."

Purlwise's squadron was Kira's only set of heavy fighters. They could carry two torpedoes—but the second degraded their performance.

"*Raccoon*-Bravo, all full, no torps."

"*Raccoon*-Charlie. One hundred percent fuel, one hundred ammunition, no torps."

"*Deception*-Delta. One hundred percent fuel. Capacitors at one hundred percent. One torp per fighter," Sagairt reported, his voice slightly more formal than the others. *He* had the Sinisters, the Redward-built fighter-bombers. They *could* have brought two of their three torpedoes, but they shouldn't be needed.

"*Darkwing*-Alpha," Ruben "Gizmo" Hersch reported. "Full ammunition, full fuel, one torpedo each."

Two more Darkwing squadron commanders counted in the last of Kira's fighter-bombers, then one last report came in.

"*Raccoon*-Zeta online and standing by," her bomber commander reported. "Full fuel. Fuel ammunition. Twelve torpedoes per bomber."

And *that* was why Kira's heavy fighters and fighter-bombers were only carrying one torpedo each. If things truly went to hell, she would call in six of the updated Fastball bombers—carrying *seventy-two* torpedoes between them.

That strike would be a serious threat to even *Deception* herself. If Kira's enemies forced her hand, she had the firepower to obliterate her target.

Of course, if she had to obliterate *Fortitude*, things had gone very, *very* wrong.

"T minus one minute," she said aloud, making sure all of the squadron commanders heard her. "If you have a concern or a problem, now is the last possible moment to mention it."

"If you forgot to go to the bathroom before we left, I suggest you double-check your flightsuit catheters," Cartman suggested on the same channel. "Because nobody is mothering anybody."

"Be good, Nightmare," Kira said. "We all know the plan. We all know the drill. We all know who we're up against."

Seconds ticked away. They were giving *Fortitude* a full minute more than they'd calculated she'd need. There was too much chance of her jumping somewhere slightly differently than expected. That kind of change would be a *smart* security precaution, though they might also think it was unnecessary.

"These people have no idea what's about to hit them," she continued. "Our reputation reached this place, enough that the Crown Zharang came to find and hire *us*, specifically, out of the entire galaxy.

"Pilots of Memorial Force, let's prove they made the right call."

Ten seconds. Five. Kira swallowed. There was no more time. No more second thoughts. She'd taken Jade Panosyan's money and she'd signed on for the Crown Zharang's cause. If the Crest was to be free of the Sanctuary and Prosperity Party...if they were going to stick a finger in the Equilibrium Institute's eye...if Memorial Force was going to have a fleet carrier this year, there was only one thing left to do.

"Memorial Force...*nova and attack*."

SURPRISE WAS TOTAL. *Fortitude* was exactly where they'd projected she'd be, and six of the Hussar nova fighters were in space.

Kira's sixty-one nova fighters emerged in a perfectly synchronized wave and activated their multiphasic jammers within moments of arrival. Old habit meant that she tried to lead the way, gunning her Harrington coils to full power and blazing forward through the chaotic mess of the jamming.

The other interceptors were with her, five squadrons of the Hoplites and their clones swooping in. The Blue Scarlet pilots didn't even begin to react before the first plasma bolts struck home.

Four of the Hussars were gone before they even started defensive maneuvering, and *Fortitude*'s defensive guns weren't firing either.

A fifth Hussar vaporized, a kill Kira was reasonably sure was hers, and the sixth *finally* seemed to wake up, unleashing a spiraling spray of fire as the pilot dodged back behind the carrier.

They didn't make it. Kira couldn't tell which of her pilots had taken down the fighter—she had no more communications in the mess the multiphasic jammers created than *Fortitude* did.

The Blue Scarlets had been slow and...almost amateurish. A far cry from the elite pilots Kira had anticipated. Even faced with complete surprise, veterans should have reacted before they died.

T plus sixty seconds. The destroyers flashed into existence at the edge of the jamming zone—but the next wave of Blue Scarlet fighters should be launching within seconds.

Kira twisted her fighter around the carrier—*Fortitude*'s engines were now online and she was laboring to evade them, but none of her guns had fired yet. The hope that her weapons would have been fully safed after the firing trials seemed to be bearing out.

She absently noted the deployment of Milani's shuttles, the boarding ships flashing toward *Fortitude* as she watched for the launching nova fighters. T plus seventy to eighty seconds had been the expectation for the second-wave launch.

Now they were at T plus *two minutes*, with the shuttles about to board…and only now did Kira see energy flares in the carrier deck to suggest the launch. The nova fighters were coming out.

And it was the worst possible time. There was no way that she could warn off the shuttles, and there was no way her people could intercept the Hussars before they found themselves right in the middle of Milani's boarding force.

Even the most incompetent pilots could obliterate half a dozen boarding shuttles with twice as many fighters at point-blank range. Without communications, Kira couldn't order anyone to intercept or break off.

Instinct took over and she was feeding power to her Harrington coils and plasma guns before she even consciously realized what she was doing, dropping her fighter in between the assault shuttles and their destination and flying *toward* the carrier.

One of the biggest arguments Kira had had with John Estanza and his fighter pilots when she'd come aboard had been over unguided landing drills. She'd demanded that her pilots learn how to land a fighter with no control from the carrier.

The theory was for if the carrier's communications were out… but it also worked for coming into the hangar bay of a *hostile* carrier.

As twelve enemy fighters tried to come *out*.

The last thing the Crester pilots were expecting was for someone to be mad enough to fly into their hangar bay. Without carrier guidance, manual landings were something kept for emergencies and desperation—and a carrier's defensive guns would make a hostile approach suicide.

Except *Fortitude*'s guns were down and Kira had a hundred and twenty lives on the line.

Her plasma guns opened fire *inside* the carrier, tearing apart nova fighter after nova fighter as they launched toward her. Debris and vapor sprayed across the deck—but the launch system carried a lot of it at *her*.

One fighter managed to open fire, and alarms *screamed* at Kira as a third of her fighter was torn away. Her remaining guns silenced the Hussar. Debris and chaos had cleared the rest.

But more alarms were screaming at her, and she finally spared the fraction of a second for her headware to tell her what was going on.

Nova drives. Gone.

Microfusion plant. Gone.

Port guns. Gone.

Harrington coils. Half-gone, but no *power*.

She had about two seconds before she blasted into the back of a carrier, the horrifically named *splash plate* of armor intended to protect the carrier from a crashing nova fighter. Her Harringtons could stop her, but her power was gone.

But her guns were still at thirty percent capacitors—and that could be fed *back* to the power systems as well.

That gave her half a second.

For half a second, Kira Demirci had full power for half of her Harrington coils. It might have been enough, but she couldn't take the chance and went for the age-old solution of a pilot who needed to *stop*.

It wasn't called lithobraking when you did it to a carrier deck.

37

KIRA FORCED HER EYES OPEN. For a moment, she wasn't sure what was going on, then it all came crashing in.

Her headware calmly informed her that she'd been unconscious for six point four seconds and it wasn't detecting major head trauma. That was reassuring…though the fact that the system felt it necessary to *say* that wasn't.

She lifted her head and looked around to see what she'd got herself into. Without power, her Hoplite didn't have an exterior view, so all she could see was the inside of the cockpit.

An interior that currently had a visible sixty-centimeter intrusion where the hull had collapsed. Nova fighters relied on maneuverability and energy dispersion networks to survive incoming fire. Actual *impact* wasn't something they were designed for.

Swallowing, Kira unstrapped herself and reached for the emergency survival kit. Urgency was added by both the faint scent of burning—and the distinct sound of blaster fire outside.

The survival kit produced a blaster pistol. The rest of the equipment wasn't necessary for now, but she *definitely* needed the gun.

The damage meant that it took her longer to get out of the fighter than she'd expected, and she emerged to discover that *Fortitude*'s crew were peppering the wreck with blaster bolts.

"Get it off the deck," someone snapped. "I don't *care* if the pilot's alive—if we don't get planes up, we're fucked."

So, they were *trying* to keep her head down. Most likely while someone brought up a bulldozer. Kira moved over to the edge of the wing and took a peek. There was a ragged line of half a dozen soldiers in unpowered armor with blaster rifles, along with maybe twice that in techs or maybe even *pilots* with blaster pistols.

She could see someone heading for the bulldozer and grimaced. While she doubted that the machine would succeed in moving her fighter—it looked *very* embedded in the deck—it would probably manage to crush *her*, cover or no cover.

So, she shot at that tech, carefully leaning over the wreck. It took her three blasts to catch the running man, but he fell with a limp finality when the third shot took him in the back.

Of course, *that* drew a salvo of fire at her position. She could smell more burning as the metal vaporized under the incoming blasts, but she returned fire.

She was staying behind cover, but she knew her role now. She was in everybody's face, which meant that *she* was the *distraction*.

And the real boarding party arrived moments later, the assault shuttle's heavy blasters crackling like rapid-fire thunder as they swept into hard landings.

Armored troopers swarmed out of the spacecraft, the armor rendering the difference between Kira's mercenaries and the Redward commandos near-invisible. They moved as a single body, setting up mobile shields and peppering the defenders with precise and deadly fire.

By the time the last shuttle was disgorging troops, the hangar deck was secure—and an unfamiliar armored suit with a *very* familiar holographic dragon swirling around its shoulders was advancing on Kira like an angry avenging deity.

"Commander," she greeted Milani. She leaned on the fighter for a moment, then winced away as the retained heat from the blaster bolts burned her *through* her armored flight suit.

"What. The. Fuck. Were you thinking?" Milani ground out.

"That if a dozen heavy fighters launched into the middle of your landing operation, a hundred and twenty of my commandos were going to die and this whole mission would die with them," Kira said calmly.

She gestured at the wrecked starfighter.

"I probably should have anticipated this, but I didn't get that far. Do we have coms off-ship yet?"

"No," Milani told her. "We're still activating the localized jammers to knock out *Fortitude*'s communications. Then we'll set up a relay at the end of the flight deck to bounce out as we need."

"McCaig and Michel should already be gone. The fighters will be gone at T plus twelve unless you give them a signal to stay," Kira said. "They'll signal the prize crew to come join us."

She surveyed the deck. Her Hoplite-IV had blocked the launch of the remaining Hussars, which meant there were still twelve of the heavy fighters aboard. By her math, that was twelve more of the advanced heavy fighters than anyone had told her were going to be aboard *Fortitude*!

"We got lucky," she told Milani. There was definitely enough space to still land the prize-crew shuttles—the only nova pinnaces her fleet had—and even to tuck them out of sight before the Prime Minister arrived.

"We won't have the people to move my fighter, but that gives us an excuse not to have Hussars out when the PM arrives," she continued. "The Cabinet aren't going to know the difference between a Crest heavy fighter wreck and an Apollon interceptor wreck. You didn't lose your landing ships, and the state of the flight deck will work for us."

"You should have *died* in that stunt," Milani told her. "You might still. I've got teams out into the ship, but I'll remind you that we are *badly* outnumbered by even the skeleton crew running a ship on trials.

"And all it takes to blow this whole apart is one person managing to get a headware com to *Penalty Fee*."

"I'll be good, Commander," Kira promised. "I'll stick to you like glue until we have the bridge. Then... Well, I guess you don't need to pretend to be a prize captain. I can conn a carrier."

"Finally, something in this mess that I *agree* is good news," Milani told her. "If I think you're going to wander off, I *will* stun you. Potential concussions be damned."

"I'll be good," Kira repeated. "I wasn't planning on getting in a ground fight today."

Milani swore. Kira didn't recognize the words—Arabic, she *thought*? —but the tone was unquestionable.

"Bertoli!" they snapped. "Get me a spare unpowered vest and a blaster rifle. If the Commodore is going to join us, she's going to need some damn party favors!"

KIRA SHIFTED UNCOMFORTABLY in the vest. Her flight suit was armored against light blaster fire and more capable of surviving it than, say, the leather jacket that had saved her life twice now. It wouldn't, however, stop the high-powered plasma bolts from a full-size blaster rifle.

The armored vest Bertoli had strapped her into *would*. Not repeatedly—not even the powered heavy armor the point troops were wearing would stop more than a handful of shots—but she'd survive a hit.

And that seemed important as Milani and their point troops hammered toward the bridge. Even against normal powered armor, the bulky suits the mercenaries around Kira were wearing seemed immense.

These, apparently, were what half a million kroner had *rented* from the Redward Army. She was pretty sure they were supposed to bring the ten suits of heavy boarding armor back, though from the hits they were taking, she wasn't sure that was going to happen.

"Okay, so, where are the real guards?" Milani muttered after several minutes.

"What do you mean?" Kira asked. "Your people are getting shot to hell."

"I *expected* that," they growled. "I *expected* to have lost at least two people on this squad, but so far, we've managed to keep pace by

rotating people out and letting the suit self-repair handle it. This is…
yard security with decent gear. I was expecting real marines."

"There should be a Ministerial Protection Detail team *somewhere* on
the ship," Kira told them. "I don't know where, though. Where would
you send them?"

"Communications," Milani replied. "Which means Major Klerken is
going to run into them."

Klerken was their borrowed commando company leader. Hopefully, she was as good as the other commando officers Kira had met.

"The pilots weren't even half as good as I was expecting," Kira
admitted in a pause in the fighting a moment later. "Like they were…"

"Political," Milani finished for her—then shoved her against the
wall as a trio of armored defenders jumped through a bulkhead that
unexpectedly slid aside. Their armored body was between Kira and
the blaster fire for a critical second.

One that saved Kira's life—and allowed *her* to open fire on the
Cresters. The armor took two shots from her rifle, and then her target
went down with a horrible cracking noise and a spray of ash across the
wall behind them.

The other two were already down, and Milani grunted.

"Commander?" Kira snapped.

"I'll live," they replied. "Pass-through burn. The suit is handling it
and rebuilding the web, but that *hurt*."

"How close are we to the bridge?" she asked. Time was getting
short. It was T plus ten minutes.

"Two minutes. I know; we're almost out of time."

"We were always going to make the call before we had control,"
Kira told him. "Even if these are political troops."

Not *military veteran* elites. *Political* elites. Pilots and soldiers and
crew the Sanctuary and Prosperity Party could trust to protect the
Prime Minister and do what she said no matter what.

She'd misjudged the Blue Scarlet Combat Group and *Fortitude*'s
defenders. That was to their advantage, thankfully, but the realization
bothered her.

What *else* had she missed?

38

"OKAY, so, we found the MPD team."

A heavy blaster thunder-crackled down the corridor as Kira helped Bertoli pull a wounded mercenary back. No one had *died* yet, but the resistance had toughened just as they hit the bridge.

"I noticed," she told Milani drily. "What's your take?"

"Four and a half minutes till *Penalty Fee* arrives," they replied. "We can probably spin it out for five minutes of 'ignoring them' after that."

There was a moment of silence and the heavy blaster crackled again.

"I make it one heavy blaster," Milani said, clearly identifying it just from the sound. "They're laying down suppressive fire—quite competently, I might add. Secondary fire suggests eight troopers. Quick glance I got showed low-profile high-density power armor, probably Fringe manufacture."

Kira whistled silently inside her helmet. You could *get* Fringe weapons in the Rim—especially if you were head of government of a wealthy system like the Crest—but they'd come a long way and they didn't travel cheaply.

"If you don't want the prize crew, you have to warn them off *now*," Kira hissed.

"We'll be fine," the mercenary replied sharply. "They aren't the only ones with wonderful toys."

A panel in Milani's armor opened up and they removed what looked like a piece of plastic, roughly forty centimeters long by twelve wide and three thick.

They held it in front of them as they closed the panel, and the dragon swirled to look at Kira.

"You never saw this, sir," they told Kira calmly—and then crushed the panel between their armored gauntlets.

Kira watched in not-quite-horror as the plain plastic block dissolved into dust—dust that took to the air and flashed around the corner at high speed.

Attack microbots were *technically* a gray area, not quite covered by the general ban on attack nanoweaponry, but most people regarded them as extremely questionable regardless.

"Non-replicating," Milani told her. "No worse, really, than regular explosives, except self-mobile. But…people get twitchy."

The explosion that echoed down the corridor as the mercenary finished speaking silenced the heavy blaster.

"What…do they *do*?" Kira asked.

"Go the target area designated by my headware, attach themselves to any available source of human-level body heat—capable of both scanning through and penetrating power armor—and then detonate on my signal," Milani said quietly. "Everyone in that hall is dead.

"We should move."

THE GORE and debris scattered across the hallway sent a shiver of atavistic fear down Kira's spine. From the suddenly slow pace of most of Milani's lead squad, she wasn't the only one looking at the nonbinary mercenary commander slightly askance now.

The bridge door was jammed open by the wreckage of the heavy blaster itself. The Ministerial Protection Detail had been using the armored hatch as cover, which left more than enough space for Milani and Bertoli to insert their powered gauntlets and pull the accessway open.

Fortitude's bridge was immense to Kira's eyes, a fifteen-meter-diameter space with two levels, focused on a central hologram tank at least five meters across on its own. A dozen techs and officers were still in there, wisely backing away from their consoles as the mercenaries entered.

"This is an outrage," a tall woman of apparent Korean extraction snapped. "And madness. You cannot possibly plan to escape the wrath of the Navy of the Royal Crest—and you have no—"

The ship's computers dinged.

"Command transfer, recognized. Captain Gyeong-Ja Moon authorizations, removed. Captain Random Sample Six, activated.

"All current officer authorizations, removed. All personnel authorizations, removed.

"Standing by for new personnel listings from Captain Sample Six."

Kira couldn't resist. She removed her helmet as she walked onto the bridge so that Captain Moon could *see* the brilliant grin on her face.

"Captain Moon, I do believe you are relieved," she told the other woman. "And you're standing next to my chair."

"How… That's…" Moon spluttered, but *Fortitude* happily informed Kira that the Crester was trying to access ship's systems…and failing.

Moon had the commanding-officer codes. Kira had the *builder* codes, the ones that would have been deactivated at the end of her trial —plus a set of commanding-officer codes and a set of *Admiralty* codes, just in case. The woman had never had a chance of retaining control of *Fortitude*'s systems once any of Kira's people were on the bridge.

"Commander, please detain these gentle people without hurting them more than you have to," Kira told Milani as she brushed past the stunned Captain and lowered herself into the command chair.

She *could* fly a carrier. It wasn't going to be an efficient or elegant process, but she could do it. Right now, though, all she had to do was bring the carrier's engines down to "we are making test maneuvers" levels instead of "we are running from a threat" levels.

Mercenaries produced cuffs from various panels on their armor and began restraining the NRC crew. None of them resisted—a combination of shock and realizing they were utterly outclassed, Kira suspected.

"Internal sensors are being fucked by our multiphasic jammers," she told Milani as they joined her at the command station. "Which is the point, I know. Any updates from your side?"

"Everyone is supposed to send runners to the flight deck," the commando replied. "I've dispatched one. Bertoli on the wounded. It looks like we aren't going to lose anyone."

"How long have you been carrying attack microbots?" Kira asked softly as she activated the codes they'd given the skeleton crew.

"I picked them up for this," Milani told her. "Redward *can* make them. They just don't."

"Most people don't," she said. "Because they're *banned*."

"Not *quite*," they corrected, echoing her earlier thoughts. "And we couldn't afford failure."

"No, we couldn't," Kira agreed. "Without the warning to break off, nova pinnaces should be coming aboard. Two minutes to *Penalty Fee*'s arrival."

She entered more commands and the holotank cleared. *Fortitude*'s multiphasic jammers were now offline, and all of *Kira's* jammers were either gone or locked to her volume of hull.

"I'm not seeing any resistance in the engineering systems," she told Milani, "so I think your people are in position. I now control the ship's software, but there are a few places where someone clever can still cause me a lot of trouble."

"Once main points are secure, all strike groups should be deploying two-commando sweep teams to track down any resistance," they replied. "The prize crew will be running a manual cable connection from the hangar relay to here to let us hail *Penalty Fee* with that if nothing else."

"I know the plan," Kira said quietly. She shook her head as she looked around the bridge of the most powerful warship she'd ever set foot on.

"Part of me honestly didn't think we were going to make it this far," she admitted. "Any concerns on grabbing the PM?"

"If everything goes right, she should just walk right into our clutch-es," Milani pointed out. "So, *of course* I have concerns!"

39

KIRA UNDERSTOOD the principles and high-level structure of the runner system that Milani was using to maintain control of the ship. The powerful jammers running on the flight deck—and now several other key structural points in the ship—weren't true multiphasic jammers, but they were more than capable of shutting out communication emerging from the ship.

They *shouldn't* be detectable from outside the ship, but Kira still held her breath when *Penalty Fee* emerged from nova, exactly on schedule.

"Will we be able to receive their hails?" she asked Konrad. Once again, she'd stolen her boyfriend from his job as executive officer and chief engineer of *Deception* to support a detached operation.

Strangely, Zoric never seemed to object. Probably because Kira, at least in her own opinion, had a solid judgment of when she needed the best engineer they had.

"No," Konrad told her calmly. "The jamming field wouldn't work if it wasn't covering the external transceiver dishes. We can't be sure no one is going to be able to hack into the communications network."

"That's why my people are setting up a relay on the flight deck,"

Milani told her. "It sticks out enough to receive and transmit, but we need— Ah!"

Two of Milani's commandos, in regular armor instead of the heavy assault suits Milani's point team was still wearing, appeared at the entrance to the bridge with a large coil of cabling.

"Get that over to the com console and hook it up," Milani barked. They looked at the screen. "Is it just me, or was *Penalty Fee* expecting to see us?"

Kira nodded. Even a presumed *friendly* fleet carrier showing up unexpectedly should have earned some kind of caution or reaction from the battlecruiser. Instead, *Penalty Fee* had emerged from nova and just...waited.

"They knew *Fortitude* would be here," she agreed. "Or at least the new Captain did."

She shook her head.

"I don't see any scans or visible energy trails that they can pick up from their location," she said aloud. "Soler?"

Isidora Soler was a pale-skinned woman with pitch-black hair and eyes who normally served as *Deception*'s senior assistant tactical officer. Today, she was the tactical officer of the skeleton crew Kira had to run *Fortitude* and was sharing XO duties with Konrad.

"I don't see anything either," she confirmed. "I *think* we're clear, but we need to communicate with them, or they'll get suspicious."

Kira concealed a smile. Soler was being careful to tell her bosses what they might need to know, but *everyone* in the room knew that. That was the price of the rapid expansion of her mercenary fleet, though. Soler had been a Redward Officer Academy dropout two years earlier.

The woman who'd *caused* her dropout had picked up a dishonorable discharge and a ten-year jail sentence almost before Soler's paperwork had finished processing, but even rapid justice didn't make it any easier to walk back into a building where someone had used physical violence to attempt to recruit you into organized crime.

Both the courage necessary to come forward after that and her mostly complete training had been exactly what Kira and Zoric had been looking for—which brought the pale young woman there, to the Crest Sector, a hundred-plus light-years from home.

"We're linked," Konrad announced from the coms console. "Relay is online and chugging. We have a copy of their message on seeing us —standard ship-to-ship courtesy."

"Send back the same," Kira ordered. "Then tell them we are on trial exercises and they are to stay at least one million kilometers clear."

Konrad nodded and pulled a headset on. Like everyone else on *Fortitude*'s bridge, he'd be holding down multiple roles until this was over.

"Time on the core?" she asked as he finished speaking into the headset.

"No idea," he admitted calmly. "Jamming is screwing with intra-ship coms, even system reports. We don't have a lot of control or feed-back systems operating yet."

"Milani?" Kira turned to the ground-force commander. "How long till we can drop those jammers?"

"My reports are slow," they told her. "I *think* we're clear or should be shortly, but it'll be two or three minutes after that's done before I have confirmation.

"At least with the cable, we have a direct link to the flight deck and can shut down the jammers quickly enough." The big armor suit didn't transmit a shrug, but Milani's voice did. "Five minutes, boss. Maybe a couple more."

"We've told *Penalty Fee* to stand off. That should cover our expected coms and buy us some time," Kira noted. Holographic control panels appeared around the Captain's chair at her mental command, and she grimaced.

Like Konrad had said, very few of the internal systems were running. The majority of the network she was trying to access was cabled, but there were *enough* wireless bridges and sensors the jammers were blocking to render the situation difficult.

The same energy dispersion networks the carrier would use to resist plasma hits were keeping *Penalty Fee* from seeing the jamming— and would keep an external source of jamming from causing this much trouble. Multiphasic jamming defined the battlespace, after all.

A commando stepped through the bridge accessway and crossed to Milani. A swift whispered conversation followed, and Milani gave the armored soldier a thumbs-up gesture.

"Do we have a crew listing, boss?" Milani asked, turning back to Kira.

"Let me check." She had full command access, but that thought hadn't occurred to her. "Yeah, here. Step closer."

She didn't quite have to touch her subordinate to send them data, but it was close. The dragon swirled attentively across Milani's armor as they processed the data.

"Listing says one hundred fourteen people aboard, but doesn't include the PM's detail," Milani noted aloud. "We have ninety-eight prisoners and thirty-nine confirmed corpses. Think the Ministerial Protection Detail brought more than twenty-three people?"

Kira grimaced.

"If they brought twenty-three, they probably brought twenty-four," she pointed out.

"We also might be miscounting bodies outside the bridge," her subordinate admitted. "Those would be MPD."

That did *not* help Kira's current grimace or general discomfort with how Milani had accessed the bridge. There were definitely *worse* deaths than that, but most human cultures had a quite-reasonable aversion to sub-visual-scale weaponry.

"Konrad, if we bring everything back up, how's the internal surveillance?" she asked.

"Seventy-three percent of the cameras are wireless to allow concealed placement," he warned. "So, I don't know. The problem is that it only takes seconds for someone to send a message to *Penalty Fee*."

Kira checked the distance.

"They're at five light-seconds right now," she said. "Headware coms can't cross that—best case for those is *three*—so they'd need to have armor systems or a portable transceiver. It's a risk, but..."

"We can't keep the jamming up forever. Not if we actually want to *do* anything with this ship," Konrad finished for her.

Kira exhaled and nodded.

"Konrad, Soler, get your eyes on those cameras," she ordered. "The moment we see *anybody*, I want to know—and if you see a transceiver or someone in armor, we shut everything right back down."

"I'm on it," Konrad replied.

"I'm in," Soler confirmed a moment later.

"Milani?" Kira said softly.

"You're the boss."

"Shut it down."

With the hardware in her head, Kira knew the moment the jamming cut out. The hardware and software had kept it from having a noticeable effect, but the return of her data channels was still sudden and obvious.

Her team was suddenly in a network in her head. *Fortitude* was suddenly in her head, her command authority linking her in to the Captain's control channels.

"We've got three solitaries scattered through the ship," Soler reported an instant later. "None have full armor or appear to have coms. Two are ship's crew, third is MPD.

"MPD officer is armed with a blaster rifle and appears to be setting up a target blind. Ship's crew are in hiding."

"I have the locations on all three," Milani replied. "Linking to my nearest teams and moving in. Gal with the blaster is *not* getting her ambush."

It took another ninety seconds for Milani's people to check back in, but then their dragon perked up cheerfully and they turned to Kira.

"*Fortitude* is secured, Commodore," they reported.

"All right, people." Kira looked around and smiled. "Next steps. We have an hour or so to pretend nothing has happened, then we jump to the rendezvous.

"We have a lot of work to do to clean up the flight deck and make it look safe for the Prime Minister and her Cabinet Ministers to land. We'll need a simulacrum of Captain Gyeong-Ja Moon that can talk to the Prime Minister's people when we meet them, and we need to make sure we've unlocked as much of this ship as we can."

Her prize crew was already studying their consoles.

"I'm not worried about *Penalty Fee*," she said softly. "I *am* worried about the two cruisers and the carrier that are coming with Prime Minister Jeong.

"So, Soler, code me the ability to fool her. Konrad…get me this damn ship's guns."

40

DESPITE WHAT SHE'D said about not worrying, Kira spent the fifty-eight minutes they remained in the company of *Penalty Fee* watching the battlecruiser like a hawk with hungry chicks at home. At one hundred and twenty kilocubics, the ship was the same size as the battlecruisers and carriers Redward was laying down, but more modern in a dozen small ways.

One of those ways was almost certainly her *sensors*, which meant that she might well see something Kira didn't anticipate.

But as minutes stretched to an hour, the battlecruiser carried on her patrol without ever hinting her crew thought something was amiss.

"You know, I would not like to be her new Captain," Konrad murmured, stepping up to her seat. "The last Captain mutinied. This one? They're going to work out that *Penalty Fee* was here after we took the ship eventually."

"They're probably loyal enough to protect them… Well, from the SPP," Kira replied. "Are we ready?"

"Cooldown complete. Nova vector for the rendezvous point set." He looked at the holodisplay and the battlecruiser hovering four light-seconds away. "If *Penalty Fee* is paying enough attention, they may realize we didn't nova very far."

"They shouldn't know that we're scheduled for a full-length nova test now," Kira said. "If they do... Well, it's a risk we have to take."

She nodded to Konrad and glanced around her new bridge.

"Make it happen, Commander Bueller," she told him.

He didn't move, grinning down at her and activating the command from his headware. A momentary chill ran through her—a smoother reaction than many ships, if not *quite* as smooth as Captain Zamorano's ship.

Then they were in deep space, a full light-week away from the *Crest's Herald*—and only two light-seconds from the rest of Memorial Force.

All of them flashed up as unknown contacts on *Fortitude*'s scanners, of course, though it quickly resolved *Deception* as a Brisingr K70 cruiser.

"Loading in the ID codes," Soler reported. "Linking in to the command network.

"Welcome home, *Fortitude*," Zoric told them all the moment the channel opened up. "It's damn good to see you. We were a tad worried about the Commodore."

"My fighter's a write-off," Kira replied. "I don't think we're even getting her off the flight deck. Lithobraking *sucks*."

"It's not lithobraking when you do it to a *carrier deck*," Cartman replied, the CNG joining channel. She'd been through the same lectures and training as Kira, after all. "What's the plan now?"

"First, we need to get the shuttles back over to *Deception* and *Raccoon*," Kira told them all. "We'll relay personnel back and forth as needed, but we don't want to have any unexpected ships on the deck when we meet *Terminal Loss* and her escorts."

"There's a fighter *embedded* in the deck," Konrad pointed out.

"And we're going to use that," Kira said. "We'll pull hands over from the rest of the Force and get everything running aboard *Fortitude* that we can. But we leave my fighter where she is. If we can sort out how to launch the Hussars *past* her, I'll steal pilots for them, but..."

She sighed.

"Crashes happen, people. We lost *more* pilots in the rush training system for Redward than we should have, but we always lose pilots in training," she said grimly. "And Blue Scarlet, as it turns out, were selected for *political* reliability at least as much as they were selected for piloting skill.

"So, they had an accident, and that's why we don't put up a combat space patrol when we arrive at Grand Prince," she continued. "That removes one obstacle to the final escape jump. A light-week nova gives us a thirty-two-minute cooldown. That would be an odd time for us to pull fighters aboard."

"The PM and her Cabinet are supposed to be aboard for three hours," Zoric said. "That does suggest more than just an inspection tour."

"It's still going to be a problem once she's aboard, since she's expecting to meet Captain Moon, not me," Kira said. "We need *everything* working. If it comes down to it, *Fortitude* may well have to fight two cruisers and an assault carrier with no easy way out."

That chilled the conversation.

"So, we make this work," she told them. "Once we're clear of the Crest, the hard part is done. If nothing else, the rest of Memorial Force will join us for the trip to Guadaloop and the dance party that's going to be our time there."

"'Dance party,' sir?" Michel asked, her tone faux-hopeful.

"I don't plan on fighting either GODCom *or* Battle Group *Final Usury*," Kira pointed out. "But we have to deliver our ransom demand, and that means we're going to be novaing around the system like crazy to evade pursuit."

"We all know that dance," McCaig said grimly. "It's not a favorite, but we know the steps."

"For now, we have twenty hours to turn *Fortitude* into a fully functioning trap for the Prime Minister of a first-rate Rim hegemon," Kira said calmly. "So, let's be about it."

KIRA SPENT MORE of the twenty-hour prep time sleeping than she'd expected. The Captain's office, attached to the bridge, had just enough space that the designers had included a fold-out bed. She crashed on it three hours after they hit the rendezvous point and woke up nine hours later.

As soon as she got out of the bed, the office coffeemaker started burbling—and the distinctive scent of Redward Royal Reserve wafted through the room. There was *no* way that Captain Moon had stocked her coffee maker with the private blend of the royal family of Redward, which meant that someone had set it up for her.

Probably Konrad, who'd done it without waking her.

A series of quick reports was already waiting for her, updates recorded or dashed off as projects were completed. Angel Waldroup had apparently just reported aboard and had a plan for the Hussars. The guns were proving recalcitrant. Konrad had rigged up his decoy nova cores for the additional Jianhong radiation.

More reports. None of them were long, but a *lot* of things had happened in nine hours. Kira swallowed down her coffee—an abuse of the good beans, she knew—and tugged a brush through her hair to make herself more presentable.

Then she grabbed a cup with a sealing lid, filled it with the Royal Reserve and went looking for Angel Waldroup.

ANGEL "BOSS" Waldroup had been the deck boss of *Conviction* when Kira had met her. She'd run that carrier's fighter tech crews with an iron fist—but not so iron a fist that she'd defied John Estanza's final evacuation order.

Kira had given the woman a choice between running *Deception*'s flight deck or *Raccoon*'s, and she'd refused to displace Tamboli from their existing role. Waldroup wasn't any fonder of *Raccoon* than anyone else in Memorial Force, but she'd turned the so-called junk carrier into an effective fighter platform.

Now she stood on the edge of *Fortitude*'s hangar deck and surveyed her new kingdom like a conquering queen. She'd set her broad shoulders back and had her hair braided tightly to her scalp, ready to get to work.

"Commodore," she greeted Kira. "You made a fucking mess of my new deck."

"Are we talking about the cannon holes or the wrecked fighter?" Kira asked.

"The fighter," Waldroup snapped, turning to face Kira. She was a large and heavyset woman in every way, looming over her commanding officer. "They've got a decent repair-drone setup here. The cannon holes will be patched at least two hours before go time."

"And the fighter?"

"We could move her," Waldroup admitted. "The bulldozer exists for a reason. It'll be a nightmare and make a giant mess. I could make this deck fully functional in twenty minutes, but it won't look *good*."

The deck boss's sharp description brought back painful memories, and Kira shivered. She'd *seen* what it looked like when a wrecked fighter was bulldozed off the deck...and in one of the cases where she'd seen it, the dead pilot had still been inside.

"I don't care what's pretty," she told the mechanic. "I have a lot of faith in your judgment of what's necessary, Angel. Your message said you had a plan for the Hussars?"

"I do," Waldroup replied. "Wouldn't work with anything less maneuverable. You can't *land* a bird through that mess," she said, gesturing to the wreck. "You need the space to run friction with the wheels and the grav-catch to slow the bird down.

"Power up the grav-catch a bit higher and you can stop the fighter before it hits the mess, but you can't take her past it," she concluded. "So, anybody that launches comes back and goes in a hangar on *this* side of the deck. Easy to launch from there, but the landing is going to suck."

"And the launch?" Kira prodded again.

Waldroup grinned.

"Despite how *you* landed in here," she said, "all of the landings and launches are going to need to be on full computer control until we clear the deck. I've checked the angles and the power on the Hussar's Harringtons and antigravs."

"They can clear it?" Kira asked.

"They can clear it. Pop up, fly over. They lose most of the velocity punch from the grav catapult, but they can get out," Waldroup confirmed.

"But we can't *put* fighters back there?" Kira said, turning to look at where the dozen heavy fighters were hidden. They were almost invisible in their hangars, and with the wreck to keep their hopeful prisoners on this side of the deck…

"Not a chance," the deck boss admitted. "We could stick another dozen fighters aboard, but we'd need to put them here."

"Which is visible to our guests," Kira concluded. "That's not going to work."

She smiled.

"Stick around, Angel. Get used to the place. See if you can make her look like the *only* thing that ever happened here was the crash."

"Can do, Commodore," Waldroup told her. "I brought my best."

"Good." Kira shook her head. "Now I'm afraid I need to go talk to my boyfriend about his guns."

41

WITH EVERY FIBER of her being, Kira Demirci wanted to be in one of the Hussar-Sevens on the hangar deck. Each of them was prepped, loaded with a single torpedo, and manned by pilots under Helmet Sagairt's command.

By moving those pilots over to *Fortitude* immediately, she *hoped* that her people had managed to organize the decks on *Deception* and *Raccoon* to avoid the problems they'd been having with too many fighters.

She wanted to lead that double squadron herself—but if the Hussars launched, so much had gone wrong. Her place, as Commodore of Memorial Force, wasn't in a fighter today.

It was on *Fortitude*'s bridge, playing the role of Captain Gyeong-Ja Moon via a digital simulacrum.

"Nova complete," Konrad said, his voice echoing oddly in the carrier's mostly empty bridge.

"Soler?" Kira asked.

"We are on target. Grand Prince is four hundred thousand kilometers away, twelve degrees to starboard, six degrees up.

"I have four major contacts and what looks like four six-fighter squadrons of nova fighters," she continued. "Twenty-eight contacts. Warbook makes the nova fighters Hussar-Sixes and Cavalier-Sixes."

"ID those ships, please," Kira ordered as a spike of nervousness ran down her spine. There were only supposed to be three. That was already enough to render this suicide if it became a fight. Who was the *fourth*?

"Confirming, seventy-kilocubic light cruiser, *Terminal Loss*," Soler reported. "One-hundred-twenty-cubic battlecruiser *Amortization*. Second battlecruiser, *Amiability*. Sixty-kilocubic assault carrier *Valiant*."

"They brought a second battlecruiser," Kira muttered. "That… shouldn't be a problem, I don't think. Are we set up to hail them?"

"Yes, sir."

Kira nodded to her limited staff and focused on the recorder. The simulacrum should make this work…*should*.

"*Terminal Loss*, this is Captain Moon aboard *Fortitude*," she reported. "We are ready for our 'scheduled exercises.' Standing by."

A few moments passed and Kira checked the data on the NRC task group. They were currently just over a hundred thousand kilometers away and closing. With no jammers, Kira could basically guarantee direct hits from *Fortitude*'s turrets at this point.

Of course, so could the three cruisers over there. *Valiant* only had a pair of single-gun antiship turrets in her defensive arsenal, but even *Terminal Loss* had eighteen guns on nine turrets. Kira pulled up the specifications on the battlecruisers and swallowed grimly.

Thirty guns in ten triple turrets. Each of them slightly weaker than *Fortitude*'s more-modern cannon but still notably more powerful than *Deception*'s.

This could *not* come to a fight.

"*Terminal Loss* is requesting an active channel, sir," Soler told her. "Simulacrum processing time shouldn't be noticeable against the time lag. You're good to go."

Kira nodded and inhaled sharply.

It was showtime.

"WELCOME TO GRAND PRINCE, CAPTAIN MOON," the middle-aged man in Kira's screen told her. Captain Tāne Król of *Terminal Loss* had ground out in his career in the NRC five years before, one of a type of officer destined to serve out a career as a Commander until seniority meant he either had to retire or be promoted—and his superiors would try *very* hard to find him a non-command billet, from Kira's reading of his file.

Except his loyalty to the Sanctuary and Prosperity Party had seen him promoted, and now he was one of their most loyal partisans in the Navy and the man they trusted to transport the Prime Minister.

"We managed to scrape together another battlecruiser to keep the Prime Minister and Cabinet safe," Król told her. "We're starting to hear some ugly rumors about the Royalists, so extra security seemed wise."

"It can never hurt; that's for sure," Kira agreed. "I'm glad to see the fighter patrol, too. We had an unfortunate accident in one of our test flights, and my deck is currently only half-usable.

"We had to send half the Blue Scarlets home on their own because it was a choice between landing *them* or landing the Prime Minister."

"Is it going to be a problem?" Król asked. "Is everyone okay?"

"No, but no," Kira said. "A Blue Scarlet pilot crashed their fighter in the middle of the hangar deck. They were killed in the crash, and I declined to order it treated like garbage with a body inside."

She shook her head.

"It's peacetime, after all. We can land the PM on half a deck and have the body extracted properly to return to their family when we get back to the Crest.

"You'll need to let the PM's pilot know—they'll have to surrender full control to our flight deck on approach. I'm told the landing is going to be extremely precise."

"I will," Król promised. "Is everything in place for the inspection?"

"Everything is brand-new and my hands have spent every moment they weren't running tests polishing," Kira replied drily. "I don't think you'll find a more ready-for-inspection ship in the entire Navy of the Royal Crest, my friend."

Król laughed.

"On behalf of my ship and crew, I would *like* to challenge that, but I suspect we're all better off if you're right," he said. "Her Excellency and the Ministers are boarding their pinnace now. I'll check with the CNG, but I suspect we'll have fighters from either *Amiability* or *Valiant* escort them over, if your fighters are down."

"Trapped behind a stack of debris, unfortunately," Kira confirmed. "Everything *else* is in order. I do hope the Prime Minister will overlook the crash."

"She was a pilot herself once," Król said. "I'm sure she's familiar with the risks of even normal flight operations."

"Thank you, Captain Król," Kira said. A pilot? She'd missed that in the Prime Minister's file…but if they'd missed it, it had been so long ago it shouldn't impact anything.

She hoped. It was too late to change much of the plan.

"For the Crest," he replied, voice heavy with sincerity.

"For the Crest," she echoed, and let the channel fall.

She turned away and looked around.

"You heard him," she told her crew. "Waldroup, get the landing program ready. Milani, get the welcome party ready. All the pieces."

"We'll be there when 'Her Excellency' lands," the commando promised.

"Stunners only, Milani," Kira warned. "We need them all alive."

That wasn't *entirely* true, but they were better off stunning the entire Ministerial Protection Detail than they were accidentally killing Maral Jeong!

"PINNACE DEPLOYED. DEFINITELY NOVA-CAPABLE," Soler reported. "ETA two minutes."

Kira was watching the entire flight deck through various cameras as the shuttle approached. It took a thought to add an optical pickup zoomed in on the Prime Minister's spacecraft.

She recognized the lines and styling instantly. Jade Panosyan had kept one of the nova pinnaces in the shuttle bay aboard *Yerazner*. Whether the class two nova-drive–equipped shuttlecraft were bought from elsewhere or built in the Crest, the Prime Minister and the Crown Zharang were clearly drawing on the same source.

"Everyone ready?" Kira murmured. It wasn't even a real question. If someone wasn't ready, they'd have told her by now—and her people sensibly ignored the question.

"Pinnace Crest Two has surrendered control to the flight deck," Waldroup's voice said instead. "We have her locked on approach to landing point six."

"Understood," Milani replied in a clipped tone.

Sixty seconds. Thirty. Now Kira could make out the two people in the cockpit of the pinnace—a fundamentally civilian ship, it had actual windows on the cockpit. The pilot was roughly what she'd expected, a uniformed MPD officer wearing a standard headset and utterly focused on their task.

The woman in the copilot seat was a surprise. Maral Jeong wore the same standard headset as her pilot but was dressed in a wide-shouldered angular suit. There was no question as to who she was, though. Kira had seen enough pictures of the petite Prime Minister over the last few months to pick her out.

Jeong was an older woman with graying black hair and skin the color of age-stained hardwood—and eyes the color of fictional acid, a bright vivid green that likely spoke to genetic modification.

A shiver ran down Kira's spine as Jeong's gaze appeared to lock on to hers through the camera for a moment. That was impossible; it was simply a fluke of the Prime Minister studying the carrier as her shuttle approached.

"Ten seconds, slowing the pinnace and bringing her in," Waldroup reported.

Several of Kira's video feeds faded out as the pinnace slid into *Fortitude*'s flight deck under Angel Waldroup's control. Everything was going smoothly—and then Kira *saw* the moment Maral Jeong saw the wrecked fighter.

It was the moment the Prime Minister who had apparently once been a *fighter* pilot clearly recognized that the wreck was *not* a Hussar-Seven.

42

KIRA WATCHED as Jeong grabbed the pilot's shoulder, and looked the complete collapse of her plans in the eye.

And went to her first contingency plan.

"Jam the pinnace's coms," she snapped. *"Now. Jeong was a fighter pilot."*

She saw the alert as the same jammers they'd used to take over *Fortitude* now flared to life at lower power, just blocking off the flight deck itself.

They had never even *considered* the possibility that Maral Jeong would be able to identify the type of wrecked fighter by sight. Kira was running back through the Prime Minister's file in her headware and swallowed a curse.

Jeong was over eighty standard years old and they'd focused on her political career and her connections with the Equilibrium Institute. There had been so much going on that even the reference to her being a pilot hadn't left Kira time to re-check the PM's file—and she had missed that the woman had served a six-year tour of duty in the Navy of the Royal Crest's fighter wings…*sixty years before.*

Apparently, she'd kept up with the field well enough to realize that the wreck was, if nothing else, an interceptor instead of a heavy fighter.

"Pilot is trying to retake control of the pinnace," Waldroup reported. "No such luck for them. Milani—they're down."

"And they're angry," Kira warned.

A dozen troops were trotting across the flight deck, but they were in stolen Crester armor. The *plan* had been to move the PM away from the shuttle and at least part of her escort before moving. It would have been far easier to stun everyone when they were split into groups and away from cover!

Kira wasn't sure if it was Waldroup or the Ministerial Protection Detail that dropped the ramp—but the MPD opened fire without any hesitation at all.

"Damn, they trust Jeong without question, don't they?" she asked as the MPD opened fire on soldiers in their own uniforms.

"They also can tell they're being jammed," Konrad pointed out. "Even those Hussars shouldn't be able to pick that up...yet."

"Please tell me they're heading back."

There were two Hussar-Sixes that had flown wing on the nova pinnace on approach and, thanking every deity that might be listening, Kira realized they were flying away toward their battlecruiser mothership.

"They're outside the range they should be able to detect contained jamming at," Soler told her. "But..."

For the second time in as many days, *Fortitude's* flight deck was the scene of a firefight. Kira's people were trying to take the pinnace's passengers alive—and the MPD was under no such compunctions with regards to Milani's people.

There were definitely fewer MPD blasters firing than there had been at the start, but half a dozen of Kira's commandos were down, and she had no way to tell if they were still breathing from here.

There was *nothing* she could do from the bridge except watch.

"Damn, that pilot's good," Waldroup snapped. *"They have control."*

"Darken the deck cameras," Milani ordered.

The system automatically obeyed, not pausing to question what the commando officer was planning—even though *Kira's* response was confusion.

Then she spotted the red dragon that marked her senior officer as they stepped out onto the deck, wearing the bulkier heavy boarding armor—and carrying a Crest-manufactured *rocket launcher*.

The launcher flashed brilliantly even on the darkened camera feeds —and the explosion a quarter-second later activated the automatic protection software to darken the feeds even *more* as one of the main Harrington-coil casings blew apart into several thousand pieces.

The pinnace hadn't closed the ramp or done more than *begin* to lift off. Now, with the Harringtons on one side of the spacecraft active and the coils on the other side *gone*, she flipped in the air, going through a full rotation and a half before slamming back down on her roof.

A half-dozen MPD officers were flung clear of the pinnace, hitting the deck in ways that made Kira wince—but her people stunned them anyway as Milani's point team advanced on the shuttle.

The stunners the team carried looked like delicate toys in the heavy boarding armor, but they were still *heavy* stunners, variable-aperture weapons designed to disable crowds or stun someone in full armor. The *shuttle's* armor could stop the beams, but almost no personal gear could.

With heavy stunners, heavy armor and the shuttle just having flipped five hundred and forty degrees in the air...the fight for the pinnace was *very* short after that.

"STATUS REPORT ON OUR FRIENDS?" Kira asked as the flight-deck situation finally came under control. It looked like she wasn't going to be landing fighters on *Fortitude's* deck for a while now—the pinnace was less embedded in the deck than her fighter but no less wrecked from the looks of it.

But...

"We've got them all," Milani told her. "Alive and intact. A few broken bones among the Cabinet. The Prime Minister actually had herself strapped in. Sensible woman.

"We're setting bones as we go and applying painkillers and tran-quilizers," they continued. "Everyone should be out for at least an hour, but we're moving them to the brig with the nice shiny Faraday cages before they wake up."

Headware wouldn't send messages without conscious instructions from its owner—but if someone was *awake*, they could send messages up to fifty or even a hundred thousand kilometers through a vacuum. Maybe even a full three light-seconds, depending on the gear they had installed.

"Thank you," Kira murmured. "How bad did we get hurt?"

There was a long silence.

"Three dead, eight wounded," Milani admitted. "Wounded are going to the infirmary. Dead…Well, the ship does have a morgue."

"We'll give them proper funerals when this is over," she promised. "If we're lucky, they're the only funerals we'll be holding."

"I can dream," the commando said. "But for that… Well, the rest of this show is yours, Commodore. I have the prisoners."

Kira cut that channel and looked over at Konrad and Soler.

"And our other friends?" she asked.

"Cruisers and carrier are maintaining position at ten-thousand-kilometer intervals," Soler reported. "Still have twenty-four fighters running space patrol around all five of us."

The main holotank had been updated. The four NRC ships were marked with the bright scarlet of hostiles, and their distance was nerve-wracking. At this range, the battlecruisers' plasma bolts would probably go all the way through *Fortitude* and out the armor on the far side.

"Nova cooldown?" she asked softly.

"Twenty minutes," Konrad told her.

"Incoming hail from *Terminal Loss*, sir," Soler reported.

"Connect them," Kira ordered. She considered. "Hold up. Do we have a simulacrum for someone other than Moon? *She's* supposed to be with the PM now."

"Building them takes most of a day," Konrad said grimly. "We don't, no."

"Damn." Kira swallowed. "Can we swap my uniform for a Crester Lieutenant's? I can fake it from there."

"We can do that. Give me five."

"Let's hope Captain Król is patient," Kira murmured. A feed popped up next to her chair, showing the post-modification version of her. The NRC uniform looked odd on her, but she shrugged and it moved with her actual motions.

"Good enough," she decided. "Put him through."

Captain Król appeared on her screen again. He looked…*concerned* was too strong a word, but he was definitely bothered.

"Is Captain Moon available, Lieutenant," he asked her.

"The Captain is with the Prime Minister, sir," Kira said, as earnestly as she could. "I can connect you to her headware?"

"That shouldn't be necessary," Król said. "We were just expecting a confirmation from the Prime Minister's pilot when they touched down, but we haven't heard anything yet. Has there been a communication problem?"

"We haven't had any problems here," Kira lied smoothly. "According to the reports from flight deck, everything should be fine. The pilot might still be in shock from our flight bay. It is impressive on first sight."

"I'd expect better from one of our pilots," Król said in a grimly derogatory tone—and that he let that show to a supposed junior officer told Kira *everything* she needed to know about why he'd been stuck at Commander for a decade.

"But you can confirm that the Prime Minister is fine? There's been no problems?"

"I'm looking at a feed of the flight deck right now, sir," Kira told him. "Everything is fine. The PM has begun her inspection with the Captain, I believe. I can connect you to the Captain, but I don't have the codes to connect you to the Prime Minister, sir."

"No, that's all right, I suppose," *Terminal Loss*'s Captain said. "Thank you, Lieutenant."

The channel cut out and Kira snorted.

"On the one hand, I'm glad I didn't have to come up with a name," she said aloud. "On the other…*what* an asshole."

She turned back to Konrad.

"Cooldown?"

"Sixteen minutes."

Everything was down to time now. How long would it take the NRC ships to get twitchy about not receiving direct communication from the Prime Minister and her companions?

An inspection should take more than sixteen minutes, after all.

———

FORTITUDE'S bridge was dead silent as the clock ticked down.

Kira was watching three things. First, the timer till they could nova. Second, the location trackers of all of their prisoners on the internal map. Third, the position of the warships around her.

"*Valiant* is drifting closer. Eight thousand klicks," Soler noted. "If I'm reading the beacons right, the fighters that are out belong to the battlecruisers. She's still got a full load of eight bombers and forty fighters."

Kira nodded.

"No one is in position to see into the deck?" she asked quietly. They could send anyone who asked a neatly edited feed of the flight deck with the pinnace parked normally, but if any of the fighters managed to line themselves up at the *exactly* right angle, they would see right into the flight deck.

"Nobody yet," Soler confirmed. "Turrets are clear, but we can only run so much power without drawing attention."

Kira had used that to her advantage on *Deception* once. It was ironic that it was going to cause her trouble today. From their current state, *Fortitude*'s guns would take a critical forty seconds to charge and fire.

The nova fighters swanning around her would take *four*. If they panicked…

"…Oh. That's not good."

"Konrad?" Kira demanded.

"We just received an encrypted Ministerial Protection Detail ping," her boyfriend said grimly. "I'm going to guess a regular check-in with a controller on *Terminal Loss*."

"And there is no way we can send the correct response," Kira realized aloud. "Cooldown?"

"Four minutes."

She stared at the NRC ships.

"If you were running the MPD for the Prime Minister of the Crest, how long would you accept silence from her personal detail?" she asked the bridge.

"Ping repeated after fifteen seconds. I'm not sure this is even something they have to respond to consciously," Konrad warned. "If it's an automatic check-in, their headware would normally handle it."

"Except that they're all in Faraday cages that block transmissions, and if we let their headware report, it would tell them enough of what happened to trigger a crisis."

"Third pulse," Konrad said. "If I was running this, I'd have an automatic check-in attached to a manual one, that I'd get an answer on even if my people were *dead*."

"Yeah." Kira looked at *Terminal Loss*. "Captain Król, what are you going to do?" she murmured.

"Sir?" Soler asked.

"Three unanswered pulses and the MPD is going to call an alert. The question is what is the *Navy* going to do when the Ministerial Protection Detail does that?" Kira told the other woman.

"What do *we* do?" Soler asked.

"Three minutes," Konrad murmured.

"Wait," Kira ordered. "Get ready to bring coils and guns to full power on my command. First target is the assault carrier—*Valiant* does not get to launch fighters."

"Ready," Soler replied crisply.

There were two responses Kira could see. Captain Król could do either or both of them…

"*Terminal Loss* has gone to max power on all reactors," Soler snapped. "Incoming hail."

The answer, it seemed, was both.

"Start powering up everything," Kira barked. "Then link him in, show him Moon."

The channel opened a moment later and she hoped the simulacrum was in place.

"What the hell is going on, Król?" she barked. "My bridge is telling me you're going to battle stations!"

She had a thirty-second edge on the cruiser from the prep they'd done. The other ships were starting to spike to battle stations as well—but *Valiant* wouldn't be able to launch fighters before *Fortitude* fired.

"Where is the Prime Minister, Moon?" Król snapped in turn. "She's not responding to messages from her detail, and we can't even raise her guards. Stand your ship the *hell* down and prepare to be boarded!"

"My duty is to protect the Prime Minister, Captain Król," Kira replied. "I will not surrender this ship to *anyone*."

"Are you *mad*?"

Kira gave him her widest, most winning smile—and then heard the chime as *Fortitude*'s systems came online. She cut the channel.

"Konrad, get us out of here," she ordered. "Soler…*fire!*"

Valiant's drift had spoken more to a less-than-competent crew than any intended threat. The battlecruisers had maintained their ten-thousand-kilometer intervals, putting both of them twenty thousand kilometers from the stolen carrier. *Valiant* and *Terminal Loss* were the close-in ships—and *Valiant* had drifted almost three thousand kilometers closer than she should have.

Six heavy plasma turrets swiveled and fired in a single motion. *Valiant* was an armored assault carrier, with fewer fighters on her cubage than a more traditional light carrier—but at *seven thousand kilometers*, it didn't matter.

Twelve bolts of superheated gas slammed into her at nearly the speed of light and tore clean through the warship. One moment, she was bringing her systems to battle stations.

The next, *Valiant* was in pieces and seven hundred people were probably dead.

Kira pushed down the reminder her brain *always* brought up as *Fortitude* plunged away from her supposed escorts. The light plasma turrets were in full automatic mode, firing on the nova fighters as the stunned Crester pilots scattered from her.

The two biggest threats right now were those fighters' torpedoes and *Terminal Loss*. The fighters' confusion meant the torpedoes weren't going to be in play fast enough.

But *Terminal Loss*'s Harrington coils were online and her turrets were showing active energy signatures, and…

"Jammers online," Konrad reported. The entire sensor display that Kira was watching dissolved into static across every radiation band and sensor—a static lit by blasts of heat as *Terminal Loss*'s first salvo went wide.

"We are evading," Soler said. "We are clear of the first salvo, but the timing was *perfect* there. They'll get some hits on the next, and we are *too damned close.*"

Fortitude's own turrets fired again, hurling plasma at their sudden pursuers. Even at this range, multiphasic jamming made targeting solutions difficult, and only half of the plasma bolts hit. *Terminal Loss* shuddered in space, twisting as she tried to both adapt to the momentum transfer from the hits and start evading.

"Battlecruisers will have guns in ten seconds," Soler reported.

"Doesn't matter," Konrad snapped. "Cooldown complete! Novaing *now!*"

43

SILENCE REIGNED on *Fortitude*'s bridge as the world shifted around them. New datacodes appeared in the holotank as the carrier's sensors updated, and Kira breathed a sigh of relief as green icons flashed into existence.

Security point six might have a trio of destroyers renewing the mapping, but the *other* five security points six light-years away from the Crest did not. They would see occasional patrols, but they were empty.

Point three was on the route to Guadaloop and was currently entirely under the control of Memorial Force. Kira's destroyers were already swimming over to *Fortitude* to confirm her status.

"Report," she said aloud. "Did we take any hits?"

"Negative," Konrad told her. "Soler ripped *Valiant* apart and managed to spook the fighters and trigger the jamming at just the right moment."

Kira's partner gave the tactical officer a confident nod.

"You made the right choice, bringing her along."

"I knew that," Kira replied. "Soler, you okay?"

The young woman exhaled sharply and nodded.

"I..." She exhaled again. "I just killed a crapton of people, didn't I?"

"Yes," Kira agreed bluntly. "And that you *register* that says good things about you, and it *should* be hard." She shook her head gently. "Dr. Devin is good at the counseling for that; we'll get you in his office once this is over."

"Are you good for now?"

She'd let Isidora Soler stand aside if the young woman needed it, but it would make *Kira's* life a lot easier if Soler stayed at her post.

A third ragged exhalation, and Soler nodded again.

"Yeah, I'm good," she said. "I'll make that appointment with Dr. Devin, though."

Ailin Devin was *Deception*'s doctor and had been *Conviction*'s doctor before that. He was Memorial Force's senior physician—but his focus was actually on psychiatry and counseling. He had subordinates for surgery.

Kira was starting to realize Memorial Force had grown large enough, she really needed to have Devin put together a full counseling team, the same way they had put together a surgery team for him.

"Rest of the fleet is assuming formation around us," Konrad told Kira, clearly keeping an eye on the tactical system while Soler recovered her composure. "Nobody else in the security point. I... I think we may have pulled it off, Kira."

"Don't say that until we've been paid," she told him. "Which means I need an all-senior-officers conference in five minutes."

"We have twenty hours where we're *probably* safe. Then we're hitting regular trade routes the rest of the way to Guadaloop. Let's make the best use of the time we've got to be ready for what's coming."

WHEN THE DUST SETTLED, Kira was going to have to rearrange officers and rationalize her org chart. For the moment, though, she had six ships in play. That meant six Captains, though since she was acting as *Fortitude*'s Captain, that didn't add anyone to the meeting.

She also had three CNGs: Cartman, Patel and Sagairt. Two deck officers: Tamboli and Waldroup—but those two were managing *three* flight decks.

Similarly to the deck officers, they currently only had four executive officers on the call. *Lady Tramp* was sufficiently important for Kira to include her Captain, but Woodcock was the freighter's only representative on the call.

Konrad was acting as XO for both *Fortitude* and *Deception*—which meant *Fortitude* right now. Similarly, Milani was the ground commander for all six ships.

There were a lot of empty spots in the org chart right now, but until they could recruit new hands to fill holes, they might have to muddle along.

"Well, folks, we've done the first two parts," Kira told them all. "We have *Fortitude*. We have the Prime Minister of the Crest and five key Cabinet Ministers in her brig. That means, among other things, we are now *the* most wanted people in the Crest Sector."

That got her a collection of awkward chuckles.

"So, first steps," Kira continued. "*Fortitude* needs to be a fully functional carrier. I feel bad about treating my old plane like this, but Waldroup...bulldoze the deck."

"It won't be pretty," the deck officer reminded her. "Not until I have time to really dig it and clean up the debris and the hole."

"It only needed to be pretty to fool the Cresters," Kira said. "Now I want it *functional*. If we pull fighters over from *Raccoon* and *Deception*, can we fuel and arm them?"

"Sort of," Waldroup admitted. "Including the light load on the twelve Hussars we *acquired*, we still have forty-eight torpedoes aboard. I can put them on any of our fighters, but I don't have a lot of them to go around.

"As for fuel, well...we need to draw from *Fortitude*'s tanks to do that."

"Which brings us to the biggest problem," Konrad continued, picking up the hint Waldroup had laid down. "*Fortitude* was fueled for trials, not operations. Her tanks were only at twenty-five percent when she *started* the trials.

"We are well below anything I would accept as a reserve," the engineer and XO said grimly. "We have enough fuel to get to Guadaloop, but we will have limited ability to nova once we get there.

"Sublight maneuvering, obviously, is an entirely different situation, but I don't think we can avoid an NRC carrier group sublight."

"We can't," Kira agreed. "But we're not going to be able to refuel in Guadaloop, either. *Fortitude* is going to draw every eye in the system when she arrives, and *Final Usury* is not going to play nice, even if the CO is a Royalist."

In theory, Kira had code words to convince Royalist officers to stand down. She wasn't going to trust them as far as she could throw the carrier, but she had them. She just trusted them even less in a system where everyone else would be able to see what was going on!

"So, we do what we have to do," Konrad said grimly. "Everyone's least-favorite nightmare. How're your hoses, people?"

Kira watched the ripple of wincing pass through the starship officers. It was *possible* to transfer fuel between two vessels in deep space, even if neither was a specialized tanker. It was risky and required precision flying, but it was possible.

"Konrad has a point," she told them. "We'll equalize fuel tanks across the fleet as best as possible, but *everyone* needs enough fuel to play nova footsie with a carrier group for weeks."

"We'll make it happen," Mwangi said grimly. "I do *not* want to see *Raccoon* on the receiving end of a bomber strike. This is a real damn Navy, not the backwater compromises of the Syntactic Cluster."

"We need to split our fighter force," Kira agreed. "Sagairt will stay as CNG aboard *Fortitude* for now, but I want at least a few more squadrons. We'll move torpedoes over from *Lady Tramp* to stockpile our magazines, but I want *Raccoon*-Charlie and *Deception*-Charlie aboard *Fortitude* before we nova again."

That would give Helmet eighteen heavy fighters and six interceptors while firmly bringing both of her other ships under their listed strength for both pilots and fighters.

"We were considering which fighters to dump off *Raccoon*, so that works," Mwangi admitted. "Even without trying to launch them, we just don't the space to have extra birds on the deck."

"We're going to have a hell of a rationalization and reorg when we get home," Kira told them. "A lot of promotions, a lot of new recruits. New fighters even if we decide to give *Raccoon* back to the RRF.

"But for now, Memorial Force is a hodgepodge of a compromise. If I had anyone else at my back, I'd be worried at the mess." She grinned. "But I have *Memorial Force*, and we fucked up Cobra Squadron.

"At this point, all we have to do is dance. I trust our people to do that for us. So, we clear *Fortitude*'s deck and load her up. We get fuel balanced across the squadron.

"And then we head for Guadaloop to deliver our ransom demand."

"SIR." Milani remained in the conference room as the meeting broke up, waiting for Kira to step over to them.

They'd switched into their usual lighter armor now, abandoning the bulky-but-effective heavy boarding armor they'd worn for the assault. The dragon flitted across the entirety of this suit instead of just the holographic projection around the shoulders they'd had on the boarding armor.

It was *probably* Kira's imagination that the dragon seemed excited and relieved to have that freedom.

"What is it, Milani?" she asked.

"Interesting call up from the brig during the meeting," they told her. "Jeong is awake and she's asking to speak to whoever's in charge."

"She realizes this isn't going to go away if she makes angry faces, right?" Kira said drily.

"From what Bertoli says, she seems to have made a pretty accurate assessment of the situation," Milani noted. "She offered him quite a bit of money to get her free and to a nova shuttle or fighter, but took his refusal calmly enough.

"That was when she asked to talk to whoever was in charge."

"I'm not sure that the Equilibrium politician fully understanding the situation is necessarily to our advantage," Kira murmured. "But I don't think it hurts for me to talk to her."

"Not my call," Milani replied. "I just shot her in the face with a stunner."

There was a disturbing level of satisfaction in the mercenary's voice.

"Milani," Kira said carefully. "Is there something I should know?"

"Nah, I just hate politicians," the mercenary commando told her. "So, any day I get to stun one is a *damn* good day."

44

IT WAS ALWAYS uncomfortable to walk into areas where headware couldn't find a signal. The entire brig aboard *Fortitude*—and most other warships—was sealed inside a Faraday cage, limiting the access of the hardware in the prisoners' heads to what their captors specifically allowed.

That also meant that their guards suffered the same restrictions, though they would cycle in and out and had communications with the rest of the ship.

It wasn't like the prison was uncomfortable. The guard post at the entrance had the same automatically adjusting seats as everywhere else in the ship, and the cells were equipped with much the same amenities as the standard crew quarters.

Even the interrogation room Kira entered had the automatic seats and an artificial-stupid mobile coffee machine that handed her a cup of steaming black coffee. It wasn't Redward Royal Reserve, but it smelled surprisingly decent for brig coffee.

She had the machine lay out a second cup just before Bertoli escorted their prisoner in, carefully sitting the petite Prime Minister on the chair and manacling her feet in place.

"Is this really necessary?" Maral Jeong asked, her tone calm. "I am eighty-five years old, and I have neither armor nor soldier boosts. I am no threat to your commander, soldier."

Bertoli double-checked the manacles, sardonically saluted Kira and then stepped out, leaving the two women alone.

"I'm not going to tell you my name," Kira said calmly. "I'm sure you'll work it out eventually, but I see no reason to make it easy on you.

"But you asked to see the person in charge, and I'm curious enough to be here." She smiled. "So, tell me, Em Jeong, what do you expect to get from me?"

The Prime Minister's vividly green eyes locked on to Kira's gaze and held it for a few seconds.

"You're mercenaries, not pirates," Jeong noted. "Someone is paying you to do this. I'm impressed with what you've managed to pull off. I wouldn't have thought this was even possible."

Kira leaned back in her chair and drank more of her coffee. She had no intention of giving Jeong *anything* in this conversation.

"Whoever is paying you, you have to realize that the Crest can outbid them," the older woman finally said. "You've achieved the impossible already, but *taking* this carrier is a far step from keeping her. You should have come to us when someone tried to hire you. We would have offered you ten times as much to work for us."

"Don't worry, Em Jeong," Kira said with a chuckle. "The Crest *is* paying us. I was going to ask for a ten-million-crest ransom for you. It sounds like I should be thinking more in the hundred-million range.

"Your advice is appreciated."

The interrogation room was silent, and Jeong's friendly demeanor faded.

"You have to know you can't get away with this," she said sharply. "My government may pay you off, but we will come for you. Whatever you think you're getting out of this, it cannot be worth the consequences.

"You will be hunted to the ends of the galaxy. My reach is far longer than your worst nightmares, mercenary. I am prepared to negotiate a peaceful solution to this that serves both our needs, but if you carry this through, you will never sleep again."

"Would that reach be through the Equilibrium Institute, Em Jeong?" Kira asked softly. "Or the Sanctuary and Prosperity Party? Or the government of the Royal Crest? I am not afraid of… Well, of any of them."

The room was silent.

"The Equilibrium Institute," Jeong echoed. "That's not a name I expected to hear in the mouth of a mercenary. Who do you serve?"

"My contract," Kira replied. "A mercenary's contract is their bond, their word, their most important tool of the business. I will not break it. And that means that you, Em Jeong, will be offered up to the highest bidder.

"Given the resources of your government, I imagine that will be the Crest," she noted. "Unless you think the Institute will find you even more valuable?"

"The Institute is a useful ally. A *tool of the business*, as you say," Jeong told her. "You seem to lay more weight on them than I do."

"Really." Kira eyed the woman. "That's fascinating to me, to be honest, but I don't think we really do have much to discuss."

"Dammit, woman, I'm trying to find a way out of this for both of us," Jeong snapped. "You're not going to kill me *or* my Ministers. You want money—we can give you money. You want power? The Crest could finance your conquest of a Rim world of your choice. You want *purpose*?"

Jeong met Kira's gaze levelly.

"You want purpose," she echoed, "I can connect you with the Equilibrium Institute. Their mission is great, their task nothing less than peace for all mankind."

Kira laughed aloud.

"We're done here, Em Jeong," she told the other woman. "I have a plan to make money from this. I don't *want* a planet—and I already have a purpose in my life."

She smiled as she rose.

"But tell me, given the chunk of your Cabinet that were supposed to be on this ship, how close *were* you to removing the King of the Royal Crest?"

The room was silent again, then Jeong sighed and shrugged.

"One of us is a dead woman who doesn't know it, I suspect," she noted. "So, what does it matter? We'd barely started planning, but the decision had been made. Six standard months at most before the King and Crown Zharang were removed and the Crest became a republic."

A republic, Kira suspected, that would have been a thinly veiled dictatorship by the SPP—a faux republic that would have been less fair and representative than the monarchy it overthrew.

"I appreciate your honesty," Kira told the other woman. "In turn, I will be honest: I don't think either of us is going to be a dead woman over this."

She gave the Prime Minister of the Crest a calm, probably not-at-all-reassuring nod and walked out.

45

"STANDING BY FOR NOVA," Soler reported.

Kira ran through the reporting metrics from *Fortitude*'s command seat. There were a few clever user-interface tricks and automatic reports in *Fortitude*'s software that she'd have to incorporate in the other ships of Memorial Force if she had time.

Right now, though, those tricks and reports were telling her the stark story of how understrength *Fortitude* was. Twenty-four fighters on a ship that should carry a hundred and fifty. Two hundred crew on a ship designed for over fifteen hundred.

But she had the reports from the rest of the mercenary battle group. Everyone was at a solid fifty-five percent fuel now. *Fortitude* had stocked up to almost two hundred torpedoes, more than enough to reload the heavy fighters repeatedly.

Everyone's drive cores were cooled down. This was almost the moment of truth—their first nova to somewhere *not* a security point. They only needed three novas to get them to Guadaloop from there, through two trade-route stops—but those stops were going to be patrolled.

"All ships report at battle stations," Konrad said. "All guns are charged, all fighters are standing by, all jammers are armed. We are ready."

Kira nodded, taking one last skim through all of the reports hovering in the air around her and then inhaling carefully.

"Order to all ships: nova on my command."

She let the silence hang for a second, making sure she had everyone on the line and listening.

"Nova."

"CONTACTS, MULTIPLE CONTACTS."

"Break them down," Kira ordered.

Civilians weren't going to mess with a carrier group. Any nova warships from the Crest's client network weren't particularly more likely to pick that fight—Memorial Force had outgunned most of the clients' nova-capable fleets *before* they'd stolen *Fortitude*.

The risk was Navy of the Royal Crest ships. Even there, smaller deployments could be either intimidated or talked down with Panosyan's code words.

Maybe.

"Forty-two civilian ships of various sizes," Soler reported. "Um… two Apollon destroyers. Looks like they're escorting a diplomatic vessel."

They were a long way from home, Kira knew. It was almost as far from her homeworld to the Crest Sector as it was to the Syntactic Cluster. But the Crest was a major power in this region of the Rim, so it made sense.

It still made her twitchy.

"I've got an NRC cruiser group at sixty-five by ninety-one," Soler barked as the data resolved. "I make it a *Banker's Acceptance*–class battlecruiser with six destroyers. Range is…three million kilometers."

"Get me an ID on that battlecruiser," Kira ordered. She had a list of people who would be safe to use her codewords on—and just *sending* them could risk the whole scheme if they went to the wrong people.

"Working on it. They will have seen us…*now*," Soler reported.

"That's the nature of the game," Kira replied. "A *Banker's Acceptance* has how many fighters?"

Kira was already taking control of the ship's sublight navigation and directing the whole squadron to start opening the distance. She couldn't open the distance enough to stop the battlecruiser's fighters reaching them—that was the whole *point* of nova fighters.

A squadron of fighters spilled out from each of her flight decks, eighteen fighters assembling into an escort formation around the fleet. If the Cresters came for *Fortitude*, her people would be ready.

"Single squadron, ten Cavaliers," Konrad reported.

"ID confirmed," Soler added. "Battlecruiser is *Interest Differential*, Captain Ella Abraham, commanding."

"She's not on my list," Kira said after a moment's review. "Damn."

"Not a Royalist?" Konrad asked.

"No. Also not an SPP lackey, from what I have," she told him. "But just straight loyalty to the flag is enough for her to come after us once she works out what's going on."

"Do we play for time?" her lover asked.

Kira studied the battlecruiser in the displays—and watched *Interest Differential* turn toward them and launch her nova fighters.

"Incoming hail," Soler reported.

"Play it and ready up the Captain Moon simulacrum," Kira told her. "Let's see what games we can arrange."

The image of a tall redheaded woman in the NRC uniform appeared on the screen.

"Hijackers aboard the carrier *Fortitude* and attendant unknown ships," Captain Abraham said flatly. "Your crimes are known and you cannot escape. Surrender now and avoid further bloodshed."

There went pretending to be Captain Moon. Well...there went expecting to *succeed* at pretending to be Captain Moon, anyway.

Kira smiled.

"Pull up the Moon simulacrum," she ordered. "Then record for transmission. Ten seconds' lag gives us space to play with."

A few seconds passed as the program activated and Kira looked down at the screen showing her outgoing message. Captain Moon—

currently in a cell in *Fortitude*'s brig—looked back up at her and blinked when she did.

"Captain Abraham, this is Captain Gyeong-Ja Moon aboard *Fortitude*," she told the Navy of the Royal Crest officer.

"I do not know what lies are being spread around the Crest, but I have been tasked with a special mission to protect the Prime Minister and key members of the Cabinet after a Royalist assassination attempt.

"I have been given specific code words to advise me that the situation at home is safe for the Prime Minister's return." She smiled thinly—an even *more* terrifying expression on the Moon simulacrum than Kira thought it was on herself—at the other woman.

"Suffice to say, calling us hijackers is not included on that list. If you continue your hostile approach, I will have no choice but to engage your task group to defend the Prime Minister.

"Please, Captain Abraham, if you are not involved in the Royalists' schemes, stand aside. If you approach within two million kilometers, I will order fighter strikes on your command."

She cut off the message and sent it.

"Think they'll buy it?" Konrad asked.

"Honestly? No," Kira admitted. "But I suspect that things are in a state of absolute chaos in the Crest right now, and even if the Crown Zharang *hasn't* moved yet, that whole spiel seems believable *enough*."

She shook her head.

"I'm not counting on Abraham believing me," she concluded. "I'm counting on her being unsure enough not to risk a fight she can't actually *win*."

FOR SEVERAL MINUTES, there was no response from Captain Abraham and *Interest Differential*. The battlecruiser and her destroyer escort continued to close, moving ever closer to Kira's two-million-kilometer line.

"Sagairt, Cartman, Patel," Kira said quietly, linking all three Commanders, Nova Group, into a channel.

"Stand by for launch. Priority target is the battlecruiser. *Raccoon-*

Zeta will make a high-speed strike with their nova bombers. Everyone else will cover them. Heavy fighters and fighter-bombers will target the destroyers with their torpedoes if they get a chance."

None of the interceptors were carrying torpedoes. Their job would be to deal with their Cavalier counterparts on the other side.

Her CNGs chorused acknowledgement, and icons began to flicker from yellow to green on Kira's fighter status report. The speed suggested that many of the nova-fighter pilots had already been *in* their cockpits, waiting for the order to strap in.

"Two-point-four million kilometers," Soler reported. "Wait. I have a vector change! She's turning away."

Kira double-checked and breathed a sigh of relief. For *now*, it looked like Abraham was blinking.

"She'll transmit shortly," Kira said aloud. "Let's see what she's thinking. Maintain battle stations."

If she had to hold Memorial Force at battle stations for the full twenty-hour cooldown, she would. Her people would be shattered by the end and she'd be in trouble if her next nova took her into even *more* Crester ships.

"Still no coms," Soler reported. "*Interest Differential* has matched velocities at eight light-seconds. The destroyers are spreading out but also at eight light-seconds."

"Spreading out?" Kira asked.

"They're attempting to synchronize active sensors to create a virtual telescope," Konrad guessed. "Aiming for a better view of the ships around *Fortitude*."

"Short of bringing up the jammers, can we stop them?" she asked. If they got a good look at her ships, they'd realize how heterogenous her fleet was—and they might even be able to ID the Redward destroyers, given that Panosyan's delegation had been sending reports back.

Hell, they might even be able to identify *Memorial Force* based on those reports and the Redward-built destroyers.

"No," Konrad said grimly. "It's jammers, which blows any chance at pretending we're friendly, or allow them to ID us."

"Which will probably also shred any chance of maintaining the deception."

Kira checked the time. They still had nineteen hours left. But...*Interest Differential* was a big ship and an older one. Bigger than *Deception*, older than *Fortitude*.

"Do we have an estimate on the *Banker's Acceptance*'s acceleration and speed?" she asked.

"On your screen," Konrad replied a moment later.

Kira studied the specifications for the cruiser. They could do it. Just barely.

"And she's matched *v* with us," Kira said aloud. "*Raccoon* and *Lady Tramp* are our slowest ships, but even they have a slight edge over *Differential*."

She shook her head.

"I don't want to kill people who are simply doing their duty," she noted. "All ships are to rotate sixty degrees to port and go to maximum acceleration. Multiphasic jammers to come online as soon as we're moving."

The icons on her display updated swiftly as her people obeyed. All six of her ships were suddenly running away from *Interest Differential* —and before Captain Abraham could react, multiphasic jamming shrouded Kira's fleet.

The *downside* of multiphasic jamming was that Kira couldn't see out. Optical pickups weren't going to reliably detect a ship at eight light-seconds at the best of times, and it wasn't like multiphasic jamming had *no* impact on the visual wavelengths.

"Adding possibility zones for NRC vessels," Soler said quietly as the icons on the main display dissolved into large colored spheres. "The destroyers *can* catch us. So can the nova fighters."

"We'll keep our fighters in space," Kira replied. "Stand the rest of the Force down to status two by laser if we can reach them. We'll maintain a combat patrol capable of handling their ten Cavaliers."

And otherwise, they would spend twenty hours running away. Kira was perfectly capable of recognizing when flight was the best plan.

46

KIRA WAS PRETTY sure Captain Abraham was *furious* by the time they dropped the jammers to nova to the next trade-route stop. The battle-cruiser group was still pursuing them and clearly had been for the entire nineteen-hour layover.

The Navy of the Royal Crest commander hadn't been foolish enough to send her destroyers or nova fighters ahead on their own, though.

Kira gave the other woman a mental salute as *Fortitude*'s nova drive engaged. She could respect that kind of determination and loyalty. She wasn't going to let the NRC task group engage her fleet, and by running away, she'd made sure *nobody* died.

Kira had even managed to sneak in a nap while they ran.

A perfect victory for any mercenary.

"Novaing now," Soler reported. "Stand by for new contacts."

It wasn't a question of if there would be contacts. They were now at the closest trade-route stop to Guadaloop and still only three novas from the Crest. There were *going* to be ships around.

"Sixty-five contacts," the tactical officer reported after a few seconds. "More are freighters; I am still resolving... We've got a GODCom destroyer and I'm definitely looking at five NRC ships."

"I was hoping for a nice quiet stopover," Kira noted. "What are we looking at?"

"Looks like…logistics-support ships, eighty-kilocubic colliers," Soler replied. "No, hold on…that's *two* eighty-kilocubic supply ships and three eighty-kilocubic cruisers."

"That's not good," Kira muttered. "Identities?"

"Give me…got them. *Reliable*, *Dependable*, and *Sensible*. They are *Reliable*-class cruisers, almost obsolete and the last of their class in commission."

Kira was running the names against the lists in her head.

"Captains Ruud, Yong, and MacDermott by my list," she noted. "They're all Royalists, at least in theory."

"That could be good, right?" Konrad asked. "*Should* be good?"

"Yeah," Kira agreed. "Assuming the Crown Zharang got their message out. Assuming that they're Royalist *enough* to turn a blind eye to a stolen carrier."

"What do we do?" Soler asked.

"Transmit to all three of them," Kira ordered. "Audio only. Advise them that we are operating under Protocol Tinkerbell Rising and they are to stand by for further information from Hook, Line and Sinker before acting."

"Does that mean *anything*?" Konrad asked.

"It means we're operating under direct authorization from the royal family and they are to stand by for further orders from NRC Central Command before taking any combative action," she told her lover.

"Transmitted," Soler reported. "What now?"

"We keep our distance and we hope that the Crown Zharang's message reached them," Kira said. "We don't let them get close. If they're older ships, we should be able to hold the range open."

"Warbook says they have updated Harringtons," Konrad warned. "They're faster than *Raccoon*."

"Then let's get that range opening now while we wait for their response," Kira ordered. "The *good* news is that I'm reasonably sure the *Reliable* class doesn't have nova fighters."

Which meant that unless the cruisers had cooled down their own nova cores, she didn't have to worry about the almost thirty light-seconds of range disappearing on her.

Memorial Force began to move away from the three cruisers. Nine million kilometers gave Kira a lot of room to play with, but it could go away in a lot less than the twenty hours it would take to cool *Fortitude*'s nova drive.

"No response," Soler reported quietly. "Cruisers are moving… toward us, but relatively slowly. They're maintaining range, not closing it."

"I can live with that," Kira said. "Confusion is enough for here and now. All I need is for them not to attack us."

"How long do you think they'll hesitate?" Konrad asked.

"Less than an hour," she admitted. "Three ways this breaks down, people. The three Captains are arguing it out right now, considering their loyalty to the Crown of the Royal Crest versus the fact that we've pretty clearly stolen a carrier.

"First way it breaks down is that they decide that our sins exceed what those code words buy us," she said. "They come after us. It's unlikely to take them an hour to get to that point, so we'll have a fight on our hands.

"Both the second and third way it breaks down, they decide our code words cover us or can't come to a shared conclusion. Second way it breaks down, they either let us go or hesitate—and they don't move against us before we can nova."

"And the third option?" her boyfriend asked.

"Someone jumps in from the Crest with an update and a shoot-to-kill order," Kira admitted. "Faced with direct orders, they have no choice but to attack—backed by whoever carried the message.

"Which could be anything from a single gunship to an entire carrier group. Depending on timing and where the messenger arrives, that might still be a bust for them."

The wild card in the deck for the Navy of the Royal Crest, Kira knew, was whether or not *Fortitude* had a full deck of nova fighters. If Kira had brought enough birds and pilots to arm the carrier, she'd have a two-hundred-plus-fighter alpha strike.

She *hadn't*, which meant that the odds were even at best if the three cruisers came after her. But the NRC didn't *know* that, which hopefully added to their hesitation.

"We'll keep the distance between us and the *Reliable*s as open as we can," she told Soler and Konrad. "That keeps options open for us."

"And if they do try to close?" Konrad asked.

"Then we send in the fighters and try to take out their engines without wrecking the ships," she said.

They could only try that once. If they didn't disable the cruisers on the first pass, a second attempt to cripple them would be too dangerous. They'd have to destroy the cruisers or risk Memorial Force's safety.

The Captains and crew over there weren't Kira's enemy and she really didn't want to do that.

But her people came first.

***

"*RELIABLE*S ARE BREAKING OFF."

Kira released a breath she hadn't realized she'd been half-holding. Seventy-six minutes had passed since they'd transmitted their code words.

"What are they doing?" she asked.

"Resuming their original patrol pattern, it looks like," Soler reported. "They…appear to be ignoring us now."

"That's the best we can hope for," Kira replied. "Let's get the range further open. If they want to ignore us for now, let's make sure they can't change their minds later."

"Will it last?" Soler asked.

"Now we're waiting to see if they get orders from the Crest," she told the tactical officer. "If they do, then it's a lot harder for them to pretend they didn't know something was going on."

Kira eyed the cruisers as they slowly jetted away from her command and shook her head.

"Go catch a breather, Soler," she ordered. "I'll keep the lights on here for the moment. Listen for the battle-stations alert."

The *look* she got from her subordinate in response to the last suggestion made her chuckle.

"I think we're fine, Soler," she said. "So, go rest. We've still got nineteen hours before the final nova, and things are going to get *fun* in Guadaloop."

"Yes, sir."

The younger woman transferred tactical control to Kira's console and left, leaving Memorial Force's Commodore alone on the carrier's massive bridge.

Someday, it would be filled with mercenary crew at all hours. Right now, they had a *battle stations* crew of five, and Kira had sent all of them, including her boyfriend, to rest.

She could fly the carrier from there. She could even *fight* the carrier from there, though not overly well without support crew.

What she couldn't do from there was see how the Navy of the Royal Crest was reacting to the theft of their newest supercarrier. She couldn't know how the judicial counter-coup was going on the Crest, or if the military forces loyal to the Sanctuary and Prosperity Party were short-stopping the Royalist scheme to retake control of their government.

She had no answers and no vision of anywhere but one trade-route stop in the middle of nowhere.

At least the code words had worked. Kira really hadn't wanted to fight the cruisers—but she also hadn't really believed that anyone would buy the "Protocol Tinkerbell Rising" thing.

47

"COOLDOWN NEARLY COMPLETE," Konrad reported.

Everyone was back on station and Kira was watching the three *Reliables* like a hawk. She'd slept in the daybed in the captain's quarters, in an uncomfortably restive three-quarters doze, all too aware things could go sideways.

"All right, everybody." Kira looked at the collection of virtual faces hanging around her. Starship Captains and nova-group commanders. Subordinates and friends.

"Are we good for the final leap?"

Nods answered her. No one was looking entirely comfortable with what came next, but they'd been planning for it for a while.

"Remember, it's a three-light-year jump, not a six-light-year jump," Kira said. "That means we only have twelve hours before we can start novaing again, and we're jumping in twelve light-hours out.

"We *should* be clear of attack until we've finished cooldown. We'll transmit our demands from the twelve-light-hour point and then begin an outer-system nova hopscotch."

She shook her head.

"We will come under nova-fighter attack," she noted. "Sorry,

CNGs, but we're looking at a minimum of five squadrons in the air at all times. Half the planes. Once we've seen off the first few strikes, they should hesitate and wait for orders from the Crest.

"*Final Usury*'s Admiral Dafina Avagyan is related to the royal family by marriage but is not on my list of officers cleared for Protocol Tinkerbell Rising," Kira continued. "So, either Panosyan briefed her personally when they were in the system, or we can assume that Avagyan will react as any rational NRC officer would."

"Assume we've stolen a carrier and attack?" Zoric asked drily.

"Exactly. Assuming that Avagyan relays our demands to the Crest immediately upon receipt, we're still looking at a minimum of eighty to a hundred hours for a response," Kira continued. Without the stopover at the security point, it was only two trade-route stops to the Crest.

"We're better off assuming a week, people. If things are looking remotely orderly in the Crest, they're not going according to plan."

Kira's next words were interrupted by an alert as *Fortitude*'s scanners picked up something new...

"Contact, contact!" Soler snapped. "Multiple contacts. I am making it..."

The young woman looked up in concern.

"I am making it a *Banking*-class fleet carrier and two battlecruisers, plus destroyers," she noted. "Full carrier group."

"They'll launch fighters as soon as they locate us," Kira said. "Konrad? Cooldown?"

"Ninety seconds," he reported.

"Your orders?" several people asked simultaneously.

There were no good options. If they were seeing the nova emergences, the carrier had seen *them* almost a minute before. Long enough ago to already be launching fighters.

"Get the fighters aboard and fire up the jammers," Kira ordered flatly. "Then stand by to repel fighters with defensive turrets while we prepare to nova!"

THERE WAS one last piece of data Kira needed before the jammers went up, and Soler resolved it for her just in time.

The carrier was *Collections Agent*. The battlecruisers were *Amortization* and *Amiability*.

Those battlecruisers' commanders had to be *furious*. They were SPP loyalists who'd watched her kidnap their Prime Minister under their very noses—and according to the files, *Collections Agent*'s Captain was of a similar vein.

As were the destroyer COs and probably most of the senior officers and crews. This was the Sanctuary and Prosperity Party's own personal carrier group.

"The SPP can't control many entire carrier groups," she muttered. "Why did you send them *here*?"

It wasn't the normal organization of the ships, either. *Collections Agent* had a completely different battlecruiser listed as her escort, but *that* ship's Captain was on Kira's list of Royalists.

The NRC had rearranged ships to create a battle group that was unquestionably loyal to Maral Jeong, and then they'd sent them to *exactly* the right place.

"That..." Kira bit off several scatological observations about their employer.

"Jammers are live, turrets are live, we are scanning for targets," Soler reported.

"Nova in forty-five seconds," Konrad added.

"They're coming," Kira said softly. "They knew where to find us. They knew where we were going. They aren't going to let us go easily."

"Nova emergence!" Soler barked. "Engaging!"

There was no time to report what they were facing. Dozens of flashes of bright-blue radiation lit up the battlespace, met almost instantly by stark-white plasma blasts. The computers struggled to provide a map through the self-inflicted chaos of the jamming zone, but Kira knew enough to pick out the bombers at the core of the formation.

"Target those bombers," she ordered. It wasn't a necessary order. *Everyone* knew that—and *Fortitude*'s lighter turrets were already concentrating their fire on the heavy torpedo platforms.

Incoming fighters died. Plasma blasts washed over Kira's ships and she watched, stone-faced, unable to do *anything*. She was a nova-fighter pilot. This helplessness went against everything she'd learned, everything she knew how to do in a fight.

"Multiple hits," Konrad reported. "Dispersal networks and armor holding. No critical damage—

"*Nova!*"

Kira had barely registered that her engineer boyfriend had interrupted himself before the universe changed, the chaos of the battlespace vanishing to be replaced by calmer void.

That void was then instantly filled with new static as their jammers threw chaotic energy into it, but there were no fighters there.

"Cut the jammers, report," Kira ordered.

"Everybody made it," Soler said instantly. "*Fortitude*'s jammers are down; trying to establish links for damage reports."

Kira exhaled a long breath.

"We made it," she murmured. "Send the canned ransom demand as soon as all the jammers are down."

It would take almost as long for the ransom demand to reach Guadaloop and its orbiting battlegroup as it would take her fleet's nova drives to cool down.

That was the plan. That much was going according to plan.

"How the hell did a carrier group catch up to us?" Konrad growled. "Even if someone from the first trade-route stop reported in, we shouldn't have seen them already."

"They used another security point to go around that trade-route stop," Kira told him. "So they could surprise us there, but they got the timing slightly wrong."

She shook her head.

"They'll be here in twenty hours, adding to the dance. And unlike Admiral Avagyan, they *know* we're the enemy."

"But...how did they know where we were going?" Soler asked.

Kira looked at her lover. From the tired expression on his face, he'd guessed.

"Panosyan leaked that part of the plan," Kira said quietly. "The key components of the Sanctuary and Prosperity loyalists in the NRC are now out-system, heading right at us, while the Crown's agents move against the SPP headquarters.

"*That* was their solution to the SPP's partial control of the military. Everything the SPP controls is coming after *us*."

48

"*PEGASUS* GOT HANDLED MORE ROUGHLY than I like," McCaig rumbled on the all-Captains channel a few minutes later. "We're still sorting out the damage, but it looks like we lost a turret and we're down almost twenty percent of our sublight maneuverability.

"The turret is outright gone, but we might be able to rig up replacement Harrington coils," he continued. "I'll keep you all updated."

Kira nodded. *Pegasus* had taken the brunt of the fighter strike, at least in terms of damage. Both *Deception* and *Fortitude* had taken more hits, but their heavier armor and more powerful dispersion networks had spared them major damage.

"Sublight maneuverability shouldn't matter too much for the moment," she told McCaig. "But we are going to need every scrap of everything we can get, people."

A mental command brought the shared sensor data up in front of everyone.

"I'd wondered why they'd sent a carrier group to the trade-route stop," she admitted. "They wouldn't have known we'd be there without knowing we'd be coming to Guadaloop, and the odds of catching us there were low.

"Now we know why."

A collection of starships in high orbit above Guadaloop flashed red.

"Admiral Avagyan was an unknown—potentially a neutral or even an ally, given her relationship to the Panosyans," Kira reminded everyone. "Unfortunately, *that*, ladies and gentlemen, is Carrier Group *Temperance*. *Temperance* is an older carrier, sister to the previous *Fortitude* who was decommissioned five years ago, but she still has a hundred nova fighters aboard.

"If she still has her regular group, she's also accompanied by the assault carrier *Diligent* to make up the numbers. We're still working on resolving the escorts, but we can confidently expect that *Collections Agent* will now be joining them in-system in about twenty hours."

There was a long silence on the channel.

"That gives the NRC three, potentially *four* carriers in-system, plus four cruisers and twelve destroyers," she concluded. "We are badly outgunned and outmatched, but the plan never called for us to fight them here."

"We were expecting to stand off their fighters, though," Zoric pointed out. "We're not going to be able to do *that* against over four *hundred* of them."

"Is there any reason we should not relocate to a *different* system to send our ransom demand?" Michel asked. "The plan was Guadaloop, but given *this* much firepower…"

"Only one, really," Kira admitted. "And that one, people, is that all of this—everything we've done—is a distraction. Our entire operation was intended to seize the Prime Minister and draw the SPP out.

"Now, I do wish the Crown Zharang had *told* us that we were going to be used as bait to lure the SPP part of their fleet out of the system, but the logic is sound," she told them. "I fully intend to find ways to convince the Crown Zharang that we are owed more money because of that."

Blackmail was an ugly word, but Kira was certainly willing to at least threaten full publicity of the Zharang's involvement to get value for her people.

"But…to complete the intent of the mission we took on, we need to keep those carrier groups out of the Crest for, mmm, at least a few days. A week would be best—and conveniently, that's how long it should take to get updated information back from the Crest in response to our ransom demand."

"That was a reasonable ask against *one* carrier group whose Admiral we expected to be somewhat ambivalent about the whole affair," Zoric noted. "Against three? With at least two flag officers and a lot of senior and mid-level officers who are loyal to the people we have locked up in our brig?

"We can only dance so much when someone has four hundred–plus nova fighters to play with."

"And that, my friends, means it's time to change the music," Kira said with a chuckle. "We had one set of dances planned, but that's not going to work.

"Which means we need a new dance, new music and a new plan."

"And you've got one, haven't you?" Zoric asked, not even trying to conceal the long-suffering sigh that followed.

MARAL JEONG LOOKED NO LESS COMPOSED after several days of imprisonment. Even given the amenities in *Fortitude*'s cells, that was surprising to Kira. She'd expected helplessness to wear on the Prime Minister more.

"So, you return to me, mercenary," Jeong said calmly after her guard had manacled her to the chair again. She ignored the coffee in front of her, focusing her strangely green eyes on Kira.

"Are you ready to deal?"

Kira chuckled.

"That's an interesting question," she noted. "What kind of deal are you thinking?"

"It's been several days and several novas," the Prime Minister murmured. "And I am reasonably sure I felt weapon impacts several hours ago, which means the Navy of the Royal Crest is catching up with you.

"You begin to feel the noose tighten around your neck and realize you cannot escape. You cannot survive the wrath of the Crest. Your only hope is to cut a deal."

"You're perceptive, I see," Kira said. "You do realize, of course, that you are aboard this ship as well? If the NRC destroys *Fortitude*, you will die."

"I know," Jeong agreed. "And I would prefer not to, which is why I am prepared to consider a deal. Surrender myself and the rest of your prisoners to the NRC. Surrender this carrier. You will be allowed to go free in exchange for our lives and this ship."

"I see your offers grow less generous with time."

"I can wait. As the reality of the situation sinks in, your desperation will grow and your negotiating position will weaken," the Prime Minister said calmly. "The Crest will not allow this to stand. We can end this, you and I, before you and yours suffer the due punishment for your crimes.

"I am biased," she admitted. "I wish to live. Therefore, I will permit you to escape that punishment and we will end this without further bloodshed."

Kira leaned back in her chair and took a sip of the mediocre coffee to conceal her smile.

"I'll make you a counteroffer," she told Jeong. "You sign a document transferring ownership of this carrier to me, have the NRC provide one billion crests in bearer chits and order the ships here to stand down.

"I'll leave you and your Cabinet in a sublight-capable shuttle on the edge of the system and leave with the carrier and the money. I'll never come back to the Crest Sector, and you'll live."

"No." Jeong stared at Kira like a trapped predator. "I will never order the NRC to stand down. We will pay you nothing. In exchange for our lives, I will permit you to leave this sector no richer or poorer than you entered it, but you will not benefit from this transgression."

Kira took another sip of the coffee.

"You realize that your stubbornness risks all of our lives?" she noted. "If I fight your fleet, your chances of survival are no better than mine."

"I will take those chances," the Prime Minister told her. "I am willing to die, if I must."

"And your Cabinet?" Kira asked.

"They may be weak, but they will follow me in this," Jeong snapped. "They have no authority to act alone, regardless of what threats you apply. I have made my offer, mercenary. Do you have anything else to say?"

Kira smiled.

"No, I think I have everything I need," she told the other woman.

49

"START THE COUNTDOWN," Kira ordered calmly. "They should receive our ransom demand in the next few minutes and spot our arrival. How long till nova?"

"Countdown is five minutes," Konrad replied.

"Are we ready?" Kira glanced over at Soler.

"We're ready," she confirmed. "If I'd known we'd be doing this much of this kind of thing, I'd have suggested we bring an actual artist."

"The thought would never have occurred to me if you hadn't done such a great job with Moon," Kira pointed out. "We'll be fine."

"There is a hundred-and-thirty-second gap between our message arriving and our being able to nova," Zoric warned from the command channel. "They may have fighters ready to go."

"And that is why we're almost three light-minutes away from where we sent the message," Kira reminded them. "Yes, they can spread out and locate us, but not in two minutes."

Plus, nova fighters jumping twelve light-hours would have a ten-minute cooldown. Shorter than the one for a class one drive, but not by much—one light-week was where the two cooldowns converged.

If they sent out a wide fighter sweep, only some of the fighters could possibly be close enough to be a threat. The biggest threat was if they sent a carrier who then deployed fighters to search.

But even that would take more than two minutes to locate Memorial Force and launch a strike.

"Message will now have arrived," Konrad reported. "Count is at one hundred twenty-five seconds."

Kira nodded silently and studied the tactical display. Even if someone jumped *immediately* to the source of their message, she wouldn't see them for three minutes. Unless someone actually landed fighters right on top of her people, she'd never see them.

"Sixty seconds."

Nothing. There was probably someone at their origin point now, but nothing was near them.

"Thirty seconds."

"Nova flare at ten light-seconds," Soler snapped. "I have a four-fighter section of Cavaliers at ten light-seconds!"

"Scouting sweep," Kira concluded. "They probably have a carrier out here, but they can't even go back for sixty seconds."

She mentally saluted the fighter pilots as the counter ticked down.

"They're going to be *real* pissed when they find out where we went," she noted aloud.

"Ten seconds," Konrad said. "We better be ready.

"Everything is ready," Kira promised.

"What happens if this *doesn't* work?"

"We die."

The countdown hit zero.

MEMORIAL FORCE EMERGED from nova in perfectly aligned formation. Parade-ground formation, even, with all of the lights and beacons and glittering array that came with that. Fighters spilled from all three launch decks and flickered into formation with perfect precision.

It was a show—and it was a show with one *hell* of an audience, because Kira's entire mercenary fleet had just appeared four light-seconds from Guadaloop itself. They were outside range of GODCom's fortresses and the two carrier groups still in orbit, but *everyone* saw them.

"You're live," Soler told Kira.

"GODCom and Navy of the Royal Crest forces," Kira told the camera. "I am Kira Demirci, commanding officer of the Memorial Force mercenary company.

"Before anyone takes any *precipitous* action, I must advise you that the Prime Minister of the Crest is aboard *Fortitude*—and her Cabinet has been parceled out across my ships," she said calmly. "I don't like using people as human shields, but I need you to listen to me."

She smiled.

"Besides, do any of us soldiers *really* regard politicians as people?" she asked. "You have received my ransom demand. If you are smart, it has already been forwarded to the Crest. If it has not, you should get on that. *Now*.

"And then we will wait for an answer, and you will leave my ships alone. And if you want to argue that plan, well... Listen to the words of your own Prime Minister."

The feed of Kira cut away to the recording of the meeting in the cell.

"I am ready to deal," the edited recording of Maral Jeong told the camera. "I feel the noose tighten. I am prepared to consider a deal," she repeated.

The editing was careful, utterly changing the woman's original intent...but the words were all Maral Jeong's.

"Very well," Kira's own voice said. "Tell your fleet what we are going to do."

That had been recorded later, but Kira wasn't in the video feed. Maral Jeong's own intentional impassivity worked in her enemy's favor there.

"I am biased. I wish to live," Jeong's recording said. "I order the NRC to stand down in exchange for our lives. We can wait."

"And your Cabinet?" Kira's recorded voice asked.

"They will follow me in this," Jeong said. "Our only hope is to cut a deal."

Kira's people, led by Soler and her work on the AI avatar of

Captain Moon, had done an incredible job on smoothing the cuts. That Maral Jeong was a politician, with the controlled and frozen body language of six decades of political life, had only helped.

Kira now smiled thinly at the camera as the transmission cut back to her.

"We're not asking for your surrender," she told the defenders. "But the Prime Minister of the Crest has agreed to our deal. We will wait to hear from the Crown of the Royal Crest as to whether her ransom will be paid.

"And we are all going to peacefully sit here and glare at each other over our guns until King Sung Panosyan has his say, aren't we?"

She cut the recording and leaned back in her chair, allowing her nerves to finally hit her.

"What now?" Soler asked.

"All ships remain at battle stations," Kira ordered grimly as she massaged the knot forming in her neck. "If they come out after us, we'll have plenty of warning."

FOR A FEW MOMENTS, Kira was worried she'd overplayed her hand. Starfighters spilled out of the two carriers in their dozens, and the escorts closed up under the defensive umbrella of GODCom's fortresses.

"GODCom has not deployed fighters," Soler noted, her voice admirably steady. "Our reports suggest they have at least a hundred nova fighters aboard the fortresses, but they are remaining in their hangars."

"Guadaloop thinks this is the Crest's problem," Kira said. "And the NRC isn't going to lean on them, not unless they really don't think they can take us."

The fighter patterns on the displays were...wrong.

"Zoric, Cartman, are you seeing what I'm seeing?" she asked softly.

"Those aren't attack formations," Cartman said instantly from her own nova fighter. "They *started* as them, but they're confused and..."

Now a pattern was starting to emerge, and Kira only half-swallowed a bark of laughter as *Final Usury*'s ships and fighters formed into a parade-ground formation facing her.

It took *Temperance*'s escorts longer to follow suit. For at least a moment, the second carrier group seemed to strain at an invisible leash —long enough for Kira to confirm that it was *just Temperance,* and her usual backup carrier was missing.

Probably because *Diligent* was chasing ghosts around the outer system, not yet warned that Kira had arrived at Guadaloop itself.

Finally, clearly in answer to an order from on high—or at least *Final Usury*—*Temperance*'s battle group joined the larger carrier in a parade-ground formation. With fighters and destroyers on the wings, the combined Navy of the Royal Crest fleet was now in the shape of a hollow swan that "swam" out of the umbrella of GODCom's fortresses.

They stopped well inside range of the fortresses' guns and well *outside* weapons range of Memorial Force, but the immense flying swan was very clear in open space, pointed at Kira but not attacking.

"Show-offs," she muttered. "Konrad, how long until the drive is cooled?"

"Twenty minutes," he reported. "Whoever was chasing us around in the outer system will be able to nova back in fifteen."

"And how long for *Collections Agent* to show up?" she asked.

"Eight more hours, assuming she'd made a full jump to get to the trade-route stop and ambush us," he concluded. "Right now, Commodore, I think everything is swinging on Admiral Avagyan. But when *Agent* gets here…"

"Admiral Matevosyan is senior to Avagyan," Kira agreed. "But he's *also* Maral Jeong's brother-in-law. So, I guess what happens *then* depends on how much his husband likes his sister."

"Sir, incoming transmission from *Final Usury*," Soler reported. "Admiral Avagyan is requesting a channel."

"Put her through," Kira ordered.

She leveled her best *not-quite-a-pirate* face at the recorder and smiled coldly as Avagyan appeared.

Dafina Avagyan was a classic Armenian-Korean-extraction Crester, with angular eyes and a sharp hawk-like nose against her shadowed skin and pitch-black hair.

"Commodore Demirci," she said quietly. "You have us at a disadvantage."

"Admiral Avagyan," Kira greeted her. "You must forgive, I'm afraid, my compensation for your larger fleets and more powerful warships. I can afford to take no chances."

"If you wished to take no chances, Commodore, you should perhaps not have kidnapped my Prime Minister," Avagyan said. "I also apparently find it necessary to remind more people than I should that Em Jeong has no authority over the Navy of the Royal Crest."

Kira let that lie where it fell, arching a single eyebrow at the Crester Admiral.

"I won't bluster and beat my chest about how many more fighters and ships I have, Commodore," the other woman continued. "We both know I can destroy your fleet. The price would be far higher than I like, but you are completely outgunned here.

"Hence your human shields."

"Indeed," Kira confirmed calmly. "The Prime Minister is useless to me unless someone is prepared to pay me for her. That requires me to be somewhere you can find me. Her orders were clear, though, weren't they?"

"And she has no authority to give them," Avagyan said. "The Crest does not traditionally negotiate with terrorists and kidnappers, Commodore Demirci. And yet, I do hesitate to blithely accept the head of my government as collateral damage."

"I have already suggested my solution to this impasse," Kira pointed out. The two fleets were a million kilometers apart. They were outside the range of the standard weapons of either fleet.

Both of them were perfectly capable of fabricating Harrington-coil smart missiles, but multiphasic jamming would render those missiles instantly dumb and blind. The moment either of their nova fighters jumped, both sides would raise their jammers.

"You do realize, Commodore, that there is no way in *hell* you are keeping that carrier, right?" the Crester Admiral said calmly. "Even if we agree to pay your ransom for Jeong and her Cabinet, we will hunt you forever for that ship."

"The Crest doesn't have the resources to hunt me forever," Kira pointed out. "*Fortitude* is nonnegotiable, I'm afraid. The only thing in question from my side is how much Jeong and her Cabinet are worth."

Avagyan grimaced.

"I have no choice, I suppose," she admitted. "Know that you cannot run and cannot escape, Commodore Demirci. We will await the decision of the Crown and Parliament of the Royal Crest.

"I will, of course, need to see evidence that the Prime Minister and her Cabinet are still *alive*, however," she growled.

"I have no intention of killing the golden goose, Admiral," Kira replied. "Give me one moment."

She froze the cameras and looked over at Soler.

"I need footage from every cell," she told the tactical officer. "For the crew and the MPD officers, too. Everyone we captured. Ten seconds, fully time-stamped. No games this time...but mute their microphones."

She turned back to Avagyan.

"We will forward proof of life for the Prime Minister, her Ministers, and all of the members of *Fortitude*'s crew and the Ministerial Protection Detail," she told the Admiral. "I will also provide a list of the known dead."

Avagyan nodded slowly and thoughtfully.

"I...appreciate that," she admitted. "The crew and detail personnel are not part of the ransom demand."

"They are not," Kira agreed. "They are not the government of the Crest, merely servants of the Crest's people, doing their duty. If we can come to a mutually agreeable solution, I am prepared to return them to you immediately."

That apparently surprised the Crester officer, who took a moment to regain control of her expression.

"I will have my people examine the proof-of-life clips," she told Kira. "And then we will speak again. We...very well may be able to come to that solution."

50

"NOVA CONTACT!"

"Close up the defensive formation; stand by the jammers," Kira snapped. This was probably *Diligent* returning from the outer system, but the assault carrier might not have received any updates from Admiral Avagyan yet.

And while Kira was certain that her offer to return the non-politicians had sealed the deal with Avagyan, things were still...fragile.

"Confirm, Crest assault carrier and two destroyers," Soler reported. "Profile matches *Diligent*. Range is eight light-seconds. She's launching fighters!"

"Don't wait for the order, Soler," Kira instructed. "The moment you see a nova flash at close range, trigger the jammers. Cartman, Sagairt, Patel." She turned to the CNGs. "I'd *love* to get through this cleanly, but if those fighters come in, *put them down*."

She wasn't sure Avagyan would let that pass—she wasn't sure *she* would in the Crester's place—but she *also* wasn't going to stand by and let Crest fighters fire into her ship.

"Nova flare—multiple fighters emerging around *Diligent*," Soler reported.

Kira sighed in relief.

"From *Final Usury*?" she asked.

"Looks like. *Diligent* flight group is holding position."

Kira forced herself to breathe as she watched the display. Eight seconds delayed. She'd know if *Diligent*'s fighters attacked when they arrived in her formation. So far...nothing.

"*Diligent* fighters powering down and returning to the carrier," Soler reported as the data updated again. "*Diligent* is bringing up her Harringtons. Course projection on the display."

The initial vector was away from Memorial Force, but Soler's projection had the assault carrier and her escorts making a long curve to join *Final Usury*'s formation.

One more crisis passed.

"Are we ready to nova yet?" Kira asked.

"Just a few more minutes," Konrad replied. "Should we start recalling the fighters?"

"Not until we're fully ready," she said. "No chances."

Seconds ticked by like years and Kira watched the displays around her. Finally, a chime and an icon advised her that Avagyan was hailing again.

She didn't even wait for Soler to tell her. Kira had the channel open herself inside a second.

"Admiral."

"Commodore."

Avagyan studied Kira in silence for a moment.

"We have confirmed your proof of life," she finally said. "I want to speak to the Prime Minister. Live."

"That's not happening," Kira said bluntly. "I have no idea what kinds of code words or other bullshit you could get up to. If I give her coms, she could play all kinds of tricks with her headware.

"Those recordings are all you're getting. You know she's alive, and you know her orders."

Kira wasn't exactly a fan of the position her mission put her in. She was trying to get through this with the minimum amount of bloodshed —but that was already far too high.

"And if I say that there's no truce if you don't let me talk to her live?" the Crester said grimly.

Kira glanced over at Konrad, who gave her a thumbs-up. She smiled at Avagyan.

"Then you don't get your spacers back and I nova out of here before you can do *anything*," she told the Admiral. "I am prepared to trade everyone *except* Maral Jeong and her Cabinet for a five-day truce while we wait for a response from the Crest.

"I don't plan on spending that five days sitting in your clear view, waiting for you to change your mind," she added.

Avagyan chuckled.

"That's fair, I suppose. I want the prisoners and the bodies, Commodore. Everyone, living and dead."

"Several of the wounded aren't safe to travel without medical supervision," Kira admitted. "While I have no hesitation in turning them over to you, I do not want to risk anyone for that."

"I had guessed from the recordings," the Admiral conceded. "I have a suggestion."

"Go on."

"My math suggests that we will require six shuttles to transfer all of the prisoners," Avagyan told her. "I will send six shuttles, including a fully equipped medevac unit with medtechs aboard, to the midpoint between our forces. You will send five shuttles, with the non-wounded prisoners and whatever security detail you feel is necessary, to the same point.

"We will transfer the prisoners between the shuttles, and your security people will board and search the medevac shuttle. Once they are satisfied it is not a trap, your shuttles and my medevac shuttle will return to *Fortitude*, and my medtechs will take over responsibility of the wounded, seeing them to the shuttle and back to *Final Usury*."

Kira could see a *thousand* different ways that Avagyan could still be plotting a trap. The parameters she was offering were fair and about as good as Kira could hope for, but it could still *oh so easily* be a trap.

But…Kira had two commando battlefield medics trying to provide serious trauma care for eleven badly wounded Cresters. They were doing everything possible, but it was still all too likely that it might not be enough.

It was a risk. But she owed it to those people, enemies they might theoretically be, to *try*.

"I agree, under one additional condition," she told Avagyan. "A nova fighter will accompany my shuttles, in case your people decided to do something *stupid*. And if any of your medtechs attempt to access anything they shouldn't, my people will shoot them dead on the spot.

"Understood?"

The Crester Admiral winced.

"I understand," she allowed. "You'll forgive me if I'd prefer your unconditional surrender."

"And you'll forgive me if that isn't happening," Kira told her. "We both have a goal here, Admiral, but the fewest people die if I achieve mine."

———

KIRA SIGHED as she watched the Hoplite-IV attach itself to the shuttle.

"Dawnlord," she hailed Patel. "Isn't that something you should be sending a junior to do?"

"Maybe," he conceded. His tone was calm, vaguely dark. It had rarely been light since Joseph Hoffman's death. "But this sounds like it might require some split-second judgment calls. Who else would I trust to do that?"

Kira chuckled.

"Nightmare drew the short straw?" she asked.

"We had Helmet flip a coin," Patel replied. "That way, neither of us could influence it. And he's disturbingly sensible."

"I won't stop you," Kira admitted. "Like you say, who else would I trust?"

Herself…but she *really* couldn't go.

She mentally flicked to another channel.

"Any problems, Milani?" she asked them.

"A few of the Ministerial Protection Detail really didn't want to abandon the Prime Minister," the commando told her. "*Fortitude*'s crew were pretty cooperative, though we had to stun one officer who tried to make it to an override panel."

Kira chuckled. None of the *Fortitude*'s former crew had the codes to override anything anymore—but normal pirates wouldn't have been able to pull that off.

"So, no *real* trouble," she observed.

"Not really. I have the team that'll search the medevac shuttle," they told her. "And we're back in full boarding armor. Unless they have something unexpected, we'll be fine."

"Good." Kira shook her head. Why did *none* of her subordinates delegate? They all seemed to be right in the middle of everything, leading from the front.

She knew perfectly well where they'd *learned* it from, but that didn't make it any less annoying sometimes.

"Good luck," she told Milani. "Get those people home safely—but get *our* people home safely, too."

KIRA WATCHED the medical team from the moment the five women came aboard. Five women, all in their early thirties, dressed in standard white shipsuits. Except...four of them looked nervous. Even more so than she'd expect from the mercenaries escorting them.

The fifth, though... The fifth didn't look nervous *enough* and Kira focused in on them.

"Milani," she pinged the commando leader. "Redhead is *not* a fucking nurse."

"No," the commando replied. "Soldier boosts. Covert commando. I'm standing by with a squad just around the corner. We're watching."

If the woman was *smart*, she'd realize that. There were ten mercenaries in standard armor escorting the five medtechs. That should have been enough to keep most people in order, but the redhead at the back of the med team was continually looking around, watching for an opportunity.

Kira's fingers twitched toward a stunner she wasn't even wearing, watching the woman make her way through *Fortitude*'s corridors. It was always *possible* that the woman was a commando medic who'd happened to be available...but Kira didn't buy that.

Unfortunately, the infiltrator knew her job and chose her time *perfectly*. The medtechs set to work as soon as they entered the sickbay, accessing the equipment they needed to do their jobs and corralling their escorts into acting as mules.

The desire to help fellow humans was strong, and Kira didn't begrudge the guards willingly helping—except that everyone, *including Kira*, missed the fifth tech slipping out a side door that shouldn't have opened for her.

"Milani, she's loose," Kira snapped. "Surveillance systems are blank... What the *hell*?"

"That's...not good," Milani replied. "We're sweeping. She's either got a worm in the system or some kind of portable jamming field."

"Konrad," Kira turned to her engineer. "Someone's playing games with our internal scanners. Find them for me?"

"On it," he told her, switching from systems management to the internal surveillance in a blink. "Oh, that is...nasty."

"Konrad?" Kira was more worried than patient.

"There's a worm in our system and it's *not new*," he told her. "Inactive until triggered by someone flashing a visible data code to the cameras. As soon as it got the right input, it started wiping that person from the internal surveillance.

"What kind of military *builds* that kind of hole into their security?"

"One in a country on the edge of a civil war," Kira said grimly. "Can you track her?"

"Not yet," Konrad admitted. "Soler, I need you. We need to burn out the virus, and *Fortitude*'s software defenses think it's part of their code."

"Damn. Milani, she's using a backdoor built into the ship to hide," Kira told her ground-force commander. "She's almost certainly headed for the brig." She paused. "Shoot to kill."

"Understood. We're sweeping," Milani replied.

Kira knew how limited their ground troops were. That was part of why she'd agreed to send the vast majority of their prisoners over to *Final Usury*. Just watching them, even with full brig tech, was wearing her people out.

"This is Bertoli," a familiar voice said. "I'm at the brig; everything is intact. I am physically sealing the doors."

"How...physically?" Milani asked.

"You're going to need to send someone with a cutting torch as soon as this is over," Bertoli said with a chuckle. "Two more entrances; I'm moving on them."

Kira's cameras now showed the exterior of the brig door—which, as Bertoli had promised, had just been flash-welded shut. She couldn't see anyone *at* the door, but the camera *did* pick up the attempt to open the door. And then the attempt to *force* it open.

"She's at the brig."

"And so am I," Milani snapped. A blaster crackled on the camera Kira was watching. She couldn't see the shooter, but she *did* see the blaster bolts flashing back up the corridor—and the responding fire.

A suit of heavy boarding armor with a holographic red dragon around its shoulders stepped into the camera view, nudging at a body Kira *still* couldn't see.

"That is really fucking weird to watch," she noted. "Is it done?"

"Handled. She's dead, though...and I shot her in the leg."

"What?" Kira snapped.

"I took off her leg just below the hip. She should be in shock but not dead," Milani said grimly, kneeling by the invisible body and running a suit scanner. "Fuck. Headware suicide charge. She self-activated when she got hit."

"I really don't like these people," Kira said flatly. "Get the wounded and the medtechs off my damn ship, Milani. I need to call Avagyan out on her bullshit."

———

"YOU HAVE TO BELIEVE ME, Commodore, I did *not* send an agent onto your ship," Avagyan told Kira grimly, her face haunted. "Please...let the wounded go. I don't know what happened, but I *will* find out...and they had nothing to do with it."

"While I may not believe that *you* had nothing to do with it, I do believe the eleven people who were unconscious in my sickbay had nothing to do with it," Kira conceded. "Their shuttle is leaving now. I kept my end of the deal, Admiral Avagyan."

"It seems you weren't so capable of keeping yours."

There was a long silence.

"You are correct," Avagyan said. "I have no excuse, only my apology. I cannot undo what was done."

"Fortunately, they did not manage to harm anything," Kira noted. "They are dead, however."

The Crester Admiral closed her eyes.

"I assumed such. I presume there is nothing I can do to regain what limited trust we had?"

"Not really," Kira told her. "Your medevac shuttle is on its way. We're going to nova shortly and keep ourselves out of *your* way until we hear from the Crest."

"I understand," Avagyan said. "May I suggest that you send a nova fighter to a nearby position every few hours for us to keep you updated? I will honor the truce, Commodore Demirci, and protect your ship, whatever it takes."

That, Kira realized, was only one step short of an explicit promise to engage her fellow NRC officers and ships to protect Kira's people. That...didn't add up with the woman only knowing what was in front of her.

It seemed the Crown Zharang *had* briefed Admiral Avagyan. Unfortunately, it also seemed that the SPP loyalists in her fleet weren't entirely under her control.

"I will forward you a list of times we will check in," Kira told the Crester Admiral carefully. "I will *not* tell you where my ships and fighters will do so, but you will know when to look for us."

She attached a file to that message as she formatted it on her screen. Once Bueller had installed a mix of brand-new Redward antivirus software and older Brisingr and Apollon software, he'd been able to identify and eliminate the worm relatively quickly.

Her extra file, labeled *Tinkerbell Protocols*, was a software counteragent that would clear the inactive worm from Avagyan's systems.

If the Crester Admiral trusted her that much.

"I hope, Admiral Avagyan, that we can get through the *rest* of our agreement more…amicably."

"You kidnapped the Cabinet of my government, Demirci," Avagyan pointed out. "*Amicably* isn't an option. I suggest you settle for *calm*."

"I can live with that."

Kira cut the channel and fired off the data package.

"That's the last talking we're doing for a few days," she told Soler and Konrad. "Is the medevac shuttle clear?"

"She's clear," Soler confirmed. "We're down to six actually important prisoners?"

"Exactly. So, let's get the fighters back aboard and get the hell out of here."

Kira grimaced.

"Avagyan agreed to a truce, but we don't actually *know* what the result in the Crest is going to be—or if Admiral Matevosyan will honor it. So, let's make some distance for this dance."

51

ADMIRAL MATEVOSYAN STRUCK Kira as the type of man who was used to being the biggest person in any given room. He was just under two meters tall and just *loomed* over his flag bridge in the recording.

Unfortunately for the Crester Admiral, Kira was used to McCaig, who was just *over* two meters tall. Plus, the reason she was watching a *recording* was that she now had a significant degree of control over the situation.

"This situation is utterly unacceptable," he growled. "But I understand Admiral Avagyan's unwillingness to risk the lives of the Prime Minister and Cabinet. Her willingness to trust a jumped-up thug, however, is beyond my understanding.

"I will accept the Prime Minister's order to stand down and await the ransom payment from the Crest when I hear it from her, in her own voice, on a live channel," Matevosyan snapped. "Otherwise, I will take the risks I judge necessary."

The recording ended and Kira leaned back in her seat thoughtfully. *Collections Agent* had arrived four hours earlier and had joined the NRC formation orbiting Guadaloop.

"We're keeping outside of his scan-and-nova loop," she said aloud.

It wasn't really a question. The novas of the fleet were scheduled and arranged so that they moved on before the light from their emergence reached Guadaloop.

"Yes, sir," Soler confirmed. "We haven't detected any dispersal of forces, either."

Kira nodded. That was the risk to their current plan. If the Cresters split their forces up, they created multiple scan-and-nova loops. They also divided their forces and would have fewer fighters to send at any given location, but since they had five or six times the fighters needed to destroy Memorial Force…

"What do you think, Zoric?" she asked *Deception*'s Captain, eyeing Admiral Matevosyan's frozen image.

"I think he's blustering for the cameras," Zoric admitted. "He knows that if he actually breaks Admiral Avagyan's deal, it'll reflect on *everybody*'s willingness to negotiate with the Navy of the Royal Crest in the future.

"But he doesn't want to be *seen* to be abiding by Avagyan's deal."

"So, he blusters," Kira echoed. "That's about what I was figuring, too." She looked back at the tactical plot.

"Let's accelerate our sequence," she ordered. "Move up to a ninety-minute safety margin on that scan-and-nova loop. Just in case he decides to be clever."

"Is there a response to his message, sir?" Soler asked.

Kira smiled.

"No, Soler," she told the younger woman. "If things are going the way I suspect and hope they are, we can leave the good Admiral to stew in his own juices for a little while longer."

She rose and stretched.

"I'm going to go take a nap," she announced. "Wake me if anything changes."

NOTHING CHANGED. There were a few more wasted attempts to sweep the spots that Memorial Force had been with heavy assault

wings, but after a day, Admiral Matevosyan seemed to feel he'd blus-
tered enough.

He'd also probably noticed the same pattern Kira was noting.

"How long since the last ship?" she asked Zoric. *Deception* had a
full tactical staff, versus Soler and two techs on *Fortitude*. This kind of
analysis was easier there.

"We've seen four ships from three systems in the last twenty-four
hours," Zoric told her. "None were from the Crest.

"The last direct ship from the Crest was thirty-six hours ago."

"How long after *Temperance* and *Collections Agent* would they have
left?" Kira asked.

"Twelve, maybe eighteen hours," Zoric replied. "Prior to that,
schedules say ships were arriving from the Crest at least every eleven
hours, on average."

"So, we're missing three, maybe four ships," Kira noted. "That's
not quite enough to assume there's a blockade, but…"

"But it's enough to flag a worry, yes," her co-owner told her.
"Something went down in the Crest about seventy hours ago, I would
guess."

"And our ransom demand is landing in the middle of it about
now," Kira said with a chuckle. She was alone on *Fortitude*'s bridge
right now, though Zoric had a full staff on *Deception*'s.

They *really* needed to reallocate staff, but there just weren't enough
spare hands in Memorial Force to do more than fly *Fortitude* home.

Forty-ish hours each way. Kira had to wonder how long
Matevosyan would stay in Guadaloop haunting her when he had to
guess *something* was going on in the Crest. What were his priorities?

"Does it change anything for us?" Zoric asked.

"No," Kira admitted. "We keep up this dance until we hear from
Jade Panosyan."

Or that Jade Panosyan's coup had *failed*, in which case Kira was
going to take whatever money the SPP offered her and get the *hell* out
of the Crest Sector.

"YOU NEED TO BREATHE," Konrad told her as he returned to the bridge. "Have you gone more than twelve steps from this room since we captured the ship?"

"Nope," Kira confirmed. "And I'm not going to, either, Konrad. I'm responsible for all of our people, everything that's happening here. I need to be here or reachable from here."

"That's fair, I suppose," he conceded. He walked up to stand next to her, looking at the holographic plot. "It's what, thirty-five hours until we're going to hear anything?"

"From the Crest, yes," she agreed. "But there are three carrier groups in this system, and while they're being cooperative right now... that could end very, very quickly."

So far, their every-four-hour check-ins had gone without incident, but that was the most vulnerable part of all of this. Kira was reasonably sure Avagyan wouldn't let the rest of the Cresters do anything stupid, but she did have to send a single nova fighter into harm's way to keep the line of communication open.

"Breathe, my love," he insisted.

Nodding, Kira closed her eyes and focused on her breaths for a minute, controlling her breathing as she tried to find a semblance of calm in the sea of chaos she swam in. There was a soft sound of metal on plastic after a minute, and she opened her eyes to see Konrad attaching something to the command chair,

"For luck," he told her, gesturing at a new version of the interceptor-over-mountain statuette he'd made for her fighter. This one had a small clamp attached to the bottom, to link it to the arms of Kira's new seat.

"I don't have scraps left from *Conviction*, but we salvaged some pieces of your fighter before we had to push her out," Konrad continued. "Waldroup helped me put this together."

That was probably why the fighter and natural mountain were both cleaner and more distinct than they had been before. Plus, she suspected Konrad had been practicing to make sure that the charm was prettier this time.

Her breath caught in her throat and she blinked away tears.

"You goof," she told him. But her fingers were already tracing the tiny fighter. "Thank you."

"It's for luck," he repeated. "The last one got you through a fighter crash alive. I figure this one is enough prettier to get us *all* home."

52

SOMETIMES, the *messenger* was as important as the message.

After over three days of a complete lack of ships and communication from the Crest, the first ship to arrive in-system was *Penalty Fee...* Captain Lorelei Simonsson, commanding.

That data barely percolated into Kira's scanner reports before the second wave of ships arrived. A full carrier group, guarding multiple Army of the Royal Crest assault transports.

They dropped into Guadaloop orbit like a descending herd of locusts. Even the fragments of messages Kira was picking up from a light-hour away were fascinating—and their scanners were able to clearly pick out the shuttles swarming over multiple ships of the Navy of the Royal Crest.

"Someone is cleaning house," Soler said with a satisfied tone. "That's...enthusiastic."

"Hopefully, they're sticking to arrests and not lining people up against walls," Kira said. She'd picked her side in this particular fight —and not just for money—but she was still all too aware of how messy and ugly civil wars could get.

In this case, speed and surprise carried the day. None of the SPP loyalists aboard the NRC ships had been expecting relief-and-arrest orders. They'd had, from what Kira could tell, the structures to convince their crews to follow them into mutiny—but they hadn't had time to activate them.

"This was all an hour ago," Kira said softly.

"Do we change our scheduled check-in?" Soler asked.

"No. We're fifteen minutes from our next nova, sixty-five from the next check-in," Kira estimated, eyeing the clocks. "We'll check in as normal and we'll move forward from there.

"The good news is that they sent Simonsson, so it *looks* like they're arresting the SPP people, not the Royalists, which means that our employer appears to have pulled this off. The bad news is that our employer already set us up once. So…we shall see."

TWO HOURS LATER, Kira pulled her key staff together.

"We have a recorded message relayed by Dawnlord," she told them, nodding to Patel. "It came encrypted under a cipher provided to us by the Crown Zharang, so this should be a good sign."

Memorial Force's ships were close enough together to talk in real-time and carry on a live virtual conference. Kira waited to be sure she had everyone's attention and then started the decrypted video.

The image of Voski, Jade Panosyan's aide and Dinastik Pahak bodyguard, appeared on the screen. The guard was in full gold-on-black uniform, with the two stars of a general on their collar.

"Just a bodyguard, I see," Zoric muttered.

"Voski was the *commander* of the Crown Zharang's bodyguard," Kira pointed out. "That would make them the second-ranked officer of the Dinastik Pahak."

The conversation was cut off when Voski started speaking.

"Commodore Demirci, this is General Voski of the Dinastik Pahak," they said calmly. "While aspects of this conversation will be obvious to everyone, there are details and elements that I think should remain private between those already briefed on this affair.

"Firstly, I wish to update you on the state of affairs in the Crest. The

Crest Planetary Police executed a search warrant on Sanctuary and Prosperity Party offices across the system five days ago.

"We were expecting some degree of legislative and active push-back," they continued. "If Prime Minister Jeong had been in place, I suspect the pushback would have been more…measured.

"On the other hand, the level and type of evidence we came into possession of might have triggered the reaction we faced regardless," Voski noted. "Several divisions of the Army of the Royal Crest attempted to seize the capital and arrest the King and Crown Zharang.

"They failed. The violence—and the SPP's clear responsibility for it —provided the final straw. Over forty percent of the SPP's members of Parliament are now under arrest, along with key supports in the NRC and ARC.

"His Majesty has officially dissolved the Parliament of the Royal Crest and called new elections for fifty-six days from today. Crown Zharang Jade's plan has worked…sufficiently, if not perfectly."

Kira nodded in silent relief. She'd figured, from the moment *Penalty Fee*'s beacon had been so clear on her commanding officer, but it was good to hear it confirmed.

"Along with that, however, I also am tasked to deal with the situation we created as our distraction," Voski noted drily. "I must note that the ransom demand we received was for significantly more money than had been discussed previously."

Maral Jeong had insisted she was worth more money than Kira thought—and Kira had been a *little* angry with her employer.

"Jade asked me to give you their personal apology for leaking your course," Voski said levelly. "Removing one of the military levers from the SPP's playbook was far too valuable to us. We hoped that you would be able to handle the situation, one way or another, but we made the call we had to.

"We will meet the increased random demand," they concluded. "One ARC transport will be at the coordinates attached to this message at the listed time. No escorts. We will retrieve the Prime Minister and Cabinet then."

Kira pulled the numbers and nodded. They were entirely workable.

"I also must confess that we did not actually expect *Fortitude* to survive this process," Voski admitted. "While we cannot prevent you from leaving with her, I am authorized to offer a ten-billion-crest ransom for the carrier herself.

"I hope to see you shortly, Commodore Demirci."

The message ended and Kira found herself glaring at the hologram tank.

"Sometimes, I would prefer that my employers be slightly *less* bluntly honest," she said aloud. If *Fortitude* had gone down to the SPP loyalists' bombers, Kira would not have survived.

"We're not taking their money, are we?" Zoric asked. "The only reason we took this damn contract was to get the carrier."

"Exactly," Kira agreed. "I mean, we also took it to stick a finger in the Equilibrium Institute's eye—mission accomplished there. But…"

She shook her head.

"No, we're keeping *Fortitude* and Voski is going to give me the papers that say that's legal," she told her people. "Because those were promised to us."

She turned to Milani.

"Get the prisoners ready for the exchange," she ordered them. "But…don't tell them anything. Let's have this all be a pleasant surprise for Em Jeong."

53

FORTITUDE DWARFED THE ARMY TRANSPORT. She was almost four times the smaller ship's size, and Kira had made sure that every one of the carrier's heavy guns was trained on the assault ship.

She was ninety-plus percent sure she could trust Voski and Jade Panosyan, but if there was a point in this entire mission where betrayal would be easiest and most profitable for the Cresters, this was it.

Still, she let them bring their own shuttle over to collect the prisoners. Milani and their commandos stood around Jeong and the five cabinet Ministers, weapons held in parade-ground stances but still clearly ready.

Kira had to conceal a smirk. Maral Jeong and her Ministers clearly felt that they were finally back in control of the situation. Money for their freedom was a transaction they could understand—and they'd have the power to seek vengeance later.

They thought.

The ARC shuttle touched down and the ramp descended. Four of Kira's commandos marched over in full boarding armor, weapons ready in case something happened.

But only three people came off the shuttle. Voski led the way, still in full uniform, accompanied by two junior-looking Army of the Royal Crest officers with attaché cases.

"They're clear," Milani announced loudly after the troopers finished their scans.

Kira glanced over at Jeong, who was looking...concerned. Not yet worried, but she clearly hadn't been expecting a Dinastik Pahak general.

Concealing a smirk, Kira crossed to meet Voski and gave them a crisp salute. She was in her own fanciest dress uniform, to live up to the occasion.

"Have you considered our offer, Commodore Demirci?" Voski asked quietly, clearly managing their voice so the Ministers couldn't hear them.

"I have, and I intend to hold you to the original contract," Kira replied. "You owe me ownership papers, General."

"And twenty million crests," they agreed. "Lieutenant Avakian. The red case, if you please. Lieutenant Hourig, both of your cases, please."

The left-hand aide checked the markers on the top of the two attaché cases he was carrying. He stepped forward and handed Voski one of them, then stepped back.

Voski entered a security code and popped the secured case open, presenting it to Kira open-side first.

The contents were sparse. A small stack of physical paper and a single black datachip. The contracts and paperwork that would confirm to all the galaxy that Memorial Force were the legitimate owners of *Fortitude*.

"I *told* them," they noted with a smile. "Congratulations on your new carrier, Commodore."

Kira nodded and took the case. It closed easily, with a small green light on the controls telling her that it wasn't locked.

Voski then took one case from the second aide and gestured for her to open the other one. Both cases were swiftly presented to Kira. This pair was *much* more heavily packed, with each of the finger-sized gray datachips representing a bearer credit for fifty thousand crests—two hundred chips per case.

Kira picked a chip at random and scanned it with her headware, confirming the contents. Then she gestured for the commandos to take the cases.

"I believe that is all but one piece of our business complete, then," she told Voski.

"Two, really," the General replied. "Despite everything, you must understand that neither you nor Memorial Force will be welcome in the Crest Sector for quite some time. Once this exchange is complete, I must ask that you leave the Sector as expeditiously as possible.

"For their *private* purposes, Jade says they hope to dine with you by the lake again," Voski added, "but the *Crown Zharang* must protect the Royal Crest."

Kira wasn't surprised in the slightest. If anything, she was actually warmed by the fact that Jade Panosyan and Voski were taking the effort to make it clear that the banishment was entirely nonpersonal.

"Very well," she told Voski. "May I ask one *small* favor in return?"

"You may ask," the General said carefully.

"I want to observe the exchange from here," Kira said.

Voski clearly swallowed a chuckle.

"Very well, Commodore Demirci. She is, after all, *your* ship now."

THE TWO ARMY lieutenants returned back into the ship, replaced by a sharp-faced group of eight middle-aged people in Crest civilian-style angular suits who could have passed for bodyguards. They spread out to form a vague receiving line in front of the shuttle.

"Milani, let them go," Kira ordered.

The heavy suit of armor with the red dragon draped over its shoulders flashed her a thumbs-up. The commandos released Maral Jeong and her Ministers simultaneously, unlocking their manacles and pointing them across the flight bay.

Maral Jeong led the way instantly, striding across the deck like she owned the place. Her glare was reserved for Kira as she reached the shuttle.

"I am glad we reached some kind of deal in the end," she noted. "But you will find there are consequences for all that has happened."

"Oh, I know," Kira agreed, then waved Jeong to the line of hard-faced bureaucrat types.

The oldest-looking of them was a woman with pure white hair tied back into a tight bun that highlighted the sharp lines of her face as she stepped forward to look down at Jeong.

"Em Maral Jeong?" she asked sharply.

"You know who I am," Jeong snapped.

"Very well," the official said. "Em Maral Jeong, you are under arrest for abuse of authority, receipt of illegal funds, conspiracy to conceal illegal funds, conspiracy to commit murder and treason."

The presumably *former* Prime Minister of the Crest just *gaped* at the Crest Planetary Police officer as a pair of handcuffs emerged from a hidden pocket of the suit and snapped onto Jeong's wrists.

The other CPP officers moved forward swiftly to sweep up the other Ministers. They were unrestrained for at most ninety seconds before the Crester police had them cuffed and were leading them onto the shuttle behind them.

And Kira stood there, watching as the most *delightful* schadenfreude ran through her.

Finally, only Voski remained on the flight deck, and they gave her a crisp salute.

"You have twenty-four hours to discharge static or refuel here in Guadaloop if necessary," they told her. "But I suggest you get on your way as soon as you can.

"The situation here will be…complex for some time, and you and *Fortitude* will make for an aggravating factor we cannot afford."

"I understand," Kira said. "Good luck, General."

54

"WELL. THAT'S DONE."

From the chorus of chuckles on the conference call, Kira's phrasing was a *little* on the excessively mundane side.

"We got paid, contract complete, ownership documents for *Fortitude* are now on digital and physical file," Kira told them all. "Guadaloop is behind us, and now we just have the long and boring trip home."

Home.

When had Redward become home? It had been a while ago, she realized.

"And the equally boring but much more intense task of finding enough crew to get *Fortitude* up to snuff," Zoric said. "Who do I need to punch out to get the captain's seat on the carrier?"

"There's going to be a hell of a reorg when we get back to Redward," Kira conceded. "And we all know that Redward is the home base until we can buy that carrier we've been promised."

"Are we going to have any money *left* after all the planned ships?" Vaduva asked, the purser still smiling as usual.

"If we sit on our butts and do *nothing* for three years while

Redward builds us a carrier, no," Kira agreed. "But you knew that, being the one who handles my bookkeeping!"

That got her more chuckles.

"So, yes, we're going to be working. And most of our contracts are going to look like this one in at least one respect: our ops zones are going to be weeks away from Redward. And, frankly, since I'm kind of attached to Redward at this point, I'm okay with that."

"Speaking as the man seconded from the RRF, I'm glad," Sagairt noted. "*I'm* not staying, but I suspect some of our traded personnel may want to make the switch permanent. On both sides."

"We'll have to sort that out with the RRF when we get back," Kira agreed. "Hopefully, the commander of the RRF's new fighter corps will be on our side."

Sagairt chuckled.

"That seems like a safe assumption," he told her.

"Four weeks home, people," Kira told them all. "Probably about the same just to get new crew and officers recruited—plus no matter what we do, we'll need to fabricate ourselves some new fighters."

Conveniently, *Fortitude*'s computers had the specifications for several of the Crest's newest nova fighters. Kira would be spending some time deciding whether the new designs were worth swapping over the entire fighter force—she liked the Hoplite-IV, but the Crest's new Wolverine interceptors were an entirely new design. They might well be superior overall.

It was the same with the Hussar-Sevens versus her Weltraumpanzer-Fünfs and PNC-115s. Most of her nova fighters were, by one source or another, contemporary to the Hoplite-IV. Given access to the latest and greatest of the Navy of the Royal Crest's nova fighters…they had some work to do.

"I guess there's one question still in play," Akuchi Mwangi admitted. *Raccoon*'s Captain looked thoughtful. "Are we going to keep *Raccoon* when we get back? The plan was to replace her with *Fortitude* entirely, after all."

"I don't know if that's a decision we even need to make yet," Kira said. "We were planning on selling her back, yes, but there's a lot to be said for an extra forty nova fighters when we get stuck in. If we rework things a bit and stop trying to cram extra fighters on her deck...Waldroup?"

She looked at their senior deck boss, who shrugged.

"She's not called a junk carrier for nothing, sir," Waldroup noted. "We can make her work *better* than she does, but I don't think we can make her work *well*. And we *do* have another carrier to crew up now."

"Well, folks, we'll think about it," Kira said. Selling *Raccoon* back to Redward—or to another Syntactic Cluster power, potentially—would free up resources for a while.

Even without it, Memorial Force was now one of the most powerful mercenary organizations in the Rim. Somehow, Kira wasn't worried about them finding work.

"Regardless, officers, friends." She raised her coffee. "A toast. To *Fortitude* and Memorial Force. Long may we fly!"

JOIN THE MAILING LIST

Love Glynn Stewart's books? To know as soon as new books are released, special announcements, and a chance to win free paperbacks, join the mailing list at:

glynnstewart.com/mailing-list/

ABOUT THE AUTHOR

Glynn Stewart is the author of *Starship's Mage*, a bestselling science fiction and fantasy series where faster-than-light travel is possible–but only because of magic. His other works include science fiction series *Duchy of Terra, Castle Federation* and *Vigilante*, as well as the urban fantasy series *ONSET* and *Changeling Blood*.

Writing managed to liberate Glynn from a bleak future as an accountant. With his personality and hope for a high-tech future intact, he lives in Kitchener, Ontario with his partner, their cats, and an unstoppable writing habit.

VISIT GLYNNSTEWART.COM FOR NEW RELEASE UPDATES

CREDITS

The following people were involved in making this book:
    Copyeditor: Richard Shealy
    Proofreader: M Parker Editing
    Cover art: Jeff Brown
    Typo Hunter Team
    Faolan's Pen Publishing team: Jack, Kate, and Robin.

facebook.com/glynnstewartauthor

OTHER BOOKS
BY GLYNN STEWART

For release announcements join the
mailing list or visit **GlynnStewart.com**

STARSHIP'S MAGE
Starship's Mage
Hand of Mars
Voice of Mars
Alien Arcana
Judgment of Mars
UnArcana Stars
Sword of Mars
Mountain of Mars
The Service of Mars
A Darker Magic
Mage-Commander (upcoming)

Starship's Mage: Red Falcon
Interstellar Mage
Mage-Provocateur
Agents of Mars

Pulsar Race: A Starship's Mage Universe Novella

DUCHY OF TERRA
The Terran Privateer
Duchess of Terra
Terra and Imperium
Darkness Beyond
Shield of Terra
Imperium Defiant
Relics of Eternity
Shadows of the Fall
Eyes of Tomorrow

SCATTERED STARS

Scattered Stars: Conviction
Conviction
Deception
Equilibrium
Fortitude
Huntress (upcoming)
Scattered Stars: Evasion
Evasion (upcoming)

PEACEKEEPERS OF SOL

Raven's Peace
The Peacekeeper Initiative
Raven's Course
Drifter's Folly
Remnant Faction (upcoming)

EXILE

Exile
Refuge
Crusade
Ashen Stars: An Exile Novella

CASTLE FEDERATION

Space Carrier Avalon
Stellar Fox
Battle Group Avalon
Q-Ship Chameleon
Rimward Stars
Operation Medusa
A Question of Faith: A Castle Federation Novella

SCIENCE FICTION STAND ALONE NOVELLA

Excalibur Lost

VIGILANTE
(WITH TERRY MIXON)
Heart of Vengeance
Oath of Vengeance

Bound By Stars: A Vigilante Series
(With Terry Mixon)
Bound By Law
Bound by Honor
Bound by Blood

TEER AND KARD
Wardtown
Blood Ward

CHANGELING BLOOD
Changeling's Fealty
Hunter's Oath
Noble's Honor
Fae, Flames & Fedoras: A Changeling Blood Novella

ONSET
ONSET: To Serve and Protect
ONSET: My Enemy's Enemy
ONSET: Blood of the Innocent
ONSET: Stay of Execution
Murder by Magic: An ONSET Novella

FANTASY STAND ALONE NOVELS
Children of Prophecy
City in the Sky

Made in United States
Orlando, FL
18 May 2022

17989810R00214